FAIR GAME

FAIR GAME

Peter Adams

Book Guild Publishing
Sussex, England

First published in Great Britain in 2006 by
Book Guild Publishing
Pavilion View
19 New Road
Brighton, East Sussex
BN1 1UF

Copyright © Peter Adams 2006

The right of Peter Adams to be identified as the author of this work has been asserted by him in accordance with the Copyright, Designs and Patents Act 1988.

All rights reserved. No part of this publication may be reproduced, transmitted, or stored in a retrieval system, in any form or by any means, without permission in writing from the publisher, nor be otherwise circulated in any form of binding or cover other than that in which it is published and without a similar condition being imposed on the subsequent purchaser.

All characters in this publication are fictitious and any resemblance to real people, alive or dead, is purely coincidental.

Typesetting in Baskerville by
Keyboard Services, Luton, Bedfordshire

Printed in Great Britain by
Antony Rowe Ltd, Chippenham, Wiltshire

A catalogue record for this book is available from
The British Library

ISBN 1 84624 058 1

Chapter One

'Maniac!' shouted Travers, as the red Mondeo swerved into his lane ahead of him, making him brake hard, pushing Molly's nose painfully into the dog guard at the back of the Mercedes Estate.

'Sorry, old girl, you all right back there?' He looked in the mirror. Molly gave a look of disdain, and this time pressed herself into a corner on top of his shooting jacket, panting after the unexpected incident. They had already been on the road for three and a half hours on this unnaturally hot and humid September morning, and the lane restrictions on the M6 were driving him to distraction. They were now back to a forty mile an hour crawl, and it didn't help when a stupid young rep raised his blood pressure still further. He shifted his position against the leather upholstery but his six foot frame was capable of little more than a shuffle, temporarily releasing the clammy shirt from his back.

It had been a very long drive from East Grinstead, which they had left at eight thirty that Tuesday morning. He would have much preferred to get to the Highlands direct from his Holland Park flat, but he had to go back to the house for the shooting gear and the dog.

He couldn't complain though. Mrs Gibbons, a neighbour at East Grinstead, had by pleasant accident effectively become his housekeeper, and for three years since the divorce had kept the house spick and span, and looked after the dog while he was at his London house, or when he was doing something else apart from shooting. He had driven down the night before, made sure he got a good night's sleep and that Mrs Gibbons had laid everything out, so it was just a case of loading up in the morning and driving off. Despite his love of shooting, these long drags across the country were no longer offset by the keen anticipation of what awaited him at his destination. The traffic, as now, had become a mechanical conga, and over the last year he found himself increasingly frustrated just by the sheer effort of getting there. It perhaps had been different when he was married – someone to chat to, or even take pleasure in a stopover somewhere. But now, he became maudlin too easily in hotel rooms, and he preferred to get where he was going without interruption.

He looked at his watch and reckoned he had about another three and a half hours to go to get to the shooting lodge at Glenlivet, and he began to think about shooting, then a million other things that were affecting the business. He wondered why he was putting himself through so much grief. Why not, as his colleagues had urged, go with the flow? What will be will be. Play out the hand, don't rock the boat, and it could all work out in the end. He thought yet again about doing just that. If the shareholders wanted to sell the business, who was he to get in the way and complicate the whole process? There was an evens chance he would lose his job as chairman and chief executive of Sunburst Soft Drinks once it was sold to a multinational, but hey, after ten years the payoff and pension would be good, and he was certain they would not be ungenerous for the enormous growth the business had enjoyed under his watch. Trouble was, could he really live with himself if he let this chance go? He was in his early forties. Would he ever get the chance to control another business that was anywhere like as much fun as Sunburst, and more to the point, could he ever forgive himself for giving up the opportunity to achieve the ultimate business achievement – a management buyout. It was different for his executive colleagues on the board. Travers had brought them all in over the last five years: they were young, probably had a good chance of being kept on by a new owner, and if they didn't, so what, finding another job wouldn't be difficult for them. They were all good at their jobs, and between them, under Travers' direction, had driven the business to enviable growth in sales and profits, which for them was the best reference of all. For Travers though, he had put too much into the business to take that attitude. He'd done the slippery pole bit and didn't fancy starting all over again. He had built this business but the job was only half done. The strategy was right on the button, free cash was generating investment and growth of the brands, and a float was definitely on the cards within the next three years. What was the matter with his shareholders? Blind or just stupid?

Unfortunately, Travers knew in reality it was neither. Sunburst Soft Drinks was a most peculiar commercial animal. It was in fact a consortium, owned by very nearly half the brewing industry. Effectively controlled by three of the six major brewers through a complicated shareholder structure of voting and non-voting shares, a further fourteen regional brewers completed the consortium shareholder base. Without doubt this did provide him with an edge in terms of loyalty from the brewers against his big soft drink competitors, but in truth the dividend payout produced no more for the brewers than the massive retrospective discounts the cola brigade sprayed at them. The fact was Sunburst had developed the brands for the youth market, and Travers felt no greater satisfaction than how, without any cooperation from the brewers, his brands had penetrated the grocery markets, thanks only to innovative product developments and heavy marketing support. But all good things, so it appeared, must come to an end. One of the major brewer shareholders, Gallant, had become the focus of attention of an acquisitive Australian brewer, and as a result the executive management and institutional shareholders were demanding focus and cost savings to drive up profits and value before the anticipated bid emerged from the Australians. Needless to say, an ancillary non-core investment such as Sunburst Soft Drinks was under the microscope, with clear indications from the board of Gallant that they intended to realise the value locked up in the company and stick to brewing beer and running pubs.

As a consortium, however, as Travers knew only too well, when one of the 'members' wants to take their ball back, the effect on the others is akin to divorce proceedings. The others were not prepared to pay anything like a decent earnings ratio to Gallant for its share, and besides that, if one of the other major brewer shareholders bought Gallant's share, they would effectively buy voting control of the whole business, which the others could never live with. The 'club' would be dead. So, spurred on by mutual distrust, very gradually, and somewhat inexorably, the major brewers holding the voting clout had decided amongst themselves that 'one out all out' seemed the right solution, and that a trade sale of the whole enterprise would bring in top dollar for everyone. Interestingly, Travers was meant to be blissfully unaware of these developments, but he had 'friends at court' amongst a number of the smaller family controlled regional brewers who saw the whole thing as an unnecessary but typical stitch up by the majors, which would force them to sell their shares to whoever came up with the cash.

Armed only with gossip and speculation he had kept as close as he could to these developments over the last twelve months, even raising the possibility of a management buyout with each of the managing directors of the three leading brewer shareholders at one of the monthly board meetings where all three of them sat as non-executive directors of Sunburst. Their response had been cynically dismissive. Travers would be told in due course if any change of ownership was seriously contemplated, and until then he should not unsettle the management by futile speculation. It was also made clear that while they had respect for Travers' tight control of the business and its development, finding someone to financially support a bid at the level they had in mind was both incredulous and beyond Travers' capabilities. Travers felt he had been patted on the head and swiftly returned to his cot. Ambition and high finance were clearly not qualities appreciated from underling subsidiaries or their executives. For all that, however, Travers just knew he had a trump card. None of these brewers had any real understanding of the soft drinks market – and nor did they want to.

Each of them was carving out his or her own career, and Sunburst was no more than a distraction in the grand scheme of things. If they wanted a trade sale, who was going to run the process and put the business in the best light to potential buyers? None of them had the time or knowledge, and they all naturally expected Travers to undertake potential career hara-kiri on their behalf. Softly, softly, and one by one, Travers had made it clear to each of them that he had his own interests to think about, and a duty to the five hundred workforce, and that he had to consider all his options, which were either to leave them to it and get out quick, or attempt to raise the money for a management buyout and join in the sale process.

Persistence had paid off, and more recently he had been told at the board that if the decision to sell was indeed made, the management might have an opportunity to bid if an auction took place. At one level Travers thought this was a bit of a kick in the face for all his efforts over the last ten years to be left at the end of the queue, but on the other hand at least the door had been opened, and now he must make sure that his boot kept it firmly ajar.

His colleagues back at Sunburst were pretty chary about the whole thing, and felt there was a severe risk of upsetting the applecart in terms of relationships with the brewers if he pushed ahead with his plan, which would not help in securing continuity with any incoming multinational. Travers, however, made it quite clear that in his view there was little chance of further employment for anyone once production had been dispersed by the new buyer, if, as was likely, it went to a multinational with production facilities somewhere in the Midlands or indeed Europe. They had reluctantly gone along with the logic, and left it to him to develop financial backing whilst the brewers pondered the future of Sunburst.

Travers had preliminary discussions with all three major brewers individually, and all three had different perspectives on the sale of the business. He felt he could use this to his advantage if only he could get firmly into the bidding ring. By sheer chance, all three managing directors of the major brewer shareholders would be present at this shoot, and he was determined to play out his hand over the next two days, and try and get a result. If the sale did go ahead, he didn't want to be left at the altar as a result of a quick bid by one of his competitors.

With all this tumbling about in his mind, three hours later he turned off the A9 just north of Aviemore, and despite being tired, was, as ever, taken aback by the sheer beauty of Strathspey as he cruised sedately now in the Merc along the twisting, undulating road towards Grantown and on eastwards to Tomintoul to the most perfect grouse moors that awaited him on the Cromdale and Ladder Hills. He had shot to the north of Glenlivet before but never on Lord Strathallan's estate.

Strathallan was a non-executive director of Albion, the largest of the national brewers. It was perhaps all too clear then, thought Travers, why Piers Tomlinson, the chief executive of Albion, had manipulated the appointment of his Lordship to the board.

Organising these shoots was no small task and perforce fell to the chairman or managing director simply because arranging the connection with the better estates would be extremely difficult if not impossible for anyone else in the organisation, whilst using an agent was really not the done thing. Add to that the nature of the grouse shoot, with wild birds probably only available in suitable numbers for three or four weeks shooting, the issue of safety, reputational risk for the estate, and last but not least, antagonistic public opinion, it is not difficult to see why most estates keep it in the 'family' with friends and reliable syndicates. At least they could be relied upon to ensure the 'right sort' of shooters. Most of the good estates had encountered the City fraternity who treated the whole experience as *'jeux sans frontières'* with wild behaviour both on and off the drives, and for something as long term as grouse management, doing without those types was not a difficult decision, never mind how lucrative.

And that, it would appear, is just what Piers Tomlinson had achieved by recruiting Lord Strathallan, who probably knew as much about brewing as Mrs Gibbons. It gave Tomlinson the chance in one stroke (but at a price) to hold court amongst his peers away from the dingy corridors of the Brewers Society in Portman Square, and then enjoy the benefits of the reciprocal invitations, which is why the whole thing was self-perpetuating. For example, each of the regional brewers controlled quite large 'free' trade accounts and tenancies where their own beer just wasn't popular enough, and consequently each national brewer wooed the regionals with discounts to stock their beer, allied to shooting if that provided the requisite incentive. Travers recalled that one of the nationals in the not too distant past, had gone as far as to actually buy a grouse moor with country hotel near Whitby, in an attempt to consolidate customer loyalty.

As chairman and chief executive of Sunburst Soft Drinks, Tom Travers was making this journey, both as a guest and as a supplier to Albion's huge pub estate. He was a good and safe shot, passable company, and for the last ten years had been a regular member of the shooting 'club', based on mutual trade. His own marketing budget funded a near six figure sum for shoot days and the requisite hospitality, ensuring he could reciprocate with the brewers and keep within the 'inner circle' and the commercial advantages it brought. He counted a number of his customers as friends (mainly the regional family brewers), whilst the social atmosphere of the shoot was perfect for defusing or resolving issues with the nationals, providing his timing was appropriate – usually between drives or over drinks in the evening. In this next two days he would have all three managing directors of the major brewers – Albion, Gallant and Caledonia – hopefully ready to listen to his plans to embark on the Sunburst buyout, or MBO as everyone referred to it.

By three thirty that Tuesday afternoon, he found himself in the one street town of Tomintoul, without much clue as to where to go to find the shooting lodge from there. He looked at Tomlinson's letter of invitation, but the only reference was to Glenlivet Lodge, as if everyone should know precisely where it was. Unfortunately Glenlivet is not a town, but a vast glen. At the end of the town he stopped next to an isolated bus stop to ask the dishevelled character sitting on the bench where his destination lay.

'Er, excuse me, would you happen to have any idea where I could find Glenlivet Lodge, apparently it's somewhere near Tomnavoulin?' From the bench the character gave a physical twitch as if someone had just switched him on. Immediately Travers saw that this fellow had fallen out of the local hostelry and was clearly very much the worse for wear. After shifting with great difficulty on the bench, and running an alcohol bleached tongue over dry lips, the fellow dragged his eyes along the car and back again to Travers.

'No doubt you'll be wanting some salmon.' This was not a question but a statement.

'No,' said Travers, 'I don't want any salmon, but I do want to find Glenlivet Lodge.' With eyes rolling skyward a broad grin transformed the middle-aged man's weather-beaten features.

'It's fresh salmon sir, straight from the Avon. A fifteen pounder, only went in the fridge last night. I'll even give you a bin bag to keep it from your wee whippet.' The fellow then stood shakily and propped his elbow on the roof over Travers' head. Travers caught sight of the old canvass gaiters that kept the man's dilapidated tweed trousers tucked in from ankle to knee, and recognised that it was probably his misfortune to have run into the local poacher.

'But don't you worry now, sir, we'll be meeting again, and I'm only asking twenty pound for the fish.' Travers said nothing, noting that the fellow was scrutinising the contents of the Merc, and no doubt putting two and two together. Realising the chance for a sale was probably gone, the fellow reluctantly gave Travers instructions to the shooting lodge of Lord Strathallan, and then, with a sweeping wave of his hand, ambled shakily off down the road in the direction of the town, extracting with difficulty his roll-up tin from the depths of his pocket.

Now nearly four o'clock, Travers, following pretty accurate instructions, made his way to the lodge and swung into the long drive, hoping he'd found the right place, as there was no sign. The loud crunching of the gravel under the car wheels shattered the tranquillity that surrounded the Gothic edifice that lay a half a mile ahead of him. Almost fairytale in appearance, with rising spires and turrets over a granite facade, this shooting lodge reminded him more of a Disney creation at Orlando. The old Queen Mum would not have been disappointed. The first thing on his mind, however, was to give Molly a run and get her fed after the long journey.

As he approached a magnificent three-arched bridge over a somewhat disappointing small stream halfway up the drive, a besuited, rotund character in plus fours complete with dog, flat cap and long shepherd's crook, was leaning on the parapet gazing at the green sward of parkland against the background of conifer and the blue braes of Glenlivet rising behind. Guest, keeper or laird? Travers wondered.

'Afternoon to you,' said Travers. 'I'm with Piers Tomlinson's shooting party, I hope I haven't arrived too early.' The fellow's posture against the bridge did not change nor his deadpan countenance, and all Travers got in reply was an outstretched crook in the direction of the lodge with the weary acclamation, *'Ignorantia excusat peccatum.'*

Travers' jaw involuntarily dropped for a moment, then he smiled, offered up the response of 'quite', and continued up to the house. As he drew up in front of the portico alongside a gaggle of Range Rovers and Land Rovers, he'd deduced that the whimsical character by the bridge may have been his Lordship, judging by the handsome hunter chain and fob draped between his waistcoat pockets, together with the incongruous vermilion spotted handkerchief overflowing from the breast pocket. Travis wondered what the poor old duffer really felt about his inheritance becoming a billet for the bloody brewers.

With Molly quartering the lawns, nose down and in quick time, Travers took the opportunity to stretch his legs and have a quick recce round the place, before he ran into fellow guests or staff. Moving round to the rear of the house showed the working nature of the estate, with Larsen traps dotted amongst the outbuildings together with a moribund collection of farm vehicles. Lines of dead crows and magpies hung from wire washing lines in a ghoulish display of the keeper's effectiveness in controlling the vermin, whilst small pens contained some immature pheasant, obviously on the way to some local lowland shoot. He moved towards the house. One of the many doors was open and appeared to be the back door to the kitchens. He ambled over, and nearly bumped into a youngish fellow with a basinful of vegetable peelings. The lad was in full chef's attire, complete with blue chequered pants and white cap, under which sweat was trickling down his forehead from the still oppressive heat of the day.

'Amazing weather,' Travers volunteered in the time honoured greeting.

'Yeah,' the lad said, looking up as if the comment was a revelation 'we could be on the bloody Riviera.'

'Any chance of a bowl of water for my dog?' said Travers.

'Sure. Come on in. I've got some pork scraps if it wants some.' With that Travers moved inside and studied the almost perfect Victorian kitchen, complete with massive pine preparation tables, copper implements hanging from wrought iron fixings around the circumference of the room, and a chain driven contraption overhanging the old range.

'Don't be fooled,' the lad said, 'this is no place to prepare food for twenty-odd people. I'm working off propane over there and there just isn't enough heat.' He pointed towards an old but large French stainless steel cooker affair where pots were steaming.

'All I've got by way of help are three stroppy local women. The natives are definitely not friendly,' he said despondently.

'What arrangement have you got here then?' said Travers, as he watched the chef pour stock into the open tops of the most perfect looking pork pies.

'Mr Tomlinson brought me up from Head Office in Derby, thought I'd enjoy the break from the directors' kitchen,' he said with more than a hint of sarcasm. 'Still, I think I know what you blokes like.' The chef worked deftly and swiftly on various tasks, while Molly scoffed at the pork fillet.

Looking at the pork pies, Travers pointed and said, 'Shoot lunch tomorrow?' The chef nodded. 'Marvellous. See you then, and thanks for the scraps.' Molly had already disappeared, and Travers felt it was high time he introduced himself to someone in the house who could show him to his room. He walked back to his car, settled the dog back in her basket until later on, and struggled up the steps of the elevated front door with his suitcase, guncase and cartridge bag.

Just opening the front door was an old friend.

'Jane,' he said. 'My God, you get more attractive every time I see you.' Jane Newgent threw her shoulders forward and laughed in her inimitable way, which Travers could only describe as the most sexy belly laugh he had ever heard. Jane was married to Bobby Newgent of Struthers brewery, based near Nottingham. The business had been in Newgent's family for generations, and following the old truism of 'location, location, location' had a collection of over a hundred managed and tenanted pubs in superb urban positions around Nottingham and Leicester together with a flourishing free trade business, which meant that the family trust that owned the business had accrued immense wealth over the years, all supplied by the in-house brewery. Whilst Newgent wasn't the brightest entrepreneur in the brewing business, he knew the value of management from his army days, as a result of which his business was run by highly effective recruits from the major brewers, who despite his arrogant style and paltry reward structure, all seemed to respect his leadership. Beneath all that, however, was something of a sad story. Although ex-army and apparently gung-ho in outlook, Newgent had an insecure personality, had acquired a distracting nervous tic on his face, in addition to being plagued by tinnitus. The end result was a premature, rather deaf Colonel Blimp whose response to any dialogue commenced with 'What? What? Speak up, man!' Poor bloke, thought Travers, he could only be in his early forties.

Jane was on the receiving end of most of this, suffering incredible rudeness from Newgent who treated her as his batman, amidst various accusations of infidelity, which in truth, so Travers supposed, were completely unfounded. It wasn't difficult to see that there was an enormous strain between the two of them, despite two kids and everything a couple could ask for, materially at least. Having sat beside Jane so many times at shoot dinners Travers had, in the course of conversation, learned all of this from Jane who was clearly succumbing to the chronic verbal barrage, and her treatment as the Newgent squaddie. Try as he might, Travers found it impossible to picture them with any sort of amorous attachment.

Travers had dealt with these conversations in the only way he thought might lift the situation, by deliberate verbal sexual provocation with Jane whenever Newgent was out of earshot, which was often, and not difficult. Newgent was always first to bed, cleaning his guns, or walking his Labs when everyone else was socialising. He was a rotten customer of Sunburst, so Travers felt he could afford to side with her version of events. Jane was about thirty-five, petite and slim with a shock of auburn hair more often than not drawn back in a bob. As he looked at her now standing on the doorstep, she did look incredibly attractive. She wore tight shooting breeks and stockings, with a close fitting cashmere cardigan, which all served to enhance her figure. A keen horsewoman. Travers could see, from her slim outline, a lithe and fit body underneath the shooting clothes, which on most women, were unflattering. But as much as anything Travers was attracted by her deep voice, which rolled almost melodically from one sentence to another without any clip. Definitely makes the old blood race, he thought.

'Jane, how's Bobby?' Travers had dropped his bags and gave her a quick peck on the cheek.

'Absolutely fine, just taking a nap. It's been a long haul up here you know, but isn't it glorious? I saw your name on the invitation, and it's lovely to see you again. Heavens, it's only three weeks since Yorkshire.'

'Great to see you too,' said Travers. 'Sweetheart, have you seen any staff round here?'

'There's a couple of old girls drifting around, but there's a rooming list on the telephone table, I think you're in Stirling. All the rooms are named after Scottish battles.'

'Strewth, I hope it's only feathers flying tomorrow. Any idea where the gun room is?'

'Down the hall by the kitchens: here let me take that and I'll show you,' said Jane. She grabbed his guncase and struggled down the corridor, plugging in the code to the combination lock on the gun room door.

'Jane, you really shouldn't. It's far too heavy. Honestly, you've actually become Bobby's ghillie!'

'Well, you know what he's like with his guns. He can never remember numbers and he's always cleaning the bloody things, so someone's got to remember the combination.'

'You're a jewel, he doesn't deserve you. When are you coming to live with me?' said Travers light-heartedly.

'Don't joke, Tom. Things are not good. You're the only confidential ear I've got. Can we have a chat after dinner?' Travers was momentarily taken aback.

'Of course. But promise me you won't get maudlin. You'll upset my shooting and I'm too old to elope.' He said this with a grin on his face to break the tension, but it may have been a mistake.

'Bugger it, Tom, I can't talk to anyone close, but I've got to talk to someone, I'm going mad.' Travers closed the door and held her by her shoulders.

'Look. If it really is so bad surely you have friends or family – you know, parents, to discuss this thing?'

'No, that's half the problem really. He misses that guidance and reassurance of the old man which clearly I can't provide. As for chums, you've got to be joking.'

'OK,' said Travers, 'when you've got a moment, face your choices and tell Bobby where you've got to. Who knows, he might turn over a new leaf.' Travers felt uncomfortable and intrusive. He was much happier with lust as far as Jane was concerned, and felt he had dropped a pound and picked up sixpence. She looked up at Travers, caught his expression, and immediately straightened up.

'Christ, I'm sorry, Tom. What must you think of me?

You've only just arrived.' She slumped her head back down to her chest.

'Don't worry, sweetheart, it'll work itself out. And I'll hold you to that date later.' He said it with a grin, but somehow it quickly evaporated. Without another word he picked up his suitcase. Domestic imbroglios were definitely not his idea of fun, despite the attractiveness of one of the combatants.

'See you for tea?' he said as he stood by the open door.

'Uhm, yes, maybe. There's something laid out in the drawing-room.'

Travers wondered if he didn't have enough on his mind. Nevertheless he was mildy pleased that Jane saw fit to regard him as a confidante. After all, despite the years, they were only acquaintances really.

Having checked where his room was, he made his way up to the second floor, which had a simple corridor as opposed to the oak-panelled landing on the first floor. Staff quarters in the old days perhaps, or is this where they put kids and the nannies? Further down the corridor a door opened, and Bill and Jennie Penn emerged from their room.

'Hello, Curly!' exclaimed Bill, who was dressed in plus twos and an over tight pullover, patting his ample girth rather like an old lady smoothing down her crinoline. Jennie, always one or two steps behind, also had a warm smile on her face. Why he called Travers 'Curly' was beyond his comprehension. Travers put it down to the difference in their respective ages and the knowledge that he was not a brewer, like Penn, and therefore worthy of some derision. He knew though that there was camaraderie in their relationship borne of their schoolboy humour, exploited on every possible occasion.

'Hello, you old tart, delighted to see you relegated to the garret with the *hoi polloi*. Jennie, my love, no one has any respect for your husband, he's such an oaf.' Travers dropped his bags and gave Jennie a big hug.

'How's those twin boys of yours, Jennie, degrees in hand yet?'

'We're waiting to hear,' she said. 'They were both home last weekend and everyone's on tenterhooks waiting for the results.'

'Now, Tom,' Bill said, with a very serious expression on his face, 'I've got to talk to you about my swing,' and with that he lifted his arms in a parabola as though aiming his gun. 'Ever since you and Sarah broke up it's gone to pot. You've got to find another filly before they take my licence away.' With that he let out an enormous guffaw, whilst Jennie looked at Bill as if he had just stood on something nasty.

'Mind your own business, Bill,' she said in a matronly way. 'I'm sure Tom's looking for the right girl, and he certainly doesn't need any help from you.'

'Far too busy for all that nonsense, Jennie,' said Travers. 'Travelling light.'

'Yes. And you have lost weight. Drawn cheeks do nothing for those debonair looks. I do hope you're looking after yourself,' she said, with genuine concern.

Travers had known the Penns from way back. Bill was an old Harrovian, but thoroughly unspoilt by it. He had been in brewing man and boy, having graduated from some Scottish brewing university and got straight in with one of the national brewers for experience. But for most of his career he had been at Grants, an old family brewery based in Putney. He had worked his way from the mash tun to the board room, but his real forte was running the considerable number of managed houses, which even outperformed the majors in the centre of town, in both numbers and quality. Bill's only real problem was dealing with the eccentric Grant family, who in truth were more suited to an eighteenth century existence, which is when the business originated.

However, Penn had had a scrape with Simon Spencer, the managing director of Gallant (which was the third largest brewery group) over Spencer's desire to take over the non-executive chairmanship of Grants from Tom Grant. Why Tom Grant ever entertained the idea was puzzling, but when Spencer started lobbying for Penn's removal on the basis of ineptitude as a managing director, Tom Grant had told him to literally bugger off and take his scheming politics with him. As far as Tom Grant was concerned, the loyal Bill Penn had a job for life, and no 'johnny come lately' was to be allowed to besmirch a trusted employee. Penn had confided all this to Travers, because at one time, Spencer had also been in the running for the chair at Sunburst, and it was only Penn's tip-off to Travers about his experience that enabled Travers to convince the board that his little company didn't need a separate chairman. That meant that Travers was not exactly flavour of the month with Spencer, but then Travers' track record with Sunburst was watertight, and Spencer knew it.

'Are you off down for some tea?' said Travers.

'Yep,' said Penn.

'OK, see you down there, and by the way, Bill, can we have a chat in the butts tomorrow?' Penn immediately picked up the request.

'Course. Don't forget the Cherry Brandy.'

At last in his room, Travers quickly unpacked his shooting gear and lounge suit for dinner, sat on the edge of the very grand carved mahogany double bed, and tried to put his thoughts in order before the socialising got under way. He had been able to buttonhole Bill for tomorrow which was good, but he would have to find time to get at the kingpins, Tomlinson, Spencer and Egan. Contrary to the perception that it might be difficult to get business done at these sort of events, it wasn't, providing subtlety and discretion were employed. To the old guard, any form of business discussion was anathema, but frankly, over the years Travers had noticed that even the old boys couldn't help themselves but gossip between the drives. The golden rule was no business over dinner, a bit like religion, politics and kids. The women could sometimes curtail business conversation, but most of them were so used to it, that they either took an interest, re-opened the novel, or pushed off to the nearest available department store with the chauffeur whilst the shooting was taking place. For the hardened negotiator, the shoot was an excellent venue for results because first, the 'target' would be in a positive frame of mind (always assuming he'd hit something in the last ten minutes), and second, because he did not want to be distracted for too long, would generally give a spontaneous, if ill-considered response. With the personal 'Game Book' of kills to be recorded after each shoot, the last thing anyone wanted was to have missed a high 'left and right' because of some other mental distraction.

But where was Tomlinson? This was his shoot, thought Travers, and a decent host would always be around to welcome his guests, however briefly. By rights, he should have been here yesterday to make absolutely sure all the arrangements with the laird, keeper and domestics were in place. Travers was concerned that for some reason he may have cried off, and would send an underling with an apology that the shares were under attack, and the chairman needed him by his side. It had happened before.

The important thing, he knew, was to keep cool and play it by ear. Being tensed up would show to these old hands, and then every question he asked would become a challenge. It was quite in the power of these fellows to give Travers a reasonably comfortable ride through to management buyout in the event of a trade sale of Sunburst, and for that a relaxed and compliant approach would be essential. Most importantly, he hoped there would be some delegatory process where one of the major brewers would take the project on, and report back to the others on progress. He could not see how a sale could be made to anyone with sixteen shareholders all wanting their 'six penneth' in the discussions.

He rose from the bed and went over to the dormer window, which overlooked the forecourt. Quite a few cars now, mostly of course Range Rovers. He could imagine the chauffeurs already waiting for the doors to open at the local hostelry. Occasionally a chauffeur might double as a loader for his boss, but moving with the times, double guns and loaders were increasingly frowned upon as being a bit too 'professional'. Travers disagreed, certainly as far as grouse were concerned. Grouse, unlike driven pheasant or partridge, tended to come across in great coveys, and at great speed. Only double guns with a loader in tow could really exploit the situation, such that for the dedicated grouse shooter, the zenith of achievement and skill was to take two in front at maximum range, change guns and take one more in front and maybe one overhead. Indeed, the keepers wanted maximum kill rates from the guns, as overpopulation – which led to the spread of the dreaded grouse worm – was the biggest factor in restricting healthy bird numbers for future seasons. However, the massacres of the twenties and thirties when over three thousand grouse could be shot in a day were long gone.

For lots of reasons, the birds were just not there any

more, and a 'bag' of two hundred brace was perfectly respectable, and still produced great sport without the need for double guns. And because these shoots with the brewers were essentially social events with the wives, Travers accepted wholeheartedly that double guns with loaders would be inappropriate. For pheasant, it had actually become infra dig to use loaders and doubles because pheasant could never be as testing as grouse, and being much more selective was appreciated by every one concerned, not least the host who would be forking out about twenty-five pounds a bird for every kill. Travers smiled to himself at the thought of all this shooting etiquette, which must seem affected to an outsider, but most of it was based on good sense and experience. Despite his business problems, Travers reflected upon how lucky he was to be taking part in this exclusive sport and reminded himself he should be in for a real treat on the moor over the next couple of days.

Chapter Two

Quarter to five. Bit late for tea, but first he had better check in at the office, not least because his mobile had been off signal since Perth. He had noticed a telephone down in the gun room, so he made his way back down, plugged in the code on the door that Jane had used, and phoned through to Christine, his secretary and general factotum.

'Chris. Checking in. Anything happening?'

'Hi, Tom. I left a message on your mobile, did you get it? Simon Spencer's been on, so I thought you'd want to know.'

'No, I didn't get it; no signal up here. What's it about?'

'I think it must be some sort of good news, he was very chatty. He tried to get you on your mobile but wanted you to know that while he wouldn't be arriving until just before dinner, it was important, given the guest list, for him to have five minutes of your time before dinner.'

Travers' pulse was beginning to quicken, and he left Christine with a pause for a moment before answering.

'Hmm. Just don't know how to take that. He's such a slippery character. Machiavelli is his role model. OK. Anything else?' Christine gave a little giggle and said everything else was fine.

'Right, I'll check in sometime tomorrow, but if I need some help out of hours, can I give you a ring at home?'

'No problem.'

Travers replaced the receiver, leant back on the counter,

and wondered what was going on now. The thought occurred to him that because every non-executive involved with Sunburst was here on the shoot, it clearly had to be on the subject of the sale, and what's more it had to be a message telling him not to discuss the subject with the others before he arrived. Why else the insistence on talking on his arrival? Or maybe it was Spencer's one-upmanship at work, just passing on a new customer or something. Though he couldn't see Spencer wasting time on that. It had to be about the sale, and he would have to wait.

He walked back up the 'below stairs' corridor, through the green baize door and into the reception hall, noticing for the first time the glass cases on plinths around the oak panelled hall. There must have been about thirty of them, each containing different stuffed items: ptarmigan, grouse, black grouse, capercaillie, huge owls that he didn't recognise, pine martens, wild cats and a whole range of huge salmon. One or two may have been impressive, but this vast collection of dead animals looked decidedly ghoulish, saying something perhaps about the Victorian obsession for collecting things.

He moved across the hall to where the hubbub of conversation was coming from, stuck his head quickly round the huge oak door, to make sure he was in the right place, and strode in. This room was vast, in the western part of the house, and the sun was streaming in through the massive double aspect mullioned windows, casting surreal rays of sunlight through the faint haze of cigarette smoke and dust that filtered through the light. The room was half panelled, with random groups of furniture, mainly huge stuffed armchairs, Knoles, Chesterfields, ottomans and equally large coffee tables. Around the room were solid Victorian sideboards and bookshelves, liberally sprinkled with silverware, porcelain and glassware, the walls covered with tapestries and what he was sure were original Thorburns. He doubted whether the room had changed one jot in the last hundred years.

At one end of the room, under the mullioned windows and next to a huge circular table laid out with the tea things, stood a group of men chatting and laughing, while sitting clustered around the monstrous granite carved fireplace that stretched to the high ceiling was the other group of mainly women, tea cups or plates in hand. He quickly scanned the room and couldn't pick up Tomlinson, so he ambled over to the ladies group, quickly moving from chair to chair with the customary greeting and peck on the cheek. No newcomers this time around, he thought. With this group, also seated, were Sir Angus Egan, chairman of Caledonia Brewery in Edinburgh, and Peter Beaufort from the Dorset family brewers, Fell and Beaufort. Interesting, he thought. One vastly experienced in the corporate world, the other most definitely not, and both gravitated to the company of the ladies. Very sensible.

He shifted over to the fireplace where Clarissa Egan was sitting and engaged her in conversation about the house, on the basis that it was on her home territory. The conversation drew in the others so that Travers was once again relaxed, and could cast an eye in the direction of the men.

Rex Bertrand, Bobby Newgent, Bill Penn (glass of Scotch already in hand), Richard Blount (no wife this time), but who was the other guy? And no Tomlinson or Spencer. It was time to make his greetings over there, so he slipped away from one group to the other, to a friendly and ribald welcome. The unknown man was Stewart Maclaren, one of Tomlinson's stooges from the Glasgow office of Albion. He immediately stood out, as he was still in his day suit while everyone else was casual. Apparently there had been a meeting in London and Mr Tomlinson was unavoidably delayed. Maclaren had been asked to explain and to make sure everyone was comfortable. He looked a little out of his depth, and Travers could see he would be itching to get away once the last guests had arrived. So only Tomlinson and Spencer to arrive. Both late. There is definitely something cooking thought Travers.

He decided to join Penn with a glass of Scotch and headed for the salver on the sideboard. He turned to survey the scene, which was full of animated conversation. The whole objective of these shoot parties, apart from making sure good birds were put up, was to create a house party feel, where anyone could go where they wanted, and do what they wanted. Very difficult to achieve in an hotel with other guests milling about. Normally, however, it was possible to take over a small country house hotel and make sure the hotelier didn't mind if the guests ventured into the kitchen at three in the morning for a sandwich. Newcomers were quickly assimilated, because the majority knew each other so well, and new guests meant maybe new custom for the men, and fresh gossip for the ladies. The presence of women was interesting, much depending on the inclinations of the host. For some of the really keen shots, there would be 'boy's own' shoots, normally in the West Country, to take advantage of the fabulous high pheasant that the geography offered. Whereas taking into account the cost, some of the smaller brewers, in offering reciprocals to the majors, would cut out the women and put their guests up in one of their tenanted pubs, which was fine, and still very much appreciated. At the bottom of the pile would be those brewers who took advantage of every invitation to shoot, and never offered anything in return. It seemed to Travers that was just plain bad business, and he for one would willingly cut eight thousand from the advertising budget to ensure he could reciprocate for a day's shooting for seven or eight of his key customers. The whole thing might be considered dubious use of shareholders funds, but, at the end of the day it brought home the bacon more quickly and surely than a double page advertisement of equal cost.

For his part, he always enjoyed the presence of the wives. He had his own circle of friends of course, but that was completely removed from business, whereas this was part of it. He enjoyed hearing the latest news of kids, builders and washing machines, and watching powerful men reduced to childish embarrassment by an off-the-cuff remark by a practical and underrated spouse. Against that, the competitive tension and conversation lapses of the 'boys'' shoot was decidedly strained, which he was happy to do without.

He returned to the group of men, wondering what lay in store, but not perturbed, and now reasonably relaxed. He especially wanted a chat with Richard Blount, who via venture capital funds had just bought a huge block of tenanted pubs from Albion, and no one knew if he would make a go of it. He liked Richard enormously, a hard-nosed accountant who had taken to the brewing industry and its idiosyncrasies like a duck to water. He suspected Blount was deeply cynical of the peculiar practices he encountered with the brewers, but as long as he got the right deal on beer supply or rent, he wasn't going to rock the boat. They got on well together because, like Travers, Blount was not a brewer, and they found affinity with each other because of that. Travers had just sealed a five year supply agreement with Blount for the supply of soft drinks to the one hundred plus pub estate, and he wanted to make sure from Blount that despite the excellent reports from both sides Blount himself was satisfied with progress.

Having buttonholed him, but before Travis could make an opening remark, Blount said, 'Tom, hi. You probably know all about it, but I'm picking up some odd comments about Sunburst from the Albion senior brass. Watch your back, mate. When these guys start to talk about anything else but beer, I get a bit windy.'

'Thanks for the tip, but honestly, Rick, Sunburst hasn't fit for the last thirty years with these fellows. Nothing new there, but thanks all the same. If they turn on me you'll be the first to know, and we can compare notes on merchant bankers, or, come to think of it, pension consultants.' Blount gave Travers a sardonic smile, but someone with his nose was seldom wrong. The trouble was that the last thing Travers wanted was a load of rumours spreading, which could be catastrophic for business. Whatever else he had to say to Tomlinson, damage limitation would be the first thing on his list.

'Elizabeth not with you on this one?' said Travers.

'No, not really her cup of tea. Watching little boys pulling wings off flies is not her thing. Besides, while I'm delighted to be here, I've got to push off tomorrow evening. Banks want to look over their covenants, which means London on Friday.' Travers then quizzed him about the terms of the loans from the banks, and Blount's equity structure.

Travers cast another quick look at his watch, and now, just before six, he thought he would take his leave, jump in the tub, and be ready to meet Spencer if he arrived at about seven thirty. Drinks would kick off about then, with dinner at about eight thirty.

He first slipped out to the car, and let Molly out for a run. It was a perfect early evening, not a wisp of breeze. The oppressive heat and humidity of the day had gone, and instead there was the slightest chill in the air. Whenever in Scotland he had noticed before just how quickly the temperature changed with the approach of dusk. The sun was now dipping down towards the Ladder Hills, and contrasted against the weaker sun, their blue-grey dominance conveyed a powerful and almost threatening permanence against the lushness of this secret green glen, framed by the conifers. A song thrush was in full voice somewhere close by, and Travers could make out, through the shafts of light breaking through a group of Scots Pine, wagtails fluttering into the clouds of dense midges that hung in the sunlight close to the trees. He could see them hovering in their midst and feasting, then darting back to the security of the trees. It reminded Travers to take plenty of insect repellent up on the moor tomorrow. If the breeze failed to show again, the huge black midges could make life thoroughly uncomfortable in the heather, biting every piece of exposed flesh. He found cigarettes the most powerful deterrent, although the keepers rightly moaned about brush fires if there were dry conditions.

Molly had now returned from her quartering exploration, and was causing pandemonium amongst the Range Rovers as her passage by wakened the black Labradors snoozing in the back of most of them. He whistled her to heel and began to prepare her evening meal under the tailgate of the Merc. Every movement they made echoed eerily off the massive granite frontage of the house, and a heavy clunk of metal on wood signalled someone was emerging from the huge arched wooden front door. Bobby Newgent appeared, striding purposely over the scrunching gravel to his Range Rover, parked close to Travers.

'Ah. Same job as me, Tom. Mustn't forget the troops.' He opened the tailgates to reveal two fairly ancient black Labradors with grey whiskers, nestled amidst the most amazing piece of joinery Travers had ever seen. Apart from the space for the dogs, the rest of the boot was taken up with a huge mahogany cabinet with many drawers and drop down flaps, each with its own recessed brass catch to keep everything in place whilst on the move. Travers was reminded of the film clips of Montgomery's battle wagon in the North African desert, and couldn't help but raise a smile as the dogs tumbled out and various compartments were methodically opened to extract the dogs' rations.

'Tom, by the way, now that we're alone. I'm more than a little concerned that your people still fail to understand our systems. You know we have rigid stock control and your stuff just cannot turn up at the warehouse without booking in first. I'm happy to take in the new range of mixers, but not if you bring the warehouse to a halt. I sincerely hope you've got it sorted.'

'Yes, I'm sorry about that, Bobby, they should know better by now. When I heard I can assure you Distribution were given an appropriate rocket.' Travers had no idea what he was talking about but did not want to get caught on the subject. What he did know was that Newgent, as a small regional brewer with very few movements in and out of his warehouse thought it would be a good idea to replicate Tesco, and insist on telephone confirmed deliveries with twenty-four hour notice. Last month, one of Sunburst's thirty-eight tonners had been turned around and sent away, even though they were delivering just a couple of pallets of drinks. Stupid, barmy and expensive, Travers thought, but they had to go along with it.

'Well, you are responsible for a good little company, Tom, of which I am a shareholder. It shouldn't be down to me to tell you how to run it.' Bloody cheek, Travers thought. He makes about half a mill profit, I make thirteen. He's in another world. Travers stopped what he was doing and stared Newgent in the face with a deadpan but intent expression. Should he let it go, or remind him to get his priorities right. Before he could, Newgent, recognising the challenge, decided to change the subject and said with a sudden smile on his face, 'Now, Tom, what have you heard about the grouse? I'm told the keepers have the worm under control, and they've dosed two thousand birds this spring. As for the Peregrines, I hear we'll see them on practically every beat, which can't be good news.'

'Well, Bobby,' said Travers, relaxing again. 'You know a lot more than me. I did hear the breeding rate was good with no late frosts, so if your swing's in order we should bring some down.'

The small talk continued until Molly had finished. Travers put down some biscuits and a fresh bowl of water in the back of the voluminous Merc, made sure some windows were open and locked the car.

'Bobby, got to go.'

'OK, old boy, see you for dinner.'

Travers wondered how on earth Jane ever fell for the pompous twat in the first place. Only forty-odd, but acts as if he's sixty. Not exactly a bundle of fun. Poor Jane.

He re-entered the house, went up to his room and drew the bath. After a long soak nothing else had crystallised in his mind. He had dressed, and was now ready to go. He looked at his watch for the umpteenth time. Right, seven o'clock, better get down in case Spencer turns up, he thought.

He made his way downstairs, and rather than go to the drawing-room where he could still hear voices, he had a nose round the other rooms leading off from the hall. Having found the dining-room, various other reception rooms and the estate office, he found what he was looking for, to the left of the grand staircase. The library. Having checked it was empty he walked in almost reverently as he took in this monument to gracious living. The room was entirely panelled with a light, unpolished cedar, and the smell was enveloping. A mixture of sweet resin and finest Havana cigars is the only way he could have described it. It was not a massive room, but that was partly because of the warmth and comfort that exuded from it. A sort of olive green seemed to be the predominant colour of the wall hangings, while the floor was covered in an extremely ancient looking Persian rug of giant proportions. The Chesterfields and armchairs were entirely leather bound and over the years had acquired an almost walnut patina. In a nook, to the right of the carved mahogany fireplace, stood a massive partner's desk with old wooden filing trays stacked on one corner with papers still in them. Opposite was a large circular inlaid table, complete with comfortable armed chairs, all positioned in front of the long wall, which was entirely covered by books, complete with a mahogany ladder running on brass rollers that could move along the entire length of the bookshelf. Row upon row from floor to ceiling. From the other walls hung, what Travers instantly recognised, were missing from the other rooms, family portraits. No dead animals here, just dead ancestors.

He was starting to examine some of the portraits when taken completely off balance by Simon Spencer appearing from behind him.

'Tom, how are you? The housekeeper said I might find you in here!' His loud polished accent rent the silence of the room.

'Good to see you, Simon, you must be exhausted. You clearly found the housekeeper, which I haven't managed to do, so let me go and get you a drink, and we can have that chat. My secretary got your message through to me.'

'Excellent, Tom. I've seen Annabel to our room, so I've got half an hour if you have.'

'That's fine, make yourself comfortable, and let me sort out a Scotch.' Travers quickly left the room and headed for the kitchens. He hated to be caught like that and however brief, he knew a minute or two was all he needed to get his brain into gear to deal with Spencer and getting drinks was a good excuse. He found the phantom housekeeper in the kitchen, and asked if she wouldn't mind delivering two large Scotches without ice to the library. He then made his way straight back to Spencer, and closed the door. Travers sat back down again and waited for Spencer to take the initiative.

Spencer had a huge frame, not fat, but well built and very tall, possibly six foot seven. He still wore his charcoal pinstripe suit, and had both charm and charisma, as many big men do. His one weakness, thought Travers, is his willingness to smile, that inability to thrust the dagger up to the hilt, which separated him from the more successful and ruthless businessmen he had met. Spencer did have a good sense of humour though, and it was difficult not to like him.

'First time I've been here,' said Spencer. 'Surprising really. With Annabel's contacts, I've shot most of the moors in this neck of the woods.' Travers was fully aware of Annabel Spencer's noble family connections, and it was clearly a marriage made in heaven, with Simon and his family supplying the cash, and she providing the connections, given her ducal relatives were somewhat down at heel.

After five minutes' banter, Travers was itching for Spencer to get going and give him the news. Spencer's somewhat maladroit attempts at the power game were beginning to get tiresome. Spencer wore his heart on his sleeve; you could see him coming, unlike Tomlinson who was an altogether different kettle of fish.

'Right, Simon, what have you got for me?'

'Yes, of course,' said Spencer, immediately lowering his voice to a gentle boom from the normal staccato. 'Now, you're not to shoot the messenger,' giving himself an appreciatory chuckle, 'but we've made some decisions about Sunburst at a meeting at the Brewers Society this morning, and it was felt I should tell you what has been decided. Piers was of course at that meeting along with Johnstone of Caledonia, but it's basically Piers you will be dealing with, as this thing moves ahead. Unfortunately he is just too tied up this evening with the shoot arrangements to break the news to you himself. But, Tom, we all believe it is crucial that you are among the first to know that Sunburst's voting shareholders have finally taken the decision to divest the business, and we would hate for you to pick up that news from anyone else but the shareholders themselves.'

It was absolutely obvious to Travers that this was a well prepared speech that Annabel probably contributed to on the long drive up. Best not to interrupt, and let him spill it all out, thought Travers.

'Now, the position is this,' said Spencer, warming to his task. 'My company, Gallant, has as you know been under an awful lot of pressure on our profits and margins, and we only just managed to beat off the Australians, for the moment, from their take-over attempt. The institutional investors have told us in no uncertain terms that we've got to get rid of all our peripheral activities, pull in the cash and focus on the pubs. Sunburst, thanks to you, is worth quite a lot, and frankly, we decided some months ago that it had to go as far as we were concerned. Now I can tell you that at one time Albion was keen to pick it up by buying out Gallant, and all the other smaller shareholders including Caledonia. The thing is though, Tom, Albion aren't the best-loved brewers in the industry, and they finally felt too much business could drop away by a lack of loyalty or antagonism if they took over the business. As far as the good Scottish Caledonia is concerned, they don't like cosy English clubs, and they want the money, if any's going.

'So, it's got to go. Goldberg's has already been appointed

as the merchant bank to handle the sale, and you will work with them in preparing the details for the Information Memorandum for Sale.'

Travers listened as though undergoing *déjà vu*. At least it was out with no major surprises. At that point there was a knock, and an elderly woman in a black dress and white pinafore poked her head round the door, with a silver salver precariously balanced above her head.

'Malt for the gentlemen?' Before the salver and the two crystal tumblers fell from her grasp, Travers sprang up.

'Here, let me take that from you, and thank you very much. Perfect.' Travers held the salver, and with his other hand held the door ajar for the woman to exit. He then turned around, closed the door, leant against it and popped the question:

'And what about my request to launch a management buyout?'

'Oh come on, Tom, you can't be serious. Where are you going to raise the money, and anyway, you've got a job for life from whoever takes over the business.'

He moved back to the table, placing one of the huge tumblers, which were at least half full, before Spencer. He took his own and sat down again.

'Wrong on both counts,' said Travers. 'I've already got venture capital funds in place,' he lied, 'and you know as well as I do that whoever takes over will close production, fire the old team and put their own guys in. They'd be crazy not to.'

'Well, we don't see it that way at all. But,' and Spencer's face now acquired the look of the cat that stole the cream, 'we have anticipated your concerns, and a package has been put in place that means you will come out of this a very happy man, Tom. I am of course talking about a serious bonus to see this thing through.' Spencer now leant back with a self-satisfied smile that suggested the whole matter had been successfully resolved thanks to his masterful exposition.

'Simon, I'm hugely disappointed in you personally, and Piers, that you could ever think I would give up on Sunburst, the management and staff, just like that, and for a few pieces of silver. You don't know me at all, which is sad. I know the pressures you and Piers are under, but that doesn't stop you discussing this properly with me first, before you run off to Goldberg's. Christ, I at least deserve that. Why should I help you if you won't help me? I feel perfectly entitled to move into a Portakabin down the road from Sunburst, and with my team, mount an MBO in direct competition with anyone else. You could put anyone you like in control at Sunburst, and try and get the best price you can. Who knows, I may be able to beat the best bid you get, which is most definitely in your shareholders' interests. I would certainly be at your AGM to ask them the same question if you disagree. How would you react to that?'

'Tom, Tom, there's no need to get upset. We have no one else who knows anything about Sunburst who could see through the process on the ground. There has got to be a way round this, but it really isn't my brief to agree it with you now. I do understand how you feel, but I'm afraid you'll have to take it up with Piers who has been delegated with the authority to act on behalf of the major shareholders.'

Good old predictable Simon, thought Travers. Spencer had just told him exactly what he wanted to hear. He could have been told to clear off, with his P45 in the post. But he didn't, and clearly they really did want him there to show off the company to prospective buyers because they had no one else who knew a blind thing about soft drinks. The playing field was levelling a bit for Travers, but he didn't want to overdo it.

'Simon, you know you've really hit me with some very bad news. I'm sorry if I seemed rude. You've told me to discuss it with Piers, which is exactly what I will do when I've slept on it. Hopefully I can have a quiet chat with him tomorrow.'

'That's the spirit, Tom. The last thing we want is for you to walk away from this, or dare I say it, get yourself pushed off the plank. On behalf of Gallant, I'm prepared to look at any solution that gets Sunburst off our hands at the best possible price. I'm sure Piers feels the same way.'

Travers could see that while Spencer was disappointed he hadn't taken the 'package' bait, there was a way through that Spencer wouldn't be directly responsible for, which clearly suited Spencer. Not a great one for confrontation, our Mr Spencer, thought Travers.

'Well look, Simon, it's gone half past seven, and you've just got time for a bath. I'm not accepting anything yet, but I'm grateful you've told me what you can. By the way, does Sir Angus know about all this?'

'Oh yes,' said Spencer. 'Caledonia have a big free trade in Scotland, and they don't want to be exclusively tied to Sunburst. Angus has made that clear. He passed it over to Johnstone to sort out the details.'

'OK see you later, Simon.' Spencer took a large swig of his malt, then huge hands on the table, pushed himself upright, beaming at Travers as he moved to the door and the staircase, while Travers, drink still in hand, made his way to the drawing-room, where people were gathering for drinks. His head was spinning a bit but his planned options were all still open, and the thrill of the chase had the old adrenalin running. Everything to play for. For some obscure reason he was elated and in a good mood. It was now a quarter to eight.

* * *

As he moved into the room, about three-quarters of the party were present, and this time the whole group stood in front of the vast windows as the sun, pale and orange, dipped behind the distant Cairngorms. Glasses were clinking, and two of the housemaids were moving amongst the party recharging glasses with champagne and distributing hors d'oeuvres. Holding centre stage was Piers Tomlinson, fresh and spruce, wearing a sporting three piece suit, whereas most of the other men wore simple dark suits. Tomlinson spotted Travers instantly, disengaged and moved towards him.

'Tom! So pleased you could make it. I'm so sorry I wasn't here this afternoon to welcome you all. Unfortunately, Strathallan isn't the most sociable of hosts. I'll introduce you to him when he deigns to appear. We're going to need you in the next couple of days, Tom. I've just come from the head keeper's cottage, and they're very confident. Birds in the right place on most of the moors, not too much wind so they should keep on track, and it hasn't been shot over since the twelfth. Some accurate shooting is what we want now.'

All of this was said in Tomlinson's low-key matter of fact way. He wore spectacles, and as he peered over them to talk, he constantly adjusted them with a brush of a finger. Whilst cutting a dapper figure, Tomlinson looked more like an academic than a brewer, with a donnish look about him, helped by the fop of black hair on his forehead that had escaped from the very trim neatness of the rest of his head.

Travers wondered if Tomlinson would mention the Sunburst developments, or whether he should. He thought better of it, simply because Tomlinson had his hands full as host, and now was obviously not the time.

'You know I'll do my best, Piers, I'll be in good company. No Henrietta? Such a pity, she would love the house and the sparkling guests you've pulled together.'

Travers made this sound slightly more cynical than he had intended, because Tomlinson never took his wife anywhere. Unlike Spencer's wife, Henrietta's family was loaded, and indeed came from Scotland. Travers, on the few occasions he had met her over the last ten years, could see she enjoyed these social gatherings, but with a few drinks she was well known for becoming a little too direct on issues of the day, especially if it related to Piers' business affairs. More than once she had referred to the 'poor bastards' whose misfortune it was to work for Piers, and that they suffered a shared affliction. Needless to say any such domestic exposure could create hairline cracks in Piers' porcelain persona, and as a result Henrietta was unfortunately rarely seen.

'Yes, you're right, Tom,' he said a little guardedly, as his eyes narrowed. 'I know she would love to be here, but she has stayed on in London.' His eyes were now shifting across the room as Travers recognised the old man from the bridge enter the room a little shakily, looking slightly bemused.

'Look, very quickly, Tom, did Spencer manage to catch you earlier?'

'Yes, Piers, and I'm unhappy and upset by the whole thing. I can't go along with your suggestion. We've got to talk.' Travers said this calmly, quietly, but firmly.

'Surely not,' said Tomlinson sarcastically. 'Not to mix my metaphors, Tom, you shouldn't look a gift horse in the mouth. I advise you to be careful. You're swimming in the big pool now. But yes, we must talk. I'm sure we'll get a chance tomorrow.'

'Thank you, Piers, I won't be unreasonable.' Travers gave Tomlinson as genuine a smile as he could muster as Tomlinson turned to attend to Strathallan. Travers now moved across the room to join the others, making his way to Rex Bertrand and his wife Lottie, whom he hadn't really had a chance to say anything but hello to earlier on. Bertrand was recharging his gin and tonic while Lottie had Richard Blount pinned in a corner. Bertrand was the chairman and chief executive of the family brewers Bertrands, from the depths of Surrey, but with a pub estate that extended into Sussex and Kent. Like most of the other regional family brewers, the strength and quality of the pubs, all on freeholds and without debt, was such that the Bertrand dynasty (stretching back to the seventeenth century) had little to fear from the major brewers in terms of competition, and like the others enjoyed a very civilised lifestyle. Bertrand was a larger than life character, always a keen spokesman for the regionals at the Brewers Society, and there was nothing he enjoyed more than tearing into the major brewers for either their greed or stupidity. Many's the time Travers had watched with great amusement as Bertrand would fence and prevaricate with some senior executive, never going quite far enough for tempers to break, and recovering the status quo with his acerbic wit.

Travers liked his wife, Lottie, very much indeed. A good twenty years younger than Rex's sixty odd years, she was devoid of malice, airs or graces, but called a spade a spade. She knew very well how to handle Bertrand's Churchillian outbursts, which was to disengage as quickly as possible. On the few occasions she had attempted to stop Bertrand's verbal assault on some unsuspecting soul, she had found she was not exempt from the shrapnel herself, so her eyes would normally roll skyward, and she would attempt to join another conversation.

'One hell of a long way up here, Rex, but by the sounds of it, it should be worthwhile.'

'Slept most of the way up, so I'm as fresh as a daisy. Only disturbance was Lottie nattering to the bloody driver. What d'you know about this fella Strathallan?' said Bertrand.

'Don't ask me, Rex, haven't a clue. Anyway, if anyone does, Lottie will.'

'Hmm. She's picked up the family history, but what does he actually do? Surely to God Tomlinson's not dropped him on the board just for the grouse and the fishing. Is he meant to contribute *anything*?'

'All I can tell you is that the family trust owns a couple of the local distilleries, one hundred and fifty thousand acres around here, half of Mayfair; and they are a big, but I mean big, shareholder in Albion. With Gallant under attack from the Australians, maybe some more of the Strathallan fortune has been pumped into Albion shares to shore up the defences, in exchange for a seat. Pure speculation mind you,' said Travers. 'Come to think of it, if you want to know, just pop the question to Angus, he can probably tell you the brand of toothpaste he uses.'

Bertrand guffawed and nodded, then said to Travers, 'By the way, saw your footage on the Tesco shelves the other day. We've got lots of capacity in the brewery for half pints and cans, d'you think we can get in there?' Before Travers could answer, Tomlinson cut in, introducing Strathallan. Both of them had surprisingly similar suits, although that's as far as the similarity went. Strathallan had a shock of white hair, held in place by presumably Brylcreem, with sprigs of it defying gravity, as though a powerful electric current had been passed through him. Several buttons were missing from his waistcoat, his shirt collar was frayed, and his stained MCC tie was hopelessly at odds with the rest of the ensemble. His huge stomach overhung his trousers, leaving an expanse of Tattershall check shirt exposed. On his feet he wore a pair of black slippers with the family crest embroidered in gilt on each one.

'Gentlemen,' said Tomlinson oilily. 'May I introduce Lord Strathallan, who has graciously allowed us to use his shooting box for the next couple of days.' Tomlinson obviously thought he'd raised the joke of the century. Strathallan raised his arm but still close to his chest, as if he were offering his tie.

'How d'y'do,' said Bertrand rather brusquely. He clearly had no time for people who didn't have a proper job. 'If this were mine, I'm buggered if I'd let it out to Tomlinson, but I'm grateful all the same.'

'Oh, what's wrong with him then?' said Strathallan in an unusually high pitched voice for such a big man. He seemed genuinely concerned.

'How long have you got?' guffawed Bertrand, completely ignoring Tomlinson. Strathallan was looking intently at Bertrand waiting for an explanation. His hand was still at his chest after shaking hands, having forgotten to put it back to his side. Tomlinson felt things could go from bad to worse, and without even allowing Travers to shake the old fellow's hand, began to wheel Strathallan away to be introduced elsewhere. Bertrand gently but firmly held Tomlinson's arm.

'Just a moment, Piers, if you don't mind, one more question for his Lordship. Tell me sir, how are you enjoying life on the Albion board?'

'Oh,' said Strathallan, relieved that he was actually being asked an opinion on something. 'Piers and the rest of the chaps are proving excellent colleagues. I've been to one meeting so far at their London offices – very close to my club actually. I'm asked to attend two or three times a year.'

'Two or three times!' said Bertrand, 'barely worthwhile I would have thought, and what's your speciality?'

'Well, I help where I can on property and estate management. My word, so many pubs, and I suspect there could be more in the pipeline,' said Strathallan, warming to his theme. By now Tomlinson had heard quite enough.

41

He suddenly had visions of Strathallan becoming Albion's 'deep throat', with all the company's secrets thrown to the wind.

'Rex, you're incorrigible,' said Tomlinson with restrained malice, leading Strathallan away.

'Christ,' said Bertrand, 'the old feller's completely gaga, shouldn't be allowed. Once upon a time, Tom, I had a lot of respect for Albion, as did my father. But honestly, the place is run by simpletons and morons, and there's the living proof.'

Travers was quietly giggling. 'For God's sake, Rex, leave it alone. You're in his house and you are about to shoot his grouse. Be grateful.'

Out in the hall a gong sounded and one of the ladies in black struggled to shout at the top of her voice:

'Dinner is served. Would you please, ladies and gentlemen, make your way to the dining-room.'

Travers glanced at his watch, half past eight on the dot. As they filtered out, they all ran into Simon Spencer and Annabel arriving at the foot of the stairs. Everything stopped while the ladies gave each other shrill greetings and air-kisses, with Simon lapping up the attention. His laughter boomed above everyone, apologising for the delay to dinner, which of course there hadn't been.

The dining-room was a sombre affair, with the exception of the the vast table itself. Huge sideboards, more Thorburns and Camerons on the walls, but bland wallpaper rather than panelling, which gave the room a rather stark appearance against the huge floor to ceiling curtains, now drawn. However, the table was a different matter altogether. Extending to about twenty feet by six feet across of solid highly polished mahogany, the centre-piece was an elongated solid silver container that looked like a small horse trough. Engraved from one end to the other with kilted clansmen and rearing horses, with pedestalled flowers and other silver statuettes within it. To either side was more silverware, like half size pheasants with long-flowing tails, miniature 'monarchs of the glen' and other assorted beasties, and magnificent candelabra. The overall impact was amazing, contrasted as it was against the deep mahogany burnish of the table. Seeing one's fellow diners across the table might prove a problem, however.

Place settings had been completed by Tomlinson, and he moved quickly around the room drawing back chairs for the ladies and ushering them into position. He had the perennial shoot dinner problem of the men outnumbering the women, and in this case ten men playing off six ladies.

As expected, thought Travers, he had got round the problem quite neatly, by placing himself at the head, with Strathallan to his right and Spencer (his opposite number at Gallant) at the other end of the table. On his left he placed Sir Angus Egan, then Susie Beaufort, Richard Blount, Jane Newgent, Travers, Jennie Penn and Rex Bertrand. Going down the table on his right after Strathallan were Annabel Spencer, Bobby Newgent, Lottie Bertrand, Peter Beaufort, Bill Penn, and Lady (Clarissa) Egan.

Travers was delighted. His end of the table was much more fun with not a stiff in sight. He could think of nothing worse than having to endure two hours with uninteresting or unsociable people around him; it was just too much like hard work. To have Jane and Jennie either side of him made his day.

As napkins were placed on laps and the small talk began, Travers' mind drifted onto his conversation with Tomlinson. Unsurprisingly, there had been some real cut to Tomlinson's response, but at the end of the day, Travers knew he could create all sorts of problems for them if they weren't amenable, and Tomlinson was open to talk, as was Spencer. He was slightly worried that Angus Egan was quite so ready to ditch Caledonia's shareholding, but accepted that despite the long relationship with Caledonia, it stood for nothing if the strategic requirements were wrong.

'Penny for your thoughts,' said Jane, who had briefly been speaking to Richard Blount. She was wearing a blue chiffon cocktail dress, with a sparse but attractive diamond necklace and earings, her hair swept back and captured at the back, all of which set off her sparkling blue eyes.

'Oh, Piers was telling me that wolves are being reintroduced to the Highlands.' He turned towards her and smiled, and with his best Humphrey Bogart said, 'But don't worry kid, stick close and you're safe with me.' She chuckled. 'How are you this evening?' said Travers.

Normally pretty abstemious, Jane still held her champagne flute glass beside her chin, and said, 'Great, great. I've been thinking about what you said in talking to Bobby, and I suppose you're right. Trouble is, can't see myself doing much about it.'

'Oh well,' said Travers. 'Come on, don't let it spoil your evening, it'll all seem different in the morning.' Travers knew he'd dropped the most frightful clanger as soon as he said it. She sat bolt upright and gave him a ferocious stare.

'Bloody typical,' she said. 'You're all the same. About as much understanding as a pound of boiled cod.'

He looked at her with a sheepish apologetic smile, and patted her free hand, which was resting on her knee. He would have removed it in an instant, but she quickly moved her hand and slapped it on top of his, pinning his hand to her knee, while still holding her glass of champagne in the other. There was a blank expression between them, with her now leaning slightly forward as if in conversation, but shielding his hand. Without a word her blank but concentrated expression slowly changed to an impish smile and then a grin.

'Well, well, Mr Travers, not quite so self-righteous now.'

Travers tried to pull his hand away again, but she wasn't letting go. He flicked his eyes to either side to see if anyone was looking in their direction. Fortunately, they were all heavily engaged with one another creating conversation.

'Let go.'

'No.'

She was obviously enjoying the moment enormously, and without shifting her eyes from his, turned her head and still with a smile took a gentle sip from her half-filled glass in her right hand. In a whisper now, Travers said, 'For God's sake, Jane, Bobby will kill you, not to mention what he might do to me. Let go.'

She still had his hand pinned down hard against her knee.

'Promise to see me later.' She said this slowly, word by word, pouting her lips.

'Bugger off.'

'If that's the way you want it.' She was now gently rocking with amusement attempting to stifle a laugh. Travers' eyes turned momentarily into dishes, and he couldn't help himself but succumb to a smile. Both of them were on the brink of laughter when he finally said, 'I give in. Now let go.' Which she duly did, slowly releasing his hand and leaning back gently in her chair, still looking at Travers.

'Jesus, Jane, I think I'm getting an embolism. You're outrageous.'

Still in the mood, quick as a flash and looking down at his trousers she replied, 'Really. I can't say it shows.' They both burst out laughing, and for a moment everyone looked in their direction hoping to understand what was quite so funny.

Jennie Penn turned from Rex Bertrand and said with a kindly smile, 'Come on, Tom, share the joke.'

Travers still creased up, gratefully shifted in his seat towards Jennie. She had given him his cue and he said to her, 'It's the one about the gamekeeper, Jennie. Far too coarse for you. Tell me, Bill looks really well. Is he over the heart problem?'

'Well, not over it, but he's had the shock of the angina, got the right pills, and at last cut down on the beer and whisky. How long it will last I don't know.'

'Well, he'll listen to you, Jennie, but no one else. Keep hammering away at him. Once he's with the boys here he's on another adventure.'

Although Jennie seemed to follow in Bill's footsteps, that actually was far from the truth. Certainly his extrovert character and boyish humour made it seem that Jennie was a bit of a wallflower, but in truth, Bill depended on her for everything. Travers had stayed with the couple one weekend at their place near Guildford, and had been really touched by their genuine affection and concern for one another. More revealing was how Bill always asked her advice or opinion on everything, even occasionally saying, 'What do you think, Mother?' obviously harking back to earlier days when their kids were growing up. During that weekend the conversation had of course ventured into business, and again Jennie was there with the low-down on Grants, and how Bill should be handling various situations. There was no doubt in Travers' mind that Bill would not be where he was today were it not for Jennie. She was a real brick.

By now the ladies in black were passing along the line of seated guests, charging their glasses with what Travers could see was a very fine Montrachet. Placed before them was the first course, which was described on the printed menu cards as 'Escalope of Cold Salmon Maitre Albert'. Travers metaphorically raised his hat to the lad in the kitchen; it looked delicious. Middle cuts of salmon covered in what looked like a white butter sauce with sorrel, mushrooms and shallots. He had no doubt at all that they were eating locally caught salmon from the Spey, which had fortunately avoided the nets of his poacher acquaintance.

As they waited for the layout of the course to be completed, Travers cast an eye around the table. To his left, Rex Bertrand and Spencer were comparing notes on gun dogs. He'd noticed before that the two got on well together, largely because Spencer was so amenable, and a fascinating raconteur. Bertrand respected him as a hard working Gallant executive, and it was true that Spencer spent a lot of time out in the pubs with his management, making sure he understood the problems.

Across the table, Travers saw that Bill Penn and Clarissa Egan were getting on famously, with the occasional raucous laughter from Bill. Heaven knows what the subject was, which was probably the same thought going through Jennie's mind, sat next to him.

Further up the table, Lottie Bertrand was in conversation with Peter Beaufort. He was only about twenty-eight, and was currently running the free trade operation at the family's brewery, Fell And Beaufort in Dorset. His father had died several years ago, which really hit all of them very hard indeed, as he was genuinely loved and admired by all of the family and staff, and was a great loss to the business. Peter's uncle had stepped into the breech as managing director, but no one believed it would be long before Peter took full control. He was a self-assured individual, quietly picking up the tricks of the trade, listening and learning. Like his father, he did not have a trace of arrogance, was excellent company, and one of the best natural shots Travers had ever seen. Across the table, Susie, his wife of about three years, was both beautiful and of the same temperament as Peter, being about the same age or perhaps slightly younger. They already had two small boys, so clearly the inheritance was in good hands, thought Travers.

Travers could imagine Lottie gently extracting all the information on the family from Beaufort. She simply had to know every detail, skeletons 'n' all. She was a lovely woman with her heart in the right place, thought Travers, but she was the most frightful gossip. He couldn't imagine Peter Beaufort giving away any information he didn't want to, as he caught Beaufort's occasional sardonic smile to some of Lottie's questioning.

The fish was excellent, as witnessed by Jane's comment, 'Yummie.'

Just as most were finishing, some quiet spluttering was coming from the far right of Travers. He looked up and saw Strathallan with both hands to his chest, coughing and spluttering, his body moving up and down with each convulsion. At about the same time, everyone else picked up what was going on, and Travers could see knives and forks begin to rest on plates as everyone waited for the moment to pass. Conversation was still taking place amongst a few of the diners, but was now muted.

Tomlinson had reached across and placed his hand on Strathallan's shoulder, but apart from that was looking on embarrassingly bemused, at a loss to know what to do next. To Strathallan's right, Annabel Spencer turned to the table and said anxiously and obviously, 'I think the poor man's choking.'

She rose from her seat, napkin in hand, stood behind Strathallan and patted his back rather than give it a good wallop.

'Is it helping?' she enquired, as Strathallan continued to quietly convulse, his eyes taking the shape of saucers.

Complete silence now, as everyone waited for the problem to pass, or for the drama to turn into a crisis. At this point, Lottie Bertrand leapt up, and, being a big woman, the chair went flying as she stood up and stepped back. Unperturbed, she moved quickly up behind Strathallan, brushing Annabel to one side, leant forward and grabbed his wine glass, and fairly shoved the contents at Strathallan's mouth, most of which missed and went straight down his threadbare shirt.

'If only I can get him to drink something!' she said with determination.

From down the table, meant more as an aside to his wife, Rex Bertrand boomed, 'Steady on, that's no way to treat a fine wine.'

That was it. Despite the seriousness of the situation, ladies' hands were raised to mouths to cover smiles, and Bill Penn let out a staccato 'Ha!', joined by an open giggle from Peter Beaufort.

'Oh, Rex, do shut up,' said Lottie. 'What can we do? He's choking to death on a salmon bone or something.' By this time Tomlinson was standing and slightly backing away as though Strathallan had the measles, a look of complete horror on his face but saying nothing.

Meanwhile Penn turned to Bertrand and muttered, 'My goodness, Rex, what an impressive woman Lottie is. A godsend at throwing out time.'

Bertrand decided not to respond, discretion being the better part of valour. Bobby Newgent clearly felt that the comment was way out of order, and with his facial twitch working overtime said, 'Gentlemen please!' raising his hand as if to silence any further interruption.

Travers thought for one desperate moment Lottie was sure to administer the Heimlich manoeuvre to Strathallan, who had now taken on a puce hue. Instead, she screamed, 'For God's sake cough man, get rid of it!' She was bent over, shouting into Strathallan's ear, and then gave him an almighty thump on the back.

Strathallan slumped forward under the weight of the blow, seemed to be vomiting, then slumped back into his chair with obvious relief. Whatever it was had been cleared.

'No signs of any bones, do you think I should give him another go?' said Lottie.

The tension broke as the crisis passed, whilst Strathallan sat on his chair fighting for breath. Lottie, realising she had been unwittingly humorous, with Strathallan recovering at her feet, blushed, drew down her dress, and with an embarrassed brush of her hair, returned to her seat.

Bobby Newgent, who had done nothing but watch until now, sought to create order and said, 'Lottie, you are a marvel, and you too Annabel. I'm sure Lord Strathallan will be eternally grateful.' They all turned round to Strathallan who, still holding his chest, raised an arm in acknowledgement. Tomlinson, who had also regained his composure, sprang forward out of his chair to help Strathallan. Instead Strathallan brushed him off, got up and went over to Lottie proffering breathless thanks for her presence of mind and skill.

The Scottish ladies in black were now all at the door, and Tomlinson without a word was gesticulating wildly for them to enter the room, and clear away the first course, so that normality could be restored as soon as possible. He then sat down quickly and everyone followed his example. Various ladies were recounting other examples of near death at dinner tables. Clarissa Egan, sat next to Rex Bertrand, led the conversation. Bertrand's response was predictable.

'Best to use a pipe and funnel on him for the main course, if you ask me. Tempting fate if we don't.' That clearly appealed to all the men at their end of the table, with a peal of laughter restoring the ambience of the party. It further sparked Bill Penn to recount the story, which Travers had heard many times, about the brewery executive who literally keeled over and died in his butt on the moor, after a splendid and memorable lunch on a brewery grouse shoot. Sadly, recounted Penn, the host felt obliged to cancel the last drive of the afternoon, which he felt was quite uncalled for, but he supposed the fellow's wife was probably a little upset, not least because the poor fellow's dog wouldn't stop licking the corpse.

The main course and dessert passed away without incident, and again, the chef had excelled himself with the local venison, whilst Tomlinson had wheeled out the most perfect Cheval Blanc to complement it, followed by a great Sauternes with the pear pudding.

Next to Travers, Jane had been happy and animated throughout the dinner, picking up on the gossip from Richard Blount on her right, and Travers on her left. As the cheeseboard circulated, Travers felt a tap on his knee, and Jane said in a conspiratorial tone, 'I know where you are. I'll pop up and see you at midnight.'

Travers, whilst not forgetting the earlier incident, had half felt it was a tension-breaking bit of fun for Jane, and for him come to that, but that she would have thought better of any hopeless tryst with him. Again, making sure there was no one in earshot, Travers turned in his seat, lowered his head and said, 'Jane, don't be daft. Bobby will ask where you've gone, and we're not schoolkids, we've both got too much to lose. I'm very, very fond of you, but I'm not going to be responsible for breaking up your marriage. That's it.'

'Well just talk to me then,' she said petulantly. She now had both a pout and a furrowed brow, and Travers could see in the brief silence she was trying to marshal her arguments of how to persuade him. 'Bobby's out like a light as soon as he hits the pillow. You know how early he goes up; I never go with him. Why are you being so horrid, when you promised?'

Travers tried to lift the situation. 'Listen, Jane, if you can't work things out with Bobby over the next month, come down to London, we'll have some dinner, and I'll do my best to help. You know, advice. You must stop trying to get me into bed, sweet pea, you're a married woman. Honestly, Jane, I can't do better than that.'

She looked at him, accusingly, and Travers could see she may have had a glass too many of Tomlinson's delicious wine, not to mention the earlier champagne. She scowled and with all her might gave a backward punch of her left hand against his thigh, fortunately, under the table.

'That feels better,' she said, and a mischievous smile returned to her face. 'Come to think of it, I get to town a lot. What's your address again?' The tension had passed, and Travers was relieved, but already he was thinking to himself exactly what he had let himself in for. He'd had a couple of girlfriends since his divorce, both introduced through business connections, and both very serious single professional ladies. In both cases the word 'expediency' came to mind, in other words meeting mutual sexual needs rather than affection. It was the old male thing about protecting Jane's vulnerability as well as despoiling her sexually, that he knew was so appealing. He turned to her, looked her in the eyes, and couldn't help but give her a smile of affection. She was not slow to pick it up.

At that point, Tomlinson rose from his chair, and asked his guests if the ladies would care to retire to the drawing-room for coffee, while the gentlemen enjoyed a glass of port and a cigar.

Travers was appalled that one or two of these fellows still indulged in this anachronism, but was equally amazed that not one of the ladies ever appeared to complain about being treated like underlings, not to put too fine a point upon it. Travers couldn't help feeling, however, that he was very privileged indeed to be in this house, and about to enjoy the finest shooting that money or breeding could buy.

The men stood, pulled back the chairs for the ladies, and off they went together chatting keenly. When they had gone, Tomlinson suggested that they all move into the library, where port and coffee had been laid out, and that if anyone wanted to take a bottle of the remaining claret, they were welcome to do so. Travers accepted the invitation, as he found that port gave him the most appalling headaches in the morning, which were difficult to shake off, and the Cheval was really too good not to indulge.

Travers tagged on to Sir Angus Egan as the men filed slowly through to the library. Egan was an old Etonian, with a military sojourn in the Scots Guards before ultimately joining the brewing business at Caledonia. Travers knew nothing about these different regiments, but from what he could see, for most of these fellows, military service was but an extension of their school days. Nothing wrong with that, he thought, particularly if, like most boys emerging from the public school system, you don't have much idea of what you want to do in life, if the family business isn't beckoning. From there, Egan returned to the place of his birth doing various jobs in ship broking, finally finishing up at Caledonia through one connection or another. He took to pubs and brewing like a duck to water, and helped by impeccable family connections rose swiftly through the hierarchy to become managing director, then chairman. Some ten years on now, Egan had a string of top notch chairmanships, and was regarded as the titular head of the Edinburgh business elite. However, Egan was not the type to rise so far by stepping on other people. Quite the reverse, he had achieved success by listening and delegating to the right people, with an innate sense and style of leadership. The Scottish Establishment held him as their icon to the English industrial power base in London, to which he was a frequent visitor.

'Tom, it's difficult sometimes to find the opportunity, but can I just say both personally, and as one of your shareholders, I really have been impressed with what you've done with Sunburst over the last ten years. It's easy for others to snipe at the pub trade and the brewing industry, but you've come up with the products, you've marketed them and produced fantastic growth in profits, that certainly none of us brewers could have thought possible ten years ago. It's a remarkable achievement.'

'Oh, that's nice of you to say so, Angus, thank you.' By now they were in the library, and Sir Angus ushered Travers to a leather Chesterfield sofa in the corner. Tomlinson himself had earlier decanted the port, and was slowly moving round the room dispensing glasses of port from a salver. The head 'lady in black' followed closely offering Havanas from a huge oak cigar box.

'I know you're aware of the consortium plans, Tom, and there may not be much you can do about it, but how do you feel?' said Sir Angus. Travers looked down at the bottle of claret he was still holding, and paused. This was either an unexpected bonus to air his views with one of the most influential shareholders, or flush his chances if he screwed up his response.

'Let down, obviously. Ten years is a long time for anyone to put into a business to have the rug pulled. But I'm absolutely convinced it's not the end of the road for me or Sunburst. I honestly owe it to the people there to find a solution that doesn't mean everyone loses their jobs, and their belief and trust. It doesn't have to be that way.

'Oh I know exactly what the pressures are on you, and the rest of the shareholders; I've known and understood for at least three years that the tie would have to go. All I'm asking is that I'm given the chance to bid alongside other interested parties, because I'm sure I can raise the money. And if I outbid anyone else, that's got to be good for your shareholders.'

'I would agree, Tom, but as ever, it's not quite as simple as that; it never is,' said Sir Angus. 'How can you mount an MBO and impartially run a Trade Sale process? It's very difficult to conceive. In principle, I have no objections whatsoever to you having a punt, but how do you do it, without frightening off potential buyers with your inside information, or simply not being around to give the details on the business?'

Travers smiled at Sir Angus. 'I am, as they say, glad you asked me that question,' said Travers, the smile quickly disappearing, to be replaced by a serious expression. Travers put the bottle to the floor and raised his hands. 'I've learned a lot about this process over the last year, and this is what I am proposing. I am very happy to work with Goldberg's, to raise the Information Memorandum, show the company to anyone who is interested and stand back until the end of round two. As I understand it, round one is sighting shots without commitment by interested parties, and round two is secured cash bids from the best of round one.

'At the end of round two, and only at the end of round two, the shareholders give me the right to put my bid on the table. I'm not even asking to know what the round two bids are, and until that stage, there is no reason or cause to tell the bidders that the management may be involved. If my bid is not good enough, I take the deal that Piers and Simon, and presumably you, have offered me. It's as simple as that.'

Sir Angus leant back. 'Give me a minute to think?'

Travers nodded and turned his gaze to the other guys in the room, laughing and joking, and gradually working their way through guns, ammo, dogs and the flight of grouse. In particular, Blount was getting ribbed about his new pub group, and that his chance of making it through the first year was very slim. Travers could see he was more than holding his own. Glad I'm over here, he thought; his conversation was much more fun.

'Well, Tom, I'm buggered if I can see a hole in that, especially if you can come up with the dosh, which is a tall order against the synergy cost savings of an industry bidder. But that's your business, and I do think we owe you a chance, if not simply to protect our investment. Can you provide guarantees of backing?' said Sir Angus.

'Yes. But it's not an issue anyway. If I don't produce the guarantee at the time I bid, you just go ahead with the best of what you've got,' said Travers.

'I'd love to say yes,' said Sir Angus, 'but I'm just not sure it can be done. Many might think it would be only too easy for you to talk the business down to buyers, but knowing you, I don't think you would. Then, if you do come up with a better price, how could we reject it based on our duty to our own shareholders?' He was smiling and enjoying the prospect as much as Travers.

'Angus, you've got to say yes, there is no reason why you shouldn't. It's in your interests. To be frank, without a yes, I'll launch from the sidelines, because I've got nothing to lose, and you will have to rely on Tomlinson to sell the business, of which he, or anyone else, knows nothing.'

Travers made sure he said this with a reasonably hard edge to his voice.

'Oh. I like that,' said Sir Angus chuckling. 'Very sweet. Nice one Tom.'

'And there's another thing, Angus. We have to get things settled within the next couple of days. I've heard even today, from within this house, someone outside the consortium tell me that Albion are selling out. I'm not going to tell you who that was, but if he knows, my guess is the Press will know by the end of next week. It's me, Angus, that has to deal with all that at Willesden, and I can, hopefully without a problem. But I won't if I'm pushed around by Piers feeding me scraps. I will say that Simon was very amenable to any suggestion that maximises Gallant's cash, so if I have your support, at least I only have to battle with Albion by the end of the week.'

'OK, you've got my support,' said Sir Angus. 'Make sure I don't regret it. Are you telling me you're not hitting it off with Piers?'

'No, no, I wouldn't say that. Piers is doing this the way he always does things, which is to bark and growl. We don't honestly need that, Angus, we need co-operation on this one from the start.'

'Hmm. I have to agree, let me think about that one. We really mustn't let that develop. Meanwhile you have my support so long as you get me some of that port that Tomlinson's waving around.'

Travers laughed, held his hand out, and shook Sir Angus's hand. A handshake was still a word of honour to the brewers, as both of them well knew. Egan knew it, and hesitated, realising that shaking Travers' proffered hand was as good as a contract. Smiling, he inched his hand forward to join with Travers'. Got the bugger, thought Travers. Absolutely brilliant, how the hell could Tomlinson turn him down now?

In fact Tomlinson had been aware of their conversation since they all entered the library. He was worried. Egan was influential, not least with Tomlinson's chairman, and Spencer's too at Gallant. Absolutely obvious what they were talking about, and most embarrassing since he was meant to be dealing with it. Travers was trying to be fly, nip round the back door and somehow get a bid accepted.

Tomlinson was determined to put a stop to that. Tomlinson approached Travers and Sir Angus with the port as soon as they seemed to have concluded.

'Angus, you'll have some port?' he said. 'Our own shipper, sixty-two.' Both Sir Angus and Travers were aware that Albion owned a string of chateaux in Bordeaux and a port brand in Porto.

'Thanks so much, Piers. Can you get Tom a glass for his claret?' Tomlinson was fuming. What was he, a bloody waiter to a soda-pop merchant?

'Er, yes, I'll see what I can do. Tom, are you sure you won't have some brandy?' Travers held up his hand to decline the offer.

Both Sir Angus and Travers joined the others who were sitting around the vast table in front of the books.

'Fancy a tilt at Sunburst on your own then, Angus?' said Bertrand. Jesus, thought Travers, everyone seems to know the 'For Sale' sign is up.

'Don't be silly, Rex. I'm just a great fan of Tom's,' said Sir Angus. Beautiful, thought Travers, the pressure is now on these boys to square me away before this thing blows up.

'Now what's the plan for tomorrow, Piers, when's Boots and Saddles?' said Sir Angus.

'Right, Angus, glad you asked. Now listen everybody, I will, as they say, say this only once. Breakfast please at about eight in the dining-room. We'll do the draw at eight forty five in front of the house. The keepers and under keepers will be assembled to introduce themselves, and if you haven't got suitable transport, you can either bunk up with the other guns or go in the keepers' Land Rovers. I'll say more tomorrow before we get underway. The only other thing I need to tell you is that the prospect for a good show of birds is excellent, and the weather forecast is not unhelpful. How's that?'

'Well done, Piers,' said Bill Penn. 'Finest MC I've ever heard. Ha!'

'Now, gentlemen,' said Tomlinson, 'I really do think we ought to get back to the ladies – they'll be wondering what happened to us.'

Bertrand replied, 'Got to be kidding, they'd carry on through the night given half the chance.'

'Thank you, Rex,' said Tomlinson wearily.

As they made their way back to the drawing-room, Blount sidled up beside Travers. He said nothing, but looked at Travers and raised and held his eyebrows, he too having seen Travers in deep conversation with Sir Angus.

Travers nodded and replied in a hushed tone, 'Fine. Catch you tomorrow in the butts?'

Blount nodded and then said, 'Tell me, Tom, how's your love life nowadays?'

'You don't want to know, Richard, you don't want to know.' Blount laughed as they all paraded into the drawing-room, completely ignored by the women, who were indeed hammering away in conversation in two groups. Fresh coffee was brought in, but the evening was drawing to a close. It was eleven thirty, and Bobby Newgent was making his way to the door with Simon Spencer to let their dogs out for a final constitutional.

Of the assembled guests, only Blount, Beaufort and Penn didn't have dogs with them. Blount certainly didn't do enough shooting to warrant the time and discipline required for a gun dog, whilst Penn never took it quite seriously anyway; he was here for the social event and trade gossip, which frankly, thought Travers, was reflected in his shooting acumen. Travers recalled on several occasions where wives in particular had tried to smuggle dogs into their bedrooms for the night, against the house or hotel rules. They generally got away with it, but it had on one occasion led to a confrontation on the stairs between an hotel manager and a certain gentleman from Caledonia. Neither would give way, especially as the chap's wife now appeared who'd requested the damn animal in the bedroom anyway, and in the end the shoot host had to intervene, having been raised from his bed, and with no thanks from either side, had to promise the hotelier to make good any damage to carpets if the animal defecated.

For most of the members of this shoot party, the performance of the dogs 'on the peg' was average to poor. In other words they were essentially pets, and although every one of them had been trained intensively when they were six months to a year old, most had lost the discipline, and were held on leads by the wives in case the dogs broke before the drive was over. The other problem, and cardinal sin, was if a dog, trained to hold his position by the peg until his master released the animal from the 'point' after the drive, watched and marked where the birds were falling, but started to whine. Once they started to do that, they could never be broken of it, and that was the end of their days on the peg. On the other hand, watching a good gun dog at work, responding naturally and also to direction from his master, was one of the highlights of the shoot for Travers. In different ways, both Spencer and Tomlinson had excellent dogs, and he was looking forward to enjoying their performance the next day.

Travers looked at his watch, and then at his fellow guests. Some of them would go on chatting until one o'clock or so, particularly the men, if they were embroiled in finding out who was selling this or that group of pubs, or that this or that national brewer was offering a new bulk barrel discount on their beer brands. He didn't fancy that this evening, or pursuing his own commercial interests with them, especially with the MBO on his mind, so he went over, thanked Tomlinson for the evening, raised his hand to the others, and to those in earshot wished them a good night. Jane, who was sitting with Annabel Spencer, raised her hand just off the arm of the sofa and gave him a little wave of her fingers, with a knowing smile on her lips. I'm not responding to that, he thought. He then followed Spencer and Newgent out into the darkness to give Molly her final run for the night.

When he got outside and moved to his car, Newgent and Spencer were in deep discussion by the back of Spencer's Range Rover. Their dogs were roaming about on the lawns. They should have been aware of someone else's presence because of the crunch of gravel as Travers went to his car, but they were in such intense discussion that Travers, unrecognised, was ignored.

As Travers stroked Molly and let her out, he could hear Spencer saying to Newgent, 'Bobby, you can't do that. We agreed the distribution three months ago, we've paid your wretched allowance, and you must hold to your word. My chaps tell me there are still fifty dispense taps stuck in your warehouse, and now they're told they can't install them. Worse, we know that Albion's premium lager has been going in willy-nilly. It's not on.'

'Simon,' said Newgent, 'it's very late at night and I should be in my bed. I'm sure your information is wrong, and I don't like your tone. If there is a problem I'll put a call in tomorrow and sort it out. Don't worry so much.' Travers could hear from Newgent's tone he was on the back foot, and probably lying through his teeth. He was obviously double-dealing the two national brewers and raking in the cash allowances at the same time.

'Well look, Bobby, I'll hold you to that. But I do want to know tomorrow, from you personally, that this distribution will be complete by the end of the month. Otherwise you leave me no choice but to debit back the allowances. Sorry if I sound a bit righteous, but a deal is a deal.'

'Well, we'll see, old chap. Pretty sure you still owe us some credits for our half pint cases you didn't return, so I wouldn't bank on seeing any of your allowance back.'

Cheek! thought Travers. He's no intention of distributing the draught lager or returning the allowance. What a sod. Pin him down, Simon, he thought.

Then, Travers heard Newgent say to Spencer, 'Simon, your bloody dog is trying to roger one of my girls! Call the bloody thing off!'

'Terribly sorry, Bobby, nasty habit he's got there. Obviously supporting Gallant's interests.' Spencer laughed and called his dog in.

'Not funny, Simon,' said Newgent, defensively, patting one of his two dogs. 'Right, I'm off to bed,' he said finally, slamming the two tailgates of the Range Rover, then walking away towards the front door and turning to say 'Night, old chap' to Spencer, as if no altercation had passed between them at all.

Spencer said nothing, and oblivious of Travers' presence, put his dog back in the car, and also headed for the house. When Spencer had gone in, Travers walked onto the lawn and breathed in the cool night air. There was a faint breeze rustling through the conifers off to his right, and an owl shrieked from the same direction. Molly, nose as ever to the ground, was circling him playfully as he stopped and took in the silence of the night, turning to see the dark outline of the huge house that towered above him.

Well, not a bad day's work, he thought. His discussion with Sir Angus, whom he had planned to get at later in the shoot, had been extremely lucky, because although Caledonia only had fifteen per cent of the voting equity, what they wanted to do had a massive influence on the others. There was much still to do, not least in terms of finance, but that would have to wait until he had some sort of undertaking agreed with Tomlinson. There was also the question of the equity stake the venture capital people would no doubt want. Several of them with whom he had already met, had used the euphemism 'feet to the fire' to describe the financial commitment the management must make before they would consider parting with their own cash or the equity in the company that they would control. He still considered this a detail in the face of the bigger decisions he needed to get first.

As he strolled back to the car, he then thought about Jane. Bobby appeared to be a true bastard, but cuckolding his wife might be a step too far. Travers nevertheless smiled to himself at the prospect and wondered if, over the coming months, Jane would actually appear in London, and whether he could ever hope to keep confidential a liaison with her. He had to admit he was tickled by the prospect.

He re-entered the house, and still heard soft conversations from two or three people in the drawing-room. He turned to the staircase, but made a diversion to the library, went over to the cabinet in the corner, which Tomlinson had dispensed from, and poured himself a large malt, and added some water. He then left and returned to his room to enjoy the drink and get some sleep.

Back in the room, he lay on the bed, skimming through a copy of *Country Life* that had been left with various other society magazines on the coffee table by the bathroom door. In fact, thought Travers, this is a very nice room, and although on the second floor, he had sofa, armchairs, walk-in bathroom and an excellent view up the glen in daylight.

It must have been about a quarter to one when Travers heard a gentle tap on the door. He had just about finished his drink, and had had enough of the shiny faces staring maniacally at the camera from the pages of *Tatler*. He thought at first it must be the staff, telling him Molly was barking. He jumped up, crossed the room and quietly opened the door using both hands to keep the latch quiet. There instead was Jane, head slightly bowed, a smile and a naughty girl look on her face. She was still in her cocktail dress, with her hair now tumbling down her back, carrying her shoes in one hand, and hem slightly lifted with the other, all the better for tiptoeing down the corridor. She raised a finger to her mouth and said in a whisper, 'Shooosh, let me in, quick.'

Travers stood there for a moment in the doorway, totally fazed and said, 'I don't believe it.' He couldn't think of anything else to say except to move the door wider open. She quickly tiptoed in, while he made an instinctive move to glance up and down the corridor to see if anyone was about. He closed the door, turned round and leaned back on the door.

He couldn't help a smile. 'Jane, you're absolutely crazy. Your husband's been in bed five minutes and you're in another man's room. We're going to get caught.' He said the last words with slow resignation.

'Don't be silly,' she said with a sparkling smile, comfortable and relaxed now she was in the security of his room. 'I went up half an hour ago, and he was snoring away. I waited half an hour in the bathroom without moving, nipped out and up the stairs and here I am.' She was clearly very pleased that everything had gone according to plan.

'Look, Jane, we're friends, and I do understand all your problems, but are you actually expecting me to jump into bed with you, or is there another reason for this visit?' She dropped the shoes now, and went over and sat on the edge of the bed.

'Oh, Tom, I just don't know. It's a thrill being with you, and it was fun being wicked over dinner. Bobby's dead to the world, and I just couldn't bear the thought of being near you for the next couple of days and then, nothing. Honestly, a cuddle would do, won't you even give me that? I tell you, Tom, sex is one thing, but being held is what I really miss, some affection. I can't remember when Bobby last gave me a hug. I just feel so, so lonely, I, I,' and her voice tapered off to silence. She had her hands on her lap now and looked really miserable. Even Travers wasn't strong enough to resist her sad vulnerability and went over to the bed, placed his arms under her, and lifted her to her feet. He put his arms around her, dropped his head to the crook of her neck and tightened the hug, his hands now moving without control, one toward her shoulder, the other down towards her bottom.

A lot of sensations hit Travers all at the same time: the warmth, softness and suppleness of her body, the feel of her breasts against his chest, the movement of her hips towards him and the smell of her. They held the hug for minutes, moving against one another. Travers was beginning to react, which Jane would have felt, and her head now looked up in a happy smile, her face slightly flushed. He looked down at her pretty face, her beautiful eyes, and with his resistance disappearing fast, kissed her gently. She responded, and within seconds the two of them were locked.

After a couple of minutes Travers forced himself to pull away, holding her at arms' length by her shoulders.

'Some hug,' he said, slightly panting. Her eyes were only slightly open with her lips apart, her arms now hanging to her side as Travers pinned them. She moistened her lips, then shook off Travers' hold on her shoulders. With no change of expression, she lifted an arm to behind her neck, slid down the first part of the zip of her dress, then with the other hand turned up behind her back, pulled it down the rest of the way and stepped out of the dress. Still without averting her gaze from Travers' eyes, she unclipped her bra, stooped, pulled down her knickers. Travers was transfixed, and now couldn't take his eyes from her body. She could see now his full appreciation, and moved forward to him, unbuttoning first his shirt then his trousers, peeling everything from him. She rose very slowly to full height with that impish smile Travers had seen before, and she pushed him over to the bed, and quietly whispered, 'Move over.'

It was one thirty according to Travers' watch, and Jane lay beside him, still naked, with a girlish bloom extending from her face, down her neck to her chest.

'Gone and done it now,' he said without emotion, and they both broke out in a quiet laugh.

He held her hand beside him, and after a few minutes said to her, 'Where, oh where do we go from here? Have you thought about this at all, Jane?'

'Nope. But I'm not going to screw anything up for you, please don't worry. This was my doing, and I thought you held out very well. I'm proud of you.' The last words she said with a slightly Newgent-esque intonation. 'It's all my problem, and I've got to sort it out. All I ask is that I can see you occasionally, and fuck you to death.'

'A not unreasonable request,' he said, and they both laughed again. With that, she propped herself up on her shoulder and studied him. He was doing the same to her, but he broke the moment and said, 'No, Jane. Let's not push our luck. I've got to get you back to your room without seeing anyone or waking Bobby. Are you up to it, old thing?'

'Absolutely.' And she flashed him a salute.

They both quickly got dressed in silence, gave each other a lingering and intimate kiss, and Travers opened the door, ever so slowly, so as to prevent any squeaks, and noticing that all the lights were still on.

'Keep to the outside of the corridor, the stairs and the landing,' he said, whispering. 'That way the boards won't squeak.'

'You've done this before,' she giggled. Travers went first, tiptoeing to the end of the corridor and the stairs, looking down and beckoning her on. She came up beside him, shoes once again in hand.

'OK, I'll go first,' said Travers. He slowly wound his way down and around the staircase, to where the thick carpet of the landing removed most of the chance of squeaky floorboards. He beckoned again. When she was with him, he said in a hushed tone, 'Right, I'll wait here while you go to the room. If I don't hear pandemonium after five minutes, I'll know you're all right. Night, sweetheart.' He kissed her and off she crept down the landing. There were no keys in the door so she opened it quietly and closed it without a sound behind her. Travers leant back against the panelled wall and breathed a sigh of relief.

Christ, what a day, he thought.

Chapter Three

Travers woke, having set the alarm clock he always carried, for six thirty. He swung his legs to the floor and sat on the edge of the bed shaking off sleep. It always took him an hour or so to be really ready for the day, and he knew himself to be a night bird rather than an 'up with the lark' type. He got up, went over to the window and looked out. The sun was already up a couple of feet up in the sky, with long shadows and a sharp yellowness to the light. Barely a whisper of wind rustled the conifers. Over to the west, some high cirrus was the only blemish on the deep blue sky, and Travers wondered if that signalled the end of this glorious Indian summer that had lasted for about three weeks so far.

Below him were the cars on the forecourt, and to his delight he saw Newgent appear from beneath him, walking briskly towards his Range Rover to let his dogs out. Everything looks normal there, he thought, as with military precision Newgent was now opening drawers from his wooden box of tricks, and the paraphernalia of dog feeding kit emerged. Travers turned from the window, stretched and headed to the bathroom for a shower. He was looking forward to the day, but there was a lot to do, starting with Molly. If she was to sit at the butts obediently, she had better run off some energy first, he thought, and he could do that well before breakfast.

Washed, shaved and the dog fed, Travers and Molly were now at the bridge about half a mile from the house. It was already warm, but the sun was not high enough yet for the sultriness of yesterday to set in. He wore his breeks, shirt, tie and a pair of stout leather walking boots only, and already he could feel the sweat under his arms. Molly was performing her normal manic perambulations, darting in every direction at full canter, sniffing out anything that might move or that had passed in the night. He stopped and leaned on the bridge, looking at his watch. Seven twenty. Time he was getting back. He wondered about Strathallan, lost in dreams on this bridge, and whether he would make an appearance today. The hills that surrounded him, and the heather, were a killer on the legs, and Travers wondered whether the old chap was up to it. But what a pity if he wasn't; it must be like losing a close friend not to be able to wander at will over these glorious moors, taking in the sheer emptiness and beauty of the place.

He strode back now, getting other thoughts in order. Thinking about the MBO, he hoped he hadn't put the boot in too hard against Tomlinson with Sir Angus. Tomlinson might yet be compliant, but if he hit a brick wall, he had to find a reason to go back to the shareholders and have another go. Tomlinson had a flaw in his personality and Travers would use that if he had to. He also thought about the 'package', whatever it was. There was just a chance, if things moved his way, that he could negotiate around that offer whatever happened. Interesting. But he knew the most important thing was to keep his options open, remain flexible and not to discount anything.

He put Molly back in the car, picked up his gun slip, entered the house and went to the gun room. He reached up and took the heavy leather guncase from one of the shelves, undid the straps and opened the lid. He stood for a moment admiring the mini masterpiece. He had bought this Holland and Holland Royal, one of a pair, at auction in Devon about ten years ago. He still kept his father's gun, which was an old BSA boxlock, but had treated himself to the Hollands on becoming managing director of Sunburst. The pair had been made in 1903, totally pristine and no wear, each with two matched pairs of barrels. One set of barrels were bored three quarters and a half, which simply put, meant they were traditional game barrels. The other was bored 'improved', in other words no choke at all, which meant they gave a fairly wide shot pattern, but little carry and killing power. An interesting combination that Travers had never worked out, unless the original owner had chokeless barrels for close quarter work on the grouse. The action was a wonderfully engraved sidelock with detachable plates, gold plated trigger, and simply the most beautifully figured burr walnut stock he had ever seen on any gun. He picked up the stock and the game barrels, pushed over the lever and inserted the barrels into the action. He then took the forepiece, attached it under the barrel and snapped it gently into place. Perfect, assembled in five seconds and ready to go. He opened the action, let the barrel pivot forward, then closed it again from the heel of the gun to check everything was smooth and in place. Satisfied, he put the gun in the leather sling he had brought from the car, and placed it in the gun rack by the door, ready to go. His cartridge case and ammo were still in the car, but he could pick those up later. He had decided, or someone had offered, to give him a ride up to the moor in one of the four wheel drive vehicles.

Quarter to eight and time for his first coffee before breakfast, so he went to the dining-room, and found the Beauforts, Spencers, Penns and Bertrands standing around the giant sideboard where some early coffee had been laid out.

'Morning everyone,' said Travers, getting reciprocal welcomes and raised cups from the men.

'Tom, if you're like Rex and prefer tea, one of the maids will get you a cup.'

'No thanks, coffee's just the ticket, all sleep well?'

'Always do in Scotland, like a log,' said Penn. 'Do you think they get any papers delivered here?' he continued. 'Be nice to keep in touch.'

'I doubt it somehow, Bill. I've rather assumed the place is locked up when there's not shooting or fishing, but I've no idea. Does Strathallan stay here much, Lottie?'

'Do you know, that's one thing I didn't ask, how silly of me. I do know he has a house in Edinburgh, and simply loads of estate houses, but where he normally lives, I just don't know.'

'Make it your task to find out during the morning then,' said Bertrand grumpily. 'Give you something to do.'

'Rex, please don't be a bore, or I won't hold your dog,' she said with finality, and he promptly took another swig of his coffee. The mood, thought Travers, was generally sombre, but it was first thing and perhaps they were all just getting into gear. Travers poured himself a cup of coffee, which tasted good, but could have been a lot hotter. He was absolutely famished after his exertions last night and the walk this morning.

'Going to check up in the kitchen and let them know we're all starving and ready to go. Won't be a minute,' said Travers, and headed off. He wasn't a great fan of comfortable silences. Hands in pockets, he sauntered off, then remembered in this company he better smarten up a bit, and headed for his bedroom to pick up his shooting suit jacket. He bounded up the wide reversing staircase and almost ran into the Newgents on the turn of the stair.

'Morning to you,' he said. 'Both sleep well?'

'Yes, thank you very much, Tom, and you look bright-eyed and bushy-tailed.'

'Absolutely,' said Travers. 'Great evening last night, and looking forward to the action.' As he passed Jane, who was slightly behind Newgent, he brushed her hand and mouthed a kiss. She looked composed and gorgeous, and gave him a big smile. Thank God for that, he thought, Bobby knows nothing, and Jane hasn't missed a beat.

Jacket on, and in the kitchen, Travers' colourful favourite young chef was there, with grill pans on the go.

'Great. Looks as though you've got a big fry-up on the go. I, for one, am famished.'

The lad turned to him and said with a smile, 'Good. Anything special you fancy? I've brought everything in the van. It's all in the fridge.'

'Black pudding?'

'You're kidding, they don't want that do they?'

'But of course. Come on, you know how it is. We all hardly eat breakfast normally, but on an occasion like this we all stuff ourselves to death. Chuck it all in if I were you.'

'Well OK, as I say, it's all here – 'bout another ten minutes.'

'Good man,' said Travers. 'By the way, any chance of one of your pork pies for my cartridge bag?'

'Don't see why not,' the chef said with a smile. 'They're over there in those tins, plenty of them.'

'Thanks a lot, I'll nip back before we go, and thanks.'

Travers returned to the dining-room, and most people were now seated, picking at toast until the breakfast tureens appeared. The atmosphere had lifted a bit, with plenty of chatter. Simon Spencer ambled up to him and said, 'Tom, would you care to join Annabel and me in the Range Rover? Richard's joining us as well, and there's plenty of room for Molly and Rex in the back.' Rex was Spencer's sex mad old springer. Thank God Molly was spayed, thought Travers.

'Love to, Simon, very kind of you, if you're sure.' Travers thought it quite amusing that Spencer's dog had the same name as Bertrand. To keep hearing 'Rex, you horrible animal, come here!' might prove quite amusing. At last the breakfast was brought in by the ladies in black, and throwing etiquette to the wind, Travers was up, grabbing a warm plate and at the tureens. Eggs, sausages, black pudding, mushrooms, bacon and even some sauté potatoes. He felt he needed to keep his strength up, and to hell with the waistband. Jane was up there with him.

'Goodness. Hungry boy. You only did it once you know.' He turned and gave her a sardonic smile, and didn't dare say anything for fear she might respond in some outrageous way. He took his plate and plonked down beside Blount who hadn't yet moved to the plates.

'Hear we're travelling together with Simon.'

'Oh, good,' said Blount. 'Want a word about the premix dispense. Don't fully understand the numbers.'

'You've come to the right man,' said Travers, and dived into his breakfast.

At eight forty-five, the front of the house was a hive of activity. Four Land Rovers had arrived and were now parked in convoy just above the forecourt ready to lead the way out. The keepers and under keepers numbering about eight, were standing in groups, with a similar number of dogs milling around. Some were Labradors, but there were also springers and Border terriers, presumably to extract the odd rabbit, hare, or maybe rats from some of the old barn buildings at the foot of the moor. Tomlinson was chatting to the head keeper, while the guests were busy around the back of their cars, putting on boots, shoes, gaiters, Barbours, filling cartridge bags and assembling shotguns.

Travers was moving over to his car, having collected his gun and a couple of pork pies for the first 'Naafi break' during the morning. He spotted that Tomlinson's man Maclaren had reappeared, still dressed in a lounge suit, and this time wellies, distributing cartons of cartridges to each of the 'guns'. He looked most incongruous, and presumably Tomlinson had asked him to tip up, before he drove on somewhere else, hence his suit.

Tomlinson suddenly spotted him, dropped his conversation with the keeper, and went striding towards Maclaren, obviously in a huff. Without any concern about being overheard, he said to Maclaren, 'What on earth do you think you're doing?'

'Just what you told me to do, Mr Tomlinson, I'm passing around some cartridges for the guests.'

'You blithering idiot. You've got those from my car haven't you? They are my cartridges, mine. Not the company's. The ones you hand out are in the gun room, where I told you. They happen to have Albion stamped all over them, you moron. Now go round, collect those up and go and do as you were told.'

The guests, wherever they were on the forecourt, couldn't help but overhear this verbal attack on Maclaren, and either turned their faces back to their car boots and shook their heads, or smirked and tittered at the unfortunate Maclaren receiving the full blast of Tomlinson's spleen. One who didn't, but stood with a deadpan face, staring at Tomlinson, was Sir Angus Egan. He was not amused. Travers could clearly see the displeasure on Sir Angus's face, knowing that such a public dressing down of subordinates just wasn't done. Sir Angus turned slowly and resumed what he was doing.

Travers saw the funny side, however, because while the 'guns' might have accepted Tomlinson's own quality cartridges, surely no one would want the cheap rubbish he was trying to distribute with the 'Albion' logo stamped all over them. They were probably a bulk purchase of

Russian cartridges, stamped up in the UK. Anyone with a decent gun wouldn't touch them, as half of them didn't even go off when the trigger was pulled, and the other half were totally inconsistent loads.

Travers was at his own car now, lifted Molly out, and told her to sit while he transferred his cartridges from the cartons to his bag. He would take another two hundred in an unbroken carton and put them in the back of Spencer's Range Rover. No need for shooting coat he thought, as it was now very warm, and he could see himself shooting in shirt sleeves at this rate. The jacket he was wearing would do. He took his cartridge belt just in case he was in shirt sleeves. With gun, bag and dog lead, he locked the car and transferred the whole lot to Spencer's car, keeping Molly to heel.

Tomlinson now called the 'guns' together for the draw, in the centre of the forecourt lawn. The ladies as usual stayed by the cars and chatted amongst themselves.

'Gentlemen, gentlemen. First let me introduce the head keeper, Sandy Macadam. He'll be in control over the next two days, and we must do as he says.'

'Morning, gentlemen,' said Macadam. 'Today we'll be driving the Cromdales. Two drives in the morning and two in the afternoon if all goes well. The beaters are already on the moor, working in. Even when you're in your butts, you'll have to expect a wait, because the beaters have about five miles to push the birds forward. The general idea is to push them north this morning, and push them back across you this afternoon. Let's hope it works. Please use the sighting sticks you'll be given, in your butts. We want no shooting down the line of the guns. Those of you on the end of the lines, remember the stops. They've been told to signal to you when they see a covey in flight, so it might help to keep an eye on them. My chappies here will help you with the pick up, so use them if you can't square your count, and please leave the grouse on your butts, the lads will pick them up later. We number from one at the bottom to nine at the top, and please move two up at the next drive. My horn will start and finish each drive. No shooting please, except behind you when you see the beaters and I blow my horn. Two blasts is the end of the drive. Good shooting, straight barrels.' He doffed his threadbare deerstalker and strode off to his cohorts, crook in hand, and a springer by his side.

Tomlinson said, 'Thank you, Sandy,' but Macadam was already gone.

'Right,' said Tomlinson. 'Now for the draw. But just a moment, where's Sir Angus?'

At that moment the 'guns' turned around to see Sir Angus emerge from the house, walking slowly over the gravel towards them. When he got close he said to Tomlinson, 'Sorry about that, Piers, last minute loo call. Don't worry, I've heard Sandy's speech before.'

Which of course he must have, thought Travers. Sir Angus was probably a regular visitor. Then Tomlinson pulled a small leather wallet from his pocket, flipped open the cover, and inside were the nine markers, with the actual number hidden by the leather sleeve. He worked around the 'guns' who were in a semicircle around him, each man taking a marker, noting the number and putting it number side up back in the wallet. Travers drew three.

Good, he thought, that means butt three, five, seven, and nine on the last drive. A good spread, and only butt nine on the outside. Not that it mattered too much. Unlike pheasant and partridge, he thought, where you could count on the centre pegs for more birds being pushed through, with grouse you never knew where along the line the birds were going to fly. On some moors they stick to the top, on others they try to flush through at the bottom, leaving the upper guns with nothing to shoot at. He was keenly anticipating what would happen here. Travers noted he had Beaufort to one side of him at two, and Sir Angus on the other side at four. Both of them cracking shots. He hoped he could keep his end up.

Having completed the draw, Tomlinson then said, 'Right, as I said last night, we don't want too many vehicles cluttering the moor, so I'd be grateful if you could fill three or four Range Rovers, and leave the others behind. Do use the keepers' vehicles if you want to.'

Travers now moved across to Spencer's car with Molly, and put her in the back alongside Rex. The old springer had his nose in her face instantly, and elsewhere too. Molly immediately sat in a corner of the boot wanting nothing to do with Rex. Sensible girl, thought Travers, keep away from the randy old sod. He got in and waited for the others to join him. He noticed that Sir Angus and his wife were joining the Beauforts, that Tomlinson, without wife or dog had joined the Newgents, and finally, the Penns and the Bertrands were together. The Spencers and Blount got in the car, engines were started, and they drew up behind the keepers' Land Rovers.

They all drove in convoy for about five miles, along country lanes with verdant grass fields, trees and whisky-coloured streams on all sides. Always to the west lay the rising moors, and the closer they got, so the dark greyness of the moor disappeared, and in the sunlight the blue sward of heather now in flower emerged into sight, with the occasional green strip, which Travers knew were the burnt areas, which in the spring and summer had produced the new shoots of heather so important for the young grouse. The Cromdales as a whole probably stretched for about fifteen miles, and appeared pretty regular, looking along the ridge, nothing like the peaks of the Cairngorms and Aviemore, not that far to the south-west. Here and there the occasional rocky outcrop, or the line of a track snaking towards the ridge. Now they were driving through a farmyard, gates opening and closing, and they began to climb, fording streams, passing sheep, with the vehicles clambering over boulders and through ruts, transfer gearboxes now in low ratios. They kept on climbing for another ten minutes until they arrived at a marshy plateau, with plenty of grass around them, beyond which the heather-clad moor climbed steeply, all the way to the ridge about half a mile above them. The lead vehicles stopped and parked alongside one another, and the other cars pulled up and followed suit. Everyone piled out of the vehicles. Indeed, the whole circus emerged with dogs yapping and the occasional peal of laughter breaking the silence and pervading solitude of the moor. Immediately Travers picked up the inimitable croak of the grouse. 'Go-back, go-back, go-back.' It really was the most eerie sound, but completely fascinating. Molly was rigid, sensing the hunt was on.

It had been an uneventful journey in Spencer's vehicle, just small talk. Simon Spencer was very keen on his shooting, and through the season from mid-August to the end of January would probably average at least a day or two a week, racking up huge mileage to get to the shoot venues. Grouse were very special though, and Travers felt his normal loquacity was probably subdued in anticipation. Because Blount had not shot grouse before, Spencer had given him a few dos and don'ts, mostly concerning safety. Unlike pheasant, coveys of grouse normally burst on the scene flying at anything up to eighty miles an hour, skimming the heather and jinking through the butts. Spencer had been saying it was all too easy to swing through the line with the gun, letting off a barrel, with disastrous consequences for your colleague in the next butt. Again, unlike pheasant, it was totally OK to take a bird behind, but success was more likely to come by using both barrels ahead, or, more likely, the second barrel overhead if the grouse had enough height. During this conversation, Annabel had merely smiled, saying, 'I'm sure it's not that scientific', which was perhaps why she accompanied Simon only on special occasions. She had probably heard this conversation a hundred times before, and had become bored stiff by it. Travers felt the lecture was probably worthwhile for Spencer, because Spencer was at peg nine on the first drive, and Blount was at eight, so he was very much in Blount's firing line!

Travers got his kit out of the car, revelling in the unique croak of the grouse in the heather calling to one another. He slung his gun slip and bag over his shoulder, and with Molly on the lead began the climb to butt number three, which was about four hundred yards away; no distance at all. For the Spencers and Blount, however, they faced a long walk up a very steep hillside, with heather almost two feet thick, before they reached their butts. Travers reminded Spencer that none of them should have eaten such a large breakfast. The other members of the shoot party fell into Indian file of people and dogs ascending the hillside.

Travers arrived both breathless and sweating. He couldn't believe how heavy going the heather was, and his six and a half pound gun felt like sixty, not to mention the cartridge bag. It was now nearly ten, and it was another humid scorcher, quite extraordinary, he thought, for this latitude. He fell against the inside wall of the butt gratefully, putting his gear on the ground and his foot on Molly's lead until the other 'guns' and dogs had passed on their way to their firing positions. He wiped his brow, and already he could feel the heather dust mixed with the sweat.

'You forget how hard it is,' said Travers to Bobby and Jane Newgent as they passed by on their way to number seven, a long climb for them yet. Jane, probably fit from her horse riding wasn't puffing, and spared a smile, while all Bobby could manage was a grunt. Travers first of all looked out in front of the butt to the south-west and along the line of the hill, to see what sort of view he had been given. Very often, in order to hide the butt from the oncoming birds, the original builders had placed them behind a bluff or ridge, so that the shooter had but twenty yards to pick up the grouse as they exploded over the short horizon, and then he would be very lucky to get even one barrel away before they were behind him.

Fortunately, from Travers' perspective, from the rim of this butt, which came up to his chest, he had a clear view ahead for at least a mile, so if he kept his eyes open, he would be able to pick up coveys or singles coming his way, which was obviously an advantage to being 'blind'. For those in butts with limited views, they had to rely on either the sound of shots from their chums, or one of the 'stops' out on the flanks giving a short blast on a whistle to signal the approach of birds.

Travers then relaxed a bit, and had a good look at the butt he was standing in. Made of roughly hewn stone blocks, with peat infill to smooth out the front of it, it was as designed, completely overgrown with heather on the front and the sides, with access from a little passage at the back. Where he stood was about two feet below the surrounding ground, so that looked at from ahead, you would only see a three or four feet high knoll of heather sticking up above the surrounding ground. How old it was, Travers could only guess. It might be over a hundred, but certainly not less than fifty years, which made him then think of the sort of individuals in years gone by who had been fortunate enough to stand where he was standing now.

The shooting party that were heading up the hillside to their butts had passed now, and Travers would be on his own with Molly from now until the end of the drive. He really enjoyed this bit, because there would be at least a half hour before the first birds came through, at which point the beaters would still be at least a couple of miles away. It was during this time that he could take in the magnificent scenery, and indeed the wildlife in the form of birds, bugs, hares and even foxes that appeared when things had quietened down.

He now looked down the hillside to the butt below him, and could see the Beauforts chatting and making themselves comfortable. They were about fifty yards away, and Susie already had a paperback in hand, gesticulating at Peter. They were completely unaware, Travers thought, that he could see their every movement from up here. Travers then looked up the hill to see if he could spot the next butt up, which should contain Sir Angus. But he couldn't. There was a small hillock between them, and all Travers could see was a small white post, which a keeper had stuck into the ground to signify the direction of the next butt. Rather nice, thought Travers, not to be looked down on.

He then turned, unclipped Molly and left her in a position just at the rear of the butt, but elevated enough for her to see what was happening without the grouse seeing her. She was already into character, sitting with her nose in the air, head still but eyes scanning in anticipation, in an almost imperious way. She knew full well what was about to happen, and would hold that position for hours, only changing her head position if a bird flew by, or received the search instruction from Travers. He now unzipped the leather gun slip and took out the assembled shotgun. Pushing the lever over and 'breaking' the gun, he reached for his cartridge bag and slipped two shells into the breech, closed the action, checked the safety was on and placed the gun carefully on the front edge of the butt, barrel forward so that he could grab it immediately if required. Because it was so hot, he took his jacket off, reached for the cartridge belt and filled the leather loops with shells from the bag, then slung it around his waist. He now took the two sticks, placed by the keepers on the top of the butt, and drove each one in to each side of the butt, so as to allow about a twenty degree 'no swing' zone to the adjacent butts on either side of him. He now picked the gun up and gave himself a couple of practice swings to make sure he had placed them about right. All done, he leant on the front of the butt, and had a good look forward.

Off to his left, down in the glen and bathed in sunlight, he could make out one of the malt distilleries with its tall metal chimney and warehouses beside a river, shimmering like silver in the sun. It was too far away to see any people, but he saw no vehicles on the move either, so he assumed they were neither distilling nor bottling, and that the amber liquid, thousands of gallons of it, was quietly maturing in the old bourbon or sherry casks. He'd never been in a distillery, and he thought it might be interesting to visit one and see how it was done, if he ever got the time. Looking forward again, and still hearing the croaking call of the grouse far ahead, he picked up the occasional bird flutter into the air and then drop down again into the heather. Presumably, he thought, some of them are getting a bit jumpy, and one or two of them might begin to fly away from the danger quite soon.

Meanwhile the midges were becoming a pest around his head and beginning to make him itch along his hairline. Despite the heat, he reached into his other bag for his flat cap and stuck it onto his head. There was a whisper of breeze on his face now and then, which had a wonderfully cooling effect on his moist forehead. He glanced down the hillside again, and spotted one of the keepers moving into a gulley between the bottom butt containing the Penns, and the collection of parked cars. He carried a red rolled flag, so Travers knew he was the 'stop' on the left flank, who would be waving that flag vigorously if any grouse tried to break out of the bottom of the line. His eye then moved to Bill Penn, whom he could just see leaning over the front of his butt, with a barrel stuck in the air. Try as he might, he couldn't spot Jennie, who was probably sat at the back somewhere, either reading or sunbathing. Moving up from the Penns, he spotted the Beauforts again in their butt, this time in a loose embrace and chatting together, their faces a few inches from one another. Travers felt like a peeping Tom, but nevertheless it was a touching sight. He averted his gaze back to the front, but couldn't help but think of Jane, and their all too short liaison the night before. He felt a growing mixture of affection and desire, and was even beginning to think of how he could plan the next encounter, and to hell with Bobby.

Then, shattering his reverie, he heard a shot high up to his right, and he nearly gave himself a heart attack, as he grabbed the gun from the edge of the butt, and swivelled round to the right, flicking off the safety catch. He quickly scanned the ground and the air in that direction, could see nothing, and brought his gaze back to his front. Yes, there was a singleton slightly to his right, about five hundred yards off, coming in at a terrific speed between him and Sir Angus's butt. He involuntarily crouched now, head and barrel just above the parapet of the butt, ready to swing the gun to his shoulder if the bird kept its flight pattern towards him. The grouse, with the occasional flutter of wing beats, but mostly gliding, was riding over the ground and hugging the terrain, probably no more than six feet from the ground at any one time. It kept on coming, and was now about two hundred yards away. Right, go for it, he thought. The gun went to his shoulder, and he was just working through the bird with the pressure coming on his trigger when Sir Angus fired. The grouse hit the ground in a cascade of downy white feathers and tumbled twice towards him before coming to a stop in the heather, with feathers fluttering down on the corpse. It had come to rest about fifteen yards just to his right, and was a legitimate target for either of them, but Sir Angus had got there first. Good shot, thought Travers, but he would have to speed up if this character wasn't to beat him to the draw on every target.

Come on, get with it, Travers, he thought to himself. He heard the clink of Sir Angus's gun in the still air as he replaced the cartridge in readiness for the next bird. This time Travers spotted a pair from the same direction, but slightly crossing from ahead and right, and which would probably pass to the left of his butt. Three hundred yards out, two hundred yards. Go for it!

He moved through both birds smoothly and quickly, firing ahead of each by a good ten feet, anticipating the lead he would have to give such fast moving birds. To his utter relief and satisfaction, both birds smashed into the heather just off to his left, and he and Molly mentally marked where they had fallen. Automatically he broke the gun and reloaded and gave the ground ahead another quick scan; nothing yet.

'Stay,' he said to Molly, who was still sat, but her paws were stamping up and down, itching to get at the fallen birds.

Now he heard the whistle of the 'stop' off to his left. The fellow was blowing maniacally. Must be a big covey coming in from somewhere, thought Travers. He looked up and down the hill, then down again, yes, yes, off down to the left about half a mile, a cloud of grouse were racing in, but high, about thirty yards off the ground. But would they break out over the vehicles? No, they were holding the heather line. Must be about fifty in this covey, thought Travers, and he knew he had to forget the numbers, pick a couple of birds and try and ignore the rest of them. Firing into the middle would hit nothing; he had to be absolutely selective. He chose a couple of birds out to the right of the covey. No. They've turned into the main pack. OK, those two, he thought. Three hundred yards out now, but high, coming to the right of butt two. Very high, distance has got to be sixty yards, too far, hold it a second, hold it. Fire! The two birds curled down, falling behind and in between his butt and Beaufort's. Then another couple of shots, and Beaufort had fired late and behind him, bringing down one bird.

Now there were quite a few singletons criss-crossing ahead and to his right. The artillery barrage was now in full swing further up the line. Travers saw a bird coming straight at him, fast and low. A gift, he thought. He raised the gun, aimed just below the bird and fired all in one moment. With feathers flying and still probably doing forty miles an hour it whizzed past Travers' head by about two feet and just missed Molly. Wow, that was close. From then on, his gun became very hot, and the action continued for another fifteen minutes, virtually without break. He was through the twenty-five cartridges in the belt, and now diving into the open bag for more. He had to stop and put the light leather glove on his left hand, because he couldn't hold the barrel any more, just too hot. Goodness what a drive, he thought.

Then a lull in the action, and at last he could see and hear the swish of the white polythene bags the beaters were using on the end of sticks to scare the grouse into flight. They were about half a mile away now, marching forward, swishing and yelling. Between them and the guns most of the birds had now lifted, and the head keeper called the beaters to a halt, to straighten the line before proceeding. Still up the line, guns were firing and birds were falling, mainly behind the guns now. Then the keeper, now about five hundred yards distant, blew on his curved hunting horn, and Travers raised his gun knowing he could only take behind from now on. A pair got up not twenty yards to his right, and Travers let them rise up and through the line, until he could see sky behind them, and fired. Missed one, got the other. The beaters were twenty yards away now, and Travers emptied the gun and put it back in its slip. As the boys walked through, he asked them not to pick any birds, but to leave them for his dog, which of course they were happy to do. About twenty yards on and behind the butts, the beaters slumped in groups, absolutely exhausted after probably walking the best part of five miles. They were probably students thought Travers, earning a bit of holiday cash as beaters, but not realising just what they had let themselves in for.

Travers was up now in front of the butt, having released Molly to pick up. He reckoned he had eighteen birds to pick, and knew for sure where about twelve of them were. It was, however, very, very difficult to see the dead grouse in the heather even if you were standing over them. They blended so perfectly into the heather, only a dog would be able to smell out the scent and pick it.

Molly set about her work with gusto, going for the close ones, bringing them back to Travers on the call, then racing off again. When she had picked the easy ones, she started to radiate in a circle, often seeming to pass over one because she had smelt another, then going back later for the one she had passed by. Within twenty minutes, Travers had the lot and was well pleased. Great shooting, and all accounted for, laid out on top of the butt.

He left Molly to happily continue her search, while he, still hot and sticky from his exertions in the butt, slowly made his way up to Sir Angus, asking if he needed any help with his pick up.

'Angus, that was really something, and you beat me to that first left and right. Very impressive if I may say so.'

'Best drive this year, without a doubt. And sorry about that pair, hope I wasn't poaching,' said Sir Angus. By this time, Sir Angus had also completed his pick, and Molly joined his small black retriever in continuing to quarter the heather. They too were having a whale of a time. Travers made his way over to the exhausted lads in the heather. There were about fifteen in all, sprawled in groups, most of them with a can of soft drink from their knapsacks. He went over to a small group and said, 'Bet you didn't realise it would be quite so hard going?'

'No, it really gets the legs. Like wading through water, this heather. Happy with the birds?'

'Magnificent,' said Travers. 'I think everyone will agree it was one of the best drives any of us has had. Where are you guys staying?'

'Oh, we're all in the barns and stables down by the fishing lodge, not exactly the Ritz.'

'Never mind,' said Travers, I bet you have a right old time in the evenings.'

'Not allowed any drink,' said the lad with finality. Travers laughed and lifted his hand in farewell. He wondered what they would be paid, for what was effectively as tough as an army route march.

Travers went back to his butt, picked up his kit and made his way back down to the vehicles, whistling up

Molly as he went. Half way down, he met a scruffy character coming up, with two huge sacks in his hands.

'I thought we'd meet again,' said the character.

'Oh, it's you!' said Travers. He immediately recognised the drunken fellow from Tomintoul, and laughed to himself that this really was a case of poacher turned gamekeeper.

'That was some fine shooting from number three,' said the character. 'I'll wager over a hundred birds in all on that drive.'

'So you work on the moor as well as the river?' said Travers.

'Ooh aye,' said the man. 'You'll find I do a bit of everything, that way they keep an eye on me. By the way, later on in the evenin' d'ye fancy some rabbit shooting? I've got some fine ferrets. Terrific sport, ye know. Being as you're a straight shot, we could get fifty in an hour.'

'No thanks, no,' said Travers with a smile on his face, 'But if you've still got that offer on smoked salmon, I'll take you up on it, providing the police don't stop me on the A9 going back.'

'Och, who's to know?' he said, perfectly seriously.

'Well, I'm off back south after shooting tomorrow, can you catch me at the lodge?'

The man doffed his cap and was off to the next butt to collect the laid out grouse. Travers now made his way to the Penns' butt, which was about a hundred yards from the cars. Meanwhile Molly had picked a fallen bird behind the Beaufort's butt and brought it proudly to Travers.

'Hi you two, get any shooting down here, Bill?'

'I should say,' said Penn, who was still in the butt with his back to the front edge, smoking a small cigar. Jennie was still reading a magazine, but looked up and smiled. 'Swarms of the bloody things. Tell you what though, can see right up the hill from here, and there was some damn fine shooting, must've got the bag off to a good start.'

'Quick word?' said Travers.

'Come in to my office,' said Penn, ushering him in. Jennie didn't move, and Travers sat down beside her.

'Bit of business, Jennie, hope you don't mind,' said Travers, as he reached for the hip flask in his bag and offered it to Penn. 'Cherry Brandy?'

'Too hot, mate,' said Penn, as Jennie got up and told them she was going for a wander.

'Bill, can I ask for your help?'

'Fire away, chum,' said Penn.

'If Sunburst is put up for sale, would you and the smaller shareholders support an MBO from me?'

Penn thought for a moment, looking round to make sure no one was listening, 'I think you're right, everything I'm hearing points to a sale. Don't know why, everybody's making money. They should leave it alone and let you get on with it. Frankly, I've got no desire to sell. But, there we are. If it is going to go, Tom, I really don't know if anyone would give up value to let it go to you, is that what you're asking?'

'No, Bill, I'm not asking for any favours on the price. The only thing I would be allowed to do is to top the price of whatever falls on the table. All I'm asking for is the right to try and raise the money and put in a bid, no more, no less.'

'Well of course you can, why not? But what do you want from me?' said Penn, slightly suspicious that Travers was going to ask him for a loan.

Travers laughed. 'Bill, don't worry, I don't want your money, we're probably looking at sixty million plus, bit more than you've got in the cigar box. No. All I want is your agreement and the other small shareholders to be allowed to top any offer that anyone else makes. That is all.'

'Told you,' said Penn, 'not a problem. Do you want me to get the others on side, is that it?'

'Got it in one, Bill. I need support from you guys, and you're all very influential as shareholders. There's a thing called oppression of minority interests, which puts the fear of God into any board. It means the big guys have got to listen to what you want, they can't ignore you, but they can ignore me. By way of a sweetener, my finance guys have said you may all be able to roll over some of your shareholding into "sweet equity" of the new company, which could be quite advantageous financially. No promises though, at this stage.'

'Christ,' said Penn, 'it's another world. Are you sure you want to go through with this, Tom? It could end up killing you. Surely to God whoever buys it would keep you. You built it.'

'No, I promise you, Bill, it won't work like that, I'll be out. I really don't mind that, all I want is a chance. I think, but I'm not certain, that Gallant and Caledonia will let me have a go, whereas Tomlinson, I'm pretty sure doesn't want me to interfere. You know what he's like.'

Travers hoped that by personalising the issue, the family brewers' backs would go up, and be more inclined to support him.

'Well that clinches it, Tom. Tell you what I'll do. By the end of next week, I'll come back to you and tell you how I've got on with the others. Shouldn't be a problem. Oh, and good luck.'

'Knew I could depend on you, Bill. Right, we better get on.'

Most of the party were now back at the vehicles, comparing notes, and waiting for the keepers to finish loading the birds on a trailer, the birds hanging by their necks from string, strung across the trailer. Tomlinson was in the middle of the group.

'Right, all aboard please, ladies and gentlemen. *Tempus fugit* and all that. Twenty minutes to the next drive.'

Dogs and kit were shoved in the back of Range Rovers, everyone clambered aboard, and the convoy set off, back down the hill.

In the car, Spencer was saying he had a pretty thin time of it at the top of the hill, but was thrilled to watch the mayhem further down. Meanwhile Blount was very happy to have brought down three grouse, and was seriously considering having one stuffed as a trophy, which everyone else thought was hilarious. They followed the convoy back down through the farmyard, and out on to the road, turning left to push on north with the hills on their left.

As they were going along, Travers was turning over in his mind the tasks that faced him. The discussion with Penn had gone as expected, and he was fairly certain the smaller shareholders would support him, particularly if there were further cheap shares to be had. He also needed to talk to Blount and tap into his city contacts. If he was in with a chance to bid, he knew he had to get the right deal from the venture capitalists, and the only way to do that was to play one off against the other, and for that he needed another two or three in the frame.

But the big hurdle was undoubtedly Tomlinson. Maybe he was worrying too much. When Tomlinson was told of the attitude of the others, why wouldn't he concur? As long as Travers hammered on about increasing value, not diminishing it, Tomlinson couldn't argue, could he?

He still felt uncertain, and was now wondering how and when to get Tomlinson on his own. It would be lunch after this next drive, and maybe an opportunity would arise. It would be difficult though, Tomlinson should be looking after his guests. They had driven about three or four miles now, and as expected the convoy turned left towards the moor. The hills seemed much higher here, but more distant, so that the incline up to the ridge was a lot shallower. The butts were therefore likely to be further apart, and probably more in sight of one another than on the steep hillside of the last drive. The vehicles climbed onwards and upwards, and Travers could see that this time, what looked like a fairly recent trail had been cut into the hillside to allow the passage of the vehicles. He made the comment to Spencer, who said, 'That's right. And that's where the big money goes on a shoot like this, especially if it's used for let days. You have to get the punters on to the moor with the minimum of fuss, although the cutting machines to make a track like this are fantastic. They literally claw their way through the heather, foot by foot, digging up at the front, grinding in the middle, and compressing at the back. Developed in the States for the logging industry.'

Spencer, thought Travers, was a mine of useless information, particularly if shooting was involved. He looked at the track zig-zagging upwards and thought what a mess it had made of the hillside. Couldn't see the local council on Ashdown Forest agreeing to that! Within another half a mile the vehicles stopped and parked on a corner of the track, where the cutting had made a deep indent into the ground above. Parked here, the vehicles would be invisible from above, if not below. Everybody piled out, and this time the head keeper did instruct the 'guns' not to let the dogs loose because he didn't want to put up any more grouse than necessary, as everyone had a long walk over to the right of their current position. Travers thought that if this chap mentioned a long walk, they could be at it for hours, and what's worse, in this heat too. He grabbed a bottle of mineral water for him and the dog, as well as replenishing his cartridge bag.

Everyone happily marched off behind the keepers, without a chance of keeping up. After a hundred yards everybody had slowed to their own pace; the heather was no joke. Tomlinson was out in front for the moment, and

Travers wondered if he could open a conversation with him on the go. If this was to be a long walk, why not?

He took a slightly wider route than the others, and walking fast, pushed through the heather. Within five minutes he was abreast of Tomlinson, having skirted by the outside of the others. He slowed down a bit and moved towards the same course as Tomlinson.

'Heavy going, isn't it, Piers? You've caught me up.'

'Well,' said Tomlinson. 'We've got a tight schedule. I do wish the stragglers would keep up. I saw you were in the thick of it on the first drive, congratulations. I saw the grouse on your butt.'

'Absolutely marvellous, a memorable drive, Piers.' A brief silence between them apart from the heavy breathing, as they both looked ahead to keep the keepers in sight.

'Piers, you promised we would have a chance to chat today about the sale of Sunburst, can we take a couple of minutes now?'

'You certainly pick your moments, Tom. We're just about to start the next drive,' said Tomlinson.

'Oh I think not,' said Travers as breezily as he could. 'Anyway, it's not the detail I'm interested in today, just the principle.'

'What d'you mean?' said Tomlinson brusquely.

'Look, Piers, I'm happy to run the trade sale for you. All I want is the chance to top any offers at the end of the process, that's all.'

'Tom, I don't think you understand what's going on. Goldberg's have already told us they're very nervous about you, and the effort you might or might not make in helping us to sell the business. Who knows what you might say to interested bidders? I have to tell you, if we had someone else who knew anything about the business, I'm afraid you wouldn't be involved.'

'Piers,' said Travers, 'frankly, I wish you did have someone else, then I could run a bid anyway from off the premises with my backers. Sadly that's not the case, and I'm offering you a compromise that gets top dollar for the business whatever happens. If you have any worries about what I may say to other bidders when they come to Sunburst, let's just make sure someone from Goldberg's is always in attendance. What's wrong with that?'

'Look, whatever you say, Tom, I've been charged with a job, and I'm going to do it. My chairman said nothing about letting you in, and it would be overstepping my authority to do so. I'm afraid that's an end to it, like it or not.'

'Piers, for heaven's sake, I'm not asking you to take this decision on your own.' (Although Travers knew he could if he wanted to.) 'All I want is your agreement to the principle, which you can get from Richards by the end of the week.'

'Tom, it's Sir Brian Richards to you, and if that option were on the table, I would have been told. No. I'm sorry. The more I think about your proposal, the less inclined I am to agree. You seem to forget you are an employee of the company, and the shareholders can do what they like without your permission. Are you actually telling me you refuse to run this trade sale?'

Travers really had to think quickly. It didn't take him long. He couldn't hold a gun to the shareholders, that sort of confrontation could only end one way, and he still had options.

'No, of course not, Piers. I just find it so difficult to understand your attitude. Apart from anything else, we've worked together quite happily over ten years with your monthly visits to the board, and I would have thought Albion, in view of all the success at Sunburst, would at least give me a chance to keep the whole thing together, rather than seeing it broken up by one of the big players.'

'Well, you're wrong,' said Tomlinson. 'At the end of the day, it's money, and the quickest way to get to it. You, Tom, would get in the way. Understood?'

'You realise I have the support of Caledonia and maybe Gallant, Piers?'

Tomlinson stopped in his tracks. The speed with which they had been walking meant that they were already two hundred yards ahead of the rest of the party, although Jane Newgent was about half that distance. While casting an eye to them and panting breathlessly he said, 'Do you mean to tell me you've been going behind my back?' By now, the sweat from his brow meant that his glasses were constantly falling down his nose, and his twitching finger was working overtime to keep them on his face.

'Don't be ridiculous, Piers. I've asked them a fair question, and they've given me a fair answer, it's you that's out of line.'

'I can't believe your cheek,' said Tomlinson. 'You take my hospitality and then mount a conspiracy against me. It's, it's, it's contemptible.' With that, and not wanting the others to maybe spot some sort of contretemps, Tomlinson marched off, leaving Travers open-mouthed.

Shit, shit, shit, thought Travers. How bad can a conversation get? He knew Tomlinson was powerful enough to sink him without trace, and he may have just sealed his own fate. Travers trudged on with Molly, all of a sudden tired, very hot and depressed.

Jane caught him up very quickly.

'Christ, Tom, what was that all about? We all saw him boil over this morning, looks as though you've done it again.' She obviously thought it was very humorous, but when she caught Travers' expression she said, 'Whoops, looks as though it's serious. Whatever it is just remember the bloke is a complete bastard.' She made sure she said, 'bastard' with as much vitriol as she could muster.

Travers flicked her a glance with the trace of a sheepish smile. 'Thanks sweetheart. Trouble is, I think you know what has just hit the fan.'

'Oh, in that case, I'd better try and cheer you up again tonight,' she said with a wicked smile. He laughed and definitely warmed to the idea, but he couldn't help feeling slightly sickened by Tomlinson's rejection.

'How did Bobby do on the last drive?' he said.

'OK, I think. Trouble is he's so competitive. When he misses, the air is blue, and the dogs actually keep their heads down. I must put it on film one of these days.' They laughed together, walking on. Travers, on hearing about Newgent's competitiveness, was quietly hoping that Bobby wasn't reading too much into his proximity to Jane. A confrontation with Newgent was most certainly not required.

They now came to a heather-clad gully, with a path around the inner rim. Set into the wall of the gully was a well of water, overflowing from a crudely carved trough. Hanging from the wall was a metal cup, which looked like pewter, which was attached to the wall by a chain. The whole scene was an absolute picture, with the blue of the heather offset by the light sandstone coloration of the gully, against which the sparkling stream ran out of the small trough, gurgling down into the sunlit gully. They both stopped and took in the scene. Her arm went spontaneously to his, and he too couldn't help touch her hand, so unexpected and beautiful was the scene.

'Quite something,' said Travers. 'Wonder how many years that's been there. Just the ticket for Molly.' He went forward and let Molly drink from the trough, whilst holding the cup under the stream of water and offering it to Jane. 'Bet it's pure, ice cold and filtered; here, Jane, have a drink.' She took a drink and he followed. While they rested, the rest of the party slowly appeared over the rim. Rex Bertrand was first on the scene.

'My goodness, Shangri-La. Don't hog the refreshments you two, let's have some for this weary traveller.' The others appeared and joined them. Plainly perspiring, the men started to remove jackets and sling them over shoulders with the guns and other bags. Travers and Jane followed suit, as the question of 'How much further?' circulated without answer.

Despite the disappointment of not ten minutes ago, Travers was again transfixed by Jane. She was wearing a Tattershall type shirt, open to just above her breasts, and tightly tucked into her tight shooting breeks. The slim and curvaceous outline of her figure was too much for Travers, and a wave of lust overtook him. She took his breath away, and what's more she knew it, looking to him and then to her watch and the others, saying, 'Come on team, our host will be getting upset.'

There was some quiet sniggering about that, but everyone fell into line again, and left the secret glen.

Within ten minutes, they were at the butts, stretching up the hillside. There must have been at least one hundred yards between each one. The first five or six butts, apart from the irregularities, were mainly on flattish rising ground, while the top four butts inclined steeply up the hillside. Travers was on five this drive, and without any further conversation, the whole party made their way to their respective butts, with the head keeper chivvying them on.

When Travers reached the butt, he looked at his watch. Ten to twelve. Time was flying. He once again went through the settling ritual, although his ability to concentrate on shooting was definitely thin. He looked forward, in the direction of where the beaters would be coming from, and he could actually see the heat shimmering over the heather.

'Very odd,' he said to Molly. He looked to his right and left, and this time, all the 'guns' were in view. Everyone seemed to have a clear view ahead, except perhaps those guns in the higher butts, where he could see it was quite craggy. He stuck in the sighting sticks, and checked the field of fire. He could see the stops to the left, down by the main heather line, and looking far behind him, he could also see one of the keepers acting as longstop for perhaps injured birds that might fly on. Whatever else he may think about Strathallan, his staff knew what they were about. He settled back again, and waited.

What could he do about Tomlinson? He was a very senior executive of Albion, and as managing director, almost no one could interfere with his decisions unless it impinged upon group strategy. Here he was, with the two other principal shareholders probably in agreement to his joining the bidding, but absolutely baulked by Albion. The others might bring pressure on Tomlinson, but so what? Tomlinson would revel in ignoring them, and would they really fight Travers' corner? Unlikely. Fuck. He had run out of ideas for the moment. But, all was certainly not lost. He kept reminding himself to stay flexible, stay cool, and play out the hand. Even if the similarity to a bad hand of draw poker was emerging.

During the next twenty minutes the occasional grouse flew over the line. Travers really did enjoy this bit the best, because if the bird came to him, the stimulus of not wanting to disappoint the others with his prowess was a pressure, not to mention the embarrassment if he missed. Meanwhile if the bird went to someone else, there was the real pleasure of having the time to watch how they took it. He was always fascinated too to see the bird fall before he heard the shot, demonstrating the dramatic speed of light relative to the speed of sound.

Now again Travers' poacher friend, acting as stop over on the left flank, was frantically whistling. The one-sided battle was about to begin in earnest. Travers looked at his belt, looked at his cartridge bag, put his left hand glove on and half raised the gun in readiness. They were at the top of the line, a huge cloud of grouse, maybe two or three hundred, were streaming over the top butt. A couple of shots finally rang down the hillside, but Travers could see no birds that fell. Who was that up there? Yes, it was Bobby Newgent and Jane in nine, two up from their last drive. Poor sod, thought Travers. To see a cloud of grouse like that, with everybody watching, and to miss it. He could imagine the blue language emanating from the butt, and the dogs running for cover. He couldn't help but smile.

There were no further big coveys overhead, but as far as Travers was concerned, that was good. He loved the pairs and singletons, because they seemed to jink more and change direction quicker. No time for long slow swings through the birds, you had to be on them, flicking through with the gun, with a lot of movement in the left arm. Wonderful stuff. Both of his colleagues in the butts above and below him were meeting the challenge, and because they could see one another on the flat ground, caps were raised and doffed in appreciation when good shots were made, or the other was beaten to the trigger. Also, when a bird was out of range, the three of them would shout 'Over!' to warn the other that a bird was entering their field of fire. Good 'Boys' Own' stuff, but without a doubt these memorable moments did forge a camaraderie amongst the shooters.

The next moment, Travers heard the unmistakable

splatter as lead pellets ripped through the heather just to the back of his butt. There was a shout of 'Hey!' from Sir Angus, one up from Travers. Someone just above Sir Angus had let go with a loose shot down through the line, which Travers felt was inexcusable for 'guns' with the experience of this party. He suddenly felt decidedly uncomfortable and wondered if Sir Angus or Clarissa had been peppered, or worse. He decided that probably no harm had been done, or the tone of the warning from Sir Angus would have been more pained than aggressive. The drive was nearing its end now, with the beaters in sight, but still plenty of shooting. Nevertheless the loose shot did detract from its enjoyment.

The horn blew, the beaters walked through and the pick up began. Molly did her thing and retrieved fifteen birds, which Travers laid out on his butt. Travers walked across to Sir Angus, and simply asked if he and Clarissa were OK. Without saying a word, he picked up his cartridge bag, holding it at arms length. Although there were no holes in it, the back of the leather had about ten spot indentations with the tell-tale grey smudge.

'Fortunately, no one in the back of the butt,' said Sir Angus casually. Clarissa was still working the dogs behind the butt, and seemed completely unperturbed by what could have been a fatal shooting accident. Travers shook his head, but said no more. It was up to Sir Angus to either complain to the keeper about loose shooting, have his own quiet word with the culprit, or let it go, on the basis that whoever made the mistake would sure as hell know he'd done it, and no further chastisement would be necessary.

Travers walked back to his own butt to collect his things. Presumably, he thought, Clarissa must have been loading for him, standing beside him in the front of the butt. Fortunately, there were quite long distances between these particular butts, so serious damage to humans was probably limited. However, he knew the shot must have been fired by Rex Bertrand in seven, because a shot from a higher position simply wouldn't have carried all the way to Travers' butt with such force. Travers thought to himself that this was the second bit of bad luck today, what would be the third?

His things gathered, he wandered down the hill. It was ten past one on his watch, and time for a well deserved lunch. He ambled over to Richard Blount, who being on eight on the last drive, was one on this drive at the bottom of the hill, fairly close to the vehicles. Despite his difficulties with Tomlinson, he might as well keep things moving on other fronts.

'Rick, how d'you get on?'

'Well, I was out on the wings again, unlike you fellows, but even so, quite enough for me to handle, great fun.'

'Good. Can I bend your ear before we get in the cars?' With a few of the dogs including Molly milling around, Travers slowly led Blount off at a tangent from the cars. 'Rick, I'm after a bit of information. When we spoke at tea time yesterday, you mentioned you'd picked up some rumblings about Sunburst. I'm sorry I was so cagey then, but things are on the move, and it's quite clear now that the big shareholders want to sell. Now, if I play my cards right, I might just have a chance of being involved if they go through with a disposal.

'Obviously the whole thing is still highly confidential and speculative. The thing is, I need to see a few more venture capital guys, and I wondered if you could give me a tip about any you've been impressed with?'

'Thought so, not surprised. OK. First thing, how big's the deal? These guys split into large and small, and don't cross over much.'

'Well,' said Travers, 'I reckon anywhere between sixty

and ninety mill, with as much senior debt as I can handle. Let's say up to fifty mill of equity finance, and forty mill of senior debt.'

'OK. That just about puts you amongst the big boys, but the really big guys don't get out of bed for anything less than a hundred. I can put you in touch with A.B.D., Bavarischer, and Freemans. They've all got funds for mid-range manufacturing buyouts. I've met the key people, and you might get a decent deal for management. I'll get my secretary to fax you contacts, addresses, and then if you're interested, I'll set up the first meetings for you.'

'Rick, what can I say? That is so kind of you, I'm very grateful. What about a merchant bank and advisors to fight for my side? Who did you use?'

'Our clearing bank. They've all got corporate finance and mergers and acquisitions in-house, and they are desperately important when some of the more arcane bullshit spews out from the venture capital guys. You'll find the venture capitalists will chop and change, do anything in fact to screw you out of the deal you thought you had with them. The merchant bank can help to prevent that, at a cost, by acting as the ringmaster, appointed by you. But mostly you're on your own, and it's you against the whole lot. Don't, for heaven's sake, underestimate what you're up against. No one's really on your side, even when you think they are.'

Christ, thought Travers, there's some experience and bitterness behind those comments.

'Rick. Thanks. It's a bit of a cheek, given that your hands are full paying these buggers back, but if I get into this, can I lean on you for some advice from time to time?'

'Sure, so long as it's just chat. If you want any more than that, Tom, I think you'd have to think about some sweet equity for me, to make the effort worthwhile – your choice.'

'Not slow in coming forward, Rick. I'm not sure I want to go that far!'

Blount laughed. 'There you are, you're getting the hang of it already!' They both laughed and walked back to the cars. As they were walking, Blount turned to Travers and said, 'One final bit of advice, Tom. I'm an accountant who fell into pubs, so I had a head start. You're a marketing man. Believe me, every day becomes a new spreadsheet for the bankers. However good you think your finance director is get rid of him and buy the best one the headhunters can lay their hands on. Someone's got to do the numbers at your end, while you think. Unless you have someone really good in-house, you're gonna get screwed.'

'Right, chief,' said Travers.

As they got back to the vehicles, everyone had returned from the hillside, and Tomlinson was calling them to order.

'Well, ladies and gentlemen, I think you've earned your lunch. Good shooting everyone, the bag is building nicely. We now follow Macadam and his keepers to the lunch spot, where I hope everything is ready. It's now one thirty, and we must be back in the vehicles by two thirty, or we won't fit in the two return drives. Please bear that in mind before your first gin! And, ladies, the farmhouse we'll be attached to has the necessary sanitary arrangements, so modesty and dignity can be preserved.'

Dogs and bodies were loaded, and the convoy set off. Within five minutes, having driven back down the track, and along a farm road, the convoy pulled up in a meadow next to one of the keepers' houses. There, an open-fronted tent had been erected, containing long folding tables complete with linen tablecloths, weighed down by a collation of cold foods and drink, mostly alcoholic. The chef from the house and the ladies in black were fussily ensuring all the tureens were in their rightful place, while in front of the tent, folding wooden tables and chairs, again complete with tablecloths, had been laid out in the cowslip-laden field. The sun continued to beat down, and had a river been nearby, it could easily have been a scene more suited to Henley than the Highlands. Tomlinson had positioned himself behind the drinks table, and was dispensing to the ladies as they returned from the loo inside the farmhouse.

Travers went up to the table and asked Tomlinson for a large gin and tonic, not knowing what reaction he would get after their contretemps on the moor. Tomlinson was in full PR mode, and as he handed Travers his drink, said, 'Tom, some very nice shooting this morning. The keeper tells me you, Sir Angus and Peter were keeping up the reputational standards of the estate. They all watch the "guns" like hawks, y'know.'

'Thanks for saying so, Piers. It's been a delight, and of course looking forward to this afternoon.' What else could he say? People were milling around the table, but from the look of things it seemed to Travers that it was likely that any further discussion with Tomlinson on the trade sale were now at an end. As he sat at one of the tables looking down the glen, he was depressed by the thought that his next contact with Tomlinson might very well be through Goldberg's contacting him next week, wanting to get on with the Information Memorandum.

He was joined at the table by Peter and Susie Beaufort, and, chatting happily about the morning's shooting, they all got up and wandered over to the lunch table buffet.

As Travers was selecting a mixture of cold meats and salad, he spotted Tomlinson's subordinate, Maclaren, drive into the yard behind the farmhouse in his red Mondeo. Travers smiled and hoped the poor fellow wasn't in for another tongue-lashing from Tomlinson. Travers returned to his table and got on with lunch with the others, but kept an eye on Maclaren. By now bottles of wine were on the tables, so Tomlinson had done his duty on the drinks table, and was hanging around with Bertrand at the end of the little queue for food. Maclaren went up to him, whispered something in his ear and gestured towards the farmyard. The two of them wandered off, already deep in discussion.

At the same time as Travers had returned his attention to his meal and the chatter, there was an almighty bang from a shot gun from somewhere very close that made all of them literally jump out of their seats. Lottie Bertrand screamed, 'What on earth's happening?'

Macadam, the head keeper, emerged from behind the lunch tent, one hand holding his battered old shot gun, the other holding a thin brown little animal with a white breast and a bushy long tail. It was either a stoat or a weasel, Travers didn't know which.

'Sorry, ladies and gentlemen, to upset your lunch, but these beasties must be dealt with.'

'Well really,' said Lottie. 'Frightened me to death. Is that really necessary?' Rex Bertrand told her to sit down, reminding her that a pair of weasels could cause annihilation of grouse eggs on a whole section of the moor if they weren't dealt with. Practically all of the men rose from their chairs and went over to inspect the creature, which Travers thought was a beautiful little thing, apart from the row of teeth in its open little jaws, which looked razor sharp. They all returned to their seats, and discussions continued from where they had been left.

Just then, Tomlinson returned, ushering Maclaren forward to the lunch spread, and walked over to Travers. He looked very serious indeed.

'Have a word please, Tom.' He spun round without

waiting, and marched off in the direction of the yard again. Travers made his excuses to the Beauforts, and followed Tomlinson. When he got to the farmyard, Tomlinson was waiting with his hands on his hips.

'It won't work y'know.'

'Sorry?' said Travers.

'I don't know what you've been up to, but don't think for a moment I'm finished with this.'

Travers also lifted his hands to his hips. He had done nothing wrong that he could think of, and was quite prepared to match Tomlinson's aggressive body language.

'Look, Piers, whatever you've got to say, get on with it. I haven't a clue what you're going on about.'

'Well let me tell you,' said Tomlinson, speaking in a quiet and measured tone, 'The chairman, for Christ's sake, has been onto the Edinburgh office to track you down. He wants to see you tomorrow in London, and me on Friday. Just when did you speak to him, and why have you gone behind my back? I want an answer.' Travers could see that Tomlinson was seething, but making a determined effort to control himself.

'Look, Piers, you've got it all wrong I'm afraid. I haven't spoken to Sir Brian for at least three months, and anyway, there's no way I would go running off to anyone at Albion behind your back. I promise you. I wouldn't do that.'

'I think you're capable of anything,' said Tomlinson. 'Our standards of behaviour are clearly not shared by you. I'll be bloody glad to see the back of soft drinks, and you with it. What a dirty trick.'

'Piers, you're wrong. I can't say any more. When does he want to see me tomorrow? You realise I'll have to leave this afternoon.'

'Would have thought you already know the details. All I've been told is you tomorrow morning, me on Friday when I've finished here,' said Tomlinson.

'OK,' said Travers. 'For the sake of appearances, Piers, I'll say to the other "guns" that we've had a flash strike in the factory or something, and that I've got to leave. No point in creating embarrassment for you or me. Might as well be sensible whatever it's about. Who knows, Piers, I might very well be getting my marching orders for all I know.'

Tomlinson's eyes narrowed. He hadn't thought of that possibility, but could Travers be right? He certainly hadn't thought it could possibly be an early exit for Travers, but he was certainly warming to the idea.

'If that were the case, you've brought it on yourself. But how can it be?' he said, thinking out loud. 'I only cleared our approach about the package for you, with Sir Brian, yesterday lunchtime, from the carphone.'

'Well, Piers, you've not even told me what that package is. Still, it may not matter any more, and you could be a happy man.'

This possibility was at the extremity of Travers' thoughts, but he knew it wasn't true. Someone must have got at Sir Brian Richards either last night or this morning about Sunburst and the trade sale. There was no way he would interfere with the plan already agreed with Tomlinson by telephone yesterday. His mind was in a spin, not knowing whether he'd hit the jackpot or was about to be flushed, but at least Tomlinson had calmed down a bit.

'Piers, I'm really sorry all this has upset you so much. Whether you believe me or not, I've had nothing to do with Sir Brian's involvement. I suppose I'd better make a move. I couldn't shoot anyway this afternoon with all this going on. I really am very grateful to you for inviting me, it's been a great party, and the shooting this morning was very, very, special. If I don't say bye to everyone, could you stick to the story?'

'Yes, all right, Tom. But don't blame me if this whole

thing blows up in your face. Albion's got no room for prima donnas, and maybe this will serve as a lesson whatever the outcome.'

You absolute shit, thought Travers. A sanctimonious bastard right to the end. If he needed a spur to succeed, Tomlinson had just given him one. See you in hell, he thought, as he raised his arm in farewell to Tomlinson.

'By the way, Piers, do you mind if Maclaren gives me a lift back to Glenlivet?'

'Go ahead,' said Tomlinson.

'And one more thing,' said Travers. Reaching into his back pocket he took out his wallet and withdrew two twenty pound notes, which he folded and held out to Tomlinson. 'Please pass this on to Macadam with my grateful thanks.' Tomlinson nodded and took the keeper's tip. 'Oh, before I forget, you will square this strike story with Maclaren? If the other "guns" talk to him, it's best we're all singing from the same hymn sheet.'

'Yes, yes,' said Tomlinson brusquely. Travers turned and walked away towards the lunch party.

'Can't explain. Literally trouble at mill. Got to go.' Travers circulated around the tables saying the same thing, explaining briefly the news of a strike that Maclaren had brought, drawing shock and genuine disappointment from his colleagues and friends. He didn't forget to thank the keeper. As he passed Jane seated next to her husband, all he could do was shrug his shoulders and purse his lips in resignation. She sat there expressionless with her mouth slightly open, as the news and the disappointment sunk in, with the spectre of a night of enjoyment disappearing into the ether.

'Bloody silly,' said Bertrand out loud. 'Could understand it if the place were burning down. Can't someone else handle it?' Travers wasn't in the mood to get caught in fake explanations, raising his hand in farewell as he made his way over to Maclaren, Tomlinson having already pulled him to one side. Having secured Maclaren's ready agreement to transport him back to the lodge, Travers picked up Molly and his gear from the Spencers car, and shoved them all in the back seat of the Mondeo. The whole group was looking at him, still in bemused surprise, but knowing that Tomlinson had brought him the news. They could at least bend Tomlinson's ear once Travers had departed.

Travers took a last look at the group, and Jane in particular. He knew, and she knew, that his final wave was for her, and he was more convinced than ever that they would be meeting again, sooner than she expected.

In the car, Travers turned to Maclaren and said, 'Bruce, is there anything you can tell me about this call from Sir Brian? Did you take the call?'

'No,' said Maclaren, 'Mr Tomlinson's secretary took the call. Because the mobiles don't work up here, I've had yet another trip. Wouldn't mind, but I never get any thanks, and I've got a job to do like anyone else.'

'Yes, sorry about that,' said Travers. Clearly nothing to learn from Maclaren, and the twenty minute journey back to the lodge was made in silence. The only thing that struck Travers at that moment was that he was now unable to take the whole salmon, offered by the poacher, back with him down south. Pity.

Travers cleared his second floor room, leaving twenty pounds for the staff on a dresser with a note of thanks. He was pleased, for the moment, to be busy getting his things together. He had the whole journey to work things out, and right now he needed the dust to settle in his brain, before dissecting all the events of the last hour.

Everything now in the car, and perspiring in the ever present heat, the last thing to do was clean the gun, which he did under the tailgate of the car. Whatever else was happening, thought Travers, the gun would be properly cleaned and oiled before it went back in the case. It was all too easy to pit the barrels if corrosive saltpetre was left there. That done, a last glance at the magnificent house, and Travers motored slowly down the drive. He wondered whether he would ever have the good fortune to be invited back.

Chapter Four

Going down the A9, Travers had just about prioritised what he had to do. It was now three o'clock on a Wednesday afternoon, so he would hit London and the flat by about eight o'clock, which was fine. The key question was the content of tomorrow's summons by Sir Brian Richards, chairman of Albion, at their small executive office in Great Portland Street, which Travers knew well. Several times in the past, Sunburst's board meetings had been held there as a convenience to the non-executive directors who had other meetings to attend in town.

The first thing on the agenda, he had decided, was to call Sir Brian, and with the very good excuse of having left the shoot, find out what time would be convenient, and what the hell was so important to cancel his attendance at the grouse shoot. Either way if he wasn't there, or wouldn't answer the question, it was worth a shot, and nothing lost. But first, he'd better tell Chris what was going on. He had a signal from his mobile now, so got on to his secretary.

'Chris, can you talk?'

'Hello, Tom, aren't you meant to be shooting? I can hear the wind noise; you're in a car.'

'Right on both counts, is anyone with you?'

'No, all clear. What's up?' she said, catching his anxiety.

'Chris, you know we've all talked about the possibilities of a sale of the business. Well, things have moved a bit quicker than planned. I've been called to see Sir Brian tomorrow at Portland Place. I really don't know what it's about, I'm still hoping it might be good news about an MBO, but I can't be certain. Tell David and John that I'll get in touch after lunch tomorrow. Meanwhile, as usual this whole thing is top secret, so make sure the guys understand that. I don't want any leaks from our end, and those two alone are all that need to know about this. Also, Chris, get Morris of Wessex Bank on the phone and tell him I want to meet him tomorrow morning at his offices, can't be certain when, but I'll phone a half hour before arrival. Finally, Chris, can you pick up Molly from the flat sometime around tennish, give her a run in the park and take her back to the office. I'll pick her up later. Have you got all that, and is there anything for me?'

'OK, got that, and no, nothing important here,' said Christine. 'It sounds as if it could get exciting, I hope it goes the way you want. Remember, Tom, give me a call here or at home if you need anything.'

'Thanks, Chris.' And he pushed the 'end' button on the mobile. One eye on the road, he then scanned the directory, and pushed the button for 'Albion'. He got through to Sir Brian's secretary.

'Is he there please, this is Tom Travers of Sunburst.' She explained that he was in a meeting, but knew he was trying to get Travers to a meeting tomorrow morning.

'Fine, can he fit me in at eight thirty, or soonest after that?' She said she was sure that would be all right. 'OK,' he said. 'Please understand I don't know why he wants to see me, and I'd be mightily relieved if I did. If I give you my mobile and my home phone, will you please ask him to ring and let me know?' She said she would try, but no guarantees, because he may not reappear from the meeting before close of play, but she would leave a message. He thanked her, and said he would see her tomorrow morning.

Blast. It would be nice to know what the hell the news was, at least then he might get some sleep tonight. There was nothing more he could now do. He'd half finished his lunch before having to leave the shoot, but he suddenly remembered the pork pie in his shooting bag, which for some reason lifted his spirits. He could have a munch on that when he let Molly out for pee break, but otherwise he could make the journey in one, without stopping. He laughed at himself. Grief, he was already getting into survival mode. But he had to admit the adrenalin charge was great, and he was looking forward to thinking on his feet with Sir Brian, who like Blount, was another quick-witted accountant. He convinced himself there was still everything to play for, and clearly, at least Tomlinson was out of the picture for the moment.

It turned into a really beastly journey. The M6 was foul, and the traffic from Luton south on the M1 was nose to tail, yet another broken down lorry. He reached his flat in Holland Park at eight thirty, and set about unloading the bare essentials from his car, namely the gun and ammo, and the dog's provisions. Everything else could stay, with the cover over it, to be unloaded when he finally got back to East Grinstead at the weekend. He had the ground floor flat and basement of an Edwardian villa, and after once more letting Molly roam the back garden to which he had exclusive use, he could at last relax and enjoy a whisky in front of the telly, with his mind in neutral for at least an hour.

He was up at six. Today of all days he needed his brain to have had at least a two hour warm up, which is why he chose six o'clock. He reckoned three quarters of an hour to get in on the tube, off at Oxford Circus, and walk up past the Beeb to Albion's office. So he would leave at seven forty-five, or maybe seven thirty to make sure. No dramas, no sweat, he would be calm, unruffled and ready by eight thirty, in front of the chairman of Albion Breweries plc.

He thought about Sir Brian Richards. Been in the job about four years, knighted last year (as were all Albion's chairmen), and another accountant. An accountant with a difference perhaps, having been recruited from a big management consultancy firm. His job was simple. To put a fire under this sleeping monolith that was Albion. Market leader in beer production, vast assets in pubs and free trade loans, hotels and overseas investments, and yet the return for investors was poor. Whether it was return on capital, or simple bottom line profit growth, everything was mediocre, spilling over to its stock market rating. Sir Brian's job was to create evolution rather than revolution in the business, but one way or the other he had to make the assets work harder for a better return. A big chunk of his problem was the management. 'Man and boy' was a phrase probably coined for Albion, where the average length of service was twenty-five years, and most of them were doing broadly the same job as when they started. Over promotion was endemic, so that limited capabilities were allowed to succeed retired or deceased predecessors. Things were happening under Sir Brian, but not fast enough. Travers had his own thoughts. Not so much the technical requirements of recovery, which any manager could pick up out of a text book or the financial press, but more about leadership and visible direction. He knew that too was overcooked by poor practitioners, but the fact was, an organisation like Albion screamed out for a figurehead, someone to point this huge and powerful aircraft carrier in the right direction, and make sure it was equipped with the latest Star Wars weapons, re-establishing confidence within the organisation, which had all but disappeared.

Sir Brian, in Travers' view, was not the man for that job. Sir Brian had spoken at Travers' sales conference three months before, and Travers had been unimpressed. One hundred salesmen need to hear some ambition for the business, and that they failed to get from Sir Brian. It was more about problems, industry constraints, perseverance – guaranteed to send a sales force to sleep. Nevertheless, for all that, it gave Travers a useful insight into the man's personality, which might prove extremely valuable this morning.

A bit of toast, two cups of real coffee, dog's bowels evacuated, and he was ready to go. He got to Portland Place by eight fifteen, and stood outside the Georgian town house. The most incongruous plate glass doors stood between the Doric column entrance, and with a deep breath he entered. A receptionist with a magnetic entry card took him through doors, stairs and corridors, until he was ushered into a mahogany panelled room, complete with original fireplace. His thoughts immediately went to Glenlivet Lodge, and he thought that Gothic Arcadia seemed to be Albion's speciality. The room was dominated by a long mahogany table, seating about twelve, leaving precious little room for anything else bar a small coffee table with a telephone on it. He was offered coffee and told to wait.

Ten minutes later, at eight thirty on the dot, Sir Brian entered the room and gave Travers a warm welcome. Milk jugs and biscuits were exchanged, and Sir Brian reminisced in a kindly way about the success of the Sunburst sales conference. Come on, thought Travers, let's get on with it, please.

'Now, Tom,' said Sir Brian, 'I'm sorry I didn't get back to you last night. I didn't get out of my meeting until late, and whilst I saw the diary entry, I didn't see my secretary's message to phone until this morning. But anyway, you know what this is about, so I suggest we make a start.' Travers wasn't sure whether he believed him about the message, but what the hell. Travers pushed his chair back a little and crossed his legs, with his hands on his knees.

'What you don't know, Tom, is that yesterday morning at nine o'clock, I received a call from Sir Angus Egan. He told me he was about to shoot with you fellows, but felt he had to make a call about you and the proposed sale of Sunburst. He suggested that the consortium, and perhaps Piers, were not approaching the problem with the right attitude, and that because the job has fallen to Albion to become spokesman and effectively executor for the sale, I should listen to your proposals, which he believed had some merit. The reason I have agreed to see you, Tom, is frankly more about reputational risk for Albion, rather than any personal desire you may have for your future. Nevertheless, if we can come to an accommodation that suits you as well as us, and that doesn't create unwelcome press, then, there is no reason not to consider it. What mustn't happen is that you as managing director destroy value in the sale process. If you do that, and our advisors substantiate it, then there is no alternative but to terminate your contract, probably on the minimum possible compensation.

'I am saying this, Tom, just so that you understand the full impact of what we must do if you fail to follow the shareholder's instructions.'

'Brian,' said Travers, 'thank you for that explanation. Of course I know exactly what you and the other shareholders wish to achieve from this sale, which is purely and simply maximum value. Depending on who ultimately buys the business, they'll want assurances about continuing service from key individuals, always assuming they are considered valuable. I would do my best with both workforce and management to ensure that those people who have contributed to the success of Sunburst continue to be available to the new buyer, if they consider those individuals an intrinsic part of the value they have put on the business.

'Frankly, Brian, there's no one but me who can deliver on that promise, because I have spent ten years developing a mutual trusting relationship with the employees that I know is valued by all of them. So let's be clear, apart from developing the value of the business as it now stands, I can also help to sustain that value with the new buyer.

'But, Brian, before I go on to tell you my thoughts of how you and the shareholders could facilitate an MBO approach as a secondary stage of the trade sale process, no one yet has told me of this "incentive package" that is to be my reward for probably selling myself out of a job. Would you mind?'

Sir Brian uttered a restrained laugh.

'Of course, Tom, you are in a precarious position with whoever takes the business over. We fully recognise that however good you are, they might want their own man in place to convert the culture, rationalise or whatever. Recognising that, we are prepared to pay you a success fee, based on three times your annual salary, if the business is sold without any hiccups.'

'I take it,' said Travers, 'that would include equivalent company pension contribution for the same period.' Sir Brian hesitated, but only for a second, realising that Travers didn't appear to be asking for any more.

'Um, yes. I think we could agree to that, which seems fair.'

'OK, thank you, Brian. Now on the same subject, I have another problem. There are only three of us at Sunburst who really run the business. That's me, David Ogden in marketing, and John Fellowes in ops. The other directors, including finance don't really matter to me in keeping the ship on course through a period of at least three or four months while the sale process is going on.

'Both of them are good, and both of them are about to jump ship because, of course, they know about the trade sale. I need them both, Brian, and in the context of a sixty or seventy million trade sale, the cost of offering them the same deal as me is minuscule. If you agree to that, whatever happens on the MBO front, I promise you we'll see it through.'

Sir Brian sat and stared at Travers, with no visible expression.

'I'm not sure Gallant and Caledonia would agree to that,' he said in an emotionless way.

'Oh, I think you'll find they will,' said Travers equally deadpan. 'And of course they have given you full discretion to resolve this matter.'

'All right, Tom, what else is on your shopping list?'

'Absolutely nothing, other than letting me enter the bidding for the business at the appropriate time.'

'And just how do you hope to accomplish that, may I ask?' said Sir Brian.

'OK, let me explain,' said Travers. 'I am fully aware of your natural concern about MBOs, in terms of having information about the business that third party buyers may not have, which may have the effect of scaring them off in the first place. There is also the tension from both third party buyers and management, of knowing that while information exchange is going on, they are going to be pitched against one another when it comes to the bids. I think we can avoid all that.'

'I'm all ears,' said Sir Brian unconvincingly.

'Very simple, really,' said Travers. 'Management undertakes not to even enter a bid until after the second round, when you have binding bids from the third parties. At that stage, you will know what bid you are inclined to accept, and all I ask is at that stage we have the right to submit our own bid. We don't even want to know what price we have to beat, because that could compromise your even-handedness with everyone involved. Either our bid is better, or it's not. Either way, the shareholders have been best served by securing the best possible price for the business. Indeed, it could be said, not least from me, that you would be doing the shareholders a disservice by not accepting the best bid, wherever it came from.

'And one more thing, Brian. I'm very happy indeed for Goldberg's to direct the whole trade sale process, and have their staff sit in every meeting that may involve third party buyers, to ensure we meet the rules of the game and are open and honest in our analysis of the business. I honestly think I have met any concern you may have about an MBO shot, and furthermore you get best efforts from me during that process, and end up with the best price.

'My final comment, Brian, is that I do think you owe me one. In ten years I've taken Sunburst from two million profit to thirteen million before tax. I know it's a partially commodity business, but even on a low earnings ratio, I've added at least fifty million to the value of the business.'

'You certainly seem to have covered most of our concerns about management involvement,' said Sir Brian. 'But again, this is wholly unconventional, and I would need the support of the other shareholders, and my own board. From the sound of it though, Angus Egan has already given you his support. For me, I'm bound to say I don't like offering MBOs. If they succeed it's my head on the block for selling off the business too cheaply to management – and I get the nasty questions at the AGM about sweetheart deals. On the other hand, if you fail and go bust it's me who's overstretched you and we should have gone for a clean sale. But, we both know we need you with a positive frame of mind to get through what will be an extremely challenging period. Knowing you as I do, I'm inclined to accept that you will play the game fairly. Nevertheless, I would be bound to take up your suggestion that Goldberg's monitor your every progress, which should keep us all honest. But I'm not sure...'

Travers nodded, and then said, 'Brian, I hesitate to mention it, but there is another reason why we must have a very quick decision on this, and I mean by Monday. Without mentioning sources, at the shoot I was told that most of Piers Tomlinson's management know that Gallant, backed by Albion, is disposing of their shareholding in Sunburst, thereby forcing a trade sale by all the shareholders. My guess is, that by Monday or Tuesday, this will have found its way to the trade press and maybe even the nationals, and I'm going to have a mountain of pressmen camping outside Sunburst by the middle of next week. Now I can handle that, it's meat and drink to me, but you can't expect me to handle it if I haven't got an answer.'

'Would you undertake to keep the MBO pitch confidential until the end of round two?' said Sir Brian.

'Of course,' said Travers. 'Then, the trade sale of Sunburst is simply about focus and concentration by its brewer owners on what it does best – brewing beer and running pubs. I wouldn't even try to cultivate press support for an MBO, or suggest that Albion had forced a sale.'

'Hmm. That really is bad news if the press are on to this before we're ready to go. We've had quite enough bad publicity recently, and the prospect of another five hundred redundancies at Sunburst wouldn't be welcome – even though Tom, you and I know that isn't true.'

Ha! thought Travers, you let that out too quick. Sir Brian knows, thought Travers, that any sort of trade sale was most likely to go to one of the multinationals, with obvious consequences for the employees.

At this point Travers just knew that Sir Brian was going to say yes to his plan for the MBO, he was over a barrel, and anyway, Egan had already agreed. Sir Brian only had to square away Gallant in the form of Spencer, which would be a pushover. Travers decided to play his last card when Sir Brian actually said yes. Meanwhile, Travers knew silence was the best policy while Sir Brian made up his mind; there was nothing more Travers could say now to swing the decision.

Sir Brian Richards sat in front of Travers, playing with his pen, with fierce concentration on his face. He looked up and smiled.

'OK, Tom, we'll do it your way. Congratulations. I'll check with the other shareholders and get back to you on Monday. I will also talk to Goldberg's and confidentially put them in the picture. No doubt they will be making contact with you. If, by the way, your bid fails, and you don't want to stay at Sunburst, can we have another chat?'

'Sounds interesting,' said Travers jovially, 'I'll make that a date. Now one more thing, Brian; we are agreed, aren't we, that success fees are still payable if the MBO wins the trade sale?'

Sir Brian's face dropped immediately.

'What! You mean we pay you for succeeding with your own bid?'

'That's implicitly what we've already agreed, Brian. If you don't agree we've got no money to put into equity, and I'd never raise any money from the venture capitalists. You really can't change the principle of success fees now. You are willing to pay for a successful sale. An MBO at top dollar is a successful sale. There's no difference.'

'Good God, you'd better leave before I lose my shirt. But I'm really not sure I can get away with that one.'

'Course you can, Brian. Come on, you owe me one,' said Travers.

'OK, OK, I'll be in touch on Monday.'

'Thank you, Brian, I'm very grateful. Let's shake on that.' Travers thrust his hand across the table. Just give me your hand, he thought, because he knew Sir Brian would never break his word, whatever the difficulties with the others. Sir Brian held back for a second, fully aware of what he was committing himself to. He smiled and reluctantly stretched his hand across the table, and the pair of them shook on it. Got him! thought Travers.

'Thank you Brian,' said Travers unemotionally. 'You won't regret it. Will you brief your in-house lawyer about a contractual Heads of Agreement on the MBO, and a contract on the success fees, or shall I do that via my lawyers?'

'No, no, Tom, we'll keep that in-house. Give us a week and we should have some drafts for you.'

'Brilliant,' said Travers, 'speak to you on Monday, have a nice weekend.'

Travers wound his way back through the corridors and stairs, emerged by luck rather than judgement into the modern reception area, and out through the glass doors into the heat and noise of Portland Place. It was now just gone ten o'clock. He moved up the pavement, out of sight of Albion's offices, briefcase in hand, and stopped. Whatever else happened over the next year, he thought, he would savour this moment. He couldn't believe it. Everything he had wanted, he had eventually got from Sir Brian Richards. He worried slightly if his veiled threats about publicity were really necessary, but then they all had to know he had some teeth. Mr Nice Guy rarely wins the race, and in the negotiations that lay ahead in terms of the MBO, he reckoned he had earned some cautious respect from Albion.

He then got his mobile out of his briefcase and put in a call to James Morris at Wessex Bank. When he had got through he simply said, 'James, got some business for you, see you in half an hour.' He then hailed a taxi, and started to make his way down to Upper Thames Street in the City.

The Wessex Bank headquarters was a blue and stainless steel edifice that certainly made a statement on behalf of the bank. Entering the building, the reality of day-to-day life was evident on the pavement outside, with piles of cigarette butts littering the entrance where staff sneaked out for a quick fag. Travers smiled, and wondered why these people spent hundreds of millions from their ill-gotten gains on the building, presumably to impress clients, but were too tight to provide a smoking area for their staff. Crazy. Inside, he faced what could only be described as a cavern of chrome and glass, with a floor area of maybe a quarter of an acre, but stretching up to the full height of the building, which must have been about twelve floors in all. All around the edges of this vast space were the offices, where from the reception area, could be seen hundreds of clerks beavering away, right up to the seventh floor, where presumably, thought Travers, the executive offices took over. It reminded him that all this had to be paid for, most likely from people just like him. Have to keep a tight rein on these buggers, thought Travers.

He was shown up to client reception on the seventh floor, where a kindly looking middle-aged man who introduced himself as Dennis, showed Travers to a conference room, which was clearly one of many of all shapes and sizes. Travers quickly picked up that Dennis was the 'man that did' in terms of looking after clients and their needs, relieving the whiz-bang executives of any tiresome butlering duties themselves. Travers had to admit though, that it was all very impressive and unforced, as he settled down to wait for Morris, having been served silver service coffee and biscuits.

Within minutes Morris appeared. James Morris was a dapper, studious looking man, shorter than Travers, wearing the pinstripe uniform, black brogues and spectacles. Travers noticed immediately that Morris had exactly the same habit as Tomlinson of flicking his glasses back into position with his index finger. They had met several times before, mostly at Willesden, when a gaggle of regional executives of the bank felt they should visit to 'kick the assets' of Sunburst, and actually see what was behind the overdraft facility. Morris had been introduced as the bank's corporate finance man from the 'smoke', and had given a short and stuttering explanation of his ability to raise finance, if needed by the company, in the form of long term loans, bonds and a host of other handcuffs for the business. Travers had learned at an early stage that while the business was doing well the banks were merely suppliers of services, and that they would dance to his tune, and not the other way around. Consequently he had short shrift for the desperate seriousness of these people, preferring to goad them light-heartedly whenever possible. This did produce results across a whole range of bank charges, simply because most business executives seem chary to push the issue. However, Travers knew that what you don't ask, you don't get, and so long as the exchange is friendly, these fellows normally responded positively in what had become an increasingly competitive market.

After brief introductions, Travers ushered Morris to a chair and suggested they get on. He first requested a letter of confidentiality from Wessex, such that all their discussions were to remain private and that contacts outside the bank were cleared with him first. Morris was slightly miffed that Travers should think otherwise, but at this stage was clearly intrigued, and agreed.

Travers then gave him a full analysis of the situation, leading to the request that he wanted Wessex to act as the financial 'ringmaster' for the whole deal, and maybe provide the long term bank debt (called senior debt, because it had first charge on the assets) and overdraft facilities.

'Tom, this is very exciting for you, and the bank. We would of course be delighted to work with you, and the equity providers to structure a deal. Given Albion's resistance to MBOs, I think you've done extraordinarily well. Presumably, we have time to run all the numbers whilst you and Goldberg's structure the Information Memorandum. If you need any help with the individuals at Goldberg's, we of course know them all extremely well. Now what about equity providers, have you got that lined up?'

'I've been to see three, so far,' said Travers. 'Only Bardons Bank actually ran some numbers, suggested the business would go for an earnings multiple of eight, and reckoned they could squeeze a management share of up to ten per cent of the sweet equity. I told them flat that was totally unacceptable. With the other two, they both decided it was pointless doing anything until I was clearly in the bidding ring. As you can imagine, I wasn't too pleased about that either – I expect to see some bloody enthusiasm from these characters.'

'As it happens,' said Morris, 'I was with Maxwell Griffin the other night, and they've just pulled a new fund together with a lot of German and Japanese money, and are itching to place it. Furthermore, it's intended for the fast moving consumer goods sector – which obviously includes soft drinks. So just maybe they might be interested.'

'Oh, right,' said Travers. 'Well, I've also got some other leads from a colleague in the brewing industry, but I won't get the details until next week. The thing is, I don't want to hawk Sunburst around the City in an elongated beauty parade for equity, otherwise it'll get out, and I'll be in trouble with Albion. How quickly can you get in touch with Maxwell Griffin?'

'No time like the present,' said Morris, and after a nod from Travers, he picked up the telephone. Within a couple of minutes Morris was shielding the telephone, saying to Travers, 'Can you make six o' clock tonight, here?'

'Yes,' said Travers, 'so long as you can let me have an office this afternoon.'

Morris waved agreement and returned to the telephone fixing the appointment.

After that was done, the two of them set about planning the logistics of what had to be done. Morris agreed to see his superiors, and discuss with them the possibilities of supplying the senior debt, or 'laying it off' with other banks. He explained to Travers that his bank might want some 'mezzanine' finance thrown in, which had some share warrants attached, so that the bank themselves could effectively have an equity interest, thus providing an upside to counterbalance the risk. All the way through this, Travers kept stopping Morris, insisting on plain English. He would never agree to anything he didn't fully understand, however complex the mechanism. They also discussed what Travers had to do, in terms of strategy papers, marketing plans, financial projections and historical performance. It reminded Travers of Blount's advice to get out and find a hot shot finance director – one more job to add to the list.

Finally, Travers asked Morris, 'Now James, what is your fee for advising me going to be?'

'Oh, I wouldn't worry about that now, Tom, it's all standard charges anyway.'

Nothing put Travers' back up more than that phrase 'standard charges'.

'You've been very helpful, James. But unless we agree

here and now what it's going to cost me, I'm afraid I've got to find another bank. I'm serious. I want to know what I'm in for before the wagon rolls.'

'Well,' said Morris, 'it's going to be about one and a half per cent, or thereabouts.'

Travers did a quick sum in his head. On 80 million that was about 1.2 million.

'In your dreams, James. The way I see it, I'm letting Wessex score on the senior debt and the mezzanine, all of which will carry a margin. You've got an excellent chance of making pots of money on that. But I'm not paying one and a half per cent, no way. You can have three quarters, and even that is generous.'

'Tom, I can't do that, it's, it's just not done. Anyway, why should you worry, it goes straight to the share premium account, not profit and loss, it'll all get wrapped up in the purchase price.'

'James, don't give me that crap. It all adds up to extra debt or more sales that I have to produce to get the return on capital, I'm not going to get screwed.'

At least his comments broke the slight tension, and then Travers said, 'Well, James, I'm here all afternoon. You go and see whoever you have to see. Either you come back at three quarters of a per cent, or else I've got to walk, which would be very sad, we're getting on so well.'

Morris sat back, obviously frustrated.

'Look, Tom, I can understand you think these are big numbers. But I don't think you have any conception of what work is involved. I'm going to have about five people working on this at any one time, and I just know it's going to take six months to completion once you take into account due diligence and bank documentation. We're all, including you, going to be on twenty hour days, and the costs on our side are huge – not to mention the salary bills of the specialists you'll have at your disposal from the bank. This is not Tesco, and after all, if you fail to win, we pick up the bill, not you.'

'I hear you,' said Travers. 'Nevertheless, you need to understand I've spent ten years building this business, and I promise you we will win this MBO, and you'll make piles of money on the senior debt margin, not to mention mezzanine. But I'm not going to get burned on costs because you say it's standard charging. The fact is I am here with you ready to deal and not speaking to anyone else. But if you don't bend on this, you force me elsewhere, and I'm absolutely certain I can get what I want if I push. It's up to you.'

Morris replied: 'OK, all I can do is ask. But I wouldn't hold your breath. We don't normally encounter this sort of thing so early in the process.' Both men leaned back in their chairs amidst a slightly tense silence, when Morris, almost resigned, broke the silence:

'Oh by the way, Tom, you must also think about lawyers and accountants. There's a mountain of work there with contracts, indemnities, purchase papers, short form reports, long form and so on. You've got to get that in place, and they've got to be good.'

'Who the hell pays for that; it's an MBO?'

'Difficult,' said Morris. 'I dare say you can work out something with them on a no success, no fee contingency basis. Trouble is, Tom, if it does succeed, you'd have to pay them a premium. If it doesn't work, you can walk away with no costs.'

'I like it, I like it,' said Travers, 'especially as you of course will operate on the same principle. Who shall I use?'

Morris was beginning to look battle weary, 'Oh, go for the best, it'll put the fear of God into Albion knowing you've got the best lawyers. I'll ring Andrews and Overton, and get them round here this afternoon, might as well meet them.'

'You're not on a kick-back are you?' said Travers.

'For heaven's sake, Tom, I'm really trying to help. We do have ethics, you know!'

Travers could see from Morris's agitation that his question was just plain rude. He bit his lip. 'Just checking, old chap, sorry. Keep your hat on,' said Travers with a smile. Morris raised his eyebrows in resignation and began to wonder what he had let himself in for. He hoped he wasn't going to suffer these barrow boy tactics, because it was not what he was used to. All he knew was that Travers' commercial record at Sunburst was spectacular, which in his terms translated into continuing growth in free cash flow over the last five years, which simply meant to him and the bank that the company's ability to take on a lucrative pile of senior debt with good security was of a high order.

It was now nearly one o'clock, and Morris said he had to leave. He told Travers that Dennis would look after his lunch, and that he could use all the facilities such as telephones or faxes, as he wished.

Dennis entered the room after five minutes, asking Travers what he wished for lunch.

'Sandwiches, please, Dennis, and a glass of Chablis?'

'Of course, sir,' said Dennis, leaving the room. He could get used to this, thought Travers, instinctively feeling that the whole of his career had been leading up to this opportunity. What's more, he would enjoy the whole thing every step of the way. He was in control and calling the shots, and every problem could be surmounted, providing he kept his wits about him, and exercised his normally subdued ruthlessness.

Things were definitely on the move.

With pen and pad on one side of him, and a magnificent tray of overfilled exotic sandwiches on the other, Travers jotted down all the things he had to do. The company accountants, who were a big London practice anyway, he could tackle next week. He'd need to phone Chris, and tell her, if she wouldn't mind, to keep the dog overnight as he may be leaving London very late that night. At some stage he would also have to address all the employees and tell them what was going on. There was nothing worse, whoever you were, not knowing what was happening to your daily routine, and he simply had to tell them at this stage that there might be new owners, which could prove better for all of them than the benign presence of the consortium. There could be nothing worse than a press leak filtering back to the employees, and putting Travers on the back foot in his explanations. He wanted to show the staff he was in control of this process as a natural development of the company, rather than a 'smash and grab' by the shareholders.

He also knew he had better speak to Goldberg's, who of course were the principal advisors acting on behalf of the consortium and Albion, in the disposal of Sunburst.

Having dealt with Chris, arrangements for the dog, and his movements that afternoon, he phoned Sir Brian's personal secretary. He asked if she had the name of the executive at Goldberg's dealing with the sale. She gave it to him, and he again got on the phone.

It was a very peculiar conversation with Geoffrey Levy of Goldberg's.

'Look, we shouldn't be speaking at all, this is very irregular,' said Levy.

'What on earth do you mean?' said Travers. 'I was with Sir Brian this morning, and as chief executive of Sunburst, you and I have to fix an agenda to get the Information Memorandum completed, so that you can get it out to prospective buyers. I am merely suggesting we get on with it.'

'On behalf of the shareholders, I must remind you we fix the agenda, not you. We will let you know when we want to see you, and we expect to have your directors on call so that we can begin to assemble unprejudiced information.'

'Listen, chum,' said Travers, 'we've never met, but let's get one thing straight. I will allow you on to the premises when I say so. You will have access to my colleagues when I say so. I am responsible for everything that happens at Sunburst until it is sold. If you're going to be difficult, I'll get you replaced, is that clear enough for you?'

There was silence on the other end of the telephone.

'We must get this issue resolved,' said Levy. 'We have a job to do, which is difficult enough without having to deal with management who disagree with what is happening.'

'Wrong,' said Travers. 'I totally support the sale of Sunburst by the consortium, so don't even try to use that one. You're an agent in this affair, no more and no less, so I suggest we get off on the right foot.'

'Well look, we haven't actually agreed when the process starts. But now you've called, I'll check with Sir Brian if he wants to get things moving. Then I'll come back to you,' said Levy.

'OK, that's a bit better. The other thing is I will not allow more than two of you on site at any one time. Nothing more upsetting to the staff than hordes of grey accountants sticking labels on the furniture. Agreed?'

'We can agree all that later,' said Levy, obviously annoyed.

'OK,' said Travers. 'Make sure you only speak to my secretary Christine, and nobody else about this matter. I'll await your call.'

Travers thought what a pompous prat the man was, but on the other hand, this was not an auspicious start with a man who it was important to get on with. Nevertheless, if Levy thought Travers was to be at his beck and call, he had better think again.

It was now two o'clock, and for the first time, Travers rose from his chair and examined the view from the huge plate glass window, which had been against his back. There was HMS *Belfast* up river, and the dirty old Thames surging past below at a surprising lick. Those vessels on the tide were moving past at a fantastic rate, whilst those against the tide were clearly struggling to make way. He was surprised by the amount of river traffic, which was fascinating, bringing the whole scene to life. He compared the scene to that of Willesden, and reminded himself that win or lose in commerce, the bankers always came out ahead and found themselves in buildings like this. Still, he wouldn't want to swap.

Dennis's head then appeared around the door, announcing the arrival of two guests from Andrews and Overton, the City lawyers. Travers told Dennis to wheel them in, and remained by the window.

'Welcome to my new office,' said Travers when they entered. He introduced himself to Paul Foot and Rebecca Wright. Foot was a senior partner specialising in mergers and acquisitions, and Wright was a junior partner, and Foot's 'right hand man'. Foot was an extraordinary character, not at all what he had envisaged of a lawyer. He was humorous, light-hearted and completely relaxed, and the two of them were obviously a close knit team, making little jibes about one another as they explained their experience and speciality.

Travers gave them the full run-down on what had happened, and the option he had been granted by Albion to bid for the business at the end of round two. As with Morris, he of course kept secret the issue of success fees payable by Albion or the consortium. In turn, Foot was impressed with the opportunity, and discussed the raft of documentation and undertakings management would have to complete to secure an MBO. Most of it was not about the actual purchase document, which was simple enough, but more to do with banking undertakings and covenants, which Foot assured him would be enough to give any sane man a heart attack. There was also the complex issue of Supply Agreements with the brewers, which would have to be agreed before any completion of purchase.

The subject of how to pay for their services if the bid failed didn't cause Foot a ripple of concern.

'No problem, that's the business we're in,' he said. 'So long as we come out ahead at the end of the year, we get on with it.' In round numbers, Travers discussed with them the cost in the event of success, and again he was horrified. The difference was that Foot simply said, 'Before you make any decision to appoint us, why not have a look around? We're here, take your time, and if you get a cheaper offer and you can trust them to get the job done, go with it. We want the business, but not if you don't think it's worth it.' Travers liked the man enormously, and thought they would get on well.

'No, I've made up my mind, Paul, I'll run with you.' Foot agreed to provide Travers with a synopsis of what in legal terms had to be completed and undertaken by management, which he advised that all the MBO team should read. Travers agreed to phone him as soon as he had received the Heads of Agreement from Albion.

The lawyers departed by three thirty, and Travers asked Dennis if he could get Morris to make an appearance before the venture capital people arrived at six o'clock. He also asked if he would be around at six to greet them. To Travers' surprise, Dennis simply said he was there as long as he was needed, and it wasn't a problem because he lived a short tube ride from the office. Travers thought the banking union would be most upset at this fellow's attitude, and wondered what on earth the bank were actually paying him; whatever it was it wasn't enough.

At four, Morris reappeared, saying that, unbelievably to him, the managing director of corporate finance had agreed the fee. Travers acknowledged what he thought was only a minor detail, sat him down again, went through his discussion with the lawyers, and told Morris how he wanted to run the process, in the context of their relationship. He reminded Morris that it was likely to be a long haul, and that Travers was determined to enjoy it and succeed. What he wanted from Morris at all times was openness and honesty with no bullshit. He told him he would stop any discussion with lawyers, bankers or accountants if he didn't understand the jargon, and that Morris must take time out to explain things to him, even at critical moments. Morris willingly agreed and reminded Travers that the converse was true, in that he had to know the workings of Sunburst better than any other advisor, so that he could fulfil his role as the 'ringmaster'. After agreeing that Morris would be present on the arrival of Maxwell Griffin, Morris disappeared again to some other job he was working on.

At six, two young men from Maxwell Griffin were ushered in by Dennis, and fresh coffee was provided. The older one, probably no more than thirty, thought Travers, was medium height, fresh faced and wearing a plain grey suit and light blue shirt. The other one was much younger, had a shock of blond hair and wore the regulation Saville Row pinstripe, brogues and cuff-linked blue striped shirt. They both looked trim and fit, each with a comfortable public school drawl. The older one was Anthony Giddings, obviously the senior of the two, and the younger one was Giles Roberts. Privately, Travers would put money on Roberts being an Old Harrovian – he was practically swaggering with self-importance.

They got down to business around the table, and it was agreed that Travers would talk about the business, its financial performance, marketing plan, and its shareholders, and then they would talk about Maxwell Griffin and the parameters they would apply to an MBO.

Travers had to admit he was impressed by both of them, but Giddings in particular. He asked all those difficult and incisive questions, be it customer relationships, product gaps, margins or managerial tensions. He wanted to know which sectors of the business were actually driving profits, analysis of consumer profiles and advertising objectives. He didn't miss a trick. Meanwhile Roberts was clearly more financially oriented, making notes of margins, gearing, free cash flow, all of which Travers could recite from memory. Travers could see he already had a column of figures from sales down to bottom line profit after tax, and while Travers spoke, he was putting his scientific calculator into overdrive on various ratios.

Travers spoke for about an hour, which was no hardship because like most managing directors, he loved the business and knew everything about it, warts and all. After this time, he thought he'd given quite enough information, including details of his meeting that morning with Sir Brian Richards, although he had been careful to keep the subject of the success fees to himself. He then invited Giddings to tell him why he should select Maxwell Griffin to finance the MBO.

Giddings gave a lucid explanation of his company's background, its backers, structure, and successes, which Travers had to agree was impressive on the basis of so many household names, which had been spun off to

MBOs. Travers asked all the questions he thought he needed to know, and then popped the Big One.

'OK fellas, you've done some numbers, what's in it for management?'

'What are you expecting?' said Giddings.

'Something north of thirty per cent.'

Giddings replied in all seriousness, 'That's a bit on the high side from what I can see. If we apply a factor of say eight to post tax earnings, realising it may go to twelve in a tight bid, we have a range of theoretical value. Because of your strong cash flow, it's likely we can gear the buyout with pretty high levels of senior debt, and therefore ratchet up the value of the equity. Let's assume we go fifty-fifty on debt equity, and that you can get this business to twenty million profit within three years, and, that it could then be worth one hundred and twenty million. If we want to make forty or fifty per cent internal rate of return on our investment, then that would indicate we could allow you to think about twenty per cent or so. But I promise you, we really can't firm up on that until we've run the spreadsheets, and built in discounted cash flows, margin spreads to investors, headroom on debt and lots of upsides and downsides on your projections.

But put it this way, Tom, right from the start we'll tell you what we want in terms of return, and you can have what falls out of that. In that way you'll have an objective eye on the price we're all willing to bid, because the higher it goes, the lower your share becomes, if we get the price wrong. But at the end of the day, it's you guys in management that've got to do the business to make the investment work, and unless you have the right incentive in terms of shares, that's not going to happen.'

Some of it was bullshit to Travers, but he got most of it, and it was the best and clearest exposition he had yet had, with at least a modicum of concern for what was in it for management.

'Do you insist on any contribution from management?' said Travers.

'Yes, we do. For our own protection. If your money's on the line and at risk, we can be absolutely certain you will do everything you can to protect it, and make it grow. If you haven't got a stake, it's far easier to bale out if the going gets tough. Tom, "feet to the fire" is non-negotiable.'

'But what if I've got no money?' said Travers.

'A first charge on your houses will do nicely, Tom. I think you mentioned you have two properties?' said Giddings.

'Suppose I'd better try and find some cash, then,' said Travers smiling. 'When could you start this process?

'The sooner the better, as long as we don't bump into Goldberg's at Sunburst,' said Giddings. 'But sooner or later they're going to know you're in the ring, so even that won't matter.'

'Well look,' said Travers, 'I have been highly impressed by the speed at which you've got the numbers, and apparently understood the business. I'm inclined to pitch in with you, but not until we have an agreement on numbers. That means that you and I have got to do some work, which may come to nothing if you whip away the carpet, and I have to find someone else. On that basis, what d'you think?'

Roberts then piped up, saying, 'There's just too much work for you to tell us to piss off if you don't like the numbers. I don't think we can live with that.'

'It's a two way street,' said Giddings, 'Yes, we can live with that. Frankly, both of us have the opportunity to pull out if it doesn't look right, paper agreements can't cover that anyway.'

Travers shook Giddings' hand, then Roberts', and finally

Morris's. They agreed a list of documents from Sunburst that would enable desk research to get under way at Maxwell Griffin, and Travers promised to supply a contact name at Sunburst for financial data and updates, which wouldn't be the finance director. He didn't go into details on that subject, but knew he had to find a replacement.

It was now nine o'clock, and Travers was relieved the meeting was at an end. It had been a long day, and he was beginning to hallucinate about a large Scotch and a long bath. It was time to go home.

On the way back on the tube he tried to get everything in the right sequence, to ensure he didn't miss any tricks on such a complicated project. His biggest concern was the people at Sunburst. Whatever happened to them he was responsible, but because he now had some control over their destiny, that responsibility was magnified, and he didn't want to let them down on his account. The livelihoods of five hundred people weighed heavily on his conscience, much more so than if this were just a personal risk, which he was happy to take. Was he right to go for this opportunity? Or would it have been better to just run the sale process? After all, he thought, maybe there's no buyers out there who will pay a decent price, then everything would revert to normal. But then he reviewed what his own position would be. He'd carry on at full throttle building Sunburst with no perks other than a good salary and bonus. No equity, no share of growth, and with the certain knowledge that as soon as someone came up with an attractive offer, more than likely he was out of a job. No, he had to go for this chance, build the business through MBO, onto flotation on the stock market three years later, and the future of the business, not to mention his own, would be secure. Good, he was satisfied.

His mind then drifted onto Jane, and their arcane tryst on the grouse shoot. This was a risk that he really shouldn't be taking. He was fairly sure it was nothing other than infatuation and pure lust, in other words he hadn't 'fallen' for her, but goodness, he couldn't help feeling slightly embarrassed that she was the best 'lay' he had ever had, and the thrill of it was compulsive. After all, she felt the same as him, and there was absolutely no advantage for her to do anything other than keeping this thing absolutely clandestine – she had as much if not more to lose than he. Nevertheless he knew emotion was a damned sight harder to control than a business project, and perhaps he should 'cool it' until the buyout was done. In business jargon she was a potential 'loose cannon' and he would have to watch his step.

At eight the following morning, he was in the office. The trip took just over half an hour, out on the Western Avenue, and round the North Circular. The factory was really more Neasden than Willesden, being adjacent to the North Circular on a twenty acre site.

Sunburst had been there since its inception in the thirties, so it was hardly a state of the art site. Nevertheless, heavy investment had gone into the plant, if not the buildings, so that Sunburst possessed high speed filling and canning lines, which could fill anything from fruit juices in cartons, through two litre plastic-bottled lemonade, cans of cola and small returnable glass mixers for the pub trade. It was highly flexible, low cost, but the real volume and profit growth in the last four years had come from a range of carbonated canned citrus drinks aimed at the teenage market and backed by a totally wacky advertising campaign led by a TV 'youf' presenter. Some of the brand varieties had the addition of alcohol at low levels, and this had opened up the trade in pubs. The beauty of it was product cost was minimal, even allowing for advertising costs and duty on the alcoholic variants, but retail selling prices were high, producing superb profit margins. The real strength of the brand now was in higher alcoholic variants, filled into lager type bottles, giving the lucrative youth market alcoholic 'delivery', combined with 'ease of consumption', because the fruit flavours tasted so good in comparison to beer.

Because of Sunburst's ownership and Travers' excellent relationship with the brewers, gaining distribution in the pub trade had not really been difficult. Indeed, one of Travers' biggest headaches over the last three years had been 'hiding' profits from the consortium.

Travers had been really concerned about this. His worry was that if he started turning in forty plus per cent profit growth every year, the shareholders would naturally expect that to continue, and Travers would be on the old treadmill of 'catch-up' thereafter. Instead, he had put a whole chain of measures in place to 'smooth out' profit growth for as long as he could, whilst other product developments came on stream. Amongst the perfectly legitimate measures he had put in place, was to write off any plant, equipment or materials that weren't bang up to date, to contract forward TV production costs, to sink huge sums into development contingency costs, provisions for unpaid customer discounts, and two months before each year end, when he knew the profit target could be hit, to slam in advertising expenditure on TV. This latter measure was wonderful, because it built sales and the consumer franchise for later, and it was easy to get past the shareholders and the auditors without any fuss. He had also thinned out the product range, disposing of acquisitions made some years ago, and putting the cost directly to the profit and loss account, depressing it more.

The net result was that Travers had consistently produced twenty per cent per annum growth for the last five years, but because his advertising budget was now running at eight million per annum, he could take money from there, or from the huge range of other contingency costs, and either boost profits after a buyout, or smooth out a difficult trading period. The shareholders were happy, because although they weren't too keen on these massive advertising revenues, who could justifiably complain about doubling sales volume in five years?

As Travers sat at his desk in the separate office building, one of his chief concerns was whether Goldberg's would pick up this range of 'golden eggs' that remained hidden within Sunburst. While the evidence was in the numbers, thought Travers, it would be extremely difficult for an accountant or banker to say that those levels of expenditure weren't necessary, that the levels could be cut, and that profits were really on a different plane. It shouldn't be too difficult, thought Travers, to persuade them that prudence and investment had grown the business, and that they would never, as bankers, understand the commercial realities. It was an old chestnut, but it usually worked, because they didn't have the commercial experience to challenge it. If they did, it would be their heads on the block, not management, if the new buyer didn't like what he'd bought. Travers knew, there was no banker in the world that would take that sort of responsibility against an obviously competent management team.

Travers was mulling all this over when Chris appeared with Molly at eight thirty.

'Hello, dog!' said Travers, and he leapt up to give his dog a good pat and loads of affection. 'Chris, thanks so much for looking after Molly, you really got me out of a hole.'

'Any time,' said Chris. 'She's so easy and good fun, and John thinks she's a hoot.' John was Chris's husband. Travers knew he worked in IT with a Japanese company in Willesden. The two of them had been married for ten years, and all Travers knew was that they had been trying for kids for years, but without any success. He could imagine that Molly provided a bit of light relief, because as they were both working, it would be difficult for them to keep a pet. Chris suited Travers very well. She had been his secretary for five years, didn't mind the occasional long hours, and, fortunately for Travers, wasn't about to get pregnant. She was discreet, fiercely loyal and had the respect of the management including the directors, as someone who couldn't be jerked around. She took a lot of responsibility from Travers in terms of report writing, as well as the normal stuff such as minutes, the diary and meetings.

'Has she had a run this morning, Chris?'

'Yes, we've been down to the warehouse by the railway, on that planted strip. Should last 'till lunch time.'

'Good,' said Travers. 'Chris, come and sit down, and let me get you up to speed. I've got some excellent news, but we're all going to be extremely busy.'

They moved to the comfortable chairs around his coffee table, and while he spoke, she listened attentively while putting on the Kona coffee machine. Molly stretched out on the floor next to Travers.

At nine thirty, Chris had a long 'to do' list jotted down on her shorthand pad. It would be her job to collect every piece of information, every report that Travers felt might be relevant to the construction of an Information Memorandum about the business. They would then clear out his cloakroom, attached to Chris's office, and use that as the 'information room', where every document taken out by bankers, lawyers or other third parties would be logged out and in by Chris.

'Do you really think you're in with a chance of buying the business?' said Chris.

'Absolutely. At the end of the day it's down to who puts most on the table, but up to that point I have enormous power to influence things in a hundred ways. It could go either way, and I won't complain unless I feel we didn't give it our best shot.' He didn't tell her about the success fees, because he felt that for most sane people, they would take the money and run rather than face the highly speculative future of a buyout. He wasn't sure she would understand that, or indeed how the shareholders could so easily part company with such a vast sum, spread across the three directors, which Travers had negotiated.

Before leaving, Travers asked Chris to wheel in David Ogden and John Fellowes, the commercial director and operations director respectively. It was time they were also brought up to speed. He would tackle the finance director, Brian Locke, later. Brian would have to go, and Travers had in mind a very generous payoff so that he could walk with dignity. He was fairly sure that Brian knew his own limitations, and that the prospect of continuing as finance director under a new regime were nil. He was fifty-five, and frankly, still incapable of working with spreadsheets and their variables. Travers felt the session with Locke shouldn't be too difficult if he handled it with sensitivity. Thereafter, he had in mind a short term executive placement from the auditors to replace Locke while the head-hunters got to work. The beauty of this, was that while 'renting' this individual (maybe a junior partner), he would be able to integrate all the information requirements that Goldberg's might need, with a shortcut to the auditors. Verification and execution all in one, thought Travers. Furthermore, only Travers would be around to explain the accounting treatments that had been applied in the past. Travers had to admit, it was a very compelling spur to action with Locke, and he must do it soon. He made a note on his pad to speak to the personnel manager after lunch, so that he could pull a package together, make double sure he was on sound legal grounds, and fix a meeting with Locke for Monday morning.

Two hours later Ogden and Fellowes emerged from Travers' office in a daze. They slowly walked back down the corridor to their offices, which were next to one another.

'Was all that bullshit or what?' said Ogden, 'Do you really believe Tom can do this thing? Two days ago he was going to shoot grouse, and all of a sudden my redundancy money's in a buyout, Jesus. Whadyathink?'

'It's only in the buyout if we win, David,' said Fellowes. 'If not, it's in our pockets whether the new owners want us or not. Don't forget that's three years' salary and pension contribution, two years more than we've got now. To me it's no lose, and I think the whole thing's brilliant. Let's face it, we couldn't have done it.'

'Just shows what a shotgun and the right school can do for you. Different bloody world. OK, let's run with this thing. Mind you, it's me that's got all the work, and what do I say to those hundred salesmen out there?' They both scratched their heads disappearing into their offices in shell-shocked silence.

It was now eleven thirty. Travers was generally pleased with the meeting with Ogden and Fellowes, only they didn't seem to ask a lot of questions. He put this down to unfamiliarity with the complex issues rather than any lack of enthusiasm. He was convinced they had the same commitment as him.

He then thought of Tomlinson, probably in Sir Brian

Richards' office at this moment. Would Sir Brian rip into him about the thinly disguised complaint from Sir Angus Egan? Or let him off the hook on the basis that if the chairman of Caledonia had done his bit, it was only right for him to do Albion's bit. Travers didn't know. What he did know was that somehow he had to patch things up with Tomlinson, because if the MBO was to succeed, supply agreements would have to be in place, and Tomlinson inevitably would be involved. He made a note to phone Tomlinson that afternoon on his mobile and try and re-establish platonic relationships. He then grabbed some of his personal Sunburst stationery from his desk drawer, and quickly knocked off a thank you letter to Tomlinson for the shoot. Mustn't forget his manners, he thought.

During the next three hours, Travers worked through his mail with Chris, and went over to the new laboratory building to see how the enlarged team of analysts in the quality assurance team were getting on. Much as he hated having to carry all the additional overhead cost, the mountain of health and safety requirements emerging from Brussels meant he had to carry this army of technicians to stay in business. From there, it being two o'clock, Travers went into the old office building, now converted to the personnel, or more properly the 'human resources' office, which had the new canteen facilities underneath it. He spent half an hour with a surprised Jacobs, the personnel manager, pulling together the termination package for Locke. Travers couldn't really explain the immediacy of his action, but certainly Jacobs was well aware of the appalling appraisals Locke had received over the last two years. Satisfied that he was on safe ground, and with a generous package, Travers returned to his office to give Tomlinson a ring.

Travers rang the mobile number, and as soon as it was picked up, heard the static of a car on the move. Tomlinson answered.

'Piers, Tom Travers. Glad I've got hold of you. I've been feeling pretty rotten about the fact that you've been caught between Sir Angus and Sir Brian, and all over Sunburst. I'm really sorry.'

'I've not been caught,' said Tomlinson. 'They want it wrapped up quick, and that's what they've done. To suggest that I might in any way hold up that process is rubbish.'

'Well I'm sure no one was suggesting you were, Piers.'

'Can't say I'm too upset about another brewer complaining about me, we're fighting in the streets with Caledonia. Just goes to show what an unholy alliance Sunburst has been. Anyway, looks as if you've got away with murder. Got to hand it to you, you wouldn't have got that from me – and don't repeat that, I'll deny it.'

Travers laughed. 'You can't tell me that you wouldn't have done exactly the same if they offered you the chance. We're pretty similar in that respect, Piers. But look, as you well know, the odds are still twenty to one that Sunburst will go to a strategic trade buyer who will want to take out a competitor whatever the cost. That still means, Piers, our people have got to get together to hammer out a binding supply agreement, which is where the value of the deal lies. Can we get on with it?'

'Yes, better do that. What've you got in mind?'

'Simple as possible, really,' said Travers. 'Take the volume base of the last year, put say a ninety per cent floor on it as a minimum, and escalate it over five years with say, a ten per cent minimum growth per annum. Also a rollover clause at the end of five years, if targets have been met.'

'Just like that, I suppose. Well, I'm not too keen on that. Why should I guarantee ten per cent per annum minimum? Aren't they just going to replace your products for theirs?'

'Probably, Piers. But that's nothing to do with me. All you and I have to do is get a supply agreement in place with Sunburst products, that's going to make whoever the buyer is pay top dollar. If they want to change that after purchase, then you'll have another negotiation, probably before completion. It's very much down to you to put some value into the supply agreement to get the price up for Albion.'

'Oh, very neat, Tom. So if you do get Sunburst yourself, you've got a fat, juicy agreement to run with,' said Tomlinson.

'Well that's the gamble, isn't it, Piers? Whoever gets the business won't pay top dollar without one, so it could be said you'd be shooting yourself in the foot if you don't. But then, I'm sure Sir Brian told you that.'

'Don't get cocky, Tom. I get the picture. OK, I'll put Armitage onto it, with your man Ogden, how's that?'

'Perfect,' said Travers. 'Always good to talk to you, Piers, see you on the next shoot, wherever that may be. Oh, and thanks so much for the grouse at Glenlivet, letter's in the post.'

Travers put down the phone and threw his fists in the air. Yes! he thought. Another part of the jigsaw in place. He now just had to repeat it with Caledonia and Gallant, which would mean that ninety per cent of his on trade volume would be guaranteed for five years. He went straight to Ogden's office to tell him the news.

When Travers was back in his office, he spent the next half hour making notes about events during the next week, and the critical go/no-go decisions that were facing him and his backers. Apart from his directors, who would all now, with the exception of Locke, be involved, he also thought about a confidential discussion with the senior management group; first, to tell them what was going on, and second, to ensure they understood the delegation that would have to take place, while the directors were spending most of their time in town. Put across the right way, he could see a very positive response to the challenge. Those that didn't, would undoubtedly descend into Travers' little black book.

Satisfied with his list, and with Molly now seriously fed up with the interior of his office, he decided to call it a day. It was the weekend: did he really fancy East Grinstead? Not really. All right, he thought, he'd give his brother a ring. He lived near Chippenham in a nice country pad with his wife and kids, and Travers would see if he could scrounge a weekend with them for himself and Molly. He could do with some social company, but not the female sort. His two on/off girlfriends paled against Jane, who was still very much in his thoughts, and he couldn't imagine any bedroom antics with either of them while he felt so strongly about Jane. Goodness, he thought, he was getting soft.

He first picked up the telephone to put a call through to Mrs Gibbons at East Grinstead, and let her know what was happening. He would tell her he would return Molly on Sunday evening, before returning to Holland Park, and remind her he would next be at home the following Friday, on his way through to a shoot in Devon over that weekend.

Chapter Five

On Tuesday, the late September Indian summer had broken. As Travers waited for the guys from Maxwell Griffin to arrive at the Wessex building, he looked out over the Thames from the seventh floor, and watched as the wind and rain whipped up little wavelets on the brown water below him. At this height, the screech of the wind around the building was loud and intrusive, but inside it was warm and cosy, Travers noticing that the air-conditioning was already quietly pumping out warm air.

Yesterday had been a simply horrible day. He felt rotten about Locke, but it had all gone smoothly enough. Locke had actually agreed with everything Travers had said, but it was the blow to Locke's pride that really showed, embarrassing Travers more than Locke. They had agreed that Locke would stay on until the man from Boulters, the company's accountants and auditors arrived, so as to spend a couple of days on the handover. The severance package was generous, giving Locke two years' money for his 'early retirement' as opposed to his one year contract. Travers also threw in the car, which Locke appreciated enormously, realising that whoever the new owners were, he would be unlikely to get this generosity from them. Travers had also agreed the circular to the staff, and the date and venue of his leaving party. Nothing had been missed. Nevertheless, it was a shitty job, and Travers wondered what he would feel when his turn came, if he lost the MBO.

Morris broke Travers' reverie, sticking his head round the door and announcing the arrival of Giddings and Roberts on time at ten o'clock, accompanied by the supremo of Maxwell Griffin, a certain Mr John Brown. Travers immediately had a vision of Queen Victoria entering the room on horseback, with this Mr John Brown leading the reins. He couldn't help a private smile. Instead, Giddings and Roberts were accompanied by a medium height dapper, if slightly rotund figure in a plain grey business suit, who carried a smile on his face, a head of thick dark hair, which was well groomed, the whole package reminding Travers of a grown-up schoolboy, in and out of trouble. When introduced, Brown had a cultured Edinburgh accent, and was already extremely affable, immediately congratulating Travers on the fantastic progress towards the buyout that he had already made. It was clear to Travers that the other two were well used to Brown's style, because they had already sat down with smiles on their faces as if about to watch a theatrical performance. During this introduction, Brown said that he had already examined the opportunity last week with Giddings, and was determined to give it their best shot. Furthermore they had received all the information that Christine had sent, and over the weekend the 'two boys' had knocked out some figures, which showed some potential. The purpose of the meeting, he said, was to run through these first spreadsheets, help them fill in some gaps, and to look at the overall value they thought might be applied to Sunburst for the bid.

Travers, appreciating the speed of his application to the task, reminded Brown that there was a long way to go, with a slim chance of success, and that none of them should be too optimistic, much as it hurt him to say so. It was out of character for Travers to play this filial role, but the ebullience of Brown was almost overwhelming.

'Och, having met you, Tom, any doubts I had are disappearing fast. I think you'll get it.'

'Well look, fellas,' said Travers, 'before you expound on value, do you really understand the figures you've been given? I won't beat around the bush, but you're looking at a forecast for this year of thirteen pre-tax, and I'm telling you that could be seventeen, and if we want, twenty next year is a doddle.'

A silence fell on the room. Giddings then cleared his throat and said, 'Admittedly, we did see some quite large provisions, but every company has those. How on earth do you arrive at seventeen million?'

'OK,' said Travers, 'if you're sitting comfortably, then I'll begin.' Over the next half hour, Travers took them through the report and accounts for the last three years, explaining precisely what had been done, how the provisions had been maintained with the auditors, and the mechanism of advertising spend, and how it had been used as a profit regulator.

'But how do you know you can do the job with six million rather than eight million on advertising?' said Giddings. 'Surely, if you get that wrong, sales could take a dive.'

Travers reminded Giddings that eight million exceeded what Albion, with its market leading beer brands, would spend on advertising that year, but he agreed it was an imponderable. It was also something that could remain a contingency in case of difficulties, but no one really knew exactly how much advertising was needed, only that it worked. It was Travers' judgement that six million was perfectly adequate to get the reach and frequency needed for his target market, which would also surpass their competitors' spend.

'Well, of course,' said Brown. 'That puts an entirely different complexion on the whole thing. I don't really understand how your non-executive directors from the brewers just allow you to spend this much.' Travers explained the benign, once a month participation of his non-execs, and the fact that he was producing results, far in excess of any growth the brewers could put on. Travers indicated that the phrase 'If it ain't broke, don't fix it' was invented by the brewers, and that as long as their dividend went in the right direction, why would they change anything?

As Travers let that sink in, he flipped open his copy of the Maxwell Griffin spreadsheets, and went straight to the back page. Thought so, bastards! Twelve and a half per cent for management. They saw him take in the figure. Giddings held up his hand: 'Tom, we really must take you through from the beginning. You have no idea yet what has had to go in the numbers.' Travers picked up the sheaf of stapled papers, and threw them into the middle of the table.

'Look, you fellas, please don't piss me around. I've had enough of that already and I'm not going to put up with it from you. I honestly thought you were going to be sensible, and give the management a fair shake. If you're going to insult my intelligence with twelve and a half per cent, let's all go home and I'll start again with someone else.'

Travers got up from his chair, and started to place papers and pads in his briefcase. The thing was, Travers half meant it, and he was also extremely annoyed that they were playing him for a patsy. Morris put his hand on Travers' arm to stop him, but didn't actually say anything.

It was Brown who rose from his chair, and with one hand gesticulating for Travers to recover his seat, said, 'Tom, what exit do you see from this business after the buyout?'

'Sorry?' said Travers.

'Do you want to float this business, which is perfectly feasible given its five year track record, or do you want to sell it, eventually, to another trade buyer?'

'I'd feel pretty silly selling it to a competitor after the buyout, no matter what the price. I want to float, and float as soon as possible, and get you guys off my back.' Travers smiled rather acidly at Brown.

'OK,' said Brown. 'What if we gave you a share that had a ratchet attached to it, that depending on the capitalised value of the float, gave you a percentage share that rose with that value.'

'Try me,' said Travers.

'Fifteen per cent, rising to twenty-five per cent if you achieve a float price of fifteen times earnings.'

Travers slumped back to his seat, and giving Brown a brief smile, quickly looked in his notes for the price/earnings ratios of his two key competitors, both of which were quoted on the stock exchange. They were above fifteen P/E ratio. Travers knew this price/earnings ratio was vital to the bankers and investors. It was a figure produced by simply dividing the capital value of a company as expressed by its share price, by the annual profit (earnings) of the company, before tax. If the company was highly rated, and had good growth prospects, the resulting figure could be high, maybe even twenty. If it was high risk, or had performed badly in the past, it would be low, say down at ten, or even lower. Fifteen seemed pretty high to Travers for a company like Sunburst, that would be new to the stock market. It meant that investors would be paying a high opening share price for the prospect of growth. It demanded a lot of faith in the company by investors. He thought some more before answering.

'Seventeen and a half rising to twenty-five, on a P/E

exceeding twelve,' said Travers. 'If we decide not to float, and hold on, we lock in at seventeen and a half.'

Then Giddings, in a fluster, broke in, 'Tom, we haven't done the number.'

Brown sharply raised his hand to silence Giddings. Silence now enveloped the room, and Brown put both of his hands outstretched onto the table, leaned forward, and said slowly and with measure, 'Seventeen and a half rising to twenty-five in a straight line based on exceeding a twelve P/E. You'll hold seventeen and a half if we don't float or sell within three years.'

Immediately Travers got up, stretched out across the wide table, and saying nothing, held out his hand. Brown took it, and with both of them sporting a hardened smile, shook each other's hand. Travers then said, 'Now, John, I have your word on that. Whatever happens, management's baseline is seventeen and a half per cent. You've made a good offer, and I'll take it. I want that locked in the top drawer, and for all of us to get on with the job. You won't mind if I have that in writing in today's post?'

'Tom, you'll find a Scotsman never breaks his word, you've got a deal. Now, can we let Giles go through the spreadsheets, and we'll start amending the forecasts and the cash flows. This is the easy bit.'

For the next two hours Travers was grilled on the factual numbers, and on his opinion of a particular course of action, be it stock levels, new product launches, advertising and a host of other subjects. He was drained at the end of it, but Giddings and Roberts seemed satisfied, both back on their old form after the heart-stopping start to the meeting. As the meeting was clearly drawing to a close, Travers said to them, 'Oh, one final bit of news. I've let our finance director Brian Locke go. You're free to interview him about everything we've discussed, but the fact is he's not up to what lies ahead, and I've got some alternative arrangements in mind.'

That clearly came as a bit of a shock to the merchant bankers.

'I'm sure you're right, Tom,' said Brown, 'But it's a brave move to push the finance director out of the boat just as the wind is rising. What plans have you got?'

Travers relayed his thoughts about a placement from Boulters in the short term, while a head-hunter search was underway for a permanent hot shot replacement.

'Sounds good to me,' said Brown. 'I agree you really must have someone good to get you through the covenants, control the cash flow and the overheads; it'll be a daily job that you can't afford to fuck up. Are you happy for us to be a part of that interview process?'

'Absolutely,' said Travers. 'All the help I can get from you guys would be welcome.'

Before the meeting closed, they all agreed that the new spreadsheets would be completed the next day, and that Morris at Wessex, on Sunburst's behalf, would analyse the numbers, and get an input from the debt people, as a fast start to looking at revolving credit facilities, and the mezzanine debt possibilities. They all agreed to meet up again on Thursday to put a range of value on the company, and for Travers to report back from his first meeting with Goldberg's, which would take place the following day.

Travers left the building feeling well pleased with the morning's work. Several pieces of the jigsaw had dovetailed nicely in to place, and he was convinced he had a hell of a deal on the equity. Further, they still hadn't asked him about his own 'ante', or in their parlance, 'feet to the fire'. No doubt they would get round to it.

He now headed round to Boulters head office in St

Paul's Churchyard. He had spoken to the partner running the Sunburst audit, and had been put on to the partner in charge of management consultancy, who also ran executive placement. He had explained his problem, to which it was made clear to him it was not unusual, and was now on his way to meet the candidate. The fellow in question had done this task three times before, enjoyed the challenge, and it was promised would review all the accounting procedures along the way, making sure the due diligence requirements of Goldberg's, and any other merchant bank, were met. If Travers didn't like the individual, they had another candidate who could step into the breach. It seemed to Travers that as long as the guy could do the job for three months, it didn't really matter whether he liked him or not. His name was Phillip Carter.

Travers spent the next three hours briefing Carter about Sunburst, the trade sale process, and of course the position with Locke. Travers wasn't too sure about him, somewhat arrogant tending towards flippancy, which wasn't his ideal vision of a big hitting accountant. He knew, however, that if he had any problem, he could trade Carter in for another one, a bit like buying a car, which appealed to Travers. They agreed he would appear at the office next Monday, on a full working week basis, and that Travers would arrange for him to meet the other directors including Locke, and then the rest of his new department. He reminded Carter that the entire staff knew that his post was a temporary one until a replacement for Locke could be found. Finally, he agreed to let Carter see the management accounts for the last three years, which he would arrange for Chris to send.

He left the building at about four, and put in a call to Chris. He was hoping that either in the morning post or that afternoon, some mail had arrived from Albion's in-house lawyer, concerning the agreement on the MBO bidding arrangement, and a draft of the success fee contract. On speaking to Chris, neither had arrived. She also reminded him to call the PR agency to discuss a reactive statement should any leak about the trade sale get to the press, and that Goldberg's were arriving at nine o'clock sharp in the morning. He told Chris he would head home and make some calls from there.

He was beginning to get worried. Sir Brian Richards had promised to phone on Monday to confirm agreement of Caledonia and Gallant to their deal, but he had heard nothing. He had assumed that they had all agreed, and therefore the lawyer was getting on with things. Unfortunately, he would have to call Sir Brian, and see if there was a hold-up. Blast, better do it now, he thought. He entered the actual churchyard by the St Paul's choir building. Although the rain had stopped, the wind was still howling round the buildings. He hoped it wouldn't drown a conversation.

He got through to Sir Brian's secretary, asking if he was there. No. Did she remember his visit, and would she recall if their lawyer had been briefed by Sir Brian about Sunburst? Cheeky, he thought, but she should know. She thought so, but would he like to speak to the lawyer? Go for it, he thought, and got the number.

His name was David Thompson. Travers said, 'Tom Travers, Sunburst. Just been speaking to Sir Brian's secretary about various agreements, and she suggested I might speak to you direct. I wonder, have you been briefed on anything yet?'

'Yes,' he said, 'looks straightforward enough, but you must realise this will take some time. Albion will do the drafting, but I will have to circulate this to my opposite numbers at Caledonia and Gallant before you get to see it. We've got to be talking two weeks.'

'Well is there a chance I can see the drafts?' said Travers. 'Speed up the whole thing.'

'Not a chance, I'm afraid, Mr Travers. You will have to wait and see what has been agreed by the shareholders.' Travers was in no position to argue.

'OK, but you won't mind if I keep in touch, David, in case this thing drags?'

'Fine,' said Thompson.

Good enough, thought Travers. Sir Brian must have spoken and agreed the principles, otherwise the lawyer wouldn't have been briefed. Just the desperate delay to deal with. He headed to the tube, and would phone the PR man from home. He was getting cold in the biting autumnal wind.

The following day, Wednesday, Travers arrived at the office at his normal time of eight o'clock. This gave him time to peruse yesterday's post, marking it up for Chris to deal with, before she and the other directors arrived at about eight thirty. Chris had left a note saying she had laid out and locked the conference room last night, with most of the documents from the 'information room', so that everything would be to hand for Goldberg's arrival. At eight thirty he wandered down to the conference room and told Chris to tell the other directors, including Brian Locke, to join him there.

At nine o'clock, Goldberg's arrived, in the shape of Geoffrey Levin and Amanda Beresford. As they were ushered in to the conference room by Chris, Travers' first reaction to the pair was Beauty and the Beast. Levin was fat, with a vast expanse of bloated shirt between the buttons of a jacket that had never been fastened since manufacture. He was clearly panting as a result of the hundred paces from reception. He had thick grey hair swept straight back, and must have been about fifty. His light, Windsor check suit, was not only ill fitting, but Travers could definitely detect stains on the lapels. Levin looked at no one when he entered the room, but instead at a very particular chair, which he was obviously about to make his own.

Two paces behind him was an altogether different vision. Amanda Beresford was tall and blonde, maybe carrying a few extra pounds, but very curvaceous. She looked about late twenties, had a two piece skirted business suit, and a white blouse stretched tightly over a shapely bosom, and she wore flattish heels to hide her height. Travers could not spot any rings on her fingers. She had a beaming smile on her face, which was finely formed and pretty, in a slightly aristocratic way. While he carried what looked like an empty but battered old brown leather briefcase, she was struggling with a rather shinier version, and an armful of multi-coloured files. Without any introduction yet, Travers leapt towards her, and took the files from her arm, saying, 'Good Lord, you shouldn't be carrying all that, here, let me help.' Travers took the bundle, and was careful to place them on the other side of the table from Levin, who, having fairly thrown his briefcase on the table, was pulling out his selected chair to sit down.

She said, 'Thanks so much; I can somehow tell you must be Tom Travers. How d'you do. Please let me introduce Geoffrey Levin.'

The assembled men, all gazing with interested curiosity at Amanda, almost reluctantly turned to the seated slob, who, rather than get up again, looked at each man in turn with his mouth open, briefly nodded at each one, and said, 'How d'you do, I'm Geoffrey Levin of Goldberg's. So you're Tom Travers,' he said, looking at Travers. 'And you gentlemen are...?' He then dropped his head to his chest with his eyes raised towards the three Sunburst directors, as though he were a headmaster. Travers intervened.

'Right, Geoffrey, this is David Ogden, commercial director; this is John Fellowes, operations director, and finally, this is Brian Locke, finance director. You see before you the executive team of Sunburst.' Levin made no attempt to shake hands with any of them. Travers then continued, 'Well I hope you found us easily enough: now, what about some coffee?' He went to the machine and held up the jug, offering a cup first to Amanda, and then to Levin. When they were all seated, Travers said, 'Right, Geoffrey, everyone in this room has heard from me about the trade sale process that has been put in place by Albion, Caledonia and Gallant, representing the voting shareholders of Sunburst, and their use of Goldberg's to achieve the best price for that sale. Tell me, Geoffrey, has anyone bothered to formally tell the non-voting shareholders?'

Levin winced ever so slightly at being on the back foot already and said, 'Not strictly necessary at this point, because everything is still confidential. But that will be done in the next few days.'

'Geoffrey,' said Travers, 'I hate to put you off your stroke but they all know. Albion salespeople have told them, or at least, that's what I've been told.'

'That is not my information,' said Levin, 'but even so, they will be told within a day or two.'

'Just so you don't forget oppression of minority interests, Geoffrey,' said Travers seriously, 'if they don't agree with the majors, they can still create a hell of a stink, as you well know, even without voting rights.'

'Yes, yes,' said Levin, 'can we please now make a start? Travers slightly raised his arms in submission and resumed his seat at the end of the table. He had Ogden, Locke and Levin on his left, and Amanda and Fellowes to his right.

'Now,' said Levin, 'we're working to a tight timetable. Your shareholders have made the decision to divest from the company, and have briefed Goldberg's to offer the company for sale, and achieve the best price from the market as soon as possible. We already have a list of interested trade parties as well as a financial buyer, and as soon as we have pulled the numbers together, Goldberg's will place a valuation on the business for the shareholders to evaluate, and then we will get on with the sale process in an attempt to achieve that price, or more if we can.

'Whoever buys the business will, I am sure, want to keep the management and staff. But, that is for you to consider with the buyer after the sale is agreed. I have to tell you, the shareholders have put no restrictions on the buyer with regard to employment. I must make it clear that management will not undertake any discussion on the subject with prospective buyers, until the shareholders agree that such conversations may take place. But you have nothing to fear, I assure you. This company is, I know, very highly regarded, and none of you should be concerned about future employment.'

Levin had made his statement in a manner that suggested he had done it a thousand times before. He had spoken very quickly, and the assembled directors were still in the process of taking it all in. He then continued: 'Now then, I must make it perfectly clear that the shareholders have demanded absolute confidentiality from the management during this process. For many of you the news may well have been received with sadness, but I'm afraid there's nothing that can be done about that. Any lack of co-operation with us, Goldberg's, will be viewed extremely seriously by the shareholders, but I am sure, Tom, you will have words with everyone on that subject anyway, because absolutely nothing will be achieved by being obstructive. Not that anyone will be, I'm sure.'

Travers was about to answer, but Levin diverted his gaze and went straight on: 'All we will be doing today is assembling information to take away with us, and we shall probably have a session with Tom, just with an overview on the business from him. From next Monday, Amanda will be here every day for at least a week conducting interviews with you gentlemen, and your senior managers where necessary, to understand some of the finer points. Please ensure she receives maximum cooperation. Once the valuation and Information Memorandum has been produced and circulated to prospective buyers – in about two to three weeks' time – you may well receive visitors wishing to inspect the site, and have discussions with Tom. Again this is only normal, but it's best not to upset the rest of the staff, so I suggest confidentiality is maintained, but more of that later.

'There will then be two rounds to the bidding process. Round one will be speculative sighting bids. That enables us to see who is interested, and serious enough to go into round two. Round two may consist of three or four buyers, who are prepared to put binding sealed bids on the table, complete with evidence of collateral, be that cash or shares. We may finally get an auction between two, but that is usually unlikely. Then, if we accept one of the offers, there follows the completion period complete with due diligence by the buyer and certain warranty undertakings by the seller.

'Then, gentlemen, the process is finished. You will have new owners and life will, I am sure, go on as before. At this stage, you no doubt will have some questions.' He now sagged back in to his chair, with a self-satisfied expression suggesting that his well-honed homily was getting better and better.

Travers leaned forward, casting a glance to his colleagues, and said to Levin, 'Geoffrey, I for one have a great deal of questions, and if I may, I will go first. Now first of all, are you aware of the MBO plan, and when did you last speak to Sir Brian Richards about it?'

'There is no MBO plan, and Sir Brian knows my view that there cannot be one. It would create a massive conflict of interest for you and the management in giving unprejudiced information to third parties, and Goldberg's recommend that no such opportunity is given. There is no such thing as a level playing field once the management are involved.'

'And when did you last speak to Sir Brian on that subject?' said Travers.

'Oh, about three or four weeks ago.'

'Well I'm pleased to tell you, Geoffrey, your view was overruled last week, and we shall be placing a bid on the table at the end of round two. Until that time, we will as you say, offer maximum cooperation to you and Amanda, and anyone else who wants to come and kick the assets. Whilst we may well become aware of the identity of the bidders, only you will know their bids. When you have made your recommendation to accept a bid, ours will go alongside it. Too little, we lose. One penny ahead, we win. All three major shareholders have confirmed this proposal from management. If they hadn't agreed, you would be running the trade sale without the directors, which might well raise a few questions with the buyers as to what we were up to.'

'If that is true, in my view it's a bad decision. I will telephone Sir Brian presently. Meanwhile, your other questions?' said Levin.

'Yes,' said Travers. 'You mentioned a financial buyer. Does that mean a venture capital outfit bidding, without knowing if the management will stay to run it?'

'Could be,' said Levin, 'Or just as easily, if you don't want to run with him, he puts his own team in – Management Buy In as opposed to MBO.'

'I see. You also made the point, Geoffrey, that the shareholders had put no restrictions on the job security of management or staff. In other words, a trade buyer will be able to buy, move the plant elsewhere and sack the lot of us, without any complaint from our current owners?'

'Yes. But you're being over dramatic. I've told you, you should all be safe.'

'Geoffrey, I have to remind you, your opinion is not worth a light to a buyer, and you've absolutely no grounds on which to say employment will be maintained. As an agent for the shareholders, I suggest you keep your opinions to yourself, if you can't back them up.' Travers raised his hands and said, 'Don't bother to answer that. You also mentioned that Amanda will be circulating amongst my management from next week. Amanda, you won't mind will you, clearing that list with me first, to ensure you speak to the right person. I want minimum disruption while this is going on, and just bouncing round the management isn't on.'

'Yes, no problem, Tom,' she said hurriedly, not willing to enter the tension zone between Travers and Levin.

'Next question, Geoffrey,' said Travers. 'You said that Amanda will prepare the Information Memorandum. Are you telling me we're not responsible for any input to it?'

'No,' said Levin. 'You and your colleagues will sign it off as being truthful and accurate, but you will not be responsible for writing it, only contributing with relevant facts and opinions.'

'But the poor girl's only got a week. How on earth can you expect her to give an in depth analysis of this company's activities and performance over the last five years, and its prospects and forecasts for the next five, in a week?'

'That is what she's paid for. You've no need to concern yourself,' said Levin.

Travers gave Amanda a concerned shrug, then turned to Levin and said, 'Now when we get to trade buyer visits, they must not be allowed to speak to anyone but the directors. And a director must accompany them wherever they go on the site. I'm not having competitors wandering willy-nilly round my factory. That, Geoffrey is non-negotiable.'

'Fine,' said Levin.

'OK,' said Travers, 'let's go round the table. You first, David, fire away.' The other directors were given the opportunity to ask questions, most of which concerned their ability to discuss their futures with potential buyers, and whether termination contracts would be met if everyone was fired. Such little faith, Travers thought. Still, everyone else would want to know the same answer.

At the end of it, Travers finally dropped in, 'One more thing, Geoffrey, that you need to know. Brian Locke, sat next to you, is taking early retirement in the next couple of weeks. I suggest you and Amanda put the accounts top of the list before he goes. He is being replaced, pro tem, with a guy from Boulters who will be here from Monday to help you as well. Between them, you should find everything you want.'

Travers had been thinking about this during the meeting, and had come to the conclusion that it would seem odd if Locke was bundled out of the door too soon. Because Locke was so incredibly conservative and cautious in his accounting as well as his personality, Travers reckoned he would put up a stauncher defence than he could to those arbitrary aspects of the balance sheet that Travers had implemented. In any event, Travers was confident that any challenge would be referred to him before any conclusions were drawn by Amanda or Levin.

Travers was also realising just how important Amanda was to this whole process. If he could manage to get on with her, she would hold all the information about the valuation, and the other buyers. As the others were talking he said to her, 'Amanda, will you be travelling out from town every day, or staying at a local hotel?'

'Well, unfortunately, I live in Greenwich.' Travers noted that she pronounced it 'Grinidge'. 'So it's a hell of a way across town. Don't suppose there's anything decent around here?' The tone of her question was slightly incredulous, as if a hotel would be quite out of place in Willesden.

'Funnily enough, there is. Just over at Harrow there's a super country house hotel in its own grounds, family run, excellent cuisine. We use it a lot for customers, and you're welcome to check in at our rate. It's only fifteen minutes away.'

'Terrific,' she said, 'I'll do that, very good of you.' She flashed Travers a girlish smile, hunching her shoulders at the same time like a teenager.

'OK, I'll get Chris to have a word with you,' said Travers, returning the smile. He turned his attention to the meeting and could see that Levin was tiring from the predictable defensive questioning from Travers' colleagues.

'Right, gentlemen,' he said, 'I think we'll break there, and let Geoffrey make his phone call. If I can remind you both, we've already laid out all the information on that table that we think is relevant, so Amanda do have a look now, and see what you think. Whatever you take, please remember to sign the book with the detail of each document and return it to Chris. Thank you. Geoffrey, would you like to make your call?'

'Thank you,' said Levin. The meeting broke up, leaving Amanda in the meeting room, and Levin, in silence, following Travers to the offices upstairs.

As Travers waited at the head of the stairs for Levin to reach him, he said, 'Geoffrey, we've made an office available for you here, next to David Ogden's. We've put a telephone and fax in there, both of which have direct lines. Any secretarial requirements, just see Chris, my secretary. OK?' Levin nodded, panting, and Travers led him to the office, ushered him in, pointed to the telephone and said, 'Soon as you've finished, pop down and see me, I'm at the other end of the corridor.' Travers then closed the door. He walked back down the corridor to his own office. Chris looked up from her desk in the outer office.

'How'd it go?' she said.

'All right, I suppose. Trouble is, as usual the right hand doesn't know what the left's doing, and he didn't know about the MBO shot,' said Travers. 'By the way, Chris,' said Travers, 'anything in the post from Maxwell Griffin?'

'Yes, it's a letter spelling out management's share based on a range of values. It's only a letter, is that good enough?'

'Don't know. I'll have a look, then I want you to fax it straight off to Paul Foot at Andrews and Overton. Make sure with his secretary that the machine's in a secure place. I'll give you a note to attach to it.' He then went into his office to wait for Levin and mull over the meeting. The obvious concern was whether Levin, the professional M&A advisor to the consortium, could throw a large spanner back in the works and destroy the buyout chance. The other thing that concerned him was Sir Brian Richards. He was chairman of a Footsie 100 company. With Tomlinson sidelined from the job of running the trade sale, surely Sir Brian wasn't taking it up? He would be far too busy for such minutiae. The thought then crossed his mind to check with Simon Spencer at Gallant. After all, had Sir Brian cleared the MBO with him? Travers assumed he must have for Sir Brian to have briefed his lawyers. Nevertheless, it was too loose, and he had better check.

He picked up the telephone and dialled Spencer's direct line at Gallant. Spencer's secretary passed him through.

'Simon, glad I've got you, Tom Travers here. Simon, I need to check a couple of things with you. Has Sir Brian filled you in about agreement to the buyout shot?'

'Tom, you're a dangerous man to know. From what I've heard, you're responsible for giving Piers a severe rap over the knuckles. I'd better be very careful what I say to you, don't want you snitching to my chairman.' Spencer had said this jovially enough, but Travers could just detect some caution in Spencer's voice.

'Nothing to do with me, Simon. But I think Sir Angus could see stormy waters with Piers, and decided on a short circuit to Sir Brian. From what Piers has told me, he wasn't rapped at all.'

'Just as you say, Tom,' said Spencer humorously, but with undisguised disbelief. 'Well, you've got what you want, and actually, Tom, I'm delighted for you. Puts you in with a chance, but still gives the shareholders full value. By the way, my ear is getting continually bent this last week by the regionals. They know what's going on, and they want you to have a shot at MBO. You've got at them too, haven't you, you bugger?'

'Not me, Simon,' lied Travers. 'They've picked it up from Albion's sales guys. By the way, when are you going to issue a statement to the press?'

'Do we need to?' said Spencer.

'I think you do. I've got a reactive statement ready, but we'll always be on the back foot. Why not make a virtue out of it, and say something like, Sunburst is now too big and successful to continue under the consortium umbrella. You, the shareholders have your hands full focusing on your own markets, and the time has come to release the full potential of Sunburst by accelerated investment. You would all earn massive brownie points if you also say the management will be given a chance to pitch at the appropriate time.'

'Sounds bloody good to me,' said Spencer.

'But look, Simon,' said Travers, 'who is running this now Tomlinson has slipped from grace? Surely not Sir Brian?'

'No, no. It's been pitched back to me. Which is all right, I suppose. But I want you working with me, Tom, not against me.'

'Honestly, Simon, I'm delighted. We've always got on, and you were the first to agree a shot at buyout. I'll always be very grateful. Thing is, I've got Goldberg's here today, and they know nothing about the MBO opportunity. In the rush, someone's forgotten to tell them. Right now a chap called Levin is trying to raise Sir Brian to find out what's going on.'

'Oh shit, forgot all about them,' said Spencer, 'better let him speak to me, and I'll put him straight. Meanwhile, Tom, you'd better come up with some evidence of support from the bankers. Don't want to frig around if you've got no money.'

'My sentiments exactly, Simon. I'll make sure Goldberg's have an undertaking from my backers by the end of the week. Thanks again, and, oh, look forward to seeing you Friday night at Bucksham Court. I'm looking forward to the first pheasant of the season, and I'm so grateful for the invitation.'

'Not at all, Tom. And do think about bringing a lady friend, lots of room, and helps the party go with a swing. See you Friday evening,' said Spencer, and rang off.

Travers was hugely relieved, and felt as if a massive weight had been taken from his shoulders. Spencer was so much easier to read than Tomlinson, and he was sure he could stay two paces ahead of Spencer on most of the issues. Furthermore, the invitation for a lady friend had sparked a thought. He sprang up from his desk to see what had happened to Levin.

Now in Chris's outer office, he was about to ask her about Levin, when he spotted him sat in the corner, arms folded, and not a happy man. Chris said, 'I told Mr Levin you wouldn't be long on the phone.' Chris, looking full on at Travers, mimed a grimace that couldn't be seen by Levin. Travers smiled, restraining a laugh.

'Geoffrey, sorry to keep you, please come in.' Levin rose with a sigh and plodded into Travers' office, and was ushered to a seat by the coffee table.

'How did you get on?' said Travers.

'Couldn't get hold of Sir Brian, and frankly Tom, if you're spinning some sort of wishful thinking about MBO, I'd drop it now before everyone gets upset. I have some sympathy with your predicament, but these games are futile, and I've got a job to do.'

'Listen, Geoffrey. Sunburst isn't just some subsidiary investment for these guys. They're selling my products every day of the week in their pubs, we share our customers, and we're in each other's company week in, week out. Most of them are friends of mine, not just colleagues, and it's about time you realised that the shitty treatment you deal out to most of your targets is absolutely misplaced here. Your arrogance as a mere paid broker is astonishing, and if you keep up this ridiculous "holier than thou" attitude, I'll have you removed, because you're just too damned rude to work with.

'Now, as it happens, I've just been speaking to Simon Spencer, who you will find has taken over the shareholder "reins" of this sale from Piers Tomlinson, on Sir Brian Richards' instructions. You really should try and keep in touch with what is going on. Now here is his direct line at Gallant.' Travers wrote the number in a huge scrawl across Levin's neatly scribed pad. 'Phone him now and sort this out. He's waiting for your call. And incidentally, by Friday you'll have letters of intent from my backers confirming the availability of funds to support the MBO. I'll leave you to it.'

Travers rose from his chair, and casting a glance to his desk to ensure there were no papers lying around, left his office and closed the door, telling Chris in a loud voice not to disturb Mr Levin until he had completed his call. Then with an earlier idea still in his mind, he strode off down to the conference room to seek out Amanda Beresford.

Amanda was alone in the room, poring over a management accounts pack.

'How are you getting on, Amanda?' said Travers.

'Oh, it all seems to be here, just a question of wading through so I can draw up the trends. Seems to me everything should point upwards OK, improving margins too.'

'Look, Amanda,' said Travers sitting down beside her. 'I've just had a thought. I've got a function this weekend with the brewers. It's a dinner party and jolly with about eight of them and their wives down in Devon. Nothing serious, but it'll give you an insight into the industry, and you'll have every opportunity to quiz them about Sunburst, if you want to. I can't think of a better way to understand how Sunburst works with its customers, and you'll enjoy it too. Back in London by Saturday night. What do you say?'

Amanda was completely taken aback, and was clearly looking for a way out.

'Tom, it sounds fantastic, and I am encouraged to get out in trade and meet customers and the like, but a dinner party? I don't know anyone, and it could be frightfully embarrassing for you.'

'Amanda. Listen. Geoffrey doesn't understand Sunburst's

relationship with the brewers, and he doesn't think an MBO shot is in prospect. He's having that confirmed to him right now by the managing director of Gallant, Simon Spencer. Simon is my host on Friday evening, and I'd very much like you to meet him and understand the trading relationship with Sunburst. It's a great opportunity. Or are you tied up with a boyfriend or something?'

'No, no, it's not that. Geoffrey may not agree with this.'

'Well look, of course it's up to you. But I would be very grateful too. You see, it gets me out of a tight spot as far as a partner is concerned. See what he says, and let me know before you leave this afternoon.' She was still leaning back from him, jaw slightly dropped, when he stood and left with a smile on his face. He reminded her of a spinning top, and she wasn't quite sure whether the next wobble would crash into her. No question, she did find him very attractive, partially because of his obvious business acumen, and the power and self-assurance that flowed from him. She had spent the last five years at Goldberg's dissecting the nature of entrepreneurs, and Travers was just about as close as she had got so far. Mind you, she thought, bit odd, and Devon too. God knows what these brewers get up to. Still, she thought, leave it to Levin to decide, although she would miss out the bit about the other wives being there.

Travers returned to his office to find Chris indicating with her hand to her ear that Levin was still on the phone. He silently acknowledged her message and sat down in the corner and read the letter from Maxwell Griffin. He then penned an attachment, and popped it back onto Chris's desk, asking her to get it off straight away, so that he might get an answer in the morning from the lawyers, during his meeting at Maxwell Griffin.

Two minutes later, Levin emerged from his office, both tetchy and with a resigned look on his face. He put his hands on his hips, and ignoring Chris, said to Travers, 'You realise this is going to complicate things. By their agreement to an MBO effort, the whole issue of conflict raises its head. If we're to go ahead on this basis, I'm going to need some legal undertakings from you and your colleagues about disclosure, and there must be no meetings with prospective purchasers without a representative of Goldberg's. Because of this, it looks as though I'll have to beef up the team, which would otherwise have been unnecessary.'

'Wouldn't worry about that, Geoffrey, I'm sure your fee will reflect the extra effort. How much are you charging for this job anyway?' said Travers with a smile.

'None of your business. Mind you, the way you chaps seem to be in each other's pockets, you'll probably know by the morning.'

'Now, now, Geoffrey, your slip's showing. Still, I'm delighted everything is sorted. Oh, anything you want me to sign, must of course go to my lawyers first. Just send a draft to Paul Foot at Andrews and Overton.' Levin's neck visibly tautened. Grief, he thought, this guy's already signed up the best M&A lawyer in the City.

'Very well, Tom. By the way, we'll be leaving shortly. We can then get started back at our office today.'

'Pleasure to see you, Geoffrey. See you next week with Amanda?'

'Almost certainly.' Without so much as a gesture, Levin rolled out of the door, making his way back to the conference room.

'Real charmer, that one,' said Travers to Chris. 'I think we'll call him the Black Death.'

'Would have thought the Fat Controller was more appropriate,' said Chris, and they both chuckled. Travers looked at his watch. One fifteen.

'Fancy a pie and a pint, Chris?' She nodded. 'OK. Nip

up to David and John, and see if they want to join us down the pub. We can have a quiet recap of this morning's jolly japes.'

At nine thirty the following morning, the Sunburst team in the form of Travers, Ogden and Fellowes, were waiting in the Wessex conference room on the seventh floor, for the arrival of the Maxwell Griffin team. Travers' two colleagues had met James Morris, but not the venture capital team. David Ogden was clearly impressed with the plush executive surroundings, and the prospective thrill of rubbing shoulders with these mystical money men he had heard and read about so much. To some extent, Ogden reminded Travers of many advertising executives he had met: he was small in stature, a couple of fashion glitches like tiepin and gelled hair, but extraordinary self-confidence. From the confused reluctance of just a few days ago, Ogden was now firmly in support of the buyout, no doubt sniffing fame and fortune if they could get through it. Travers noted without surprise that Ogden tended to blow in the wind. If his sales and marketing management team wanted something, Ogden was a good boss, and fought hard for what they wanted. If there was something that Ogden personally felt needed doing, he would never follow through, unless he knew he had support from his senior managers or Travers. The fact was he couldn't live with conflict, or more precisely the courage of his own convictions, beneath the bluff exterior. It had led to some second rate decisions in Travers' opinion, but he felt on balance that the team leadership that Ogden provided, plus to some extent his analytical and debating skills, balanced the equation.

Fellowes was a different kettle of fish. He was a plain speaking Yorkshireman, tall, bespectacled, with something of a beer belly, who saw things in black and white. With the buyout opportunity, as with many other issues, Fellowes had weighed up the pros and cons, and made a decision. A decision he would stick with through thick or thin. His only shortcoming, Travers thought, was surprisingly, his 'thin skin'. He had come a long way since being a bottling line manager with one of the brewers in Yorkshire just ten years ago. Now the executive director in charge of production and distribution at Sunburst, he was wary lest he make a mistake that could knock him off his perch. He was particularly wary of any smooth talking southerner who may be playing games with him, and as a consequence, rather like a clam, could go into a silent defensive mode if he detected a threat. Nevertheless, Travers was happy to be entering this arena with these two colleagues, and felt their overall strengths were up to the challenge.

Once the Maxwell Griffin team had arrived, complete with John Brown, and after everyone had been introduced, the agenda for the meeting was tabled by Giddings.

'We've got some numbers for you, based on what has been supplied, and Tom's comments concerning various, shall we say, conservative accounting policies. There are any number of gaps still to be filled in, but we are getting to grips with the business, and have a range of valuations to show you.

'That done, we want to listen and learn about various issues we have identified. If we can understand that, then we will have a grasp of the company's strengths and weaknesses, threats and opportunities. That will allow us to flex the numbers depending on a range of probabilities, and build that formula into the spreadsheet along with the volume sensitivities. Then, as the forecasts change, we just press a button, and out drops the new valuation.'

Ogden was nodding vigorously at all these laptop gymnastics, proffering the services of a computer 'wunderkind' that resided in the Sunburst commercial department. Travers interjected, and turning to Morris of Wessex Bank said, 'James, correct me if I'm wrong, but I'm under the firm impression that you will be our analyst and advisor on any of these projections. These formulae are gobbledegook to me, and if they're a pile of crap, I expect you to tell me. Now have I got that right?'

'Absolutely, Tom. We'll take those spreadsheets, and the same program if we may, and run them through with the senior debt people. In fact, it would be a great idea to stick to one set of assumptions at a time for the program, then both sides know the score.'

Travers could see from the look on the Maxwell faces, that this wasn't a welcome development.

'I can see you're over the moon about that, fellas,' said Travers. 'Excellent. Well I'm sorry, but that's just the sort of check and balance I'm after, and you will agree to that won't you?' The heads on the other side of the table nodded.

'OK,' said Travers, 'take us through this, but slowly. I want to know every wheeze you're up to.' Giddings and Roberts were clearly somewhat affronted, but Brown was thoroughly enjoying Travers' direct approach.

Giddings then started what was to prove a marathon session on his spreadsheets. First came the reams of paper specifying volume projections, by product category for the next five years. Then came the accounts forecast down to profit after tax and distributions. Then cash flows and borrowing requirements, and last, the investment analysis.

From this, Travers and the others learned that Maxwell Griffin would be 'selling down' equity participation to other financial institutions, whilst funding about twenty-five per cent of the equity requirement themselves. Each tranche of equity had warrants attached in terms of conversion rights, together with an annual 'coupon' of twelve per cent in the form of preference shares to sweeten the pill for investors. Travers could see there would be an enormous burden of repayments layered onto the company.

The equity formed about fifty per cent of the funding requirement, with short to medium term bank debt making up the balance. Fifteen per cent of that 'senior' debt was down as 'mezzanine', in other words, this part of the bank debt had share warrants attached, to sweeten the deal for the banks. Travers turned to Morris and said, 'Do you think, James, your guys will go for this sort of deal?'

'They're expecting something very like this, yes. You've got to understand though, Tom, they will want to run their own fine tooth comb through all of this, and you will be in the centre of it. Basically, the risk for the banks is far higher than for the equity boys, because the return is so much lower. Apart from the mezzanine sweetener, they only get a margin on your borrowings, maybe two per cent above base.'

From the other side of the table, Brown grimaced and said, 'Surely to God not two above base. I can pick up the phone and get one per cent from any Scottish Bank.'

'Oh,' said Morris, 'one per cent on fifty mill, just like that. In your dreams.'

'Steady, boys,' said Travers smiling, and enjoying the jousting, 'We've only just started!'

Further attachments to the spreadsheets outlined discounted cash flows, internal rate of returns, enterprise value and overall return on capital employed.

'What level of return are you hoping to achieve on this deal?' Travers said to Brown.

'You can never tell, Tom. But to get the cash invested in buyouts you have to look at thirty per cent plus, otherwise the risk of loss is just too high. We only run on a fifty-fifty success rate.'

'Well I have a valuation here of seventy million, with

a return of thirty-five per cent. What management share have you assumed on that?'

'At this stage, seventeen and a half per cent.'

'Seems to me I could be squeezing you for a lot more than a range of seventeen and a half up to twenty-five. If you've legged me over, John, I will find out, and it would be an understatement to say I would not be pleased.'

'Tom, how would you like to risk thirty-five million with an evens chance of losing the lot? Remember, these bank boys pick up all the bits and pieces after a failure, we get nothing. They could even come out with fifty pence on the pound. Deals like this can't be sold for less, believe me.' Travers screwed up the corner of his mouth and returned to the numbers. He just didn't know whether to believe a word any of these fellows said.

At the end of the session, Brown said to Travers, 'Now, Tom. Success fees. We know how much you chaps are getting, it's the most wonderful deal I've ever heard of. But just putting that into the pot isn't good enough. It's manna from heaven, been given to you, and you can afford to lose it. We want something else from each of you. We need 'feet to the fire'. We need some pain on your side if this doesn't work.'

Travers was stunned, and for the moment silent. They have to be joking. Over three quarters of a million, which could go into their pockets, would go into the buyout. What did they want? Blood?

'John, you've got to be bloody mad. Have you any idea what three quarters of a million means to us? You have to be joking.'

''Fraid not. No deal unless we get a more personal commitment. Success fees are not personal commitment,' said Brown.

'No deal then. I'm sorry, John, but if you don't feel three quarters of a million from management is enough, we're with the wrong people anyway. Don't you understand, we have no other cash between us anyway.'

'Look,' said Brown, 'this is not me speaking, it's our investors. This is standard stuff. A first charge against your mortgages would be OK. Look, don't make up your minds now. Think about it and let us know. There isn't a way round this, whoever you go with.'

Travers looked at his two colleagues, who both seemed unfazed, and to Morris. He would certainly bend Morris's ear about this after the meeting. Travers thought the proposition was plain unfair, and depending on what his colleagues felt, was indeed prepared to look elsewhere, as a double check, at least.

'Jesus, you'll want the shoes off my feet next,' said Travers.

'Very probably,' said Brown.

After this the mood of the meeting was more sombre, and there was still more on the agenda. Giddings and Roberts wanted a series of visits to the factory to understand the production side of things, and make their own evaluation of depreciation levels and management systems. They also booked field visits with Ogden to get out in trade, and actually see the brands on the shelves and in the pubs. Morris wanted the Sunburst team to make a presentation to the senior debt people, and to select a house broker, so that if the buyout did come off, there could be a fast track to flotation.

The Sunburst team's diaries were filling fast, and it caused some amusement to the advisors when Travers mentioned his shooting programme was under pressure. He then had to explain just how important those engagements were, but only received further scepticism for his trouble. Travers was also requested to meet a series of key investors over the next four weeks, so that they could get a feel for the chief executive of this potential investment. Brown insisted it was vital, even at this early stage. With all these pressures on their time, Travers also agreed with his colleagues that a full staff briefing in the factory had to take place, to keep the goodwill, or at very least some understanding from the employees. A delegated programme for the senior management group would also have to be implemented the following week, if they were to spend so much time in the City, and away from the office. Someone had to steer the ship in their absence.

By the time they were finished, it was four thirty, and the huge table was strewn with curling sandwiches, coffee jugs and mounds of jettisoned paper. Nevertheless, there was a feeling amongst all of them that a lot had been achieved, and just as importantly to Travers, a camaraderie had been established that seemed durable enough to withstand some slings and arrows that were bound to come their way as this thing progressed. They agreed the next meeting would take place when all the parties to the buyout would be represented, including the lawyers and accountants. Travers (he thought humorously), suggested an early booking at the Mansion House to house them all, but couldn't help but be concerned at the huge professional fees that would have been racking up if all these people were on a charging basis. He began to see how fees on mergers and acquisitions for even his small size of business were reaching the two million mark.

As they left the conference room, Dennis was as usual, on hand to help them on with coats, collection of bags and the ordering of taxis. Travers' mind was already jumping ahead to tomorrow, and whether Amanda Beresford would enjoy his shoot or not.

Travers was in the office on Friday morning at his usual time. He worked quickly, scribbling notes on yesterday's mail for Chris, checking and responding to internal e-mails, and looking at his notes from yesterday's meeting at Maxwell Griffin. He was moving fast to enable him to leave the office at around ten, drive down to East Grinstead to pick up Molly, some clean shirts and ammo, and then drive north to Greenwich to pick up Amanda Beresford around lunchtime for the long drive down to Bampton in Devon, and the Bucksham Court Hotel. He had phoned the office on his way back from Wessex Bank the previous evening, and been informed by an incredulous Chris, that Amanda had confirmed the dinner date, and had left her home phone number and address. Chris, with very matronly concern, had told him to be good, and if he couldn't manage that, to be very careful. Travers tried to reassure her that the date was strictly business, and that they had to make some friends at Goldberg's, if the Fat Controller remained so implacable in his animosity to the management.

At eight thirty Chris arrived, stuck her head around the door, asking if Travers was still on for a ten o'clock departure. He nodded without lifting his head, and said as casually as possible for Chris to phone the hotel, and ensure two single rooms had been booked for him and his guest.

'And what if they don't have singles?' she smirked.

'Then jolly well book two doubles. Really, Chris, you've been reading too much *Cosmo*.'

He had left the office on time, called into West Lodge for clothes and ammo, and moved on a couple of hundred yards to Grace Gibbons' thatched terraced house to pick up Molly. He had stayed as long as possible, jawing to Mrs Gibbons, telling her he would probably be back on Saturday evening, and would be spending Sunday at West Lodge before returning to Holland Park.

Following his A–Z, he had found Amanda's flat, which was a converted warehouse building overlooking the Thames and the Isle of Dogs. It seemed to Travers that he was in Deptford rather than Greenwich, but could imagine how important an address was to the svelte Amanda. Travers could only park twenty yards from the building, and then had to walk up to some serious looking ornate cast iron gates, which were twelve feet high, with a speaker phone attached to the pedestrian entrance. He pushed the button for her flat number, noticing that in this security conscious building, no tenants names were actually displayed.

Amanda answered the intercom.

'Yep?'

'Amanda? Tom Travers. Your carriage awaits. Shall I come up?'

'No, no,' she said, 'I'll be down in ten minutes if you don't mind waiting.'

'Fine,' said Travers. 'Oh, Amanda, you will bring some casual clothes for Saturday, and some wellies if you've got them? We're going to be shooting.'

'You have got to be joking. You never mentioned shooting.'

'Yes, sorry about that, but I know you'll love it, the weather forecast is actually very good.'

'Shit. Well, you better give me fifteen minutes,' she said angrily.

'Take your time,' said Travers as casually as he could, just pleased she hadn't come out with an outright refusal. He turned and walked back to the car, and let Molly out. She immediately dived into a cultivated border while Travers looked self-consciously around for any locals. Defecating dogs were probably a capital offence in this neck of the woods, he thought.

She finally emerged from the electrically operated gates with both arms overloaded. In one arm she had two zipped dress covers, a make-up bag, voluminous Harrods plastic carrier bag, and wellies, and in the other, a very large suitcase. He leapt to her aid, grabbing the suitcase and wellies. Her short blonde hair had fallen down over her face, and as she looked up from the exertion, blew out of the corner of her mouth to remove the hair from her eyes, which didn't actually work.

'Tom, you're a client and all that, but I've a good mind to leave you in the lurch. I'm sure most girls would. You didn't tell me anything about shooting – what if I can't stand the noise and the death?'

'No problem,' said Travers cheerily. 'Ear plugs and look the other way. Now don't be such a blanket, Amanda. We both know you're going to love every minute, and enjoy some fabulous hospitality from Gallant Breweries. Just lie back and think of excess.'

She smiled, but only thinly. 'That's all very well, Tom. I told Levin this was an official brewery dinner for Gallants' suppliers that you thought would be interesting for me. If he finds out I've been bagging pheasants, he'll go bananas.' Travers was now loading her kit in the back of the Merc.

'Bagging? Have you done this before then?'

'My father's got his own shoot at our place near Shrewsbury. "Man and boy" as they say.' She still wasn't happy, and spoke with her hands on her hips. Travers noted she was wearing another two piece, but this time plain dark blue over a white blouse, which had the effect of making her look much slimmer than he remembered. Very nice, he thought.

'Well come on, Amanda, that's great. You can give me a few tips, and bring a few down yourself. And please don't worry about Levin. Just blame me, I couldn't care less, honestly. By the way, d'you know what we call him at the office?'

'Oh my God, this is my boss you're about to rubbish.'

Travers turned from loading and straightened up, facing her with a broad smile.

'The Fat Controller.'

She leant back and laughed with her hand to her mouth.

'Good, isn't it?' said Travers, then whistled up Molly. The dog emerged from behind some parked cars, and sniffed around Amanda's legs.

'What a beautiful little springer, what's her name?' said Amanda, as she crouched down and ruffled Molly's neck.

'Molly, and she loves female company. I can see you're going to get on famously. You'll like her in action too; she's a great little gun dog.' Travers opened the passenger front door of the car and ushered Amanda to her seat, then instructed Molly to lie in the back.

Travers drove down to the M25, then around to the M3 in traffic that was still light. Then onto the A303, heading for Honiton and branching off through Taunton. Along the way, Amanda's misgivings about the trip evaporated, having decided she would indeed blame Travers if her boss found out.

Travers did his best to keep the conversation light, avoiding the subject of Sunburst altogether. Nevertheless they both exchanged personal details, Travers telling her about his early career, marriage, divorce, no kids, East Grinstead and Holland Park. For her part, after leaving LSE with a first in Economics, she did a year's post grad in Business Studies, worked for her father's business in agricultural engineering for a year, got fed up with the Midlands, and through a family connection joined Goldberg's as a statistician in corporate finance. One thing led to another, and for the last three years had worked for Levin in various capacities, finishing up as his investment analyst in mergers and acquisitions. She went on to say that she loved the work and its variety, and that Levin had been very supportive. Yes, she suffered his bluntness, but explained to Travers that as the only real boss she had ever had she was used to his rudeness and remoteness. He was, however, extremely highly rated by his contemporaries, because he got the job done, and more importantly, executed these sale deals efficiently and for top dollar, which is what the clients wanted. As no surprise to Travers, she said he was rarely involved in acquisitions because his style wasn't as compliant as many clients would wish.

At this stage, Travers couldn't resist a question: 'What were your impressions about Sunburst, before you tripped up on our doorstep, Amanda?'

'Well obviously we had been well briefed by the three major brewers at various meetings. They do rate you very highly, Tom, and they know there's a risk to your career if the trade sale goes through. I shouldn't say, but I got the distinct impression one or other of them would offer you something if you were cast adrift. But at the time there was a very clear agreement not to let you pitch for MBO, not because of conflict so much as the negotiating hassle you might cause them because of your relationship. With third party negotiation, everything would have been kept at arms' length. In fact, and for your eyes only, it was Levin's suggestion for the success fees to keep you sweet. Presumably, now you're going for MBO, they've been withdrawn?'

'Dunno,' lied Travers. 'But a sale is a sale whoever it goes to. One for Sir Brian Richards at Albion, methinks.' Travers wanted to move off that subject pronto, and said to Amanda, 'I'm not being patronising, Amanda, you're twenty-eight and gorgeous, but your life in the fast lane must wreak havoc with your love life. How do you manage on the romantic front?'

'Sore point, really, I don't. Oh I meet plenty of nice eligible men in the City, but I really can't afford to get involved. Can you imagine the M&A grapevine? Who? Amanda Beresford? Oh yes, goes like a train. I don't think so. I value my career too much.'

'Amanda, that's terrible, and completely wrong. You've got the nous to spot those guys, and I'm sure they're not all as bad as that, for heaven's sake. Christ, these should be the best years of your life. Anyway, whose talking about jumping into bed? If you begin to get involved, you'll know whether he's a kiss and tell type long before you drop your drawers – not to be too crude of course.'

She laughed, the first genuine, carefree laugh she had made in weeks.

'Maybe you're right. But I'm sorry, I'm not that gorgeous at all, and I'm so bloody hopeless with men, I wouldn't even know if they were straight or queer. To be honest,' and now she was giggling, 'I've even made that mistake!' They both turned and laughed at one another, but Travers was still curious.

'Amanda, I'm being nosy, but I'm curious now, and do tell me to bugger off, but how long ago was your last amorous attachment?'

She flushed, and with a watery smile turned to Travers and said, 'I don't know why I'm telling you this.' She paused. 'College.' Travers said nothing and kept his eyes on the road. She could have answered with any rubbish, but she didn't, and Travers could tell it was a painful subject, and all, presumably, because she felt her reputation might be at risk. That, or she was incredibly shy with men, which she clearly wasn't.

'Amanda,' he said, 'live dangerously. For Christ's sake don't take life so seriously. Mind you, with a divorce and a string of ex-girlfriends behind me, I've got no room to talk.'

'Well, Tom, that's the difference between men and

women in business. No one thinks the worse of you, but can you imagine what people would say if I had your notches on my belt?'

'Look,' said Travers sheepishly, 'I'm not quite as bad as that, I may've overdone it.' He was feeling decidedly hurt. She laughed again, throwing her head back and running her fingers through her hair.

'Little boys, you're all little boys.' Then she propped herself against the door pillar, arm on the window, and just looked at him. 'Tell you what though, Tom,' and her serious look turned suddenly into a smile, 'You do have a way with you. You're very direct, aren't you? And somehow ... disarming. I'm not used to it.'

'Listen, Amanda, I'm forty-three and past caring. But it's very sweet of you. You really must meet some decent blokes.' He took his eyes from the road and turned to her with a smile as she was propped in the corner of the seat. From the corner of his vision he saw that her skirt had ridden up, and he could just make out the darker line at the top of her tights. Grief, he thought, get a grip, this really would be taking advantage. Her head turned towards the road ahead, as did his, as the light now began to fade. The companionable silence lasted for the next twenty minutes, until the turnoff to Bampton came into sight.

The next ten minutes were spent cross-checking maps and instructions, until they found the stone-pillared entrance to Bucksham Court. They were pleased it was still just about light, or they would have certainly missed it. They could just make out the house, high up the hill, as they bounced over the ruts and potholes of a dilapidated private drive. A bend on the hill, and now the house was in full view. It was a late Victorian Gothic monstrosity, completely failing in any charm, unlike Glenlivet Lodge. For all the world, this building could have dropped out of the Hammer

Horror film set. It was a very tall building, with wings and circular high-pitched turrets in odd places along the roofline. Many of the lower floor windows had stained glass in the upper mullions, and old red brickwork mixed uncomfortably with stone pedestals and pediments. The place had a slightly run down feel to it, and as they swung onto the forecourt, muddy puddles and weeds covered the once gravelled drive.

Travers stopped the car and turned off the engine.

'Suggest you don't leave your room tonight, Amanda. God knows who wanders the corridors after twelve.' She laughed. As they got out of the car, from the arched front door strode Spencer. He made quite a sight. He was wearing his shooting breeks and a very brightly coloured pair of shooting socks with a yellow check around the tops, and an enormous pair of highly polished brown brogues on his feet. Over his tall frame he wore a heavily embroidered wool pullover, complete with scenes of flying pheasants around the shoulders, with dogs chasing birds around his waistline. Travers didn't think that anyone other than Spencer would dare wear such a creation, which in fact was close to a work of art.

'Tom,' he bellowed, 'glad you could make it. I say, do introduce me to your lady friend.'

'Simon, good to see you again. May I introduce Amanda Beresford. Luckily for me she accepted a very late invitation to even up your numbers. Amanda, by the way, works for Goldberg's, and is collecting up all our numbers for the sale. I thought it might give her a break, and get to know how the brewing industry ticks.'

'Delighted to meet you, Amanda. What a very clever idea of Tom's. Have you been shooting before?' Once Amanda had informed Spencer of her family's interest, Spencer led her away to the hotel entrance in animated discussion as to the identity of her father. You old snob, thought Travers, who was left with the job of unloading the car. It was most unlikely any footmen or staff would be on hand to help in a place like this, so Travers got on with the job, making two trips to the entrance while Molly bounded about in the plentiful undergrowth. When he had finished unloading, he put Molly back in the car until he could feed her later, and made his way past a few other Range Rovers to the entrance hall.

It was a quarter to five as Travers entered the reception hall. Classical music at quite a loud volume reverberated around the house, and Travers noted that the hall, which had a high ceiling, had been made into an informal drawing-room, with a huge staircase off to his right leading to the upper floors. To his left, in the large open room, sofas formed a quadrangle around the open fire, which cast a bright and warm glow from the blazing logs balanced between the old iron firedogs. Various rooms led directly off from the hall, with a main passageway barred by two oak swinging doors giving the general direction of the working part of the hotel. The half panelling and tall pointed windows, complete with stained glass crests gave the room the atmosphere of an eerie museum, heightened by the music echoing from the high ceilings.

Amanda and Spencer were still in happy discussion by the fireplace. Both had a cup of tea in hand, and Travers, spotting the service laid out on a table against one wall, made his way over and poured himself a cup, pinching a scone, and then joining the other two.

'Staff won't appear for at least another hour, Tom, so I'll show you both to your rooms after tea. I know where you are. Just two other guests arrived so far, who of course you know, Alan Jenkinson of Bishops Brewery, and John and Elizabeth Hardy of Oakham's. In fact, John put me on to this place last year on one of his 'boys shoots'. As you can see, it's terribly romantic, food's good, and we've got the whole place to ourselves.' Travers could think of a better word than romantic, but it was certainly very unusual and did have a Wagnerian charm. Spencer then leant forward to Travers, and in a muffled but still thunderous voice said to Travers, 'Wait 'til you meet the owner. Funny chap, "Johnny Foreigner". Just about understand him. Come six thirty, we all meet up for drinks in the cellars, and guess what? We all get to sample his wine cellar. Brilliant idea, and a damn good selection, if memory serves. Different anyway, then we're all over there in the dining-room. Wife's the cook, and excellent she is too, though long wait between courses.

'By the way, Tom, shooting eight tomorrow on the Clutton Estate. Marvellous birds, but of course you've shot there before. Alex Trimble is running things as normal, and we meet up in his yard at nine tomorrow.'

'Well that's great, Simon, sounds like a lot of fun. Who are the other "guns"?'

'OK, there's Tommy Bradford and Belinda from Albion, Rupert Holmes from Blackburn Brewery, Edward and Samantha Munson from Victory in Durham, and finally, yes, finally Bertie and Patricia Duke from Wiltshire.' Turning to Amanda he said, 'Sorry to say, Amanda, bit short on the ladies, again. There's three of us without partners, which is a damn shame. Still, a pretty gal like you won't be short of conversation.'

Travers noticed that Spencer had obviously taken a shine to Amanda, not least because she was one of the few women who stood as high as his shoulders. Travers looked at Amanda. She stood happily enough with her hands in the little jacket pockets, and she seemed to be managing. But Travers wasn't really sure, difficult to tell. Travers then said, 'Right, Simon, gun room? Then maybe you could show Amanda to her room?'

'Absolutely. Down through those swing doors and to

the right of the kitchen, can't miss it. Oh, and Tom, you're in number fifteen, first floor, halfway up on the left – good view. Amanda, I'll take your cases and lead the way. All finished?'

'Yes,' she said, smiling. 'You're looking after me extremely well.'

'Remember, you two,' said Spencer, 'on parade six thirty, just through those swing doors, and the cellar door to the left.' Travers put down his cup and saucer, and went back out to the car. He let Molly out once more, and prepared her food under the tailgate. He looked down on the countryside below, but tall trees surrounding the forecourt hid a lot of it, and what he could see was all hills and valleys. He had no idea where he was in relation to the Clutton Estate, only remembering the precipitous drives and rushing river valleys that always showed such excellent high pheasant. He remembered too that most of the 'guns' were, in truth, second division customers of Gallant's, which is why perhaps Spencer had taken a bit of a chance with Bucksham Court. All his guests were, however, the cream of the crop in terms of shooters, and they would, without exception, appreciate Clutton, especially under Alex Trimble. Being a top marksman himself, Trimble ensured all of the pegs were in testing positions, and was not averse to the odd derogatory comment if the 'guns' failed to do his birds justice. He had inherited the estate many years ago, but from what Travers had heard, the property side of things had gradually been chipped away, so that most of the old estate farms had gone, leaving Trimble with a thousand acres of shooting rights in prime Devonshire countryside. It had become his full-time job during the season, letting out the estate for shooting, the rest of the time engaged in forestry. Travers whistled back Molly to the car, made sure she had some air and returned with his gun to the hotel.

When he got to his room, he quietly chuckled at what met him. The room was entirely Victoriana, from the bed to the 'po' underneath, the wallpaper, the old ewer and stand, dressing table, wardrobe and chairs. The lavatory and bath, in the adjoining room, were massive and imposing, with a thick mahogany seat on the loo, and chromed steelwork pipes overhanging the bath. The floor of the bathroom was solid stripped pine, but not tongued and grooved. Consequently Travers could see light below from the gaps in the old plasterwork of the ground floor ceiling. The entire floor creaked ominously, and even the smell of the room was musty. His eyes were drawn to the black and white lithograph prints, framed and faded on the walls, most of them depicting sentimental Victorian scenes of children and swans, and mannequin faces. Whether the owner had 'inherited' this time warp condition when he bought the place, or whether he created it, would be an interesting question for his host over drinks. Travers noted there was no telephone or TV, which he actually applauded. He sat on the overstuffed bed, practically disappearing down the slope to the middle, and thought for a moment about the guests. He knew them all, and he was racking his brain for problems reported with any of them. None that he could think of, but what about opportunities? He began to run through the individuals, getting up from the bed and moving to the bathroom to draw an early bath. He would set himself some priorities while soaking.

His thoughts also returned to Amanda. Providing she got through this evening, and enjoyed the shooting tomorrow, he reckoned they should be reasonably close, which could be extremely useful over the coming weeks, particularly if she was to be on her own at Sunburst. He might well be able to push her on the response to the Information Memorandum, and who knows, maybe the range of the bidding. He clearly wouldn't get any help from Levin. Spencer himself might also be a source of the odd snippet. He was the sort of character who couldn't resist spilling a few beans if it brought him some kudos or one-upmanship. Finally, he thought about the minor shareholders. There had to be an information conduit to them in terms of progress of the trade sale, and perhaps he could keep a tab on events through Penn.

He turned off the ancient taps, which was accompanied by a cacophony of rattling unsecured pipes, got in the bath, and found that he could stretch out from head to toe in the cavernous cast iron monster of a bath. He took a breath and shut out the world underneath the enveloping water.

At six thirty, dressed in an ordinary lounge suit, he left his room and walked down the bare corridor with his footsteps echoing all the way. Plenty of voices and laughter from below, and as he descended to the large hall, he could see that Spencer had already broken out some champagne prior to the wine tasting in the cellars. Everyone was in one large group in front of the massive fireplace, except for Alan Jenkinson, who stood by the old stereo system, on which the turntable was churning out the non-stop collection of classical music, with the odd jazz classic in between. He was reading the sleeve of a Gershwin LP as Travers approached.

'Hello, Alan,' said Travers, extending his arm. 'How are you? Long way from home.' Jenkinson looked up with a smile.

'Hello, Tom. Good to see you. What an extraordinary place. I've never seen so many LPs in one collection.' He pointed to the bookshelves behind the player, which Travers hadn't noticed before, but which contained hundreds of LPs running for about five yards over six shelves.

'Wow,' said Travers. 'Amazing isn't it? Fifteen years ago no one had heard of CDs, now we're looking at a genuine collection that most of us would've thrown out. Probably worth a bob or two now.'

Jenkinson was managing director of Bishops Brewery in Suffolk, having taken over the reins on his father's retirement. No fool, Jenkinson had pushed the business ahead with selective pub acquisitions largely in Essex, and with an efficient brewery, supplied a wide free trade business, including some of the tied estates of the majors. Unlike most of his contemporaries, Bishops was a fully listed PLC, and Jenkinson had been forced to learn the ropes under the full light of public exposure extremely quickly. Travers had noted he had achieved this pretty well, especially as Jenkinson was a somewhat reclusive, retiring character. Travers suspected he enjoyed his own company just as much as being thrown together with his largely extrovert peers. Surprisingly, given that Jenkinson was now about thirty-five, he had never married, although he remained highly eligible. Travers knew his passions were obviously not in his loins, but in shooting, fly fishing – normally salmon in Scotland – and cricket in the summer. He too was a shareholder in Sunburst.

'Tell me, Alan,' said Travers, 'has someone contacted you about the Sunburst trade sale?'

'Well, Bill Penn told me last week, and I got a letter just yesterday from Simon. I'm delighted to see they're going to let you pitch, if you can, after the formal process. I think it's bloody good of you to run it for them – not sure I would. Still, knowing you, you'll pull something out of the fire. Incidentally, Tom, if you do win, can I keep my stock and convert it? I'll be very happy to run with you, and I know a few others would too.'

'Good Lord, Alan, to be honest I hadn't even thought that far. It's terribly flattering, though. Come to think of it, why not? I would imagine the venture capital people will be hugely impressed and welcome it. Real sign of confidence from the trade, and some underwriting too. Can I ask how many of the others you know might be interested?'

'I'd say pretty much all of them, after all, they got their shares for practically nothing, and they get a good dividend that goes with the business: why wouldn't they?'

'Well, brilliant, Alan, I'll get my people on to it, and at the right time I'll circulate something. I can't really do anything formally at the moment so would you mind passing that around if the opportunity arises?'

'No problem. And, in case I forget, the very best of luck.'

The two of them joined the others, and Travers quickly passed amongst them with greetings. Then Spencer moved slightly to the middle of the room and pinged his glass with a teaspoon.

'Attention please. Welcome to Bucksham Court everyone, I hope you're all comfortably settled and have found your way around. Now we're starting the evening slightly differently from usual, as our host has kindly offered to let us sample his cellar with a tasting before dinner. The ladies may wish to grab a wrap or something, because it's not terribly warm down there. But I assure you it's worth the visit. He's assembled a very fair library of wines from around the world, and I'm sure those of you with wine interests will find it fascinating. Dinner will be at eight by the way, and for later, the gentlemen should remember the billiards room over there. See if we can't get some tournament going. That's it. Would you now care to join me?'

Spencer then led the party to the cellar door, for all the world like Japanese tourists. Spencer didn't mention the name of the hotelier, because he couldn't pronounce it anyway. Travers wasn't certain either, even when the fellow introduced himself, but it was something like Ghoulash, and yes, he was Hungarian. He looked extremely serious, and was attired in a dark suit, adorned by a very bright, technicolor brocade waistcoat. He had thick dark wavy hair, with eyes that darted all over the place. He mumbled and gesticulated, but as Travers was at the back of the party with Amanda he couldn't pick up much. Anyway, he had started with the lighter, sweeter white wines, progressed through the drier ones, and on to the reds. Spittoons had been provided, but no one was using them except the Hungarian. There were however some real wine buffs in the audience, especially Bertie Duke from Dukes Brewery in Wiltshire, who ran a thriving wine wholesale business in the south-west, together with a number of dedicated wine bars across Dorset and up to Bristol. He folded his arms across his chest, and very studiously listened to the Hungarian, quizzing the man on vintages and viniculture. After twenty minutes, Travers was getting bored, and noticed that Amanda, arms crossed, had some goose pimples on her. He gave her a nudge and raised his eyes upwards, together with his glass. She nodded and smiled, and they both quietly retreated to the warm library upstairs, which also doubled as the hotel bar. It really was very snug, with another fire blazing, and as no one was around, Travers went behind the bar and poured a gin and tonic for Amanda, and a whisky and water for himself.

'How are you getting on?' said Travers as sympathetically as he could. 'I was beginning to have second thoughts about letting you in for this lot, not exactly your generation.'

'Tom, I'm having a wonderful time, really. They're all so nice, and what's more I'm not on my guard. Some of the women are a hoot. Would love to be in my shoes, and show the men how it's done. Seems to me they don't rate their husbands too highly on the cerebral front.'

'Phew, I'm so glad,' said Travers. 'But you're right, they are a nice bunch, and pretty easy going. If you fancy chatting up an eligible bachelor, have a go at Alan Jenkinson, he's the one with the specs and slightly receding hair.'

'Thanks a lot, Tom, sounds a real catch, I don't think.' They both chuckled.

'Best to avoid Rupert Holmes, if I were you. He's the little fella on his own, also with specs but with light, wispy hair. He runs Blackburn Brewery and thinks he's God's gift to the corporate world. D'you know, I met him about ten years ago, just when mobile phones were coming in. In those days, you didn't just get a little handset, you had a big black box it clipped onto for batteries and the booster – huge thing. It was at a formal dinner of some kind, black tie, the whole bit, and that prat came into dinner holding this thing, and putting it on the dinner table in front of him. Absolute dick. It never did ring. Mind you, he's in Albion land up there, and he does cause them a major headache in his pubs. He regularly sells the beer for a pound a pint and causes no end of trouble to the bigger brewers in the free trade too. Funny thing is, never seems to take his wife anywhere, suppose she hates shooting. Who knows? By the way, he's the only one of this little group who isn't a shareholder in Sunburst. He was never interested, always says he wants to play the field; bet he's regretting it now.'

'Funny you should say that,' said Amanda. 'He's already had a word, and you're spot on. Even asked me to send information to his merchant bank, to 'run the rule' over Sunburst. I got the impression it was bullshit when he said it.'

'Hmm,' said Travers. 'On a lighter subject, have you been introduced to Edward and Samantha Munton yet? Edward, unbeknown to himself, really is one of the funniest men I've ever met. Such a plum he can hardly string a sentence together. But absolutely charming, would have been in his element a hundred years ago. With his uncle, they run Victory Brewery in Durham. Just like stepping back in time. Edward still has a coal fire going every day in his office at the brewery, from September to April, I've seen it myself. The thing is, any conversation with him is so deadly serious, however light-hearted the subject. I think it's his way of showing an interest even if he hasn't a clue about what the hell you're on about. If you laugh, he laughs, if you shake your head, he'll do the same. He does exactly the same with his pub tenants. God knows what they think of him, probably kindly for all I know, he's so ... paternal to everyone. Can't help feel it won't last, which I suppose is sad. You'll like her too, Samantha. Very "County", but with it. They're a good match really: she looks after his interests, on the social side at least.'

'Goodness,' said Amanda, 'you really do know them all so well. It's much closer than just business, isn't it?'

'Hmm, don't know,' said Travers. 'The thing is I see these people more on these social events than I do in a business environment, like their offices or mine. When I do meet these chaps in a work environment, they're so much more guarded, frightened they're going to get ripped off, sometimes even cold. It's an extraordinary transformation, which I don't understand at all.'

'Well I do,' said Amanda. 'You can be pretty intimidating. Remember, I've seen you in action with Levin. If I were one of these brewers and Tom Travers had come a long way to see me, I'd be worried about just what I'd have to give away – or buy from you.'

'Really?' said Travers, 'Good Lord, I hadn't looked at it that way. But I'm always so nice to them, I've never put any one of them under pressure, I know that would be a waste of time.'

'Yes, Tom, but you're still seen as high powered, with your background and everything. Seems to me you have the perfect setting, here on their own turf for any issues that need solving.'

'Very perceptive, Amanda. You'll go far. Another gin?'

At about the same time, other members of the shoot party were now joining Travers and Amanda at the bar, and Travers was in the right place to act as barman. The alcohol of the tasting was having the desired effect, with the volume of discussion and laughter rising so that for once, the sound of classical music had become incidental.

At eight, Spencer called them into dinner. Everyone stood chatting in the dining-room until Spencer, with a scrap of paper in his hand, had ushered everybody to the seat he had selected for them. The dining-room was positively dingy, with a chandelier high above the long thin table, casting a bare minimum of light. Candelabra with fluttering flames were positioned along the table, but because of the massively high ceiling, the effect was eerie, with the guests' shadows flickering against the walls behind them. This place, thought Travers, would be the ideal location for one of those whodunnit murder weekends.

Travers wasn't happy. He had drawn the short straw as far as the seating plan was concerned. Spencer, as usual, had taken the head of the table at one end, with Alan Jenkinson at the other. Travers was positioned to his left, halfway down, but because of the shortage of ladies, he had Tommy Bradford to one side, and Edward Munton on the other. Amanda was beyond Edward, sitting next to Jenkinson, the bachelor, at the end of the table. Travers was the only man to have men either side of him. On his right was Tommy Bradford. Travers knew him well, being the northern sales manager for Gallant. He wasn't a director of the company, but his family used to own a small brewery in North Yorkshire, which was bought out by Gallant. Bradford remained employed, but the attraction to Spencer was the fact that the Bradford family shoot had been maintained near Yarm, and he was here this evening no doubt as insurance for a reciprocal to the North Yorkshire shoot. Unfortunately, Bradford was a very dull man, with little conversation behind the willing smile. With the fossilised Munton on his other side, Travers felt he was going to have to work hard for his supper tonight. And so it was.

Each course slowly followed the last, and in the end, Travers found himself joining the conversation on the other side of the table.

In particular, Patricia Duke became embroiled with Rupert Holmes, who was adamantly maintaining that the era of the family brewer was coming to a close, unless like him, aggressive moves were made to move ahead, to borrow money and sweat the assets. He was arguing that it was impossible to stand still, and that because his colleagues were so lazy, they would all inevitably go backwards into decline and failure. Patricia, who was a small but feisty lady, had an original view of things, which probably reflected those of her husband.

Her view was simply that the brewing business, and the meat of that business, the pubs, was exactly the same as landed estate. Whatever else may happen in the world, as long as it was maintained and cared for, it would look after itself. Travers decided to throw his weight in support of Patricia, urging Holmes not to underestimate the endurance of the pub, if it was properly located and managed, and who could dispute the wisdom of the various Dukes of Westminster for the maintenance of a landed property estate when all their peers were selling up. Holmes, typically, became over aggressive on the whole subject, which at least provided some light entertainment at Travers' end of the table.

Otherwise, the subject of conversation with Bradford and Munton revolved around shooting, fishing and dogs. Travers was fading fast. He was mightily relieved when they all moved into the drawing-room for coffee, rather than the port routine with the men; he'd had quite enough of the dining-room.

Travers, coffee in hand, went over to where Amanda was sitting, and planted himself on the arm of the massive stuffed armchair she was sitting in.

'How's it going? Any proposal from the eligible Mr Jenkinson?'

'No,' she laughed. 'But I like him, he's very interesting, honestly. I've never met anyone who shoots and fishes quite so extensively from Scotland to Cornwall. I can see why a wife would cramp his style.' Travers looked at his watch. Gone eleven, he must let Molly out for a run.

'Well, Amanda, I'm glad you enjoyed your evening, mine was bloody hard work. Look, I've got to see to the dog in a minute, but are you OK for tomorrow? Seems the forecast is all right, if a bit windy. Have you got the right clothes, you know, Barbour and pullovers? If not, we can go on the scrounge with some of the ladies, bound to have some spares.'

'No really, I've got everything I need. Will I be going round with you?'

'Well yes, but only if you want to. None of them would mind you wandering around their pegs, or you could do a couple of drives with the host, Alex Trimble, you'll find him amusing. Otherwise, you could load for me, no doubt you're an expert.'

'Great,' she said, 'I'm really looking forward to it. See if you're as good as you think you are!'

* * *

Travers slipped out of the room, leaving Amanda to look after herself. If she needed rescuing he would pop back in after seeing to the dog. He was glad to get some air, despite the chill of the early October evening. He let Molly have a good run for twenty minutes, and reminded himself to take her for a really long walk on Sunday, back at West Lodge. Turning toward the house, he could hear some of the men had migrated to the billiard room, in a wing adjacent to the front door, and even from here he could just make out Spencer's booming voice cajoling some one to get a move on. He thought to himself how the usual rhythm of a shooting party had been upset by the events of the trade sale. He should be relaxed, but wasn't. He certainly should be looking after Amanda and being more attentive, but wasn't. He just wished now that things would get a move on; a million things had to be done, but he could only go at the pace set for him. It was frustrating in the extreme. He took a deep breath and blew a stream of warm condensed air up into the chill of the night. Remember, he thought, stay cool, stay flexible and don't let the buggers grind you down. He whistled in Molly, made her snug for the night, and returned to the house.

Back in the drawing-room, a few couples were left, deep in conversation, discussing safaris in Kenya that winter. No Amanda to be seen. Good, thought Travers, she's gone up, and so can he. He raised his hand and bade his fellow guests goodnight, repeated the exercise in the billiard room, having declined to join them, and moved towards the staircase and bed.

At six thirty in the morning, his little alarm woke him. Always groggy first thing, he swung his legs with a deal of effort from the enveloping mattress, and let his legs swing from the height of the bed. Yes, he was feeling pretty good apart from back ache from the horse hair mattress, and was looking forward to doing battle with the high pheasant. First things first: shave, dog, then a shooting fry-up.

At eight thirty, Travers had the car loaded, Amanda sat beside him in full shooting gear, and the engine running, ready to depart in convoy behind Spencer and all the other Range Rovers.

'Tom,' said Amanda, 'I'm so glad I came with you. I've only been on driven shoots a few times. My father's shoot is basically walk up. Half the time we're blanking in the covers with the dogs. This is a real treat.'

'Well, we should both be in for a treat. Trimble reputedly puts down twenty-five thousand birds every season. With the perfect terrain here, this is very much a commercial shoot, and there's an army of beaters, maybe thirty of them. It's the only place in the country that I know of where the local authority actually puts up roadsigns telling you to beware of pheasant!' The convoy set off towards the Clutton Estate. Along the way they passed through magnificent West Country scenery of wooded valley bottoms, tumbling rivers, fords, and then rising up to the fringes of moorland, and diving back down to the valley floors. The sunshine was weak, and with a fair breeze. Ideal conditions, thought Travers, to get the birds up and flying.

They reached Clutton Park, turning off the main drive for what must have been half a mile to reach the old stable block. As they approached it, Land Rovers were everywhere, complete with the customary scene of dogs racing about, and men in battered Barbours and gaiters. The stable block had in fact been converted to house Trimble and his family, and while one end of the building was used to house vehicles and farming implements, the rest of it made a very attractive residence, with magnificent views across the old deer park. Trimble appeared, doing a very reasonable job of car-park attendant, making sure the guns didn't block his drive and the exit for the beaters' Land Rovers. Travers suspected Trimble worked off a very short fuse. He remembered the fellow getting very upset if 'guns' or beaters didn't do as they were told, made all the worse by Trimble's stutter, which worsened with his blood pressure. For most of the time though, he was very amusing and excellent company, with a store of shooting anecdotes, both of prowess and stupidity. It hadn't slipped Travers' memory that in a recent edition of *The Field*, Trimble had been rated as one of the top six game shots in the country.

With thirteen people in the party, some reshuffling took place to keep the number of vehicles down. Spencer again asked Travers to join him with Amanda, while the other two single men, Jenkinson and Holmes, both of them without dogs, bunked in with the Bradfords in their vehicle. Trimble told everyone that they would be returning to the house for lunch, so if they wanted to drop any kit, they were welcome to do so. That done, and all loaded up, Spencer assembled the 'guns' in front of the house for the draw. This was always done by Trimble, who served up the usual homily about safety, reminding everyone that because of the height of the covers and therefore the presence of beaters, no shots should be fired without sky behind the barrels. He would start and finish each drive with a whistle, and he was hoping to get in eight drives during the day, five in the morning and three in the afternoon. All 'guns' would move up two on the pegs after each drive. He then went round the 'guns' with the draw pins, Travers drawing five. Oh well, thought Travers, better be on form, because he was likely to be in the thick of it on the first drive. That done, everyone mounted up in the vehicles, and a fresh convoy got under way, led by the keepers and Trimble.

Within five minutes the party arrived at the first drive, which was a river valley with a flat meadow, bordered on every side by precipitous forestry of larch and conifer. A river tumbled and crashed at the foot of one side of the valley, and it was here that the pegs were placed, right beside the river, with huge beech and oak trees almost overhanging the shooting positions, which were stretched out over about five hundred yards up the river valley.

While Travers was decanting cartridges to his bag from the back of Spencer's Range Rover, he said to Amanda, 'Have you ever seen a drive as high as that. It's called Cathedral, for obvious reasons.' He stopped for a moment and pointed to the ridge, high up above the river. 'They'll be working them in from way over there. Along the top, if memory serves, are the game crops at something like seven hundred feet. Very slowly, the birds will break from left to right, over us, heading towards the pens, which are over here behind us. Most of these birds are at forty to seventy feet over our heads, so the kill ratio is never going to be much more than four to one, cartridges to birds. It's simply stunning.'

'How on earth do they keep them up there?' said Amanda.

'Beats me,' said Travers, smiling. 'Moving the birds around on this terrain must be a nightmare, heaven knows how many wander off to Somerset and Cornwall.' With gun bag and slip slung over his shoulder, and Molly on her lead, Travers and the party moved off in the direction of the river, with each 'gun' peeling off to take up his position. The meadow was extremely boggy, and it was only after some exertion that the pair of them, with Molly, reached the number five peg.

'OK, Molly sits out there, ahead of me. She'll spot a lot, but is bound to miss quite a few because they're going to fall way behind us. Trouble is, I'm not going to spot anything until they're clear of these trees above us, so it's snap shooting, with a fifteen feet lead through the bird. Do you want to load?' She nodded. 'OK, you stand here to my right and...'

She raised her hand and smiled imperiously. 'I do know how to load, you know.' He smiled and handed her the heavy cartridge bag. She slung it over her neck with the bag open over her tummy, cartridge in each hand.

'Just make sure you eject in front of me,' she said.

'I beg your pardon?' said Travers in mock seriousness. 'Look, put the bag down for a while, it's going to be at least ten minutes before they work this lot in. Shove me in a couple.' She slid the two cartridges into the open breech, and unhitched the heavy bag.

'There's quite a tension isn't there?'

'Well, hopefully we'll have a twenty-minute drive with a procession of birds over. Trouble is, if the beaters spook them too quickly, we'll have clouds of birds, which are unshootable. But they're so good here, they don't make many mistakes. And if you spot some birds before I do, yell out. Because they're gliding down off the hilltop, they're going incredibly fast, which is always the big mistake people make when they first shoot here. Got to get ahead of those birds.'

The only sound now was the rushing, tumbling cacophony of water over rocks. Travers could see Edward Munton to his right, on number four, and beyond him Bertie Duke at three, both with their guns pointing up from the waist, ready to take the overhead shots. Over on his left, about forty yards away were John and Elizabeth Hardy on six, trying to calm their Golden Labradors, who wouldn't settle. Travers could not see number seven hidden by a turn in the river, but beyond he could just make out the massive tall figure of Spencer at eight, leaning backwards in an awkward position, but clearly determined to take the first bird that appeared. The birds were being driven off the top of the hill from beyond Spencer, and Travers could just hear the beaters, moving step by step at this point, trying to raise the birds with their voices, calling 'Curr, curr,' repeatedly. Travers had a quick look behind him, and about two hundred yards back, Trimble was standing, leaning on his long crook, chatting away to his keeper. Beyond them, in the rising wood, were four or five other figures. They would be the pickers-up, thought Travers, spotting the injured birds that would fly on.

He nudged Amanda to look back at the figures in the wood.

'See those guys, Amanda?' She nodded. 'Unfortunately, when you get such high birds, you get a lot of injured birds too, mostly pricked up the backside. On a drive like this, they'll probably bring in at least twenty-five per cent of the kill when they drop in the wood. They've all got dogs, so they don't miss much.'

'I'm impressed by the military precision,' said Amanda. 'Not exactly relaxing though, is it?'

The sound of two discharges echoed across to them from the left. As they both looked, Spencer was already breaking his gun and reloading, screaming at his dog to stay put. Travers and Amanda saw a solitary high pheasant, fully eighty yards above Spencer, glide on without a wing beat to the security of the opposite wood. Missed, thought Travers, but at least he's pulled the trigger and got rid of the jitters. Then number seven was opening up, number six, and Travers raised his gun to within three inches of his shoulder in expectation of birds coming over.

'Left!' screamed Amanda, and instantly Travers was on to it. It broke over the trees at a phenomenal rate, maybe forty yards up. Travers wanted to make sure, so he gave it both barrels, having worked through the bird in a smooth but quick movement, firing about ten, then, fifteen feet in front of the bird. The second shot crumpled the pheasant, its head turning under, and dropping in an arc towards Trimble, way behind Travers. Molly, while still sitting, had her neck craned over her backbone. She'd marked it. It hit the ground, and bounced twice, stone dead.

'We're off,' said Travers, breaking his gun. The two spent cartridges ejected up in to the air in front of Amanda, and Travers held the breech open about six inches from her two hands, each of which was holding a cartridge. She popped them in, he closed the breech, and had the gun up at the ready, all within a second or two.

'Over!' she yelled. He caught sight of them in the same instant above his head. Four of them, all gliding fast. Take the lower two, he thought, and give them a hell of a lead. He worked through the back one, pulling the trigger gently, and without stopping the swing went on through the leading bird, pulling the trigger through the line of the bird fully fifteen feet in front of its head.

'Not bad! said Amanda, 'left and right!' Travers eyed where they were dropping, but was already breaking the gun to reload long before they hit the ground.

'Amanda, come on!' said Travers irritably, as she stood with the two cartridges in her hand, transfixed as she watched the birds drop.

'Ooh, sorry,' she said, with an apologetic look on her face, thrust the cartridges into the open breech.

'Left, left!' she screamed. This time Travers looked and picked up a lower bird, that had glided down over number six, who hadn't seen it, and was now climbing again with wings whirring to the wood beyond. It was a long crossing shot, with plenty of sky behind it. Travers instinctively knew it wasn't flying so fast, so as he worked through, he gave it less lead and fired. The bird twitched in the air, the tail feathers dropped for a millisecond, but the bird flew on.

'Mark!' came the shout from Trimble behind him, who had raised his crook and was outlining the birds' flight so that the pickers-up behind could follow the birds' trajectory to the wood.

'Oops! Pricked it,' said Travers. Travers could now hear shots to his right. Craning his head upwards, he said to Amanda, 'Keep an eye on the right, they're starting to break down the line.' No sooner said, than six birds, in line astern like Stukas, broke over his head, gliding off to the right. He tried to pick up the last two, but he knew before he fired they were moving out of range, but he tried anyway, and missed.

'Damn! Too slow!' he said to himself. Amanda reloaded, and the action continued. After ten minutes, Travers said, 'Here, Amanda, take it.' And he thrust the gun, barrel pointed upwards, into her hand, and unhitched the gun bag from around her neck.

'No!' she yelled. But Travers had already taken the gun bag, and moved behind her.

'Gun up!' he yelled. 'Over!' He thrust his arm in the air, and she raised the gun to follow the bird. She fired and missed. She broke the gun, and Travers shoved another cartridge into the breech.

'Get ahead, next time,' he said coolly. Another pair broke overhead, not gliding this time, but beating their wings and climbing. 'OK, take your time, swing through and pull, ten feet in front of the leader.' She followed his instructions, and just when Travers thought she had left it too late, pulled the trigger. The bird stuttered, tried to fly on, but headed earthwards, still fluttering. They both watched. It was badly pricked. Trimble moved forward quickly, as Travers reloaded the gun, picked the bird and jerked its neck, then dropped it back on the ground and resumed his position.

'Use both barrels, Amanda, lots of ammo.' The tension for her was such that she had only remembered to pull once. The next bird she crumpled fair and square, and thrust the gun back to Travers.

'Done it, enough for now, please, here,' she said.

He took the gun in one hand, gave her a broad smile, and regardless of the birds overhead, said, 'Well done! Knew you could do it.' He put an affectionate hand on her shoulder in congratulation. The action continued for another ten minutes, and then from behind, Trimble blew a long blast on his whistle. Travers unloaded, put the gun back in the slip, issued the search instruction 'Hilos!' to Molly, who raced into the meadow, and started retrieving the heavy pheasant.

Trimble ambled up and said, 'Well done you two, some nice shooting there. Don't mind a bit if you carry on,' he said to Amanda. 'Bit more practice and you'll knock spots off him.' She laughed self-consciously, but Travers could see she was delighted to have acquitted herself so well. Molly was now darting back with birds, and dropping them at Travers' feet.

'Lost count there,' he said. 'How many d'you reckon?'

'Seventeen, including my two,' she said without hesitation. 'I'm used to counting and picking.'

When Molly had accounted for all the birds, they each struggled to carry five pheasant in each hand back to the vehicles, until Trimble told them to leave the birds in a pile for the pickers, who would follow through.

'Any unaccounted for?' he asked.

'No, clean pick apart from that one you marked, which flew on.' Trimble raised his hand in acknowledgement.

Travers turned to Amanda, 'Some drive, eh? They aren't

all as high as that, but it certainly gets the adrenaline going. From memory, the next drive is extraordinary. We take the birds as they fly over cottages! Funny thing is, before I come on a shoot I have trouble remembering any drives. As soon as we get going, they all come flooding back.'

They returned to the cars, to a hubbub of conversation. They all agreed that Devon was the place to start the pheasant season, and how clever Spencer had been to select Clutton.

'Obvious, really,' said Hardy, who was a local brewer from Exeter. 'There's nowhere else to shoot decent pheasant.'

The shoot progressed through the morning, each drive different from the last, with the bag mounting steadily. By lunch time, the party had shot two hundred and fifty pheasant, five partridge, and two woodcock. Arriving back at Trimble's stables, it was clear to see some fatigue from the 'guns', having ascended and descended quite a few hills that morning.

Travers was feeling pretty well pleased, not just because of his passable shooting, but because he had been able to sound out most of the 'guns' on their intentions, should Travers win the management buyout. Between drives he had managed words with Hardy and Duke, who like Jenkinson from the previous evening, were happy to roll over their investment should the facility be available. Edward Munton wanted to cash in, which was no surprise to Travers, whereas Holmes at Blackburn Brewery, not being a shareholder, asked Travers if he would stay on if Blackburn pitched for the business. Travers had held back a smile, but said to Holmes that if equity were included in his package, he might consider it. Travers knew full well that Holmes would never part with equity to an employee, they didn't do that sort of thing in Blackburn.

Lunch was a very jolly affair in Trimble's drawing-room. His wife had cooked three casserole dishes, and everyone pitched in to serve it up on their long dining-room table, which was complete with the full family silver. The wine and beer flowed plentifully, which Travers never had second thoughts about, because his swing always got more fluid after a half bottle of wine. Amanda fitted in naturally with the shooting party, and was engaged in conversation from all sides. It was after two thirty before the 'guns' were back on the pegs, and a quarter to four when the eighth, and last drive finished. The sun had dipped now, and the breeze had become cold and biting.

When they returned to the stables, the final count amounted to three hundred and eighty pheasant, which was an absolutely cracking day for the guns. Everyone was dog tired, and not looking forward to their return journeys, especially the Muntons who were going for Durham in one go that evening, without a break. Diaries were compared to see if venues crossed for meeting again, tips were left with the keeper, and the whole entourage mounted up into their vehicles for their respective voyages home.

'Right, Amanda,' said Travers as they made their way down the main drive, 'I'll get you back to Greenwich, drop you off, and get myself down to East Grinstead with Molly. Enjoyed yourself?'

'I can't thank you enough, Tom. I've had a wonderful time really. It's been a super day and a wonderful weekend. But look, for heaven's sake, let me buy you dinner when we get back to London. I can get on the mobile and book somewhere, it'll be my special treat. You will, won't you?'

'Amanda, I'd love to, but I can't. It's not just Molly,

my brother's staying the weekend, and I promised I'd see him tonight. Maybe another time?' Travers had lied through his teeth. The thing was, maybe it was arrogance, but Travers knew one thing would lead to another, and he'd finish up doing something he shouldn't. His conscience pricked him. It was one thing to manoeuvre himself into a close working relationship with Amanda to further his own business interests, it was quite another to cold-bloodedly exploit it to the bedroom. Besides, it may backfire for one reason or another, and do him no good at all. He just hoped she wouldn't see it as rejection. She clearly had some funny ideas about the male of the species.

'Tell you what, though. What about an evening next week, if you decide to use the hotel at Harrow?' said Travers.

'Yes, OK,' said Amanda. But Travers knew she was disappointed. Bit rough to leave her on her own on a Saturday night. The thing was, though, he knew he was doing the right thing.

It had taken four hours to get to Greenwich, going up the M5, then M4, and through the City. Travers gave Amanda a big hug and a peck on the cheek when he helped her through the wrought iron gate of her apartment block. He hadn't given her a chance to respond, turning and waving goodbye, and telling her he would see her Monday. She had raised her hand in farewell with a wan smile. He didn't dare look back, and concentrated on finding his way to Croydon, and the A22, down to East Grinstead.

Chapter Six

Monday morning saw the start of an extremely busy week for Travers and his colleagues. Amanda had arrived at eight thirty, and after thanking Travers for the weekend once more, had set herself up in Levin's allocated room, complete with a mountain of management accounts information. Travers was relieved that Amanda appeared completely relaxed and at ease with him after the weekend. He was worried there might be some guilt or embarrassment, but no, he felt their relationship was nothing but stronger. She told Travers she had everything she needed, and would be busying herself with financial analysis over the next three or four days. Travers then gathered his executives together, and between them thrashed out the itinerary for the week, including plans for a full employee meeting in one of the warehouses for Thursday. Whilst there was still nothing in the newspapers about the sale, Travers felt that with so many strangers wandering around the offices and production lines, forewarning the staff about the trade sale was eminently preferable to a rearguard action. After dispersing his colleagues, he set to with telephone calls to the various advisors, confirming meetings, the agreement to the share terms with Maxwell Griffin, and securing outline agreement for the minor shareholders to retain their interest in the business if the buyout was successful, by securing roll-over terms on the same basis as the venture capital underwriters.

He was in the process of developing a slide presentation

for the employees, when Chris rang through that Jane Newgent was on the line. Travers was momentarily very much on the back foot. With everything else going on he had to admit Jane had slipped a bit further back in his brain cells.

'Jane, you're the last person I expected to be talking to on a dank October morning. Lovely to hear your voice, how are you?' He was indeed genuinely pleased to hear from her, but somehow, the old salacious banter seemed inappropriate. He was instantly concerned too, that Jane hadn't made some irrevocable decision with regard to Bobby.

'Tom, I really am sorry to have to ring you at work. I know how you all hate it. You never seem to be at Holland Park, and I didn't dare leave a message on your bloody machine.'

'Listen, sweetheart, I'm jolly glad you did phone me here. Sure as hell I can't call you, in case Bobby answers. Needless to say, you've been on my mind. How are things?'

'That's why I'm phoning. Really good, and I want to tell you all about it. I'm coming down to town tomorrow, staying at the Cadogan. Do please say we can meet?'

Travers quickly glanced at his diary.

'Yep. In the City tomorrow. Could meet you for tea, say, four thirty at the Cadogan?' said Travers. 'But you've got to tell me, you have sorted things out with Bobby?'

'Well that's it, I did as you said. I told him that unless he lets me lead my own life, and stops these stupid accusations, I'm leaving.' Travers, with one hand on the phone, immediately put his other hand to his forehead. Christ, he thought, she's gone and done it. She carried on: 'Told him I'd seen my doctor, who'd said I'd have a nervous breakdown if things don't improve. He took it like a lamb, begged me not to do anything silly. I tell you, I even felt sorry for him given his worst fears about me have come true.'

'What d'you mean?' said Travers.

'You and me,' said Jane, 'between the sheets, so to speak.'

'A suitably delicate turn of phrase,' said Travers cautiously. 'But maybe we ought to let this new situation settle down a bit before you risk everything. I'm not that keen on shot guns at dawn with your husband.'

'Look, Tom, don't worry. I knew you'd react this way. Everything's going to be fine with Bobby, I'm not going to leave him. Besides, I've got two teenage girls at boarding school – they'd never speak to me again. But I'm not giving you up unless you say so. You're too good to miss, and I promise not to be silly.' There was a pause before Travers answered.

'Look Jane, you know how I feel about you,' he said quietly and sincerely, 'but one thing leads to another, and yet we hardly know one another. We're risking everything for a one night stand in the Highlands.'

'I know, and I'm not risking anything. I'm only asking that we be there for one another. You've got no idea what it means to me. Tom, don't flatter yourself, I'm after your conversation and your body. That's not too much to ask is it?'

'Oh, thanks a lot, sweetheart,' said Travers. 'Nothing like letting me down gently.' She laughed.

'That's the Tom I know and love,' she giggled. 'Look, got to go, blacksmith's here. See you tomorrow. Love you to bits.' She hung up, leaving Travers completely bemused with the telephone still to his ear. He put the telephone down and sat back in his chair. Where on earth would this lead? No question, Jane was special to him, but he could do without the complication of an embittered husband. He could still get out of this platonically with

Jane, but another night of passion would begin to make it very difficult. Was discretion the better part of valour? He had no time to think. Chris came through on the phone telling him that James Morris was on the telephone about tomorrow's meeting at Wessex Bank.

'Tom, that you?' said Morris.

'Hmm? Yes, hello James, all set for tomorrow?' Travers tried desperately to realign his thoughts and get back on track with Morris.

'Yes,' said Morris. 'Trouble is, it's going to be a big meeting, could be thirty people in all, so we've moved the venue to Andrews and Overton's offices. They can handle the numbers better and it's definitely more neutral ground for the Maxwell circus. Now, to continue. You've met the senior debt people from the bank, but they've asked me, Tom, if you wouldn't mind updating the meeting about where you are with the shareholders on the trade sale, and whether or not you have a workable relationship with Goldberg's. It's still difficult for people to grasp that you've tagged the MBO on the end of the trade sale.'

'Sure,' said Travers. 'But nothing's changed. Goldberg's are working on the Information Memorandum right now, and they seem to be doing it all by themselves. They're simply not risking any conflict by asking me anything. Must say, suits me, with all our meetings going on.'

'Remarkable,' said Morris. 'And please, do try not to upset them. They could put you on gardening leave tomorrow with David and John, and make it very difficult for you to get information from the business. Which is another reason why I've called.' Morris then proceeded to give Travers a long list of information that wasn't already in their possession. Travers promised to get it for them, and would get Chris straight on to it.

* * *

The following day, Tuesday, at eleven o'clock, Travers, Ogden and Fellowes turned up at Andrews and Overton's offices in St Paul's Churchyard. No wonder, thought Travers, the partners boasted the biggest legal salaries in the City. They certainly had opulent offices to match. They waited on leather Chesterfields in the reception area, noting the depth of the carpets, the plethora of original oils on the walls, and the huge hide cigar box and silver cutter awaiting the clients' pleasure on the coffee table before them. The only thing it did for Travers was to squirm at the fees that were paying for it all. Ogden was more intent on studying the feline grace of the couture-clad Mayfair gals that adorned the huge mahogany reception desk.

After a fifteen minute wait, they were ushered into one of the many client conference rooms that occupied the entire fifth floor. All three of them stopped dead on entering the room. It was a vast room, with an entire wall of glass overlooking St Paul's Cathedral just to the right. The oval table filled the room, much like a United Nations convention, and in the empty space in the middle stood projection equipment, if required. They looked around the table, and it seemed as if every chair was occupied by pinstripe-clad executives, most of them no older than thirty something. Paul Foot jumped to his feet, and with James Morris, introduced the trio to those members of the meeting whom they had not met before. Morris reintroduced the senior debt team from Wessex, numbering three. In turn their lawyers were introduced, also numbering three. Then Maxwell Griffin and their team of lawyers. Then the mezzanine debt people, numbering three, plus two lawyers, then a team of four from Boulters, the auditors, who would be looking after the long form reports and due diligence for the bankers. Then the brokers, whose advice in terms of institutional interest would be sought. Then, finally, a financial PR outfit who would advise the management team on dos and don'ts with the press during the MBO process. Including the Sunburst team, the meeting numbered twenty-three.

Travers and the others were ushered to three vacant seats, but before Travers sat, he couldn't resist saying to the assembled entourage, 'Gentlemen, Sunburst is truly honoured to have so many professional advisors. Just don't tell me what the hourly rate of you lot amounts to.' Mild titters only, thought Travers. They're used to that old chestnut from other clients, he thought. Morris then asked Travers to give the meeting a brief update on events from the Sunburst perspective, especially as to progress with Goldberg's. Morris was keen to buy as much time as possible for the buyout team, and they were all anxious to know what parameters Goldberg's had placed on the bidding process for trade buyers.

Travers held the floor for half an hour, working through his brief. He finished by saying he was certain he would know the identity of the bidders because of the factory visits Goldberg's had planned, but that no surprises were expected over and above the three competitors who obviously had the wherewithal to extract value from the synergies of an acquisition of Sunburst. Travers and his colleagues were then asked a few questions, and for the next four hours said absolutely nothing. The lawyers, bankers and accountants went into the very depths of gobbledegook covering every legal and financial aspect of the MBO, and Travers was surprised that his sales and profit projections now went unchallenged, as if they had become papal edicts. The final surprise for Travers was that Maxwell Griffin would also shortly be writing their own Information Memorandum for prospective equity investors, but that they would wait to filch the best from the Goldberg's version, when they could lay their hands on it. The lawyers meanwhile seemed to have an obsession about Chinese walls, ensuring that the compliance departments of the various banks were making independent assessments of what their corporate finance colleagues were showing in the figures and who, specifically, had had access to the information. It seemed to Travers that the insider dealing fiascos of the sixties and seventies had really cut deep, with the result that there was now a huge duplication of effort, with everyone checking everyone else.

By four o'clock the meeting was still going strong, and Travers was bored stiff. He got up and wandered over to Morris and said, 'Sorry, James, got to go. Give me a call tomorrow so that you can fill me in on some of this.' Morris nodded agreement, Travers gave a silent wave to the meeting, and departed. Can't take too many more of these, he thought. Fortunately, his two colleagues seemed to be enraptured, and he was happy to leave them to it.

Travers grabbed a cab and went to Sloane Street and the Cadogan. He really was looking forward to seeing Jane again, sharpened by the atrophying boredom of the last five hours.

She was sitting in the small section of the dining-room, which had been laid out for tea. She was radiant, with a happy smile on her face, and looking very attractive. Her auburn hair was drawn up as usual in the informal way that left a few wisps framing her face, and she was dressed in a soft oatmeal coloured Tweed suit with a single pleated skirt just on the knee, under which she wore brown Cuban-heeled boots. Under her jacket was a beige heavy roll neck sweater over which a string of pearls shone above the rise of her bosom. As he approached, she leant forward in her chair, and still cross-legged, uttered that distinctive guttural chuckle of welcome.

'Hello, sweetheart, you look good enough to eat,' said Travers, leaning down to kiss her on the cheek. She lifted her chin in response, and deliberately planted a kiss on his lips. 'Have you checked in?' he said.

'Hello, Tom. It's good of you to come.' She was clearly not yet quite sure what mood he might be in after her news of yesterday. 'Yes, checked in, done a bit of shopping, but so looking forward to seeing you.' She raised her hand lightly to Travers' sleeve and held it there. He raised his hand and covered hers, gently squeezing her hand.

After a few moments, still standing over her he said, 'Right, better have some tea. Is there someone around?' He slid into the chair across the table from Jane.

'No, let's not. Can we go up to my room?' she said enquiringly. 'And I'll tell you all about things.' Travers smiled and nodded, got up and drew her chair back. Instead of taking the rickety lift, she walked up the stairs beside the lift, leading him by the hand from the first floor landing. On the second floor, she extracted her key from a bag, and as she opened the door said to Travers, 'Christ, I've missed you Tom.'

As soon as they had entered, she threw down her bags, kicked the door shut and leapt upwards with her hands around his neck. 'For God's sake, give me a squeeze,' she said. He held her round the waist, her feet still clear off the ground, and sunk his face into her neck, taking in her warmth and smell. One of his hands instinctively went to her bottom out of lust and for additional support. She pulled back her face, and with that impish smile said, 'Now, I want it now.' She pushed him away and slipped down to the ground, then pointed to a coffee table and chair the other side of the double bed. 'Sit there and don't move, I want you to enjoy this.' She waited with her hands on her hips and a wicked smile until he had sat down. Travers couldn't help a boyish smile of anticipation, as he obediently did as he was told. She slowly removed her jacket and threw it on the floor.

'Sweetheart, I really need a shower, it's been a long day,' he said apologetically.

'No. Stay.' She was looking him right in the eyes, and began to peel off her jacket as if commencing a burlesque routine. Travers could see she wasn't about to be interrupted. He decided to sit back and enjoy whatever came next.

At seven o'clock Travers rang the San Lorenzo, and managed to get a table for nine o'clock. To put it mildly, he was whacked. But very, very, happy. Sex was clearly a vital ingredient for Jane, but between the action she reverted to normal everyday discussion, before one or other of them made the next move. She was, thought Travers, undoubtedly the most natural and spontaneous sexual partner he had ever had, with none of the post coital coyness or silence that deflated the experience with some other women. She really was, he thought, quite a lady.

At the restaurant they discussed her situation with Bobby Newgent. While Travers accepted that Newgent may have backed off from the net he had thrown around Jane, he was not the type to give her free rein without continuing to check up on her. Jane explained to Travers that she had independent means, so that she frequently stayed at various hotels or friends in town, with nothing attributable to Newgent's bank account. Travers again pushed her on how long they could keep up this tryst without something going wrong, but she was adamant that for her at least, the present solution was a new dimension to her life, which she intended to enjoy to the full, at least until her teenage girls had finished their schooling.

'And what about me?' said Travers. 'What if I want to

make our relationship more permanent. What if I want you to come and live with me?'

'Listen, Romeo,' she said with a knowing smile. 'I've dragged you kicking and screaming into this, and I can see you weighing up the odds the whole time, as if this is another one of your projects. I also know from Bobby what you're trying to do at Sunburst. You don't want complications any more than I do. Nice try, *mon petit chou*, but this arrangement suits us both, so why change anything?' Her expression suddenly changed to concern, and she leant forward touching Travers' hand. 'You do want us to keep this going?'

'Oh yes,' said Travers wistfully. 'But I'm very, very fond of you Jane. What if we fall in love? Not sure the old macho genes are up to sharing you with that jerk of a husband. And anyway, sooner or later someone's going to spot us. It'll come out at some time.'

'Of course we're in love! But you know better than me these things don't always last. I may have led a sheltered existence, but I'm not stupid, Tom. Enjoy it for the moment, and let's see where it takes us. And we'll just have to be careful. But it's all such fun, I love it. By the way, how often do you think we can meet?' Travers looked at her, smiled, and shook his head slowly.

'You're like a gambler at Monte Carlo. Keep going until the chips run out. We must be careful, Jane. Whatever the future holds, let's stay in control of things. We're going to have to be pretty clever to keep this thing on the road, so it's no good bullying me. I think you're right though. Obviously I've got Holland Park, and I'm always in the City. So long as you're careful, and I don't know ... keep the trips down to twice a month, we might get through. What d'you think?'

'Hmm. Might be able to do a little better than that. That's no more often than I do now.'

Travers broke in, saying, 'Well fine. Let's see how that goes. My God, we're like a couple of kids scrumping apples. I must be mad.'

'Ah,' said Jane, sticking her bosom into the air and quietly giggling, 'But what gorgeous apples.'

After dinner, they returned to the hotel, and Travers stayed until two in the morning. He slipped out past the night porter, who hardly raised his head from the desk. Well used to these nocturnal trysts, thought Travers. He picked up a cab in Sloane Square and made his way back to Holland Park.

On Wednesday morning, he was in the office at his usual time, somewhat the worse for wear. Chris had left a note of a whole series of meetings she had booked for the morning, being unable to get hold of him on his mobile. She was clearly annoyed that he hadn't kept in touch. Travers reminded himself to be a little more diligent in future. He couldn't leave the poor girl high and dry with so much going on. He would apologise as soon as she came in.

During the morning he worked steadily through meetings, caught up with Ogden and Fellowes, and spoke to the two sets of bankers about yesterday's meeting. Everything seemed to be going smoothly enough. Phillip Carter, the temporary finance director, was clearly having a whale of a time, spending a lot of money on new financial software and systems to fill the void that Brian Locke had left. He was certainly getting on with things, arranging deputations from his City headquarters to come down and work through everything from the asset register and depreciation rates to salesmen's expenses, as part of the due diligence process that both Levin and indeed his own bankers would shortly demand. Fortunately, the daily sales analysis showed that sales continued to perform above target, with the added bonus that the new alcoholic drinks range were successfully flattening the customary high summer seasonality of the soft drink range. This was doing wonders for cash flow, at a time when high production levels in the factory in readiness for the Christmas period, usually depleted cash. He reminded himself to re-examine sales and cash requirements for his own MBO forecast, but leave things as they were for Levin.

After lunch, he went down the corridor to see how Amanda Beresford was getting on.

'Amanda. Hi. Are we ever going to see Levin? Seems to me he's falling down on the job.'

'Hello, Tom,' said Amanda. 'No, he's fine. I'm in touch with him the whole time. I'll be honest, Tom, everything's pretty clean, I don't need his help. But he does want to speak to some of your customers.'

'Oh, what for?' said Travers aggressively.

'We need to know from the retailers just what they think of Sunburst, and its future prospects. Don't worry, it's nothing unusual.'

'But, Amanda,' said Travers patiently, 'you can't just go and casually discuss the sale of Sunburst with them. Half of them will take fright that we're going bust and switch elsewhere. I'm sorry, but you or Levin must make no contact with my customers without my say so. If you're determined to do it, I'll select some key buyers by trade sector, and I'll put you in touch with them, and at least tell them in confidence what's going on before you or Levin go in with your hobnailed boots. I'm sorry, but there's no way my customers are receiving cold calls from Levin.'

'But Simon Spencer has already released the story about the sale of Sunburst. What's the problem?' said Amanda.

'Because my customers are far too valuable to get some half-assed story from Levin. Amanda, be reasonable or it's no go.'

'OK, I'll tell Levin what you've said. But we should select who we speak to. Otherwise, we'll just be speaking to your chums, won't we, Tom?' Amanda now sat back in her chair giving Travers a fairly brutal stare.

'Amanda, that's not very charitable.' He smiled. 'I hadn't realised you could be so cynical. But OK, you let me know first who you want to see, and I'll set it up.' She smiled, nodded, and returned to her hunch over the desk. Then she looked up.

'Oh, one more thing,' she said flatly. 'It seems to me there's at least another couple of million to be made on profit, year in year out, if you weren't so prudent with provisions, and profligate with the marketing budget. The same things keep reappearing, never seem to be used, and the pile keeps growing. Talk about cash under cultivation, you could put Alan Titchmarsh to shame. Your marketing budgets are also extraordinary. A quarter of a million a year on sales conferences seems somewhat excessive.'

'Well I'm sorry, Amanda, but it'll take you a lot more time to properly understand this business. You have to look at the results. And just look at the size of our competitors. Do you really believe we could compete on an accountant's marketing budget? You must remember who we're selling to. Teenagers mostly. It's a fashion business, and that costs money. Whoever buys this business knows the entry costs as well as I do. I'm absolutely certain none of them would raise an eyebrow at what you consider excessive. Mind you, be careful how you express an opinion. I'll undertake no warranties whatsoever if you or Levin start to falsely inflate profits. Given the profit record, I just don't see how you can argue. As to provisions, you must understand this is a highly seasonal business. Forty per cent of our volume in June and July alone. We have to be prudent. Otherwise one bad summer would wipe out our profit record, and you'd never unload this business to anybody.'

'Hmm,' said Amanda, 'but don't you think we could lift the current results by even a million?'

'No I don't. For God's sake give it a rest. The best way to lift profits is to go on raising the top sales line, otherwise the whole brand franchise will fall away. Honestly, Amanda, I don't think it's your job to speculate on such a complex area that you have so little knowledge of. The buyers will make their own judgement.'

'I know, I know,' said Amanda. 'But it's the starting point that worries me. The value of this business starts and finishes with the earnings multiple, and it would be nice to pitch that first figure of value at a higher level. But I do see your point. Geoffrey was keen for me to persuade you to put your name to a higher figure.'

'Sorry to disappoint you, but no way,' said Travers finally.

'Well I suppose with the MBO lurking you're bound to say that, aren't you?' said Amanda somewhat disdainfully.

'Look, Amanda. You must know I've been entirely consistent over the last five years with all your areas of concern. This is not a case of pulling rabbits out of a hat in the last twelve months to depress profits in advance of a trade sale or MBO. It's a bit insulting that you think I would stoop to that. You should know me well enough by now.'

'No, I'm sorry, Tom, you're quite right of course. You have always been consistent. Let's forget it.' Travers breathed an inward sigh of relief. Thank God she'd moved off that one. The thought obviously hadn't occurred to her that he had consistently depressed profits in order to invest for growth and keep the revenues out of his shareholders' pockets.

'How's the hotel, comfortable?' said Travers.

'Oh yes, super thanks. And they've given me a small meeting room, which allows me to write up in the evenings. It's all working very well.'

'How long to publication of the Memorandum?' said Travers.

'Er, maybe end of next week if I can keep going at the current rate. That lops a week off what we said before. Mind you, I've got to go through it with you and the other directors, and you've got to sign it off.'

'OK. What about some dinner tomorrow night at the hotel? My treat, keep your nose out of those books for five minutes. You can bend my ear on whatever else is on your mind.'

'Great. I'd like that, Tom. Very kind of you. Eight o'clock?'

'Look forward to it. Right, got to dash. Don't forget to attend the workforce meeting in the warehouse tomorrow, and let me have that list of customers.'

Travers returned to his office, and was glad he had seen her. Over dinner, he would try and extract from her which buyers were interested, and see if there were any surprises. Goldberg's must have started the search weeks ago, and the Information document was actually only the formalised start to the bidding process. Presumably, he thought, he would begin getting visitors from interested parties the week after next. That would be fun, especially as he might be bidding against one of them. He wondered if any of them would try and persuade him to stay on if they were successful in their bid. He thought the prospects were slim once they were informed about his buyout plans. That was clearly a major downside if his buyout failed. The possibility of his first bout of career unemployment was nevertheless sobering.

The next day he was making final adjustments to his speech to the employees, which would take place at twelve o'clock, running into their lunch break. With over five hundred employees, including half the sales force who were within reasonable proximity, the only place he could talk to them all was in one of the finished goods warehouses, where a large space had been cleared, and a stack of pallets provided for Travers to stand on. Travers much preferred these impromptu meetings to the 'bells and whistles' conferences, which many of the shop floor correctly deduced were highly contrived. He had also decided against a slide show, which he usually used as a prompt for himself as much as the audience. Instead, he had a series of headings on a scrap of paper, and that would see him through. Out of courtesy, he had arranged to see the three shop stewards at eleven o'clock to forewarn them of what he had to say. Not that there had ever been much friction between Travers and the three trade unions who represented the various members of the workforce. Apart from the annual ritual of wage negotiations, Travers had built a grudging trust even from the most radical 'lefties' within the unions. Travers was quietly pleased that half the workforce whom he himself could name, called him by his Christian name. The brewery non-executive directors, on their infrequent visits to the shop floor, thought such familiarity demeaning, but Travers would have none of it. Anything to break down the old 'us and them' barriers was good news as far as he was concerned.

Fellowes had told Travers that the shop floor was rife with rumours, and that the trade press releases orchestrated by Gallant several days before had put the cat amongst the pigeons. When Travers met the shop stewards, their first and only concern was employment. What guarantees was Travers going to give them? What about their productivity bonuses? Were their pensions secure? Travers knew what was coming, but wanted to hear it all, so that when he actually addressed the workforce, at least he wouldn't miss anything. When they had vented their views and calmed down a bit, he first tried to explain the reasons for the sale, being unusually a result of the success of the company and the value now locked into it as a result of everyone's hard work. He explained the pressure on the shareholders, and the belief that the company should be capable of standing on its own feet under new ownership. He pulled no punches though, on who might become the new owners. It was fairly obvious. Because of that he was in no position to offer any guarantees, but he would make sure that whoever bought the company clarified the position with regard to employees as a first priority.

Travers left what he thought would be the good news until last. He told them that the most secure route for the employees was undoubtedly the option he had been granted to launch an MBO, which at one stroke removed the possibility of wholesale rationalisation. If it succeeded, said Travers, he would make sure that everyone, through a share scheme, could participate in the continued success of the company. The prospect of an MBO certainly surprised the stewards, but they were not slow in casting doubts on Travers' ability to match the purses of the international cola companies, or several other very large home-grown competitors. Travers agreed with them, but like Churchill, all he could offer them was blood, sweat and long hours to reach that objective, and the rest of it was out of his hands until he could negotiate with the trade buyer, if that was the outcome. The only thing that Travers could promise was that the pension fund was secure and independent through the Trust mechanism, and that no one should be concerned on that score.

Apart from the usual bellyache about profit and fat cats

playing dice with their livelihoods, Travers felt they took the news responsibly, and they agreed to have regular weekly meetings as well as the notice boards to keep everyone informed of developments that may affect them.

As soon as they had left the room, Travers looked at his notes, made a few amendments and went over to the warehouse to address the employees.

He took about half an hour to slowly and painstakingly explain the precise background to the trade sale, the process they were currently engaged in, and the slow progression to a result, which might be as much as six months away before all the final contracts and undertakings were signed. He told them of the MBO shot, which probably had a twenty per cent chance, and how much work was involved. For that reason alone, he urged them to accept the situation, and allow the management and the stewards to strike the best deal they could for the employees as a whole, and that absolutely nothing would be achieved by disruption of any sort. Indeed Travers said he was relying on them to get on with their jobs, so that he could get on with his, and either buy the company, or if he lost, to make sure they were all treated fairly. He invited questions, but knew there wouldn't be any with such a big gathering. He was pleased. He had their attention from the start, and although the mood was sombre, he could definitely feel that this motley group had realised the threat from outside, and firmly supported their boss in his intentions. Without the MBO lifeline, it would have been a very different meeting.

Travers had a brief meeting with his colleagues back in his office, triggering the departmental briefings that each senior manager would deliver to his staff over the next few days. He implored his directors to cap the gossip, and keep people working normally. Information was undoubtedly the key, and as long as they kept up a regular and meaningful discourse with the staff through the management, Travers was sure they would be supportive.

He then walked down the corridor in search of Amanda Beresford. She had returned to her desk.

'Very impressive, Mr Travers. Not sure you needed to treat potential buyers as such big bad wolves, but that's your call, I suppose.'

'Amanda, seriously. I never bullshit the staff. They know the time of day, and they know there's going to be some blood letting whoever buys this business. There's a long way to go, and unless we have some trust from them, the whole operation will start to fray at the edges. I've seen it before. You have to have a few monsters to keep everyone pulling in the same direction.'

'No, I do understand, Tom. No complaints, honestly. You've got a nice line in "fight them on the beaches". Personally, I'd follow you anywhere.' She was broadly smiling now.

'I do believe you're taking the piss. I wonder why I bother at times.' Travers feigned offence.

'I've seen that little boy lost look already, Tom. Put it away for another day.' They both laughed.

'See you tonight, eight o'clock.' Travers raised his hand and left. He wondered if he had the measure of Amanda at all. Her solitary lifestyle meant she had developed a shield around herself, which was difficult to penetrate. He had seen glimpses of the more vulnerable personality underneath, but it was now buried so deeply beneath her serpentine world of finance and intrigue that her natural instincts and reactions were overwhelmed by that calculating intelligence, no doubt exploited and refined by Levin. Travers felt genuinely sad that such a vital and intelligent young woman, although apparently succeeding in a male dominated environment, was destined to burn out and degenerate into an embittered old spinster if she wasn't careful. Not his problem, he thought. Nevertheless, he couldn't help feeling that had his affections not been dominated by Jane, the sheer challenge of igniting a life spark in Amanda would have been irresistible. After all, she was a highly attractive and desirable woman.

Back at his desk, he broke out of the reverie. Chris was now leaning against the door smiling, with her arms crossed.

'Report?' she said.

'Oh yes,' said Travers. 'What are the vibes?' Whenever Travers spoke to the employees, or issued some new announcement within the company, he asked Chris to do what she could to take a sounding of opinion, particularly amongst the secretaries and clerks. They were quick to pick up sentiments from management and shop floor, especially once they had a chance to congregate and gossip around the coffee machine, or in the canteen.

'Well,' said Chris. 'They love the informal style, some of them are swooning, must be your voice. They all felt you were talking to them personally. I think, Tom,' she said chuckling, 'the girls will follow you over the top if no one else will.'

'That's good,' said Travers, still stony faced. 'But do they understand this sale process, and what I'm trying to do?'

'Not really. Honestly, most of it's way above their heads, they just think businesses carry on. They all recognise you were talking about a threat to their jobs, but they trust you, and are absolutely certain you'll pull off what you want. Most people think what's good for you, is good for them. Look at the last ten years. Apparently some of the shop floor think it's a ruse you're pulling to cancel all the productivity bonuses. But that's mainly the truck drivers in distribution, and everyone knows what they're like.'

'Might have known,' said Travers. 'Do you realise some of those buggers are earning thirty thousand a year? One of these days I'm going to scrap those stupid agreements, and subcontract the whole lot. Forget I said that, Chris. OK, thanks. You will tell me, won't you, if you pick up anything destructive. It'll give me a chance to nip it in the bud.' She nodded and returned to her desk. He picked up the phone to Fellowes, and told him to spell out to distribution that all productivity agreements were safe until the next round of wage negotiations, and to try and lift their thoughts for five minutes from their wage packets to the future of the firm. He also phoned Morris at Wessex Bank to tell him that the staff were notified, and that the factory visits for the hordes of bankers could now go ahead, subject to arrangement with Fellowes. He then busied himself with the mountain of routine, amongst which was completing the briefing notes for the head-hunters to get on and find a hotshot finance director.

Later that evening, after an extended period at his desk, Travers drove to the hotel in Harrow where Amanda was staying. The staff and owners were well known to him, and greeted him like a long lost friend. He hoped they were looking after Miss Beresford well, as she was a VIP as far as Sunburst were concerned, to which of course they assured him they would. He found her in the small library, which doubled as the hotel bar, where she was sipping on an orange juice.

'Grief, hope I can get you onto something stronger than that. Would've thought a dry martini was more your style. All work makes Jill a dull girl you know.'

'Mustn't, I'm afraid. Remember, I've got to write the narrative after dinner.'

'Well for heaven's sake do tap me for information at the office. It's all in here you know,' said Travers, tapping his head. 'You've only got to ask.'

'Yes, thank you, I will. Some of the background is thin, and I'd especially like to understand how you got to the current strategy with the alcoholic pop. It's obviously working a treat, but also, where from here?'

'Well, you've got the strategy document, but naturally there's a lot more on the stocks than is contained in that. Some of it, though, is purely speculative, without research or development. Not sure your buyers would be interested in flights of fancy until we've put a few research markers down.'

'I don't need to remind you, Tom, that you do have a duty to your current shareholders to maximise the value of the business. Anything, but anything that is relevant to that, I want to know about.' She was leaning on the bar as she spoke, but at least, Travers thought, she had said it without a trace of hostility.

'Absolutely, Amanda. I'll spill the beans on that whenever you like.' He noted he had become an accomplished liar in the last few weeks. 'Levin still happy?'

'Oh yes,' she said, 'everything's on schedule, better in fact, as I told you.'

'What happens after this job, Amanda? On to the next one, or do you get a break?'

'Difficult to say,' she said, running her hands through her short blonde hair. She looked very tired. 'Sometimes there's another one to jump straight into, other times it's helping other teams with desk research, and just occasionally, I'm sent on holiday if there's nothing cooking.'

'But more or less,' he said, taking a deep swig of his double whisky and water, 'you've been flat out on this sort of work for the last four or five years?'

'I suppose so, yes. Why d'you ask?'

'Because, young lady, you need a break. It does show, you know. It's different for me. I run Sunburst at my own pace, and I delegate. No point the chief executive not allowing himself thinking time. Good for the soul and the business. I rarely work past six, until this lot came along. You haven't got that luxury, and believe me, I do understand the pressures you're under on each and every job. Have you thought about a sabbatical?' She laughed.

'I'd get short shrift on that one, and probably lose my job for asking. Don't think you quite understand the work ethic at Goldberg's. That sort of thing, I'm sure, would be frowned upon.'

'Well that just shows how wrong you can be, Amanda. You really ought to talk to other guys in other firms. I know for a fact in your line of business sabbaticals are treated as a worthwhile investment in the management by any reputable merchant bank. Good Jewish outfit like Goldberg's would always look after the staff. Bet you've never even thought about it.'

'Well no, I haven't. But anyway, there's nothing wrong with me. You're only saying this because I'm a woman, and you don't think I'm up to it.'

'Amanda, don't be a cretin. I think you're an absolute whiz, and so does Levin. But you're going to burn out if you don't look after yourself. Why don't you take six months off, do the Grand Tour, or chill out in the Bahamas. You're not short of money, and you'll come back recharged, and probably with a better job. It's time you started making a few demands, by the sound of it.'

'I'm afraid, Tom, you're over elevating my importance, and anyway, what the hell would I do for six months?' Sitting on the bar stool, her body was now slumped against the bar, with her hand supporting her head, looking at Travers. He casually looked into her face and noticed for the first time her smooth unblemished complexion, devoid of make-up, and her piercing light blue eyes with the same old tuft of blonde hair partially obscuring an eye. Travers couldn't help the thoughts that were rushing through his head. He was already mentally undressing her. What a terrible waste, he thought. But he must stop this nonsense of leching after women who crossed his path. It wasn't natural. Or was it because fate had thrown these two attractive women into his path? Either way, he really ought to show some moral fortitude.

'Hmm,' said Travers. 'Please do think about it. It's a terrible waste.'

'What d'you mean a terrible waste?' she said inquiringly.

'Oh, nothing,' said Travers. 'Sorry, wrong words. Now what about dinner? Have you seen a menu round here?' She smiled brightly at him without changing her position, and Travers felt distinctly uncomfortable as he felt her brain analysing his last comment. He also felt sure she was about to say something, but after what seemed ages, she pulled herself upright on the stool, but still kept a knowing smile on her face.

'Yes,' she said quietly, 'I think we'd better have dinner.' And once more that smile was thrown in Travers' direction, before looking ahead, losing the moment, and taking another sip of her almost untouched orange juice.

As they walked slowly into the dining-room, Travers couldn't help but notice that Amanda had relaxed completely, smiling naturally and readily with the innocuous conversation, her hands again in the little jacket pockets above her hips, and her head flashing between glances at Travers and the floor ahead of her. Travers had no doubt whatsoever, however arrogant it might appear, that this woman wanted him, but couldn't quite muster the confidence to get on with it. Intriguing. The right proposition from him would, he knew, clinch the situation, but he equally knew he wasn't going to make it. It simply wouldn't be fair on any one, and would be a major betrayal of Jane. He almost laughed to himself at his own pomposity. Here he was, cuckolding a customer's wife whilst 'doing the right thing' by Amanda. Ridiculous.

Thankfully, dinner passed pleasantly and enjoyably. A friendship had certainly developed between them, but Travers could feel that his greater experience of life was leading them towards a more filial, as opposed to romantic, relationship, or so he hoped. Perhaps, that was the best outcome. But after all this was over, Travers was determined to keep in touch with her. They should be friends, and it would be good for both of them.

'Believe it or not,' said Travers at the end of the meal, 'I too have some papers to look at before tomorrow. I must love you and leave you. Thanks for having dinner with me, I really enjoyed it, we must do it again.' He went to kiss her on the cheek, but drew back. 'Oh to hell with it, business or not you deserve a kiss, may I?' She laughed and nodded, and he gently took her by the shoulders and gave her a quick peck on the cheek. He didn't fail to notice that her hands had gone up to either side of his waist.

'See you tomorrow, have a good night's sleep,' said Travers, spinning round and heading for the exit.

The following morning, Friday, held some unexpected surprises for Travers. At nine thirty he received a call from James Morris. The senior debt people had met again with Maxwell Griffin, and between them, were in a position to offer the management a finance package for the senior and mezzanine debt. Morris said he couldn't believe how fortunate the Sunburst team were, but that it was basically down to the confidence of success that Travers and his colleagues had generated. Do get on with it, thought Travers.

'So this is the deal,' said Morris. 'Basically if the purchase price falls between sixty and seventy-five million, in other words a maximum post tax earnings ratio of nine, they'll go for fifty per cent gearing, plus working capital headroom to see you through the peaks and troughs. They're offering all this, wait for it, at fifty-five basis points over LIBOR!' Travers listened to this barrage of gobbledigook, but managed to decipher its contents. So, the bank were willing to put up half the purchase price as bank debt – the fifty per cent gearing – and another borrowing facility over and above that to finance the normal monthly overdrafts, as goods were bought and sold. The fifty-fifty basis points over LIBOR simply signified that they would charge a little above half a per cent over bank base rate for the duration of the loan. Having decided that, Travers could readily understand that Morris was wetting his knickers with joy.

'Sounds good, so the interest rate is half a percent over base?' said Travers. 'What about the mezzanine portion, what do we get that at?'

'Not too bad actually. They've agreed to put in another fifteen million for an equity attachment of eight per cent. They want to make that convertible preference shares at a roll-up of twelve per cent.'

'Can I have that in English please?' said Travers wearily.

'Well, yes,' said Morris, who thought he had made himself quite clear. 'If the bank are putting up this much extra money above the senior loan, they want some shares for free, in addition to the repayment of interest. They're willing to accept eight per cent of the issued share equity in a special class of redeemable preference shares for the extra fifteen million quid. For that, they'll charge you twelve per cent per annum because of the extra risk over and above the senior debt they'll put in. They know you may have difficulty paying back all this bank interest, so on this portion they're willing to roll it up – in other words the interest will just accumulate and you can pay it off when the company repays all of its bank debt on flotation – simple.'

'Just a moment, James,' said Travers cautiously. 'That sounds a hell of a lot. Why are we paying half a per cent over base on the senior debt, and one and a quarter on the mezzanine. And we never talked about eight per cent of the equity, it was always five.'

'Tom,' said Morris with some exasperation. 'You must understand this is one hell of a deal. Have you any idea how much this cuts your interest charges, it's huge. Giving a bit more away on equity to get it is a great move, I think Maxwells have done a brilliant job to get this from my banking colleagues, I really do. Remember that although senior debt and mezzanine debt are two different departments in the bank, they've obviously done a fix between them on the margins. But don't worry about that, that's their business. Tom, I promise you this is a great deal.'

'Is it in writing yet, and have our lawyers seen the terms?' said Travers, still cautious.

'Strewth, no, not yet. This was only done yesterday.'

'Well look, James. When you think about it, Maxwell Griffin is holding the equity, and they have a keen eye on reducing the operating costs through interest charges, to actually make sure we can keep up the payments on debt on our progress to flotation. They have done a good job, but whose equity have they given away to get it?'

'I don't know, Tom, but that's not your concern; they'll have to chisel some of their underwriters or investors. Honestly, they deserve a pat on the back.' Travers then discussed a number of other issues, and agreed to visit the Wessex offices on Tuesday or Wednesday the following week to ensure all of this was agreed with the lawyers. He thanked Morris and rang off. He was of course pleased, but without an interpreter for the spreadsheet, it was difficult to work out just how much that three per cent give away on equity had cost the shareholders, particularly if the real value of the business was realised on flotation. They had all talked about a one hundred and forty million pound flotation, which meant that the three per cent was worth nearly half a million pounds. He would fax Morris to do the calculation properly, and make sure they weren't paying through the nose for this mezzanine slice. He had to admit, though, the half over base on the senior debt, instead of one and a half, would probably save in the region of one and a half million a year in interest charges on the profit and loss account.

Within ten minutes he got another call from Anthony Giddings at Maxwell Griffin.

'Tom, we've done a great deal on debt with the bank, but we've hit some other problems. Any chance you, David and John can pop up this afternoon? It's really important.'

'I've already heard the news from Wessex, sounds as though you've done a good deal. But what exactly is the problem?' said Travers flatly.

'Sorry, Tom, really pushed for time here, can you make three o'clock?' Travers reluctantly agreed, with a strong feeling of foreboding. He couldn't believe they were going to muck about with the management's share, because he and the boss of Maxwell, John Smith, had shaken on it, as well as issuing a piece of paper to the lawyers confirming it. He decided not to prejudge, but went straight down the corridor to his colleagues to make sure they could join him, and also to tell them of his worst fears. They would all need to put their thinking caps on, just in case.

* * *

They arrived on time at the Maxwell Griffin offices in Great Salisbury Street, just off London Wall. They had all been there several times before in the last few weeks, and were already recognised by the reception ladies. They were shown up to the impressive, fully panelled board room, complete with generations of Maxwells and Griffins from the Victorian and Edwardian era, who looked down from their portraits with a general disdain on the observer. Within five minutes Giddings and Roberts bustled into the room, arms full of papers, spreadsheets and electronic gizmos. Travers genuinely liked Giddings, whom he found straightforward, very bright and civil. On the other hand, his junior partner Roberts, whom Travers was convinced was ex-Harrow, was an arrogant and aggressive young sod, who seemed to regard the rest of the human race as a lower form of life. Fortunately, he said little, and on the occasional arm movement from Giddings, was generally kept silent and stuck to his calculator.

'No John Brown?' said Travers quizzically.

'No,' said Giddings. 'Unfortunately he couldn't make it. Now what about some tea or coffee?'

'Coffee please, Anthony. This can't be very important if John's not here. Are you sure I needed to come? We're very busy with Goldberg's on site you know,' said Travers, a little tetchily.

'Yes, it is important, Tom, we have to make some decisions, but let's wait for the coffee.' Giddings pointed at Roberts to go and organise it. 'So how are things going with Goldberg's, and the lovely Miss Beresford?'

'Look, bugger that, and bugger coffee. Get on with it, Anthony. What the hell are you fellows up to now? Spill the beans.'

'Ah, nicely put, Tom. OK, if you insist, let's get on.

James Morris will have told you we met with his banking people yesterday, and we think we've negotiated a highly advantageous debt facility for Sunburst. I think you know the details. Now, one of our problems is that we had to sweeten the equity offer on the mezzanine side of things to get the overall package that we wanted. That cost us three per cent of the equity, but we think it was more than worth it. Unfortunately, on top of that, the syndicate we've pulled together to underwrite the equity are not quite as enthused as us about the company's prospects, and in particular, regard Sunburst more as a commodity soft drink supplier than a strong branded franchise that can compete effectively with the top three. We've therefore had to effectively offer them a discount to hold them in, which really is regrettable, but necessary. I'm afraid, Tom, and I'm sure you'll understand, as a result the sweet equity is hopelessly squeezed, and we've all got to lower our expectations...'

'I thought so,' said Travers casually. He then leant forward over the table using his outstretched hands. 'You disreputable bunch of bastards are going to break your promise and hack back the management share.' Travers sat back and said in a level and controlled voice, 'Over my dead body. We have a deal. If you choose to change it, fine, take it out of your own share. Personally, I think the mezzanine deal stinks. You didn't need to give it away, and you did. Again, that's your business, not mine. You say your syndicate doesn't like Sunburst. Fine. Go and find some others that do, I'll even help you if you don't know how to sell the company.'

Roberts interjected: 'Tom, you're in no position to dictate the financing package. Your job is simply to run the business and be very grateful we're putting up the money. The management share changes on all the deals we do, it has to. This is the tail wagging the dog.'

The room went silent as Travers turned to Roberts. Giddings' hands already covered his face. Travers gave Roberts a withering look, sat back and still with a calm voice said to Roberts, 'I really do suggest, Giles, you speak when you're spoken to. I'm not interested in what you have to say unless it's about the spreadsheet. But I'm glad you've raised these points of principle. What you're telling me is that having the word of your chief executive isn't worth a light because you're going to change it anyway. That I've got to do business with liars and cheats and be grateful. Well I'm sorry, I don't think I want to do business with you, nor do my colleagues.' Unfortunately for Travers, both his colleagues were at this point slipping down further and further into their chairs, and were using their hands in the same way as Giddings. 'Let's get this straight, gentlemen,' said Travers. 'Deals like this don't come along every five minutes, you need me more than I need you. After what you've told me, you leave me very little option but to take up the discussions where I left them with your competitors. It'll be interesting at least to see if they can match our former agreement, particularly as the debt facility is now in place with Wessex. Good heavens, come to think of it, it's practically a done deal. Thanks for your help, though, I appreciate that.'

Having spoken, Travers got up from his chair and packed his pad into his briefcase.

'Obviously, Anthony, I'm hugely upset at your duplicity. Whatever you've got to say, I'm in no mood for it now. By all means chew the fat with David and John, if they want to stay, but I've got a few telephone calls to make. I imagine I'm going to be very busy from Monday. I'd be grateful for a call from Brown too. I think he deserves a piece of my mind.'

'Just a minute, Tom,' said Giddings, rising from his seat. But Travers was gone.

Travers left the building with a high sense of exhilaration. He had used the 'good cop, bad cop' routine with his sales director to great effect with some of the supermarkets, but he truly wondered if he had overshot the mark on this occasion. He had told his two colleagues how he would react if their share was squeezed, on the basis that any negotiation at that time would inevitably lead to a compromise figure, which Travers just wasn't interested in. Having read Rommel's North African war diaries, he knew that keeping the enemy guessing, and the element of surprise were two key factors for success with inferior forces, which he felt were highly appropriate measures to employ with Maxwell. The only trouble was, Ogden had failed to use the 'good cop' part of the routine, and actually try and call Travers back into the meeting. He'd never make the stage. But Travers wasn't bothered. He was genuinely upset at their duplicity, and Roberts had played into his hands and had opened the full Pandora's Box of what was clearly pre-planned duplicity. If it worked, Travers knew that his perceived sensibility and unpredictability would guarantee they wouldn't try it again, but if it failed, time was slipping away, and Travers was extremely pessimistic about the chances of filling Maxwell Griffin's shoes with another equity provider. Jesus, he thought, what had he done?

As per the arrangement, he went round to Andrews and Overton to wait for Ogden and Fellowes. When he arrived, he asked to speak with Paul Foot, who readily emerged and ushered Travers into his office.

'Paul, I've got the shakes. Have you any idea what I've just done?'

He explained to Foot what happened at the meeting, and instead of sympathy, Foot just burst out laughing.

'I don't believe it. My God that's brilliant. Christ, you've got some balls. But Tom, they do the same thing with every management team, and not just once. If they spot another little wrinkle, poof, there's another couple of per cent gone. But if any one can pull it off, you can. You do have a knack of putting the wind up 'em. My guess is you'll win. Are the boys coming here afterwards?'

'Yes,' said Travers, still shell-shocked by his own actions. 'Tell you what, though, if we do win this, I want a watertight agreement on equity that you're going to draft for me, that overrides all this crap. Why didn't their last written undertaking stick?'

'Because, Tom, it's full of the bog standard caveats of commercial viability. I'm sorry, I should have made the holes in it more obvious to you, but as I say, it was bog standard. I'd be delighted to ring-fence the shareholding if they reinstate it. No problem. Meanwhile, I think you need a drink.' Foot got up, still chuckling, and went over to his drinks cabinet.

'Tell you another thing, Paul,' said Travers. 'If we do win this, they're not having a penny over and above the success fees that the brewers are paying us. They can be grateful for what we're already putting in. That's the price of their duplicity.'

'Difficult, difficult,' chuckled Foot. 'Worth a try though, Tom.'

'Good,' said Travers. 'I don't mind backing up the warranties and verification notes with some sort of extra commitment, but only in the event of breach. No breach, no further undertaking.'

Two hours later, Ogden and Fellowes turned up at Andrews and Overton, and found Travers waiting for them in reception. It was six forty-five. Ogden looked like the cat who stole the cream.

'How d'it go fellas?' said Travers.

'Pretty bloody good,' said Ogden. 'Any chance of a drink first?'

'Well actually, Paul Foot wants to hear the outcome too, David, so let's try to get to his office and his drinks cabinet.' Travers went to reception, and within five minutes they were all in Foot's office, drinks in hand.

'When you left,' said Ogden, looking at Travers, 'Giddings went for Roberts. Tore into him for saying the management share was always diminished. Roberts went a funny colour and left. Giddings followed him, without saying anything to us other than he would try and get hold of Smith. Just left us on our lonesome. We were there for an hour with nothing, until they all reappeared with John Smith. Smith was good, he really was. Said it was a tragedy, would never double-deal you, real commercial pressures, all that stuff. We said nothing, just listened to him and got rather embarrassed, didn't we, John? Anyway, he then said the matter had to be put right, and he wanted to get in the limo and for all of us to go to your house at Holland Park! Can you believe it! We said, well, being the weekend, you'd probably gone straight to East Grinstead, no telling where you were. But I said – good move I thought – I would spend the weekend tracking you down, but with what message? I said there was no way you'd compromise, because you had a gentlemen's agreement with Smith, and you were funny about that sort of thing. Then we got to it. So you should be, he said, and no matter what difficulties Maxwell Griffin suffer as a result, he would reinstate the seventeen and a half base, with the twenty-five per cent share on a float of one hundred and forty million. Just like that. No mucking about. Said his reputation was more valuable than some margin, and that this would prove their honourability. We said thanks a lot, see what you say, and we'd be back to them on Monday. He gave me his Surrey home number, and said if we do track you down, would you please phone any evening over the weekend. Not a bad day's work, Tom!' He handed Travers the telephone number.

They all laughed, and raised their hands, as if the home team had just won the Cup Final.

'Oh, I say, that's splendid, splendid,' said Foot. 'I'll have the share ring-fence agreement in draft for you on Monday,' said Foot.

Travers explained the next move to legally tie them in when Fellowes interjected:

'Only thing that worries me is will they try and get their own back somehow? There's a long way to go isn't there? They're so bloody slippery, makes you wonder what they'll screw us on next.'

'I don't think so,' said Travers. 'This cuts a bit deeper than you think. They obviously try this every time with management teams, knowing that it is too late for them to change backers, or even more likely, that management actually believe their cock and bull story about the numbers not adding up without a squeeze on the management equity. The thing is, that we know just how attractive this deal is to them, particularly as they now know we can squeeze another couple of million onto profit at the stroke of a pen once we've completed the deal. And I have to say, I did give a bravura performance! What perhaps you don't know is that I'd told Giddings last week that I'd had 3i and Electra on the phone, asking if I would back a pitch from them. I would hope that also made him nervous about pushing us too far. Who knows? But I'm confident they've got to do the right thing from now on. It does remind me though, Paul, will you phone David Thompson, the Albion lawyer, and see where we are on the success fee agreement? We must put that to bed before we start seeing trade buyers, which could be the week after next.' Foot agreed. They were all tired, and had to get out of London on a Friday evening. The meeting wrapped up with a promise to meet the following week to review progress.

Travers got a train out to Willesden, picked up his car, and drove to Holland Park. He then made quick preparations for a weekend at East Grinstead, loaded the car, and headed off. It was midnight before he arrived at West Lodge, but the journey had passed quickly. In fact, there was so much on his mind with the buyout, he'd practically been on autopilot since leaving Foot's office. West Lodge was cold and dank. To hell with it. He didn't bother with the heating, just jumped into bed and crashed. He would pick up Molly in the morning, and get out onto Ashdown Forest, where they could both get some exercise.

On Sunday night, at nine o'clock, Travers telephoned John Smith on his home number. A perky Scottish lady answered, informing Travers merrily that her husband had been awaiting his call. Brown came on the phone and inquired immediately if Ogden and Fellowes had been in touch. Good, massive apologies, shouldn't have happened, my word is my bond, won't happen again, you won't regret it. Travers accepted the apology, informing Smith that nevertheless there would be a small document to sign for the irrevocable share participation of the management team. Brown admitted he was in no position to argue, and readily agreed, keen to re-establish the trust that they had inadvertently allowed to slip. Job done.

Chapter Seven

The third week in October was wet. All week it rained. Every day and every night. Travers wouldn't have normally minded, or even noticed, but for two reasons: first, a Caledonian Brewery shoot he had been invited to in Yorkshire midweek was cancelled because the birds were waterlogged; and second, time was dragging on the buyout, and he had spent too much time looking out of windows ruminating. It wasn't as if there was a lot to do. There was. With the end of the fiscal year approaching, the strategic plan approved by the board in the summer must now be converted into targets and budgets for the new year, and by rights, he should have addressed the senior management group by now, spelling out the key goals and objectives for the year ahead. Buyout or trade sale made no real difference, the company needed its budgets and the control they gave.

However, Travers was distracted, and felt uninvolved. He wanted a result, a conclusion, which would either have him searching for a new job, or diving into the very heart of Sunburst once more to extract further cost savings to offset the huge interest burden the company would face with an MBO.

Quite a lot had actually happened that week, but instigated elsewhere. Giddings had been on the telephone on the Monday morning, and without a trace of apology, had been delighted to hear everything was back on an even keel, despite the investment pressure it would cause for Maxwell. Travers told him that to cheer up his day they would be receiving an irrevocable undertaking on the share agreement as soon as Andrews and Overton had completed the draft. Also on Monday, Wessex Bank had delivered outline terms for the senior debt and mezzanine arrangements to all parties concerned. This seemed obvious and simple enough to Travers, until on the Tuesday, he had seen the gargantuan legal documents that all three sets of lawyers would pore over for the next two weeks. Travers was given a copy, fully one hundred and fifty pages long, but was ground to a halt after five pages by the unintelligible legal prose, and the constant reference to other clauses and schedules, which he couldn't find anyway, by which time he had lost the meaning of the original clause. Instead, he decided to wait for the briefing from Foot, when he had removed the 'wrinkles' from the contracts.

On Thursday, Foot had also received the success fee contracts from Albion's lawyers, fully attested by Gallant and Caledonia. Foot was completely happy with the document, which spelt out the payments to Travers and his two executive colleagues, the tasks and conditions they were expected to fulfil in bringing the company to an executed trade sale or buyout, and the time and mode of payment, including bank account co-ordinates. The draft had been returned, and they now awaited the signed and sealed originals for their signatures. Albion also wanted Travers and his team to sign a separate confidentiality agreement concerning the success fees, to make sure they were all gagged about what was happening.

On Friday, Amanda Beresford had delivered her first draft of the Information Memorandum. Some sixty pages long, beautifully bound and complete with the Goldberg crest on its cover, a quarter of its content was narrative, and three quarters endless financial schedules. Travers had to admit it looked impressive, but it was a dry document. It failed to record the conversion of a well constructed strategy six or seven years ago into the strong and profitable commercial success that was the hallmark of Sunburst at the current time.

Not that Travers was too offended. The document assumed a stance that the company had a string of lucky successes with new products, but that its core business must remain vulnerable to the economies of scale of the larger producers. That was fine by Travers, and he hoped it would temper the bids by third parties. Travers knew, however, that the popular tenet of 'Critical Mass', that volume scale was everything, meant nothing without the lowest unit cost. The sheer profligacy of the larger international companies beyond the shop floor, through the benchmarking comparisons he had undertaken, meant that Travers could maintain overall lowest cost operator status, even in the commodity end of the business, and from lower volumes than the internationals enjoyed.

Travers was particularly pleased that Amanda had raised the absence of supply agreements in the 'on' trade, in other words with the brewers, as a weakness of current trading. No supply agreements were in place, so her document said, the company relying on its shareholders to maintain volume. The inference was that once the brewers had sold down their shareholding in Sunburst, the business and its brands might fall apart in the 'on' trade. Clearly Amanda was unaware of the rollover arrangements Travers had agreed with the regional brewers, or the five year supply agreements with the three major brewers that Ogden and his team were developing. No mention was made of the competitive strength of the brands themselves, or the strong trading levels with brewers who were non-shareholders. Amanda must have been aware of all this, but throughout the document he noted a caution in detailing anything that could be construed as hyperbole, or not absolutely verifiable.

From Travers' perspective, the final damning observation of the Memorandum, was an extremely large question mark over the duty regime Sunburst had secured for its alcoholic pop concoctions. Because they were using industrial alcohols approved for beverage use, as opposed to brewed alcohol, Travers had secured a new class of duty treatment from Customs and Excise that fell between the very low level of cider duty and that of beer. He had been delighted, because this level of duty was one tenth of what it could have been, had customs applied wine duty to the products. The Memorandum queried the durability of this arrangement, a comment that Travers felt was completely groundless, but would nevertheless set the hares running.

Amanda had asked Travers and his colleagues to study the document over the coming weekend, so that a review meeting could be held on Monday with Geoffrey Levin. By the close of play on Friday, Travers had already warned his colleagues to keep their mouths shut on Monday, unless they found something that was departmentally incorrect in the Memorandum. It was not their document, and they must all sink their pride in terms of the dispassionate and analytically dubious treatment the company had received at the hands of Goldberg's. It might ultimately save them ten or twenty million on the purchase price.

Over the weekend the weather depressions that had lashed the country the previous week had sped off into the North Sea to be replaced by a ridge of high pressure that brought cold and frosty conditions, but a welcome return of clear skies and sunshine. As Travers drove to work on the

Monday morning he was pleased to hear that the high pressure would remain for the week, with bright sunny periods and cold frosts. Things must be looking up, he thought.

The meeting with Goldberg's was scheduled for ten, and was underway on time. Levin sat alongside Amanda and got the discussion going.

'Gentlemen,' said Levin, 'both Amanda and I have been very pleased at the level of co-operation we have received from you and your colleagues throughout the business in the preparation of the Information Memorandum. Unlike estate agents, our biggest concern is accuracy rather than opinion, which we leave to potential buyers to assess for themselves. With your help, Amanda has, I think, drafted an excellent document, which once approved by the shareholders this week, will be distributed to interested parties. Now, this morning I want to work through the document section by section, just to ensure we haven't made any blindingly obvious errors or omissions.'

'I agree,' said Travers, 'that Amanda has written a first class document that should serve your purposes. The three of us have had a chance to study it over the weekend, and there are a few comments, which we can discuss when you get to them. If you lead, we'll follow.'

Levin proceeded to work through the document, looking for comments from the management. Travers suggested that the background to the company and its strategy was thin, but perfectly understood the need for brevity. And so it went, through the narrative, until Levin reached the section concerning supply agreements.

'Now, I understand,' said Levin, 'from a conversation with both Simon Spencer and Piers Tomlinson on Friday, that discussions are nearly complete regarding the implementation of supply agreements after the trade sale?' Bugger, thought Travers.

'Yes, Geoffrey,' said Travers, 'that's one of my comments. I think there should be something in here about the progress we've made so far on that subject. Nevertheless, you mustn't expect to see anything in place until after the sale. If, for example, another *brewer* tried to buy Sunburst, I'm sure the current shareholders wouldn't want supply agreements in place that positively helped their competitor to get ahead. I've already covered that possibility with the shareholders, and they agree. Probably then, the best you could put in here, is that supply agreements *may* be negotiated after the sale and as part of the completion process.'

'Oh, I think we must have something stronger than that,' said Levin.

'Up to you of course,' said Travers. 'Depends on whether you put a direct competitor, in other words another brewer, into the sale process. Are you planning to do that?'

Levin shuffled uncomfortably in his seat. 'To be honest, Tom, you have to know sooner or later, and I was going to discuss this later, but we have four indications of immediate interest, and one of those is a brewer. If we get the Memorandum approved in the next day or two, some of them could be visiting by the end of the week, and we'll need you to see them. You'll see no one less than the managing director of each bidder.'

'Well,' said Travers, 'I'm both surprised and relieved. Relieved that you're pushing ahead and we can get this thing over with, but surprised that the ink isn't even dry on the Information Memorandum.'

'You wouldn't expect us to sit on our hands over the last three weeks,' said Levin. 'Most of these people already know an awful lot about you, but won't really need detailed information until round two, when we'll set up a proper information room for them to clamber over the details themselves. The Memorandum is only really intended as a thumbnail sketch.' Travers nodded his understanding, and the meeting progressed.

'What about this duty treatment, Tom? Could it go wrong?' said Levin.

'Well, yes, I suppose so. The thing is, customs know these products have gone through the roof in sales terms, but not as a function of price and their lower duty level. We make a huge profit margin on their premium pricing. Customs may well believe they're entitled to a larger slice of the cake and raise the duty level next March. But that's a lottery, I'm afraid.'

'You know, of course,' said Levin, 'that the brewers have been lobbying very hard to have that rate of duty increased? They see it as unfair competition against beer.'

'Indeed I do, Geoffrey. And they are very powerful lobbyists, both with customs, and in The House. You may well be right.'

Travers was pleased to play along with Levin's doubts. The reality was that there was no love lost between customs and the brewers, not least because of the brewers' activities with MPs in Parliament, paying them to lobby for lower beer duty and sod the other alcoholic drink producers. The brewers' arrogance infuriated the customs hierarchy and the Paymaster General whom they reported to. As a result, Travers had an undertaking from them that they would never stifle his attempt at competition with the brewers, without at least a period of three years' derogation before implementing any change to the relativities with beer duty, which would allow Travers time to either alter his margin structure, or take an increase in duty on the nose. None of this could be committed to writing, but Travers had already arranged an interview for Giddings at customs, to hear the same view 'from the horse's mouth'.

'So,' said Levin, 'an increase in duty could kill these

products off, which, by the way, produce twenty per cent of your net profit?'

'I suppose it's possible,' said Travers. They continued to work through the document, in particular the sections covering the sales forecasts and cash flows for the next five years, the Sunburst executives raising only small issues of detail, which were factually incorrect.

When they had finished, Levin leant back:

'Thank you, gentlemen. That's been most valuable and I'm very grateful to you. Now let's just talk about the sequence of events from here. As I've said, we may be able to arrange visits from interested parties towards the end of this week. In the strictest confidence, and not to go beyond this room, we have, as I've said, four runners. Having done the trawl already, we really don't expect any more, but you never know, someone may come out of the woodwork from the limited distribution of this.' Levin held up the Memorandum. 'We have a brewer, a UK soft drink producer and wholesaler, a US soft drink company, and a financial buyer.'

'What d'you mean financial buyer?' said Travers.

'A venture capital fund, who will either ask you and the rest of the employees to run the business for them, or they'll parachute in a management team to take over from you. I have sanctioned them to give you a call before they come down, to quiz you Tom, on whether you'd be interested in supporting them if they win the bid.'

'Do they know,' said Travers, 'that we're mounting our own MBO?'

'Yes, we finally decided that your activity must be disclosed, even though you would not take part in the early bidding. I don't think that changes anything for them. They would hope to offer at least the same as you're getting from your existing backers, and you'd get a result in round two instead of after. Even if you don't join them, they may, as I've said, go ahead and replace you if they win. You need to think about it, discuss it with them, and let us know.' Levin said all of this in an emotionless and abstract way, such that it was but a small decision for Travers to make. In reality, Travers knew it might change their whole approach if they were to side with this new venture capital outfit. He'd better discuss it with Morris at Wessex as soon as he could.

'I see,' said Travers. 'And has this brewer got any other soft drink interests at all?'

'That's for you to ask, and for them to tell. I can't say any more,' said Levin.

'And the American cola company is the one we think it is?'

'No. Funnily enough, it's not. It makes a disgusting concoction that's put it into the number five slot in the US, and which is not sold here. They want to buy a distribution vehicle over here, and they think Sunburst can provide it.'

'But what happened to the big guys?' said an astonished Travers.

'They don't want your commodities or production lines, and they're confident they can develop their own premium brands. In other words, Tom, they probably intend to rip you off and copy everything you've got,' said a rather smug Levin.

'Well they've singularly failed in the last five years, but I'm still surprised they're not in. I sincerely hope, Geoffrey, they won't be receiving a copy of the Information. That's highly confidential and sensitive commercial information that could do us a lot of harm in competitors' hands, especially if they've said no.'

'Don't worry, Tom, they won't get a copy, or any of the others either, we're not novices at this game you know. Now, I think we've covered everything. I'll be in touch with you later in the week. But please keep Thursday and Friday open, all three of you please.'

'OK,' said Travers. 'But one more thing on our MBO. Is the letter of comfort concerning fund backing from Maxwell Griffin and Wessex Bank sufficient evidence of wherewithal for the shareholders?'

"Yes, it all looks kosher, Tom. Well done, you're over the first hurdle, always nice to have hard evidence of backing.' Travers nodded, and stood from his chair, thanked Levin, and gave Amanda a special thanks for all her hard work.

'I'll be here for a week or two yet, Tom,' she said. 'I'll be sitting on your shoulder during all buyer visits, and I have to prepare more information for round two, when we get there. You haven't seen the back of me yet.' Travers smiled at her, then led Levin off into reception and away. All in all, Travers was delighted with the meeting and that the Information Memorandum remained woolly and vague on two key operational subjects, supply agreements and duty. It was now down to him to gently put the boot in when the visitors arrived.

His brain was now spinning with the identity of the brewer, and the UK soft drink producer. He knew the American company, and they were a real wild card. They were obviously looking for a European manufacturing base for their leading brand, and had presumably deduced that the acquisition of Sunburst would give them a fast start as a manufacturing and marketing base. The price could go through the roof if they really wanted the business, but they would need local management, so maybe Travers and his team could seem lukewarm or even hostile, and put them off. He had to be careful though; he and his colleagues were certainly not irreplaceable, and he could end up in court if he didn't expedite the shareholders' instructions. And what of this financial buyer? Who the hell were they, and why hadn't he picked them up earlier? Maybe he should talk to Wessex and Maxwells about it. It would certainly upset Maxwells, knowing there may be another backer in the wings ready to go, but at the same time, maybe they could find out who it was. Fascinating. At last things were hotting up.

Having returned to his office, Travers asked Chris that he not be disturbed, and proceeded to draw a matrix of the interested parties, and fill in as many possibilities as he could. He needed more information, and one of the first things to do was to put Amanda on the spot. The identity of the financial buyer and the brewer were uppermost in his mind. The UK soft drink producer was probably Clements & Sons, who had made vague approaches to Travers in the past. They were a hotchpotch of a company, who, because of the weakness of their brands, had attempted to control the supply chain by developing the wholesale side of their business, particularly to the 'on' trade. It was, and always would be, a bankrupt strategy. Travers failed to understand how they thought they could be successful wholesalers to the 'on' trade, and sell their brands to the brewers. The brewers themselves were the biggest wholesalers to the entire 'on' trade, and simply saw Clements as annoying low grade competition, who must inevitably be squeezed out. Clements' approach was an act of desperation, thought Travers, but dangerous, because of that. But could they raise top dollar on the basis of their balance sheet? He doubted it.

As to the brewer, could it possibly be Rupert Holmes of the Blackburn Brewery? He had, after all, asked Amanda on the Clutton Estate shoot to send him details. But surely, thought Travers, that was all bluff and bluster. Where on earth were the synergies of tagging a national soft drinks company on to the back end of a regional brewer? Didn't make sense. But, just maybe Holmes was arrogant and loony enough to have a go? But sixty or seventy million to buy it? Surely he could never raise that much, thought Travers. Then again, it might be someone much bigger, maybe even a national brewer who was not currently a shareholder. Mulligans, the Irish stout producer, were attempting to break out of the beer strait-jacket, and had launched various non-alcoholic concoctions through the 'off' trade, with varying degrees of success. Their major problem, with a range of stout, ales and lagers, was that outside of Ireland they were head to head with the British brewers, who of course controlled the pubs. Perhaps by moving into soft drinks it would be seen as a non-threatening move by the UK brewers, and Mulligans would then benefit from the already well developed distribution channels to the 'on' trade provided by their stout. It was certainly a distinct possibility.

Then the US cola company. They could outbid anybody if they wanted the business. No question. But could they parachute in an American team to run Sunburst if Travers was uncooperative? Possible, but unlikely. The quickest way to buy a 'pig-in-a-poke' would be to buy overseas without the benefit of committed local management who understood the market-place. There was one upside, however, in Travers' thinking. If they were keen to keep Travers and the team, he could see himself negotiating a million plus remuneration package over a two year period for himself, and a fancy deal for the others. Wouldn't exactly land him in Carey Street if he joined forces with the Americans, and the employees would be safe too. He needed to think more about that option before kicking it into touch.

Travers looked at his watch. Nearly lunchtime. He wandered down the corridor and found Amanda in her office.

'Well, well,' she said with a cynical smile. 'I was wondering when I would get the benefit of your presence, Mr Travers. And no, I'm not telling you anything.' Her smile lingered, but then she returned to the papers she was studying.

'Amanda, there really is no need to be so aggressive,' said Travers. 'I've come here to take you to lunch at our wonderful local, and all I get is abuse. Come on, take a break, grab a coat, my carriage awaits.' Travers stood by the door, his arm outstretched in the direction of the car-park.

She looked up at Travers through the fallen shroud of blonde hair, looked at her watch and said with a smile, 'Fall for it every time. OK but treat me gently, Tom, I'm really not meant to give you any help.'

'Help? Who mentioned help? Amanda, I want information, that's all. I'm going to know everything at the end of the week, I just want to know a couple of things a bit earlier, that's all. Don't be such a grouch. And you know I'd always treat you gently. You're my very favourite merchant banker.' She chuckled, stood up and retrieved her jacket from the back of the chair. For once, Travers was able to appreciate her tall figure, as she swung the jacket around her shoulders putting one arm in, then the other. Her tight white blouse clearly outlined her bra and her full breasts, and she caught his look. For the first time in years, Travers flushed like a schoolboy, and instantly averted his eyes. He hoped she wasn't offended by the stare.

'Honestly,' she said with a smile, 'how old are you, Tom?'

'Never too old to appreciate beauty. Sorry about that. Very rude. Won't happen again.' He ushered her out of the room.

When they got to the pub, Travers found a corner table, and they agreed on a simple sandwich each, with fruit juice. When he returned to the table, Travers said, 'Amanda, do you think I've got any chance at all with this MBO?'

She sighed and looked at her drink. 'Not if Geoffrey has anything to do with it. He sees management as getting in the way of a clean deal, complicating things, hiding relevant facts, putting off the bidders. But then, you know that. Personally, I really hope you do get it. You've built this business, and you know where you want to take it. The employees respect you, and under your leadership I don't doubt you can float it. You could be a very rich man as a result, and so could your shareholders. You also deserve it, and it really would be wonderful to see you do it. But, it's David and Goliath. I can't see how, on conventional valuation, you could put more in the pot than a strategic buyer, who can cut and splice with his own brands and extract the cost savings that you just can't make. The fact is they can get a satisfactory return at a far higher price than you could.'

'Hmm,' said Travers. 'But maybe they don't appreciate the intrinsic value of the business in the first place. Obviously if I can find ways of extracting more profit in the future, then maybe I can justify a higher price than them. Strikes me, there's everything to play for.'

'Tom, I don't doubt it, and I do know the rules of the game you're playing. That's the advantage management will always have over consultants like us, and other third party bidders. As long as you don't withhold information, or deliberately deceive, you are in fact pushing the price up because you know what's locked up inside. Just don't over do it. Most MBOs come seriously unstuck when the forecasts turn into dreamworld, and the banking covenants are breached. First your equity will disappear to the banks, and then they could screw you on false warranties about the condition of the business. I suppose you know the risks.'

'My God, girl, you'll have me cutting my throat next. Now look, please tell me who the brewer is. Scout's honour this only goes as far as me. It's not Blackburn, is it?'

'No, no.' She smiled. She looked Travers in the face. 'I trust you not to repeat it, but you'll know on Thursday anyway. It's Mulligans.'

'Shit,' said Travers, 'they're big. Suppose it makes sense for them to extract more value out of their distribution channels in the "on" and "off" trade.'

'Hole in one,' said Amanda without emotion. 'And don't forget Ireland. They practically own the place. A soft drink range complete with the alcoholic fruit pops would probably go down a storm. And don't forget, they're just down the road from you.' Travers nodded, picking up Amanda's reference to the Mulligan stout brewery in Acton, which was a vast and under-utilised facility built in the thirties. His brain was whizzing now. He knew the UK managing director of Mulligans, and had shot with him several times. Nice enough fellow, but not quite the dynamite they seemed to breed from the head office in Dublin. He looked a thinker as opposed to a doer, which Travers felt was probably right for Mulligans in the face of tricky competitive pressures from the British brewers.

'OK, Amanda, thanks. Now what about this financial buyer?'

'No, no, no. Not telling you,' she said, flicking the hair from her forehead. You'll have to wait for them to contact you. If I told you, and you told your backers, it'd be round the City in five minutes. Sorry.'

'But how can they just jump into the ring with no management support? They're flying blind, and with none of the cost synergies of the trade buyers. I just don't see what chance they've got without an inside track from the management.'

'You might be right,' said Amanda. 'But normally, they can either pick up the management later and give them a little sweetener in terms of equity, or drop a team in. Just as often, they're there to break up the business and sell on the parts, or to use it as a vehicle for other acquisitions. There's so much money on the loose in venture capital nowadays, they're like bookies, place a bet on anything.'

'So because I didn't take the deal to them, whoever they are, you think they'd offer management bugger all?'

'That would be par for the course,' said Amanda, slowly nodding her head. Great, thought Travers, another bunch of bandits.

'Finally, then, we have to be talking Clements, as the UK soft drink producer?'

'Correctimundo,' said Amanda, taking another bite of her sandwich.

'But surely they can't go to their shareholders for a Rights Issue. They're only capitalised at fifty million, and it's such a shaky business, the banks wouldn't lend them the money, would they?'

'Don't know,' said Amanda, 'but if they really want to get into round two, they'd have to produce an underwritten bid, same as you.' Travers nodded. He almost thought he could write off Clements, no one would be foolish enough to support them.

'What's your own view about price, Amanda?' said Travers tentatively.

'Impossible to tell, Tom, it really is. All in the eye of the beholder, and all that. Could go for sixty, could go for ninety.'

'Well yes, I know that,' said Travers, 'but you must have talked about a realistic figure with the shareholders, what's the ballpark?'

'Well, they've got to sell, and there's clearly not a floor, because they all bought in years ago for peanuts. I'd say a realistic minimum is sixty, which let's face it, Tom, is an exit P/E of six even on your deflated profits. I really don't think it could drop any lower, commodity products or not.'

'Well, as ever, Amanda, I'm indebted to you.' He leant across and gave her a quick kiss on the lips. She was flustered and embarrassed.

'You are a swine,' she said angrily. 'Your only interest is information. You mustn't do that! Good thing I like you.'

'I'm sorry. Another mistake,' said Travers. 'And that's simply not true. I'm actually very fond of you, and that was just to show my appreciation. Please don't take it the wrong way. Look, I want us to be friends long after all this nonsense has gone away. Forget it, won't do it again. Forgive me?' She looked him in the eyes, and her anger slowly evaporated. Her hand moved to his on the table, and slowly tapped his knuckles with her fingers. She was about to say something, Travers could tell, but she withdrew again.

'Come on,' she said, 'time to get back.' He retrieved his keys from his pocket, and guided her to the door.

Later that afternoon, Travers received a call from the venture capital fund who were 'in the ring' for the bid. His name was Harry Markovitch, and he represented Citadel Venture Capital, an American banking conglomerate operating a venture capital fund in the UK.

'Now Mr Travers,' he said with an American drawl, 'we're considering a bid for your company, and I'd like to know how you'd feel about working with us. If we can work something out, we need to get together real soon to look behind the numbers. We're giving you the chance to keep running your company, Mr Travers, I guess you could say we're your guardian angel. Goldberg's do know of our approach to you.'

'What've you got in mind?' said Travers coldly.

'Well,' said Markovitch, 'that we get together, say this week and...'

'No,' said Travers. 'I mean, what's in it for management,

what's the equity participation you're offering me and my management?'

'Oh, well it's difficult to discuss that sort of detail at this stage. But rest assured there could be nine or ten per cent if the numbers look right. We like to incentivise our partners.'

'Listen, chum, I think you're wasting your time. Unless the figure has two digits, and the first one starts with a two, I'm not even remotely interested. We are, as you well know, mounting our own MBO, and unless you can beat that figure, let's forget it. Good luck, and if you've got the right number, give me a call, you know where I am.' Travers put the telephone down. God, how he hated arrogant Americans.

He then picked up the phone to Giddings at Maxwell Griffin.

'Anthony. Tom. Thought I'd tell you I've been approached by Citadel, who apparently are making a sighting shot in round one. I don't mind a bit if you have a word with Amanda to confirm what I'm saying. The point is, they're trying to woo my support with a very attractive offer, because I think they understand they're not going to get very far without an inside track. Because you and John Brown have played the white man over the shareholding for management, I want you to know I've told Citadel I'm not interested. A deal is a deal, and I want all of you at Maxwell's to log that. Obviously, it would have allowed me to get straight into round two, but so long as you keep playing straight, I'm sticking with you.'

'Tom, I don't know what to say, that really is very good of you. It's nice to know you'll stick with our partnership, which of course we will too, no more nonsense, I promise. But Citadel, you say? Well, well. Loads of money and no where to put it. They're very new over here and they're already muddying the pitch with silly deals. I'm glad you gave them short shrift. What did they offer you?'

'Best not to ask,' said Travers. 'As you say, loads of money, and they wanted a fast start on this one with us, the management. Let's just say you'd have been embarrassed.'

'What d'you think they'll do now?' said Giddings.

'My guess is they'll still go ahead and put in a silly figure for round one, just to keep in the game. After that, they might come back to me again and have another go. But I do think the shareholders have got to be careful. If Sunburst did go to an outfit like Citadel, and they simply break it up and lay everybody off, the PR would be a nightmare. Big bad brewers, and all that, taking the money and running. It's something I may be able to work on with Spencer and Sir Brian at Gallant and Albion. They're very sensitive about their image at the moment.'

'Good, good, Tom. Well thanks again for telling me. You've done the right thing and you won't regret it.'

Travers came off the phone and meditated. There were so many balls in the air, he was worried about dropping one. He looked through his 'bible', the A4 notebook he always carried, and made yet another updated 'to do' list. It then occurred to him, that he hadn't spoken to Jane since their assignation at the Cadogan last Tuesday, nearly a week ago. He had told her not to use her house phone or her mobile to contact him, just in case her husband examined the telephone bills, and the same number kept reappearing, which could blow the whistle on them. That restricted her ability to contact him, but he had told her wherever she could get to a phone, it was perfectly safe to leave a message at Holland Park, or West Lodge at weekends. There was no one to intercept the calls at Travers' end. But nothing. Perhaps her ardour was waning? The release from Newgent's strait-jacket may have gone to her head; heaven knows what she might be up to. Should he telephone her? It could be tricky if she didn't answer the phone, and somebody else did. Then if he put the phone down, whoever had picked it up could do 1471 and find out who it was, unless of course, he called from a public phone box. He didn't feel good about it. She wore her heart on her sleeve, and yet no contact for nearly a week. She must be going off the idea, or maybe found someone else to enjoy her new found freedom? All sorts of irrational thoughts were now racing through his head, but he did need to know. He looked at his watch: four o'clock. Nothing more to do today that wouldn't wait, and he decided to leave.

Parking his car outside Holland Park, he walked to the end of the road to the telephone box. It was four thirty, and Bobby Newgent should still be at work, he hoped. He retrieved the number from his diary and phoned the number. It was ringing, but no one answered it yet. Then at last, a strident 'Hello?' on the other end of the line.

'Jane? Jane, is that you?' said Travers nervously.

'Tom,' she said finally, and quietly, 'it's good of you to call.'

'What's the matter, Jane, you don't sound right, is there anything wrong?'

'Of course, you've no idea,' said Jane breathlessly, and perhaps tearfully, thought Travers. 'Tom, Bobby's had a heart attack over the weekend. We've managed to get him into Harefield. It's touch and go. It's all my fault. Tom, I feel so guilty. What if he dies, what shall I tell the girls?'

'Calm down, sweetheart, please,' said Travers. 'What d'you mean it's your fault, that's nonsense.'

'He'd do anything to keep me, Tom. He doesn't want me to be unhappy, and he really has been so sweet over the last few weeks. But it's killed him, Tom, it's killed him. It's just eaten away at him, and killed him.'

'Don't be silly, Jane,' said Travers pleadingly. 'He's not dead and he's had a heart attack. That's not your fault. Probably genetic. How old was he anyway?'

'That's the thing! He's only forty-five! No one can believe it, and why? Because I drove him to it. All his worst fears, it just ate away at him, and it's my fault.'

'You haven't told him, for Christ's sake!' said Travers.

'No, no. But that's all you think about isn't it? Have I dropped you in it or not? God, you're a bastard, Tom, I should never have done it, look what's happened.'

'Jane, that's a terrible thing to say, and you know it's not true. I honestly thought you had no feelings for him, and we did make the running together, you know. But what happens now, what d'you want to do, and is there anything I can do? Hang on, let me put some more money in.' Travers loaded in another three one pound coins.

'Oh, I'm sorry, Tom. I do love you, but I didn't want it to turn out this way. I'd never forgive myself. What I must do is look after him, if it's not too late. The girls are due back from school today, the housekeeper's husband has gone to get them. I'm sorry Tom, I can't see you any more; it's all been a mistake.'

'Well, I'm sorry if that's how you feel. But of course, it's up to you. I've a feeling you'll feel differently in a month's time when he pulls through. They'll probably stick a pig valve in him and he'll be right as rain.'

'Oh I do hope so, Tom. But look, I must go. More things to take to the hospital, and it's such a long way. Thank God my brother's around. I wouldn't have been able to cope without him.'

'All right Jane, I'll go now. But you do promise to phone as soon as you can? I do care for you despite what you think now, and I want the best for you. Do get in touch when you can.'

He rang off and slumped against the door of the

telephone box. He would never understand women. Years of verbal abuse and practical captivity, and now he's about to snuff it, she's back all over him. Still, even Travers wouldn't wish him to die, despite being an absolute bastard. Oh well, he told himself, it was all part of life's rich pattern, and maybe the muse, or fate, was sticking an oar in. After all, it could be for the best. But the lovemaking! What a shame. She was so exciting, so erotic. What a bloody shame, he thought to himself. He pushed open the door to the box and walked slowly in the cold darkening air, back towards the house. The rush of the traffic a few yards behind him, against the cold silence of his house ahead of him, made him suddenly feel very, very lonely. He was wrapped up in this chase for Sunburst, but what for? He had no one to share it with, no one to spoil if he won; no one's shoulder to cry on if he lost. And would anyone thank him if he did win? Unlikely, he thought, just more demands from the employees, with the banks crawling all over him, waiting for him to trip. What was it they said about the banks? Can't wait to loan you an umbrella in the sunshine, but instantly repossess it when it rains. For maybe the first time, Travers recognised he could rely on no one but himself. Success or failure was down to him, and no one else. He walked back in to the house, aimlessly. Bugger it, he thought, no more papers tonight, he'd just sit back and watch the box, and send for a pizza.

On Thursday morning, he was awaiting two meetings. Yesterday, Levin had told him the shareholders had approved the Information Memorandum, and the details would be sent out. Today, Goldberg's were making a fast start, and two of the prospective bidders would meet him. First, the managing director of Mulligans UK, and this afternoon, The Southern States Soda Drink Corporation of Mobile, USA.

Travers was strangely relaxed. He saw his job as giving away as little as he could without being hostile. Both might probably offer him a job, which he must listen to, because otherwise he could be on the dole with no immediate prospects of employment. But he didn't have to impress, why should he? Anyone who cared could see his achievements over the last ten years, and if they didn't, he wouldn't work for them anyway. He had enough cash reserves to keep everything going for two to three years, so at worst the world was still his oyster. In fact he was feeling positively chipper, and was intrigued how each of these prospective buyers would set about questioning him, without yet having studied the Memorandum.

At ten to eleven Amanda knocked on his door and said, 'Ten minutes to go. May I come in?' Travers gave her a warm smile, and ushered her in with his hand.

'Coffee? Ask Chris to make a fresh brew will you, Amanda?' said Travers, as he walked over to the coffee table and armchairs that would serve for the interviews. Amanda would of course be in attendance to monitor the discussions, and ensure that Travers didn't rubbish the company. Funny, thought Travers, it's like being a criminal at a parole board. She reappeared with notepads and copies of the Memorandum, and took a seat.

'Sorry to put you through this,' said Amanda apologetically, 'but it's absolutely standard procedure.'

'Don't mind a bit, old thing. Glad to have you along if the conversation lags. Remember though, I know John Frobisher from the shooting circuit, and in the past we've discussed some joint ventures that didn't make it. So we're reasonably well acquainted.' She nodded, understanding, but still looked uncomfortable. 'Found anyone new to put in the frame?' said Travers. She shook her head, opened a notepad and began writing some notes. Travers casually studied her, watching as the swatch of blonde hair again fell over her face. 'It's so cute,' he said, 'but it would drive me mad.' He leant forward and flicked her hair with his finger, smiling. 'Doesn't it annoy you?' he said pleasantly. She leant back a little, and flushed, then looking over to him she smiled and flicked the hair from her eye, and then looked down again to her notebook, whereupon her hair promptly fell down again.

'I don't notice it. Don't worry, it's the price of fame for us "It" girls.' She was rather pleased with her repartee, and flashed him another smile, before returning to her notepad.

On the spur of the moment, Travers said to her, 'Oh, by the way, I've managed to get a pair of tickets for a new show in town, next Tuesday night I think. Do say you'll come?'

She looked up at him with her mouth slightly open. 'Sorry, what?' she said, surprised.

'Theatre and dinner, next Tuesday night. Best seats. Thought you'd appreciate a break. Do please say yes?'

'I, I don't know. You keep taking me places when you shouldn't. I don't know. But it's very kind of you, I don't know what to say.'

'Do stop worrying, Amanda. That's a date then. Pack a frock at the weekend and bring it with you on Monday. I'll pick you up from the hotel on Tuesday evening, say six thirty?' At that moment, Chris brought in a tray of fresh coffee with three cups and saucers on it, setting it down on the coffee table.

'Mr Frobisher's in reception, Tom,' said Chris. 'Shall I go and get him now?' He thanked her and nodded, and she left the room.

Amanda hadn't answered Travers, but he took her acceptance for granted and said, 'Oh well, here we go, wonder what the size of their purse is? I feel like a pimp.' He spoke with a touch of bitterness.

Chris led Frobisher into Travers' office, and everyone stood. Travers gave him a hale and hearty welcome, introducing Amanda, whom he had met before in the City, and ushered him to a seat, between himself and Amanda.

'Well, John, this young lady is here to check I don't tell porkies, but anyway, fire away, what can I tell you?'

Frobisher was a studious looking man, with neat greying hair, spectacles, dapper pinstripe, probably about fifty-five. He leant forward in his chair, thought for a moment, then looked at Travers and in a gentle tone said:

"This must all be a dreadful shock for you, Tom, like vultures around the corpse. I can imagine what you must feel like, after putting your heart and soul into this place. Just remember, though, I'm here to discuss a new beginning for Sunburst, not an end. I've watched you over the last ten years, and every achievement of the company is, I know, down to you. I hope your shareholders are grateful. If this business is for sale, we want to buy it, and we want you to run it. The rest, to a certain extent, is detail. But I suspect I don't need to tell you how we could expand this business, and how it dovetails into what we're trying to do. With your help, it could be a perfect fit. I know you're having a tilt at MBO, and good luck to you. If that doesn't work, all I'm saying is that we want you to keep running it for us, along with your team. Think for a moment, Tom, about the opportunities it could open up for your career. Sunburst is one thing, Mulligans may be another. It's a big firm and we're always looking for talent. Make a go of Sunburst under our ownership, and who knows where you may end up. What d'you think about that?'

Frobisher struck Travers as probably a genuinely nice

man. He'd heard good reports about Frobisher, who was clearly a strategy man as opposed to a street fighter. He had some excellent people working for him, and Travers felt they could probably work together. But Mulligans was now a monolith in the industry. It had an international presence around the globe, and Travers hadn't particularly enjoyed his early marketing career with the big companies. Other mysterious people called the shots, inertia could be painful, and everyone passed the buck. The idea that some grey figure in Dublin could be telling him how to run the business was not an attractive prospect.

'Of course I'm interested, John. This place, as you say, has been my life over the last ten years, and if I can't buy it, I've got two choices: continue to build it with someone I trust, or get out, and do something different. It's a bit early yet though to say what may happen.'

'Of course, I understand, I understand. Could you trust Mulligans? Do you think we could work together to build the business?' said Frobisher, in his gentle enquiring way.

'Put it this way John, from what I know about you and Mulligans, I would put you ahead of most other employers in the industry. But neither you nor I dictate what happens at head office in Dublin. Clearly if you did win, and you were still offering something, I'd want to hear it from the horse's mouth, so to speak, before jumping.'

'Absolutely, couldn't have put it better myself. And of course that is exactly what would happen. All I need to know now is that if we win this auction, and we offer the right package and the rest of it, you'll seriously consider my offer. Is that fair?'

'Yep. It is,' said Travers. 'But what you haven't yet told me, John, is what your plans are for the employees. Your brewery is about four miles down the road, and it could gobble up Sunburst twice over. Would you close Willesden?'

'Tom, you know as well as I do, that's impossible to

know at this stage. Productivity and efficiency rule our lives, and there's no escape, no easy option. Your guess would be as good as mine – what would you do?'

'I'd close it, you'd have to. Got to be two million a year cost saving if you already have the sunk costs of plant and equipment, which I'm pretty sure you do. But let's not forget, John, I have a statutory duty both to the shareholders *and* the employees. I can meet both best with an MBO.'

'Yes, yes, no argument. But frankly, Tom, you've just said it, what hope have you really got if I've got two million cost saving from the shop floor, and probably another million from the sales force, not to mention marketing. If this business goes for a P/E of eight, I can already afford to outbid you by twenty million. I don't want to disappoint you, but facts are facts.'

Travers could only nod. That's all he could do against the irrefutable logic that Frobisher was expounding. Thank heavens, thought Travers, he doesn't yet know how much real profit lurks in the accounts.

'Well look, it's your turn,' said Travers. 'What else can I tell you?'

'Not a lot, Tom. We *will* be in round two next week or the week after,' said Frobisher, looking at Amanda. 'And then we'll camp in the information room before a binding bid. The only thing that really worries me is the duty treatment on your new drinks. I think customs will stuff you next March. It does rather draw a veil over your recent successes in that field.' Travers just raised his eyebrows and shrugged.

'I suppose you're in a better position than me to know the answer to that one. After all, you spend a lot more time at Kings Beam House than I do.' That address was the location of Customs and Excise on the south bank of the Thames. The two looked at each other, and Frobisher smiled.

'Quite so,' he said. 'All right. Can I now turn to the numbers and ask you to take me through a few things, from your point of view?' Frobisher was opening his copy of the Memorandum, and proceeded to ask some very perceptive questions concerning the alcoholic pop brands, research costs and capital expenditure. Travers knew he was after the qualitative decision-making that lies behind the numbers, as if to deduce the thought processes that had driven the company's growth. Frobisher patiently absorbed everything that Travers said, and an hour quickly whipped by.

'OK, good,' said Frobisher. 'No point taking up any more of your time, Tom. I'm very grateful indeed that you've got the right attitude about this, and I mean what I say. If we win, we want you to stay, and I'll fix a couple of days in Dublin as soon as I can. We'd make a great team.' They all rose, shook hands, and Travers took him to the door of the office and asked Chris to escort him down to reception. He turned to Amanda.

'Short and sweet. But he seems very keen,' said Travers.

'I think you should be very pleased,' said Amanda. 'He obviously wants you as part and parcel of the whole thing, and clearly respects what you've done here. You should be very flattered.'

'But the staff get the bullet, and I stay a paid employee, more than a few steps from where the decisions are really taken. And if I don't conform, I'm out. Can't say I'm enthralled. Oh well, but you're happy with how that went?' She nodded. He raised his hands. 'OK, Amanda, see you this afternoon at two for the Americans.' She smiled, picked up all her things and left.

When Chris returned, he asked her to get on the phone to the advertising agency and get hold of two tickets, best seats, for whatever was the hottest show in town on Tuesday. He then went off down the corridor in search of his colleagues, to tell them of the situation with Mulligans.

At two o'clock on the dot, two Americans were ushered into Travers' office by Chris. Travers was faintly amused by the characters standing in front of him. The first one was a small, thin, wiry man, maybe mid-fifties with spectacles, wearing a huge dark blue overcoat, over a typically American two-piece suit that had a funny sheen to it. Travers wondered whether it was a cashmere or angora blend, or maybe even some sort of dreadful plastic yarn. On his feet were a pair of huge black shiny Oxford shoes with enormous rubber soles, that must have been at least an inch thick. The second one was very different, apart from the overcoat. He was massive, greasy hair with sideburns, and a hooked nose. Probably the same sort of age. He reminded Travers of the Peter Sellers mafia character in one of the Clouseau films, minus the fedora. He had another shiny suit in a strange light blue colour, and a white shirt, which also seemed to reflect light.

'How *do* you do, Mr Travers,' said the short one, with the emphasis on the first part of the sentence. 'It's a real pleasure to meet you.' He walked forward with an arm extended.

The other chap was right at his heels. 'Mah name is Davis, George Davis, and ah am the Chief Operating Officer and President of the Southern States Soda Drink Corporation. Mah colleague right here is Sam Carluccio, Vice President in charge of Finance. We've come a long way to see your little operation, Mr Travers, an' I hope you don' mind us having a nose 'round. But if you don' mind, we'd rather not take our coats off, an' instead, we'd like to chat with you as we walk round the plant. That way we'll get to see twice as much. Now what d'you say to that, sir?' Travers smiled warmly at these two southern boys, shook their hands and introduced Amanda. He told them he was at their disposal, and whatever they wanted to do was fine by him. The two men were looking at Amanda.

'Young lady, it's cold out there, and it will not be necessary for you to accompany us. We'll take real good care of Mr Travers, fear not,' said Davis.

Amanda, equally disarmed by these two caricatures, smiled sweetly back, and in her finest Cheltenham accent replied, 'Not at all, Mr Davis, it's my job, you see. I'm quite happy in the fresh air.' She turned, picked up her notepad and waited expectantly by the door. The two Americans gave each other a frown, then the short one said: 'Very well, young lady, but you'll need a coat to keep warm, it's cold out there.'

Travers put his jacket on and said to Davis, 'Oh, I don't know, Mr Davis, it's sunny and crisp out there. I haven't got a coat with me anyway, and besides, we Brits are a hardy lot.'

The two Americans seemed equally bemused that anyone could venture outside in British weather without insulation, but dutifully followed Travers and Amanda. As they walked slowly across to the first of two large production warehouses, Davis said, 'We have a number of options, here in the UK, Mr Travers. Had you not been for sale, we might well be talking to you right now about some sort of distribution deal, to get us into your food stores and bars over here. So far, we ain't had success with that route, and I guess we have chosen the wrong people to work with. The other option we have is to buy an operation like yours, Mr Travers, get the benefit of local manufacturing and competitive pricing, and control what the hell goes on. That's why we're here today, of course. From what I can see, the logistics of your site are not good. You seem to have a mass of buildings here. Seems to me there's a lot of unnecessary movement on this site.'

'The company has been on this site since nineteen twenty-three, Mr Davis, but remember where we are. We're on the edge of London, with the main arterial routes to the north and west within five miles. The shape of the site makes it physically impossible to tear it all down and build an integrated manufacturing, stockholding and distribution centre from one building. Instead, we've used what we've got, re-clad to modern standards, and used covered moving trackways to get materials and finished product to where we want it to be around the site. It may look Heath Robinson, but it works. I suspect, too, we're using the very same equipment to bottle and can the products as you do, perhaps on a smaller scale.'

Travers showed them around the filling lines, then onto the finished goods warehouses. 'We're using the latest high lift, high density racking, with robots. As soon as our order system receives an instruction from the customer, it's automatically entered on the production schedules, it's picked, packed and invoiced all without human interference, and then the computer logs it on to the right vehicle to achieve the greatest payload and geographical delivery efficiency. It may not look pretty, but it works.'

The four of them spent about an hour going round the site, before returning to Travers' office. It was absolutely clear to Travers that these guys weren't interested in any of Sunburst's branded range of goods, but only in its manufacturing capabilities, as a UK base for their 'cough medicine' cola, which Travers doubted would ever appeal to British tastes.

When they were back in Travers' office, he said to them, 'Gentlemen, in all honesty it seems to me if you just want manufacturing I wouldn't start at Sunburst. Find yourself a greenfield site somewhere near Milton Keynes, get your people across to kit it out, and buy yourself a sales force. You'd be buying Sunburst on an earnings multiple of products you don't even want. You'd save at least half of what Sunburst will cost by setting up yourselves with exactly what you want, don't you agree, Amanda?'

She looked slightly flustered, but rising to the challenge, she said, 'I'm not sure I agree. Distribution to the right retail outlets is the key. You yourself always tell me distribution is nine tenths of the law. These gentlemen know how difficult it is to build distribution, even if they make it themselves over here. Sunburst gives them that distribution opportunity through existing channels, at a cost.'

Travers nodded, smiled at Amanda, then turned to the Americans.

'She makes a very good point. If that's what you want, I have a suggestion. Wait and see if I win the MBO. Then, we'll get together again, we'll strike a distribution and manufacturing deal, and I'll get your brand, guaranteed, into those outlets that account for ninety per cent of soft drink volume. Meanwhile, you can get on and plan a European production base, and take manufacturing back from me when you're ready. As long as I make fifteen per cent net margin on a five year rolling contract, and you pay for advertising, I'll do a great job for you. What d'you say?'

The big guy rippled his shoulders under his overcoat, and in a thick Manhattan accent said to his boss, 'That ain't such a bad idea, George. What the fuck do we know about British supermarkets? We're a long way from here, and I gotta think about the cash. Mister, er, Travers here makes good sense. Suck it an' see with a good partner makes sense to me. Then spend the cash.' He snorted by way of emphasis, and rolled his shoulders again. Travers leant back and almost had to restrain himself from laughing at the mafia style finance director, who kept reminding him of Peter Sellers.

Then Davis said, 'Young lady, ah apologise for my colleague's language there. Sam, I do keep telling you about that. We're in England now. But tell me, Mr Travers just what d'you think this business will sell for anyway?'

'You may ask,' said Travers pleasantly, 'but I couldn't possibly say. Amanda?'

'Well, I'm sorry,' she said, 'but that really is up to you. This is an auction, and value is relative to the buyer's needs as much as the earnings or asset value.'

'Couldn't have put it better myself,' said Travers.

'I just love the sound you two guys make. Real pretty. Ma wife is a real Anglophile. Such a pity she ain't here to hear you guys.' Davis then pondered his next move. 'Well, I guess we're going to have to contemplate our options, I'd say. We're heading back to the Dorchester right now, young lady, and our advisors over here will be in touch with you just as soon as they can. I like you, Mr Travers, I really do, and it's been mighty generous of you to show me around your fine business. Ah have to say though, ah am wrestling with the practicality of your dinky little site – it's all sorta squeezed in, no room to breathe. But ah have to admit you've done a fine job with your numbers. Impressive to say the least. Now you take care, y'hear?' The two men stood, and everybody shook hands. The two characters made their way down to the waiting limousine.

In the office, Travers turned to Amanda and laughed. 'What did you make of those two? What a scream. Are they for real? But it's ludicrous, Amanda – why on earth would they buy Sunburst? It'd be money down the drain.'

'It may be,' said Amanda in a rather schoolmistress-like way, 'but it's not up to you. I'd say you overstepped the mark, Tom. Their decision is nothing to do with you.'

'But, Amanda,' said Travers in a boyish way, 'you heard him. He said he had two potential routes: via distribution deal or acquisition. What he really needs is a decent partner to get him penetration of the market without getting burnt. All I did was to put a marker down if he doesn't bid, or he doesn't bid enough. What's wrong with that?'

'Geoffrey would not be pleased, Tom. The question is, should I tell him?'

'Oh come on, Amanda, don't be rotten. I've played the white man pretty well through all this, don't put the boot in – it could really muck things up. It was harmless. And anyway, if those two want to go ahead they will, no matter what I say. Please don't do anything silly?'

She gave a tut under her breath, and as she picked her things up, turned to Travers and said, 'Well, don't do it again, you'll get me into trouble.'

'Scout's Honour,' said Travers, smiling and giving her a salute. She was not amused. 'By the way,' he said, 'what happens now? I mean, what about Clements and this spivvy venture capital outfit?'

'Well, it seems,' said Amanda, 'that both will make a stab at round one, but neither are interested at this stage in looking around the place.'

'Sounds a bit cavalier to me. Are you sure they're really interested? Surely you have a look at the goods before you buy.'

'No,' she said, 'it wouldn't be unusual at this stage to leave inspections and the like until you can do it properly in round two. Mind you, they have to get there first. If they're not in the right ballpark, Geoffrey won't let them through. He keeps telling them that.'

'Oh does he?' said Travers. 'But all they have to do is put in a silly high figure to get to round two; they won't be held to it.'

'Doesn't quite work like that,' she said. 'Each of them is represented by merchant bank advisors. They have a reputation to keep. You can fall back from a figure, for all sorts of reasons, but if you cry wolf too often, no one believes you any more. So the opening bid must retain some relationship with round two, otherwise it's bad faith, and people get upset.' Travers was taking in all these pearls of wisdom.

'OK, and when do you make your mind up as to who goes through into round two?'

'If no one else appears from the distribution of the Memorandum, probably the end of next week.'

'And how long for round two?' he said.

'Depends on how many go through. Once they've done some diligence and put in a bid, if there's three or four of them, we'd tell them if they're off the mark. If it's two it's equally quick, you know, nudge and a wink, not enough, and so on. However, your shareholders may decide that someone has put in the right figure, they're safe and have got the money, and may just go for it. It's up to them. This is a private sale not a plc, and at the end of the day, your shareholders can play this any way they want.'

'OK, well thanks, Amanda, very useful. You are here all next week, aren't you?'

'Just can't stay away, Tom.' She smiled and left the room. He went to his desk and slumped in contemplation. Try as he might, he couldn't help feeling elated. Mentally, he'd written off Clements as a busted flush. Sure, they'd like to buy Sunburst to get themselves out of trouble, but as a public company they wouldn't be able to raise the money from their shareholders, and would the banks ever risk a one hundred per cent leverage on borrowing? He didn't think so. Citadel was a loose cannon, but how on earth would they achieve value on the deal? A new management team would take a year to get their feet under the table, and unless they already had a buyer for the Sunburst brands, where would be the value in breaking it up and selling it on? There was precious little value in the physical assets. As long as he held them off in refusing to participate, he couldn't see how they could win. Mulligans was clearly the biggest threat, and the most credible. Frobisher didn't bullshit, and he wouldn't be wasting his time unless he was serious. Travers knew he couldn't outbid them, but they did have this major hang up on duty, which Frobisher clearly thought could kill off Sunburst's alcoholic pop. Travers didn't agree, but realised all they had to do was to trip along to customs and ask, just as Travers had done. But just maybe, relations were so strained with customs, that they might think they wouldn't get an answer. So, left as it was, Mulligans would have to discount their price in anticipation of losing a big chunk of profit earning capacity from Sunburst.

And finally the Americans. Well, it occurred to Travers they didn't know what they wanted to do, and that buying Sunburst had a touch of wishful thinking attached to it. The 'grass is greener' syndrome had led a lot of companies into trouble, based on the false assumption that because it hadn't been tried before, it must be the right solution. But Davis seemed a wise old bird despite his rustic southern drawl, and surely he wouldn't buy something that had a basinful of products he didn't even want? On the other hand, buying Sunburst would be pocket money to them. And increasingly Americans were learning the creed of controlling their own destiny by ownership of distribution in overseas markets, rather than relying on distributors. Travers couldn't really rule them out yet. Not by a long chalk.

Chris came through on the phone. 'I've got Mr Davis on the line from The Southern Drinks Corporation. He's speaking from the Dorchester. Shall I put him through?'

Travers was surprised. 'Yes, Chris, how strange. Yes, put him on.'

'Hello, Tom. May I call you Tom? Are you on your own?' Davis's drawl was unmistakable.

'Yes, yes I am. You can only have just got back. What can I do for you?'

'Well, Miss Beresford is a pretty little thing, but sort o' got in the way. We know about your buyout shot, so we know if we want you, we gotta do somethin' special. She kinda made that difficult. Can I be frank with you?'

'Fire away,' said Travers.

'Well, it's like this, Tom. We've been chasin' our tails in the UK for too long. Your market's growing, and we're still nowhere. I can't afford to wait three years to build plants over there, and it still doesn't get me into the market-place. Now what I didn't say this afternoon is that my marketing guys like what you're doing with those new products of yours. There's nothing like 'em in the States, and sure as hell someone's gonna have a go soon. We can do that. But the real key is what you said to me. You can guarantee to get us into the market-place, and I reckon, using syrups direct from us, diluted and bottled off by you, you can pack off anything we want, real good. But the key, Tom, is you. You shoot from the hip, and that's what we need. We want to see some action. Are you still with me?'

'All ears,' said Travers.

'Well, this is the pitch. If we buy Sunburst, we want you to run it. All you gotta do is get your ass over here once a month, the rest's up to you. You hit some targets, and you're in the Big Time. For starters, I'm talking a two year contract. We'll pay you half a million dollars a year, and one million dollars if you complete that term on target. On top of that, you'll get a bucketful of Southern Drinks stock, all part of the executive package. Throw in overseas allowances, some real estate here in the States, and you, sir, could be in clover. After that, Europe maybe. Whad'ya say?'

'That's a, um, an astonishing offer, George, I'm still trying to take it all in. So apart from majoring on your brand, I keep the Sunburst range alive and kicking, have I got that right? And my management and employees stay as is, yes?'

'On the button, my friend. But, Tom, the other side of all this is that we don't want you biddin' 'gainst us with this half-assed buyout. That'd be crazy. You just back off from that when the time comes. If someone else beats us, then you go right ahead and borrow what the hell you can borrow, that's up to you, boy.'

'I see,' said Travers, 'and if I don't withdraw from the MBO?'

'Then it's been nice knowing ya, and we're outa here. We've gotta have you on board, Tom, or the whole thing's shit.'

'OK,' said Travers. 'Well I can't make up my mind now, how long have I got?'

'We're goin' back to Mobile on Monday afternoon. We're playin' some golf, if it ain't frozen over, at your Sunningdale this weekend? So you just let me know on Monday mornin' what y'all gonna do, and we'll go from there. Deal?'

'Deal,' said Travers. He put the phone down, completely stunned. This is not the real world, he thought to himself. He tried to see it from their perspective. If this was a solution for them, Travers could see they could get in a horrible mess without local knowledge, both of the workforce, and the market-place. Travers did a quick calculation that showed he would probably cost them five per cent of the purchase price after two years, which was probably a small price to pay for insurance of that calibre. But much more interesting, Davis had made it clear they would draw stumps on Sunburst if Travers was not part of the deal.

So, the choice was clear: he could take a chance that it would work out with the Americans, and even if it didn't, be very comfortably off. Or take an even bigger chance that he could win the buyout, float the company and pay down the debt, but control things himself. It didn't take him long to decide. He would telephone the Americans on Monday, and tell them it was thanks, but no thanks. He then thought about Goldberg's, and how they might react, if nothing came through from the Americans, even in round one. Should he tell them the offer that was made to him? Then at least they would understand the reason for withdrawal, with the added benefit that they would begin to understand just how determined Travers was to win. On the other hand, it would be a breach of confidence to the Americans. Travers was already wondering if, when he told Davis of his decision, he should repeat his first offer made during their meeting, of taking on the distributorship of Southern States Soft Drinks? After all, Davis would otherwise be going back to the States empty handed. This way, he could offer Davis a mid-term solution, always providing Travers won the buyout. Nothing ventured, nothing gained. Travers would put just that proposition to Davis on Monday morning.

Travers was completing his ruminations when there was a knock on his office door, and Amanda popped her head around.

'Tom, may I have a minute?'

'Of course, come on in,' said Travers.

She closed the door quietly and rested her back against it, her hands still holding the door knob.

'Tom, very quickly, I just wanted to tell you that I can't make that date on Tuesday. I'm really sorry but it's just not right, I can't.' She lowered her head and looked him straight in the eyes. She said quietly but firmly, 'I'm meant to be monitoring you for fair play and disclosure during this process. Any closer association would do neither of us any good. I'm sorry, Tom, but that's the way it's got to be.' She opened the door with her hands still behind her, spun round and exited without another word, closing the door behind her. Travers slumped onto his elbows on the desk, holding his head in his hands. All of a sudden, his love life had taken a nose dive. First Jane, and now the attractive possibility of Amanda. Sod it, he thought, life could be very unfair. He reminded himself to tell Chris to cancel those tickets.

On Friday, Travers was at a bit of a loose end. He phoned round all of the advisors to keep them in the picture about the trade buyers, and how he felt it had gone. He did tell them about Davis's proposition, but only because it might layer on another income stream for Sunburst as a distributor, and therefore maintain or even strengthen banking support. When he got round to Paul Foot at Andrews and Overton, Foot had told him he would need two days of his time next week, with his colleagues, to work through the senior debt banking contracts, which contained all the banking covenants and repayment schedules Travers and his team would have to undertake. They were very onerous, and Foot insisted that each of them must fully understand what the implications for the company were in the event of MBO. Travers didn't relish the prospect, but at least it spurred him to chase the head-hunter, and push for progress on the finance director replacement. He would take along Phillip Carter to the meeting, the placement from Boulters, so at least there was someone within Sunburst who could update the internal spreadsheets with the banking details.

He left the office after lunch to head down to East Grinstead and pick up Molly from Mrs Gibbons. He was due in Dorset that evening as a shooting guest of the Dukes and their excellent family shoot near Blandford. He needed the break, and he was looking forward to the mixed shooting of partridge and pheasant. It would also give him the chance to gently curry support amongst the regional brewers, and maybe even recruit one or two more.

Chapter Eight

Two weeks had passed since Travers had told the Americans from the Southern States Soda Drink Corporation that he would continue to drive for the buyout. They had been civil enough, and noted Travers' offer to distribute their cola, but would be considering their position back on home ground. Meanwhile, Goldberg's had kept him and his colleagues, and his entourage of advisors, in blissful ignorance. Now into the second week of November, there had been no news of the start of a formal round two, and only Mulligans had sent a team of advisors and their own finance men to scour the documents in the 'information room' Travers had set up for the purpose. Even that had been brief. They were not allowed to photocopy anything, but six of them had beavered away for two days making copious notes and asking a lot of questions, before disappearing. That had been a week and a half ago, and no news.

Morris at Wessex Bank, and Brown and Giddings at Maxwell Griffin, were getting extremely worried. The odds looked more and more as though Mulligans may have come in with a killer punch, leaving the rest of the field for dead. If that were true, the chances for the buyout were slim in terms of matching it, but even worse, if that were the case, why weren't they asking Travers for his bid? Travers had telephoned Spencer at Gallant, and Sir Brian Richards at Albion, to ensure he wasn't forgotten, that they wouldn't default on their agreement to let him pitch. He had been assured by both, with good grace, that everything was going according to plan, and that Goldberg's would be in touch when they felt the moment was opportune. In other words, they had both 'passed the buck' to Goldberg's, and Travers knew he would never get anything out of Levin. Amanda was as pleasant as ever, but refused to say anything with regard to Mulligans and the MBO. She finished up simply turning her back on Travers when his pestering got too much. She also indicated her work was nearly complete, bar some outstanding requests for more detailed information.

It was even worse for the employees of Sunburst. The weeks were going by, and nothing new could appear on the notice boards or in the regular meetings. No news was bad news, as far as the staff were concerned. They felt the owners had stitched up a deal and left Travers out in the cold, and their fate was to be determined by the horde of pinstriped youngsters who still regularly burrowed away in various parts of the plant.

On another subject, Travers had telephoned Jane the week before to find out from Jane, who spoke in hushed tones, that Bobby was back home, but that major surgery was needed after his recuperation, to replace a string of arteries around his heart. He needed constant attention, and according to Jane there was no possibility of her meeting Travers, as there was nothing to discuss. Travers was never one to push water up hill. Even if he persuaded her of the life of drudgery she was committing herself to, to a man she didn't love, could he actually make any firm promises that would leave her better off? She was, to say the least, a little highly strung and the reality was that they knew precious little about one another. It could equally well end in tears. Travers had to admit it was a clear case of the head ruling the heart and letting it go. He would look the most awful shit if he were found to be responsible for foundering the marriage and perpetuating Bobby's illness. He knew there really was no other option.

Meanwhile Travers had got the annual round of budget briefings and preparations underway, in order to keep the management heads down, and on the job. Everyone recognised it was probably a waste of time, but Travers insisted the business must be run as normal, and they would thank him when the MBO had been confirmed. A major part of his job right now was simply keeping up morale, and he made a point of stepping up the departmental wandering, taking every opportunity to encourage whoever he ran into.

On the Monday of the third week of November, Travers received a call from Levin. Would Travers, his colleagues and advisors, care to join Levin at their head office in Cheapside to discuss the management bid? At last. The whole thing was on the move. Levin had suggested the Tuesday morning, ten o'clock.

Travers was straight on the telephone to Morris. Was everybody ready? The call had come.

'Odd, very odd,' said Morris. 'I know Levin is strange, but why the formality and why you guys? It would be more usual for me to be called in on your behalf, informally, just the two of us, or maybe with Maxwell Griffin. Pulling you guys in only heightens the tension, after all, whatever you put on the table, they're bound to say it's not enough.' Travers and Morris had already agreed a figure of sixty-four million, cash, as the opening bid for management. The advisors, to a man, had been very cagey with Travers about just how far they would go. They clearly wanted to control the bidding without management getting emotionally involved. Nevertheless, at a pinch, Travers reckoned he could squeeze them up to seventy-five million, and still keep the banking interest cover ratios just about in control. Anyway, the point was, Levin was calling the shots, and everyone had to dance to his tune. Morris agreed to corral the rest of the advisors for ten the following morning, and suggested that Travers revise his valuation spreadsheets, just in case Levin was in a mood to negotiate. When he had finished the phone call, Travers went in search of Amanda, but was told by Ogden's secretary that she had phoned earlier to say she wouldn't be in. Sensibly, Travers supposed, she had decided to stay well clear of Sunburst until the meeting tomorrow. He called a quick meeting with his colleagues, and put them in the picture, advising them both not to say anything to their staff, as it was more than likely to drag on for further weeks, and there was no point in raising hopes at this stage.

The following morning at ten, Travers, Ogden and Fellowes were taken to the seventh and top floor of the Goldberg building in Cheapside. Another massive circular table, complete with plate glass panorama of St Paul's Cathedral. Apart from the central circular table, which could probably seat thirty, four raised areas in each corner of the room contained a smaller coffee-sized table, each with four chairs and a telephone. Along one wall was something like a bar, but instead of drinks, a couple of ladies in black were on hand behind it to dish up hot drinks and biscuits, and presumably to serve lunch, if required.

Brown, Giddings and Roberts were already seated, chatting to one another, and beside them was Paul Foot, who gave Travers a wave and a smile as he entered the room. Morris was across the other side of the room talking to Amanda, who was wearing a smart new black suit, complete with black tights. With her blonde hair and tall, voluptuous figure, Travers thought she looked a knockout, and went over to say hello.

'Can I get you some coffee, Tom?' she said with a bright smile. He nodded.

'Thanks, Amanda. My God but you're lovely, you should be on the catwalk, you'd knock 'em dead,' he said, smiling broadly. 'OK, where is he?' said Travers. 'Awaiting the Grand Entrance no doubt?' Amanda shook her head with disapproval, but made no excuse for her boss. If Levin was going in for theatricals this morning, Travers wasn't sure he could keep his cool. But under these circumstances, he knew it was not his place to attempt any control of the meeting. This was bread and butter to Morris and Brown, so Travers knew he had better shut up and let them get on with it. It certainly didn't come naturally, but he had no idea of what sort of war dance these fellows went through before actually engaging in negotiation. It would be quite an experience, he hoped.

In a few minutes, Levin appeared on his own, with bundles of papers, made his way to the end of the table opposite the window and sat down without saying a word to anyone. Then, as if only just noticing every one else in the room, he said, over the top of his glasses, 'Come along ladies and gentlemen, do please take your seats, anywhere you like.' For all the world, thought Travers, he was making it look as if they were late, not him.

'The shareholders of Sunburst believe the time is now right to receive the management's offer for the purchase of the company, in accordance with the agreement that was struck with Tom Travers. Presumably, Tom, you won't mind if I ask James Morris to put the offer on the table.' It was not a request, but a statement.

'Very good news, Geoffrey, and thank you for inviting us here,' said Morris, 'but before we get going, do you mind telling us just where you are with the round two contestants? Have you finished with them, are you still waiting for any bids, how many others are in the frame?'

'You're not entitled to any of that, I'm afraid. All you need to know is that the shareholders want to hear your bid.' John Brown, sat over the other side of the huge table, rustled in his chair, and had a strained smile of disbelief on his face. He raised a hand in Levin's direction.

'Come on, Geoffrey, show's over, can we get on with this please? We all know how this works. We want to bid, and you want to hear it. Along the way we exchange some useful information. With this client, you're the selling agent, with other clients we'll be the selling agent and you'll be buying. It cuts both ways. Now do you mind playing the game? The shareholders aren't even here for God's sake.' Brown was clearly running out of patience with the charade Levin was playing.

'I'm sorry, John, but I won't be bullied. You all know my feelings about MBOs. They sail far too close to the regulatory wind for my liking, and I refuse to give any concessions to management over and above that which they already have. As a senior partner of this firm, I will not allow us to drift into any cosy arrangement on an MBO, so I suggest we get on?'

Travers made a note on his pad that in future, any more such meetings must be attended by the shareholders to keep things moving sensibly. Levin was being plainly destructive, and Travers determined to do all he could through Spencer, to spike this objectionable individual. He slid his note, observed by everybody, across the table to Morris, who nodded.

'Well we're not happy with this, Geoffrey,' said Morris. 'It's just common courtesy to give us a status report. *My* client may be forced to go back to his shareholders and find out for himself what you refuse to tell us, which would make you look a bit silly, wouldn't it? And as the MBO advisor, why aren't you and I having a quiet discussion rather than this circus?' Brown at the end of the table raised his hand to his mouth to hide his smile. He was now enjoying this, and mentally patting Morris on the back.

'That would be totally irregular and prejudice the impartiality of the shareholders. They have their own shareholders to satisfy in terms of accepting the highest secured bid, and you seem to be suggesting they should drop that impartiality.'

'We're not suggesting any such thing, Geoffrey,' said Morris. 'Only that you afford us the same courtesy you would give to anyone in this bidding situation. This is not a closed bid – you have a chance to ramp it up. You have a funny way of going about it.'

'Well I'm sorry,' Levin said, clearly becoming perturbed. 'I am resolute on this. Now can I please have your bid, or am I to report there isn't one?'

'Very well, Geoffrey, but I don't think you've heard the end of this, I really don't.' Morris opened a file and slid a typed piece of paper across the table to Levin. 'There is a figure of sixty-four million cash, subject to the usual caveats of disclosure, warranties and due diligence. The offer is fully underwritten by the advisors sat around this table.'

Levin leant forward and picked up the paper, studying it. Without emotion he looked up over the rim of his glasses and said, 'I must tell you straight away, the shareholders of Sunburst will be offering no warranties. Mr Travers has run this business for the last ten years, and as such is in a far better position to warrant the figures than my clients. That is not negotiable, gentlemen. As to the bid, it falls a long way short of what is required. It is nowhere near sufficient. Is this your last offer?'

The three guys from Maxwells were talking amongst themselves in open contempt of Levin. Travers could see Brown's blood was boiling, but there was nothing obvious he could do to deal with Levin. Morris meanwhile had his hand to his jaw, looking at Levin in sad disbelief.

'No, it may not be our final offer,' said Morris with exasperation. 'Would you care to give us any clue at all as to what might get us closer to whatever is required, please.'

'More cash of course,' said Levin, now enjoying his power over the meeting. 'No I won't. I've told you it's not enough, and you will have to do considerably better. How long do you need to revise your offer?'

At this point Travers intervened. Without emotion, he quietly said to the meeting:

'I think, gentlemen, we're wasting our time with this fellow. Seems to me he's doing his client, my employer, a disservice. What does annoy me is that he wouldn't have this job at all were it not for me building value in this company over the last ten years. Unlike him, I think my shareholders would like me to win this bid with the best offer, and satisfy everybody. I suggest we go away and discuss it, and plan our next move as best we can. Thanks for nothing, Geoffrey. We'll contact you later in the day.'

Travers rose, as did everybody else, except Levin. Amanda was red with embarrassment, and busied herself with her papers. Travers looked across the table and said to Morris, 'Everybody to your office?' Morris and the others nodded. It was eleven o'clock, and no one had even had a coffee, never mind the jammy dodgers. They paraded out while Levin rose, appearing to be quite unconcerned that his meeting had broken up in disarray.

Outside the building, in a tight group and in a biting wind, Morris apologised to Travers for Levin's behaviour. Travers told him not to worry, and that Levin may have dug his own grave. Nevertheless, as Travers explained, Levin was quite within his rights, as, in truth, he had never expected to actually know the precise level of the other bids, and unfortunately had made that plain to the brewers. Travers suggested they all grab a couple of cabs, get out of the cold and meet up at Wessex to plan their next move.

When they arrived, Dennis was on hand to take their coats and bags and usher them into the familiar meeting room on the seventh floor overlooking the Thames. The mood had relaxed, and there was a camaraderie borne of the earlier friction with Levin. Morris checked that no one was under a time constraint and asked if everyone would stay for a Wessex lunch of overfilled sandwiches and some of their Chablis. They may be down, thought Travers, but they certainly weren't out. He went to the end of the room, grabbed his diary and pulled out Spencer's number at Gallant. He picked up the phone and dialled the direct number. Spencer's secretary answered, and Travers was put straight through.

'Simon, Tom. We've just had a very difficult meeting with your charmer Levin. Can you speak?'

'Hmm,' said Spencer. 'Not sure I should be having this conversation, but go ahead.'

'Look, we met Levin this morning to put in our bid. We were really hoping it would be friendly, but Levin was just so antagonistic, Attila the Hun personified. Simon, we've put a bid on the table of sixty-four million, but Levin says it's no good and more is required. We can put up more, but we've got to have a clue. The normal form on this sort of thing is to be nudged in the right direction, for everyone's benefit. Levin is just plain uncooperative, doesn't want to know. My people have never seen anything like it before. All we're asking, Simon, is not who else is in the ring, but how much further do we have to go? I deserve a nudge from you, surely?'

'I don't know, Tom. It's really not just down to me,

there's Albion and Caledonia to consider. That's why Goldberg's are there.'

'Simon, I deserve a bit more than that. It's me who put the value into Sunburst, remember? Look, I'm not asking much, just give me a clue. Have I got a chance, and how much?'

'Of course you have a chance, Tom, but not where you are right now. I shouldn't say, but it's got to be at least another five, more like ten. You do have competition.'

'Simon, we haven't had this conversation, thanks very much. That's all I was asking for. The rest is down to the finance goblins. But one more thing, Simon. Can you please, please, make sure you are around to attend our next meeting? Levin's so full of himself, he's really not doing you any favours, honestly. I really would appreciate your being at the next meeting. I can tell you for nothing you'll get more out of my side if you are there.'

'OK, OK, I'll think about it. But I hope that's helped, Tom, it's the least I can do. Good Luck.' Travers put the telephone down, and felt relieved. He'd certainly done his bit in this manic circus. He fell into a chair and recounted the conversation to the others.

John Brown listened to what Travers had to say. He then said to Travers, 'Tom, you know, we must be careful here. Levin and the shareholders know how much you want this business. It shows – your heart's on your sleeve. It would be all too easy to be talked up, when the reality might be very different. For example, you say that only Mulligans came down and inspected the information room. What happened to the others? Were there any others, and if there were, could they get letters of credit from their banks? There could be any number of reasons why there is no one bidding at all, and we're just being played along because they know we're hungry to buy the business. Spencer says we have competition. Do you believe him?

And somewhere between five and ten million more. I don't know, it could be a con trick, and we're playing a bad hand of poker.'

'All I can say is,' said Travers, 'I know Simon Spencer pretty well. He's no poker player. I'm sure he wouldn't tell me an outright lie. If he says there's competition, I have to believe him. I also heard, first hand, the managing director of Mulligans wax lyrical about Sunburst. They have some reservations on duty, but I'm convinced they're in the ring. As to the others, you may be right. I think the Americans have probably gone away, Citadel have no leverage, and Clements almost certainly can't raise the money. Is there anyone else? Unlikely. So it could be a two-horse race. Now, one more thing we surely have to consider is this: I think we all agree seventy-five million is a reasonable price for this business. On a forward post tax earnings multiple, we're still only talking a P/E of six. For God's sake, are we going to throw away this opportunity because we couldn't get it for peanuts? You all tell me we can float this business on a P/E of between ten and fifteen. On the earnings growth we're looking at, that makes a hundred and fifty million float tag clearly within our grasp, and maybe only a year away from now. Gentlemen, forget the competition for a moment, we're still talking about buying this business for a song at seventy-five million. Right now we're stuck at sixty-four. Let's go seventy, and then play poker. We'll be within a gnat's bollocks of Spencer's price, and maybe I can do the rest by twisting his arm, one way or the other.'

Travers looked around the room at his colleagues and advisors, anticipating a positive response. There was none for the moment, each individual weighing up what Travers had said. Morris at last piped up.

'Difficult to dispute what you've said, Tom. I think *our* problem,' he pointed at Maxwell Griffin, 'is that it's so bloody annoying to appear to dance to Levin's tune. I think though, that we must try and put him behind us, especially if you say that Spencer will attend the next round.'

'I agree,' said Brown. 'I'm still trying to get to grips with Levin's attitude. He's getting fees based on the sale price, and doing nothing to ginger it up. Either he's taken a very great dislike to you, Tom, or he really is serious about MBOs, which is just plain stupid. Whoever heard of a bookie with morals? But I suppose I have to go along with what you say, and maybe we should try seventy million, with fast completion conditions.'

'Can I come in here?' said Giddings. 'There's something not quite right about this whole thing, and it's bugging me. We couldn't get a thing out of Levin, which is madness, for him and for us. Now what if they haven't had a response from Mulligans yet? What if they're thinking about this duty thing, and also the whole subject of supply agreements. Both are big issues for Mulligans, and why should they be in any rush? What if they haven't had the right answers so far from the shareholders, and want more time. That perhaps might explain why Levin has refused to give us any information, because he simply hasn't got any. Maybe, they've said to themselves, OK, Mulligans need more time, so let's see what the buyout team have, then we can offset that against Mulligans when they finally divvy up a bid.

'So now let's put it all together, from our side. What if, Tom, you go back to Spencer tomorrow and tell him your advisors are furious with Levin, and it's almost impossible to talk about another meeting with Levin, let alone put another figure on the table. Tell him it's going to take time for you to sort it out, but when you are ready to put another number on the table, we might put it straight to him, rather than Levin. That way, I don't see how we can lose anything. They know we've got more to put on the table, but we've got a real problem with Levin. If we hold off for a week, maybe we can level the playing field a bit, by getting more compliancy from Levin, who will have to ask where our bid is, by which time maybe Mulligans will have come in with their final offer *if* they haven't done so already. Either way, it also indicates we're getting close to our upper limit, which is a signal worth sending.'

'Can't argue with that,' said Morris. 'But maybe just another twist? What if we actually say to Spencer that Levin's behaviour clearly indicates to our side that Mulligans haven't come in, or if they have, there are some massive strings. We don't want to play a stalking horse for Mulligans, and therefore we won't come back in for another week, and then, only to Spencer?'

'No. I don't think so, James,' said Brown. 'That's just double guessing Mulligans and really playing games. If we stick to what Anthony has suggested, it's kosher. We *are* upset, offence *has* been taken, and it will take a lot of effort by Tom to get the show back on the road. When the improved offer does come, everyone is inclined to pitch it at a shareholder, Spencer, rather than Goldberg's. We've got a justifiable beef with Levin, let's use it, but not to threaten the shareholders with Mulligans. Does everyone agree with that?' There was firm agreement round the table.

'OK,' said Travers, 'I'll call him tomorrow. Tears will be streaming down my face. Full emotional overload. I'll see how that goes. But I can't see Spencer taking responsibility for receiving the bid. He'll squirm out of it. But at least he'll have to tell Levin to get his act together, and be more cooperative. If he does do that, it fulfils the same objective for us.'

'Well that's that,' said Morris. 'Now while we're all here,

what about those outstanding issues on the banking covenants; shall we go through them again?' From the thrill of the chase, the mood dipped somewhat, as Foot distributed yet another mountain of paper for them all to examine.

The next morning, Wednesday, Travers was back at his desk at Sunburst. He was trying to make sure he could be convincing with Spencer, and was preparing to call him at nine, hopefully before the fellow was locked up in meetings. Travers was at least pleased that his side were taking some initiatives over the negotiating process, rather than merely reacting to requests for a price. It was time to give it a go. Spencer's secretary put him through.
 'Simon,' said Travers, 'I'm sorry to bother you again, can you give me five minutes?'
 'Of course,' said Spencer. 'What's happened now?' Unfortunately Spencer already seemed on the defensive.
 'Simon, it's really hard to explain just how difficult our meeting was with Levin yesterday. My guys haven't experienced such animosity in a long time, and there's almost a feeling that we're wasting our time. The fact that Levin won't give a shred of assistance to our side is making us very nervous, and there's a feeling that he's working off some other agenda, and to hell with the management. John Brown is simply furious, and while there's more in the pot, I'm having a hard job persuading him that improving the offer will be worthwhile. Simon, because of Levin, it's all getting very personal, and I think I've got to let my guys cool off before we can come back. Meanwhile Brown is saying he doesn't see why he should deal with Levin any more, and when we do come back, he wants to put a revised figure direct to you, and avoid another confrontation with Levin. The trouble is, I'm

stuck in the middle of this. All I want is my company at a fair price. Simon, how the hell do I handle this? Have you got any suggestions?'

'Oh dear,' said Spencer. 'You are in a pickle. You must understand Levin is doing his job. He has got an extraordinary reputation for doing deals, and I'm just not sure what I can do. I'm certainly not prepared to take bids from you personally, that's out of the question. Goldberg's are being paid to run this sale, and nothing will alter that.'

'I hear what you say, Simon, but my guys are old hands at this too. They're saying Levin's job is to ramp the price up by giving us a few clues, you know, as you said to me yesterday. But if Levin is just going to spit in Brown's face, he'd rather give the revision to someone else. The point is, we have more money, but everyone feels we're being taken for a ride, not least by Levin. He doesn't need to be so rude, unless it's part of his strategy, or there's nothing else on the table to tell us about. But you've said to me, Simon, we are up against competition, and I must believe you. It's all very, very difficult unless you can bring Levin to heel, or give us a reason why he's acting this way.'

'Well, Tom, I'm sorry you've been put in this position. There are manoeuvrings going on, but that's what they're paid to do. I'll have a chat with Levin, and see if we can't build a few bridges. When can you put your next offer in?'

'Frankly, Simon, I think we're looking at next week, unless we get some sort of help from Levin. But I want you to know that just because we're dealing with prima donna merchant bankers, doesn't mean there's not more cash. There is, if we get an explanation from your side of this antagonistic treatment.'

'OK, OK,' said Spencer, beginning to weary of the

whole subject. 'I'll tell Levin to be nice to your people, and see if we can't get your revision on the table. I really can't do any more.'

'All right, Simon, thanks. And I'm sorry to be a bore. I can't help feeling that if I sat down with you and someone from Albion we could get a deal done in no time. But I'm afraid we're stuck at the moment. Good luck with Levin.' Travers put the phone down.

What to make of that? thought Travers. In capital letters, scrawled on his pad, he had the word MANOEUVRINGS. Spencer had admitted there was some sort of game being played, and Levin was paid to do it. But had anything changed? The only thing Spencer had agreed to do was to get Levin to maybe apologise to Brown. Big deal. But they'd bought themselves another week, and if Mulligans' bid was finally in, maybe the other side would be more receptive to Travers' bid. It was all getting far too convoluted for Travers, and he really worried whether they would lose the plot altogether at this rate. The only consolation was that Morris, Brown and Giddings had been through this a hundred times before. He only hoped they knew what they were doing. He reported his conversation to Morris, who seemed pleased enough, telling Travers he would pass the message on to Brown and Giddings. Meanwhile, Morris told him to sit tight and get on with running the business; it was all going to plan. When Travers came off the phone, he went along to see his colleagues, to get a gauge of their reactions.

It was not until Tuesday of the following week that Travers heard anything. He received a call from Giddings saying that Levin had contacted Brown, but that their conversation had been prickly, with no apology from Levin, just fresh demands for the revised bid. Levin was looking for a meeting on the Wednesday, and Giddings asked Travers if he thought the time was right to put the revision on the table. It was Travers' turn for histrionics, telling Giddings that they were the chess Grand Masters, and why ask him? Giddings tried to explain that they had achieved what they set out to, but that they could perhaps gain a greater initiative by continuing to play hard to get. Travers disagreed. He couldn't see the point. They had made their stand. Hopefully Mulligans' bid, if there was one, was on the table, so why prolong the agony? Giddings tended to agree, and said he would discuss it with Morris before agreeing to the meeting. If there was agreement, they would opt for an afternoon meeting, so that they could all get together in the morning and discuss tactics. Travers said he would telephone Spencer, to ensure his attendance, if the meeting was called.

At three o'clock on Wednesday afternoon the buyout team again entered the Goldberg revolving door on Cheapside, and made their way up to the seventh floor. The mood was sombre, because there was a general feeling that even seventy million wouldn't clinch the deal, and maybe Mulligans were just too far ahead. The worst of it was that if there was no feedback from the other side they were still fighting blind and the double guessing would continue.

They entered the meeting room to find a full quorum representing the shareholders. Spencer was there, Levin, Amanda, their lawyers and another chap talking to Spencer, who Travers didn't recognise. Travers went over to Spencer to say hello, being as friendly and positive as he could. He was introduced to David Johnson, who was Albion's internal mergers and acquisitions man, and a lawyer to boot. Travers never knew he even existed. He was young, mid-thirties, donnish and bespectacled. He had a ready smile and conversed in a relaxed way with Travers. Generally,

Travers was pleased that Albion as well as Gallant had a representative at the meeting. Surely that must be a good sign. Whether it was lack of confidence in Levin to get the job done, or simply that the time had come for serious negotiation, Travers didn't know, but there was certainly sufficient authority at the meeting to get a bid accepted.

Not surprisingly, Spencer, not Levin, opened the meeting. Spencer revelled in this sort of situation, where his ready banter and boardroom experience captured control of the meeting before Levin knew what was happening.

'Ladies and gentlemen,' said Spencer with a broad smile. 'Thank you for coming. The purpose of the meeting is for the shareholders of Sunburst to receive a revised bid from the management. I took the opportunity to invite along David Johnson from Albion corporate planning, so that between us we have some authority to react speedily to what you may put forward. Now, it is no secret there have been other interested parties, so Tom you must understand we can only accept an offer from you in relation to what else is on the table. I make no apology for saying price and cash is the key determinant here, without any strings attached. We will find out soon enough whether what you have got is good enough. Is that fair, Tom?' Travers was momentarily surprised to be brought into the conversation, and slightly off balance, replied:

'Er, yes, Simon, thank you. You'll hear from James Morris in a moment that we've made a significant upward offer, which I sincerely hope will be acceptable. All I would say is that we're on the limit. The buyout team have worked for months on this opportunity, and we know better than most what it's worth, by way of what we can get out of it. There's a lot at stake for us, and the employees. I really hope you fully consider that in your deliberations. Selling to the management is good PR for the shareholders. I'm not sure you're aware, but the minor shareholders, practically to a man, want to roll over their investment into the new company, and surely their wishes count for something, even if they don't carry voting shares. Just as importantly, the company remains independent, with a view to flotation, as opposed to the possibility of being sold to a competitor of yours. Obviously I'm fully aware of the presence of Mulligans in all this. The company has served the shareholders well over the last three decades, and by selling to management, that will continue. Perhaps I can now hand over to James Morris of Wessex Bank to detail the offer.'

'Thank you,' said Morris. 'Gentlemen, before I put our figure on the table, may I enquire if you already have an offer, which you are minded to accept? Or are you dissatisfied with everything received so far?'

Levin shuffled on his chair, clearly agitated. He leant forward, and trying to be as civil as possible in the company of his peers, said to Morris, 'James, that is not your concern. We're waiting for your price.'

'But that's the point,' said Morris calmly. 'Help us a bit and maybe we can go that extra mile. It takes two to negotiate, Geoffrey.' Then Johnson quietly interrupted. He had a biro in his hand, and while occasionally looking around at the combatants, twirled the pen between his fingers in a relaxed, casual way. He had been here before, and had an authority about him.

'We do have an offer that we could accept. Plain and simple. But we're waiting for your next offer.' He gave an encouraging smile to Travers, which had a calming effect on everybody.

'OK,' said Morris. 'When we last met with Geoffrey we put sixty-four million on the table. Cash, no strings, speedy completion. Today we're putting up seventy million, which is a very significant advance. Have we done enough?' Morris then slid the formal offer on a piece of paper across the desk to Levin.

Johnson, who was clearly experienced in these matters said, 'Gentlemen, do you mind if we withdraw to discuss this? We'll be back in five minutes.'

Everyone on Travers' side nodded, and the group of six representing the shareholders rose, and left the room. When they had gone, Brown said, 'If we believe them, then we are up against another bid, probably Mulligans. It looks tough. But Spencer kept mentioning "no strings". That seemed a little odd to me. There shouldn't be any strings with an offer, unless Mulligans have put some on. We're still in with a chance, I hope.'

'But what if they say no, John. Are you willing to put up more?' said Travers.

'Not without clearly seeing the finishing line. What's the point? They could keep this up until we get to ninety million, which is definitely not going to happen.'

'Coffee anyone?' said Travers. 'Might as well be comfortable.' He rose and made his way to the vacuum flasks, placed on the bar.

There was nothing much any of them could say. The atmosphere was tense, but a little small talk amongst themselves managed to keep most of them relaxed while they waited for the other side to return.

Spencer and his entourage then re-entered the room, Spencer, as ever, with his evergreen smile. They seated themselves without a word, and then Spencer, looking at Morris said, 'I'm sorry to say the offer is not good enough. But fear not,' said Spencer with a bigger smile. 'All is not lost. David has a suggestion.' Johnson was laid back in his chair, twiddling again with his biro.

'Yes,' he said. 'Just a thought, and it's up to you of course, but there may be a way through this that makes it far more attractive to us. As things stand, if we accept a price for Sunburst from you, the whole disposal value is taxed, and we, the selling shareholders, all lose thirty per cent of the value. If, however, we took as much as possible of the sale proceeds as a retrospective dividend, we would only pay a nominal amount of tax on that dividend. As you know gentlemen, that's called a dividend strip, and very efficient it is too. That could make a material difference to your offer. I think it still needs some sweetening though.'

Everyone on Travers' side was now leaning forward in their chairs. In one step Johnson had taken them from nowhere to within an ace of winning the bid. The whole device of a dividend strip was lost on Travers, but he would keep his mouth shut until afterwards. Morris and the Maxwell Griffin team looked quietly happy. Morris piped up, 'Speaking for myself, I have a rough idea of how much could fall into a dividend strip, but I'm not an accountant, and I don't know what impact it might have on the balance sheet. Have you got any thoughts on that, John?'

'Not really,' said Brown. 'But it sounds like a good idea to me. Tell you what, why don't we get hold of the auditors, and go through it with them? It might take an hour, and we may only get the principle straight, but it's got to be worth a shot if we can get an agreement.' Brown then looked towards Spencer and said, 'Are you all prepared to wait until then?'

Spencer looked at Johnson, and the two of them nodded casually. 'Very well,' said Spencer. 'One hour, and we meet back in this room. Rather exciting isn't it?' Travers leapt up, and went round the table to thank Spencer.

'I really am very grateful to you both,' said Travers. 'I'm sure we'll find something, see you in an hour.' Levin had already gone. Heaven knows, thought Travers, what he thought about all this.

The buyout team were now left on their own at one end of the huge table.

'Right,' said Travers. 'How do we play this? Shall I get on to the audit partner and get him round here, or try and tackle it on the telephone with him?'

'Time's a bit short,' said Morris. 'It's four o'clock now. Let's hope your man is still in his office. What say I try to explain the problem on the telephone, maybe find out how much we have to place in a divi' strip, and get him to agree the principle, subject to verification?'

Everyone nodded. 'Go for it,' said Travers.

Morris spent half an hour on the phone to Goulding at Boulters' head office, which actually wasn't far away in Cannon Street. Travers was impressed with Morris; he was very cool under pressure, and very little, apart from Levin, seemed to unsettle him. Travers supposed that if you were doing his job seven days a week, fifty weeks a year, you would have to pace yourself, or drop dead with the strain. He could see, though, how it got into the blood, the thrill was addictive and no doubt every week brought new companies and new challenges. From what Travers could hear, Goulding appeared to be saying it was perfectly kosher, but that more work would be needed to be precise about how much could be 'stripped' from reserves, and theoretically at least, paid out as dividends in lieu of an element of the purchase price. Finally, with Morris making frequent references to the bound prior year accounts packs, a figure of fifteen million was agreed to be 'safe' to be declared as a retrospective dividend. A special resolution of the board would be required, which Caledonia would have to agree to, but that could all be predated to agreeing the deal. There was also an implication for the smaller 'A' Class shareholders, but basically, they could be included, if required.

When he came off the phone, Morris regurgitated the

detail that the others hadn't been able to pick up from his conversation. It looked as if they had a runner.

'So how shall we structure this?' said Brown. 'What about sixty million purchase price, and ten million dividend strip. With the tax benefit, that makes it about seventy-four million. I reckon that's going to do it.'

'Johnson wants us to sweeten the deal some more before he'll say yes,' said Travers, 'Can't we put on another three or four million to make sure?'

'We're not a bloody charity,' said Brown. 'We're giving them something that Mulligans wouldn't do, which means our offer's gone from sixty-four to seventy-four million. That's one hell of a hike, and they'll be happy with that, mark my words.' No one in the room looked terribly convinced, but it was basically Maxwell Griffin's money, and Brown, as the boss, could call the shots. They went through every aspect again, until Morris felt it was safe to face the shareholders. He picked up the internal phone and got hold of Levin, telling him they were ready. It was five o'clock.

Within fifteen minutes everyone had reassembled in the meeting room. It was already dark outside when they all trooped back in, with generally expectant looks and smiles on their faces. When everyone was seated, Brown, by agreement, put forward the new terms, saying he felt confident the shareholders of Sunburst would accept this generous new offer. Instead, Johnson was shaking his head.

'No,' said Johnson. 'No, that's not good enough, I told you. You're close, but not close enough.'

'There is no more,' said Brown. 'We've moved from sixty-four to seventy-four. We all know that's a brilliant price for Sunburst. You should be very happy.'

'Sorry,' said Levin, with a sickly false smile on his face. 'But as you've heard, it's not enough. Now time is getting on, you've been given every assistance, and it's time to put up or shut up. What's it to be?' Spencer meanwhile had lost his smile. It was very clear to Travers that Spencer was genuinely disappointed that Travers' team hadn't sweetened the pill a little further.

'We've come a very long way,' said Brown. 'I don't think we can add any more.' Levin got up from his seat, went over and leant between the seated Spencer and Johnson, and whispered something to them. They duly considered, and answered. Levin went back to his seat.

'Right,' said Levin. 'The shareholders have agreed to give you one more day, tomorrow, to put more on the table. A decision will be made tomorrow. It's up to you whether you get it or not.' Travers looked at his colleagues. Unbelievably to him, they seemed to have accepted this second rate solution, and were shuffling their shoulders in resignation.

'Now just a minute,' said Travers. 'I've had enough of this. This is crazy. We're there bar a few bob, we've got to finish this. Christ, I've got a business to run and we're arguing coppers. Simon, what do you want? A million? What? Just tell us, but tell us now.'

Johnson interjected, completely calmly. 'Another four,' he said.

'One,' said Brown.

'Three,' said Johnson.

'Two,' said Brown.

'Split the difference, for Christ's sake,' said Travers. 'Two and a half.'

'OK,' said Johnson. 'Seventy-two and a half million, of which twelve and a half is dividend strip, agreed?'

There was silence around the room. Travers leaned forward on his elbow, giving Brown a piercing look, silently demanding a response. Still Brown played with his pencil, until finally he looked up, smiled, and said, 'Deal.'

'Thank God for that,' said Travers, rising from his chair

and going around the table to shake hands with Spencer and Johnson. 'Let's have your hand on that, Simon, it's the best thing you've ever done, you won't regret it.' They shook hands, and then Travers shook Johnson's hand. 'Thank you very much everybody,' said Travers. 'I'm very grateful, well done to you all.' Everyone was smiling and joking with the noticeable exception of Levin, who said:

'Right, I think we'd better hear now from the lawyers present, precisely what happens next. The shareholders will be driving for a fast completion, but a lot has to be done between now and then. Mr Foot, perhaps you'd be kind enough to give us your itinerary?'

Foot began to speak about all manner of things from verification to final accountants' reports, to signed sealed banking deals and equity provision, all leading to a completion date that could be as little as five weeks away. By now Travers wasn't listening any more, and got up to see if the bar actually contained any drinks of the alcoholic variety. Halfway to the bar, and while the others were still in discussion, he asked Amanda if there was any chance of a drink. She smiled, nodded and joined him at the bar area.

'Well done, you,' she said, 'I thought you were never going to get there. Terribly exciting though, isn't it?' She rummaged in a cupboard for a bottle of whisky and a glass.

'Jesus, Amanda, I can do without it. Still, it's absolutely brilliant, and thank you too for all your help and hard work.' She turned away a little embarrassed, but Travers could see she was as pleased as he was. She poured him a drink and said she must return to the table to take notes for Levin. He nodded, took a swig from the drink and said to Amanda, 'Don't forget, we must have another dinner date soon.' She gave him a smile and returned to her seat. Travers had just about had enough for the day. Reluctantly, and drink in hand, he resumed his seat.

Chapter Nine

A week later, into December, Travers realised the enormity of the decision that had been made with the buyout. Over the months it had of course become an objective in itself, but the reality was, it was just the beginning. The beginning of a very precarious and dangerous journey that would either end in flotation, a trade sale or ignominy if they breached the banking covenants, and the management started to lose its equity. The investment banks had based everything on five year projections, in terms of return on capital and revolving credit facilities, but they made it clear to Travers, that because of Sunburst's excellent profit record over the last five years a drive for flotation was in everybody's mind, and the sooner the better. Travers couldn't disagree. Whilst he was confident the business could sustain and pay down the debt burden, sooner or later a key decision to float would have to be taken, and if so, why delay? Over the past months, they had become attuned to the pace, as had the business, with middle management taking far more responsibility than would have seemed prudent just a few short months ago. Why not, thought Travers, keep this fighting structure together, and drive straight on to flotation, in one smooth progression, while the organisation was in place to do so. Whilst that decision had not been formally made, it was clear to Travers that come the new year, he would instruct the advisors to get on with a flotation of the business in say, twelve months' time – always assuming he could keep the business on track commercially.

Meanwhile, there was still much to do to complete the buyout. In particular, Maxwell Griffin now had the job of selling down the investment to other investment banks, much as a bookie might 'lay-off' bets on the race track. Brown had decided to hold on to twenty-five per cent of the equity for Maxwell Griffin internal funds, and sell down fifty per cent to other investors. The balance was of course held by management, providing they hit the flotation capitalisation target, which would entitle them to twenty-five per cent of the equity. The sales process undertaken by Maxwell Griffin fully involved the management who were required to give formal presentations to interested investors, be they in Scotland, London or Bristol.

Huge swathes of time were required from Travers and his colleagues to meet these obligations, which after the first half-dozen, became extremely tiresome affairs. But some presentations did have their humorous aspects. At one presentation, at the Maxwell Griffin offices in Great Salisbury Street, Brown had invited a consortium of Japanese banks to take a look at Sunburst. There were about thirty of them, most of whom had just flown in from Tokyo, and only a few of them actually understood any English. It was at the time when the Japanese stock market had taken a bath, following the collapse of liquidity that accompanied the property and stock market meltdown. Without a spark of understanding from his audience, Travers had worked through the presentation, hoping that at least some of the slides may have made some sense to them. At the end, questions were invited from the audience, but none were raised. Indeed, all that Travers and Brown received by way of response was blank faces. Finally, Brown had said to one of the gentlemen whom he knew understood English, 'Well that's the news about Sunburst. What's the good news from Japan?'

The elderly Japanese banker replied sombrely, 'Only good news in Japan *is* Sunburst. I think we take five per cent.' When they had gone, Brown noticed that the Orientals had stolen every one of the tooled leather-covered jotter pads that resided in front of every chair around the table.

Apart from helping Brown to recruit equity participants, Travers also had to do the same for the senior debt people at Wessex Bank who were again 'laying off' some of the debt with other banks. American, Canadian, French and German banks all finished up with a slice, which really worried Travers. If they did default on debt interest, Travers knew there was not a hope in hell of working an extension, or gaining temporary relief, when so many banks were involved. It would be simply impossible to organise it with so many participants, and a single breach of payment would trigger the whole debt structure to collapse and foreclose as quickly as a house of cards. He passed none of this onto his colleagues, as there was enough pressure already.

Back at Sunburst, the mood was jubilant about the buyout. Mostly relief that no mass redundancy programme would be put in place, but also genuine optimism and enthusiasm following the news that all employees would participate in a share scheme, which would be extremely valuable to them all if held through to flotation. Travers also took the time to drum home to employees just what the extra financial burdens on the company were, and how those costs must be neutralised. 'No pain no gain' was readily understood and applied, even from the radical socialist element on the shop floor. Productivity had never seen such improvements as a result.

Overall, the response from customers was also excellent, with most buyers or senior executives wishing them success and undertaking continued support. Travers even commissioned a trade press advertising campaign along the lines of, 'We liked the company so much, we bought it', which caught the mood, destroying the cheap attempts by the competition to denigrate the viability of Sunburst.

In addition to all that, Travers and his colleagues were forced to burn the midnight oil by both Maxwell Griffin and Wessex lawyers, on rafts of undertakings presented through verification notes and warranties. Advised by Foot at Andrews and Overton, the general objective for Travers was to whittle down a four inch thick warranty document that the banks demanded, to maybe half an inch thick. It seemed to Travers they wanted him to warrant that if the sun didn't rise, it was his fault, and he would have to pay. No wonder the fees were going to be so high when there was all this pointless discussion of whose fault it was if something went wrong. Nevertheless, Travers, Ogden and Fellowes held out, achieved what they wanted in terms of reasonable warranties, and had to pay no more than their success fees for their agreed share of the equity. The finishing line was in sight when all the sale and purchase agreements would be signed by all parties at the Andrews and Overton offices before Christmas. It had become an endurance race, where sheer tenacity and patience became more important than creativity and swashbuckling negotiation. However, Travers had enjoyed the whole thing, a truly memorable experience.

Then finally, just a few days before Christmas, everything and everyone was set up to attend the completion meeting. Every tiny detail had been resolved, the money was ready to move by electronic transfer, the ownership of the company was now about to change hands.

There were maybe fifty people in the huge meeting room at Andrews and Overton on the appointed day. Representatives from Albion, Gallant and Caledonia were there. Lawyers and accountants, each representing different client interests were milling about with papers. The equity providers and senior debt bankers were also all there in force, each with their own advisors and juniors. And finally, the PR people were there, ready to announce that Sunburst was now owned by the management. A local television crew was on standby, journalists from press and radio were being held in an ante-room, awaiting the news that at midday the papers had been signed.

Travers, Spencer, Sir Brian Richards and Sir Angus Egan were sat separately from the others, on a table large enough to take the mass of documents that had to be signed. Foot had gathered them all together on another table, and simply asked if they wished to know the nature of each document they would be signing. Because if they did, the whole process would take at least an hour, requiring Foot to explain each document that came before them. The answer was a categorical no, whereupon Foot started to layer the documents across the table. There were four piles, each stack containing about fifteen documents, so they were being asked to sign four copies of each document. Foot said the signing could get under way, explaining where each party had to sign, or even initial, where a last minute change had been made to a page. Travers was the last in line. The documents passed from one to the other, around the table, finishing with Travers. After ten minutes of non-stop signatures in the appointed place, Foot announced that the deal was complete, and the company was now in new ownership.

From out of nowhere chilled bottles of champagne were produced, and without hesitation Travers rose from his chair, and to the smiling, happy audience, many of whom he had never met before, he gave his heartfelt thanks for this momentous occasion in the development of the company. He didn't have tears in his eyes, but it was a close thing, especially after Spencer responded with the 'safe hands' routine in relation to Travers and his management. He then went round the room shaking hands with each advisor, knowing that within a few days the most horrendous bills would be landing on his desk, amounting to the grand total of three and a half million pounds.

Still, he had done it, and battle could recommence. He was now looking forward to the next stage, flotation.

It was very nearly a month later that Travers happened to find out the truth about Mulligans' bid. He had prised it out of Amanda. Mulligans had in fact put in a higher bid than the management at eighty million. However, they had imposed a condition that completion would not take place until after the Chancellor's Budget in March, or failing that, that the price would be renegotiable if there was a movement of more than ten per cent in the duty regime applicable to alcoholic soft drinks. For the shareholders, according to Amanda, that was an intolerable 'hostage to fortune', which is why they were determined to achieve a quick bid from the management, even if they couldn't secure an equivalent price. In addition to that, so she said, Mulligans was far from the ideal purchaser for the shareholders, as it was in open competition with them in the stout market, and Sunburst may have built Mulligans a more powerful portfolio of drinks with which to force distribution of their stout and other beers into the shareholders' pubs.

As Travers predicted, later still, in March, the Chancellor made no changes to duty differentials between drink classes, which was to prove the touchstone for the final decision to push on for the flotation of Sunburst sometime during the summer of the following year.

During this period, Travers had a phenomenal workload, ranging from employee share schemes to television interviews, regular visits to new fund managers interested in taking a slice of Sunburst stock, to completely revising the budget platform for the company's financial performance. The boys from Maxwell Griffin had wanted to ante-up the profit projections so that a blinding set of results could be declared just prior to flotation. Travers fought long and hard against this, refusing to give up his war chest in anything other than a controlled and progressive way, determining that profits would progress from thirteen million in year one, to sixteen and a half in year two, and on to twenty million by year four. As far as he was concerned, he was in this for the long haul and not just a whiz-bang on flotation. He was all the more resolved on being told by Morris that Maxwell Griffin were bound to bale out completely on flotation, taking whatever gain they could.

Nevertheless, this period was hugely satisfying for Travers. He was in control, he knew the business and its people, and as long as he kept up the marketing assault on Joe Public, he could steer this little gem to long term prosperity. Acquisitions were now a real possibility, and that prospect fired his imagination.

He kept in close contact with Amanda, whose internal reputation at Goldberg's had been enhanced by what had proved to be a fairly rapid and successful sale process, which had netted the company an extremely handsome fee. Levin, however, had not yet been thrown another major project, so she found herself seconded to other teams, pro tem.

One evening in April, Travers picked up the phone to Amanda at her Greenwich flat.

'Amanda, it's me. I've just had a wonderful thought, and I want to bounce it off you.'

'Oh my God, do I really want to hear this? Surely you've got enough on your plate over there. You're not going to get me into trouble are you? I've been doing so well. I can hear from your voice you've got some arcane idea you want to unleash on an unsuspecting public. Go on then, hit me.'

'Well really,' said Travers. 'There's no gratitude in this world. I pick up the phone to a trusted friend and all I get is derision. Not sure I want to tell you now.'

'OK, sorry. I'm all ears.'

'That's better,' said Travers. 'Now look, this affects us both, this is one of those life enhancing decisions. They only come our way occasionally, and it could set a new pattern for the rest of our lives. Amanda, I'm deadly serious about this, and you must promise me you'll say yes.'

'Tom, what the hell are you on about?'

'Well look, I've planned an itinerary for you and me. It's something we both must do, but mostly it's for you, because I really do care, Amanda, more than you probably know.'

'Tom it's very nice of you, but I'm quite happy at Goldberg's. I really don't think I could fit in at Sunburst. You and I are far too close for a start...'

'No, no, no. You've got the wrong end of the stick, Cara Mia. Look, you force me to be blunt. You've got to come away with me on holiday. Everything's fixed and I won't take no for an answer. You're gonna love it, I promise. Surely you haven't forgotten that hotel in Harrow, when I said you've got to take a break. You actually agreed with me. Well, I've fixed it. We both need it and you'll destroy the whole thing if you say no. I'll be heartbroken, totally unloved and no doubt pitched into a nervous breakdown. Tell me you'll say yes.'

'I can't believe it.' At least Travers detected some humour in her voice. 'What makes you think I'm going to jump on a plane with you? We might not get on, we could argue. It might go horribly wrong, and no doubt you probably want me in your bed without so much as a by your leave. Tom, we are not really an item, if you know what I mean. Nice girls don't do that sort of thing.'

'Now don't be silly, Amanda. Of course we'll get on. We've operated together in an emotional battlefield and come out of it the best of muckers. The bed sharing thing is optional, but it would be a terrible waste. But I'm really not pushing that, up to you. Look, a week in a flash hotel by the Pitons in St Lucia, just to get acclimatised you understand, then two weeks on a skippered yacht drifting around the Virgin Islands. The very best of everything, and I've thought of everything, promise, you're going to love it.'

She at least was chuckling. Travers hopes began to rise.

'And what if I can't get away? Unlike you, I don't run my own business. I have commitments and things; it could be difficult.'

'Oh come on, I know that's not true. You haven't had a break for a year – you told me – and you're not working on anything important. You could take three weeks tomorrow, and you know it. Amanda, I honestly thought we had something. Am I wrong? Or was it all just business for you?'

'Ooh, you bugger, you know that's not true.' There was a silence now between them. Travers kept quiet and crossed his fingers under the phone.

'Oh, you're right, I suppose,' she said. 'It's something I could never do on my own, and I do deserve a break. When are you going, Tom?'

'Well you could sound a bit more enthusiastic, sweetheart. I'm talking romance here, you know – Antony and Cleopatra. You make it sound like pie and chips at the dog track. I've made it my personal ambition to release your soul, light the spark, wash away that Goldberg grime.

We leave in two weeks, first class to St Lucia.'

'Tom, I am sorry, it is a wonderful thing, and I am hugely flattered and grateful. I don't know what to say except I'd love to come, honestly. It's brilliant of you and you're a very kind man. In fact, can't think of anyone I'd rather go with. Oh God, does that sound patronising? I don't mean it to be, honestly. We both know we have a thing for each other, I just couldn't believe anything would come of it. I really would love to come.'

'Well great, you've made my day,' said Travers. 'Tell you what, let's have dinner tomorrow up west, and I'll fill you in. Hope your passport's up to date. I'll pick you up tomorrow at seven thirty. Oh, and do give me a ring any time at work or at home – it's good to talk, according to the ads.'

Travers replaced the receiver. All of a sudden his life felt complete. Just go with the flow, he told himself. No questions, no analysis, go with the flow. No complications this time, life could be very sweet.